JOHNNY PORNO

by Charlie Stella

STARK
HOUSE

Stark House Press • Eureka California

JOHNNY PORNO

Published by Stark House Press
2200 O Street
Eureka, CA 95501, USA
griffinskye3@sbcglobal.net
www.starkhousepress.com

ISBN: 1-933586-29-X
ISBN-13: 978-1-933586-29-8

Visit CHARLIESTELLA.COM

Text set in Figural. Heads set in Champion
Cover design and layout by Mark Shepard, SHEPGRAPHICS.COM
Proofreading by Rick Ollerman

The publisher would like to thank Ed Gorman for all his help instigating this project.

First Stark House Press Edition: April 2010

0 9 8 7 6 5 4 3 2 1

AMICI:

A few years ago, after reading an article about the tragic life and death of Linda Susan Boreman (a.k.a., Linda Lovelace), I noticed a documentary had been made about the film responsible for her becoming an overnight celebrity and household name. *Inside Deep Throat* was a masterful exposé that detailed the many variables at play behind the making of the film and how its political persecution became the driving force behind its financial success. Immediately after watching the documentary, my wife and I looked to each other and said, *"Next book."*

In 1973 Richard Nixon was inaugurated for his second term as President; the U.S. Supreme Court, in a 7-2 vote, legalized abortion with their decision in *Roe v. Wade*; U.S. involvement in North Vietnam ended with the signing of the Paris Peace Accords and Willie Mays hit his last home run (#660). Among these historic milestones was a decision by NY Criminal Court Judge Joel Tyler to ban the pornographic film, *Deep Throat*. Tyler wrote, "This nadir of decadence...this feast of carrion and squalor...this Sodom and Gomorrah gone wild before the fire... this is one throat that deserves to be cut."

As films go, one has to acknowledge *Deep Throat* was nothing more than a campy, cheaply made porno that showcased the "sexual talents" of a young woman stage-named Linda Lovelace. With a soundtrack comprised of silly parodies and jingles and a plot born of male fantasy, the movie might well have come and gone without the slightest notice had the government ignored it. Instead, political directives from the White House launching a moral crusade that had much more to do with distracting the public from the war in Southeast Asia and an ever growing Watergate scandal guaranteed the film's iconic success. What it also did was provide organized crime with a new way to make a fast buck. It is fittingly ironic that the name given to the secret informant (FBI agent, William Mark Felt) who provided information that would eventually take down the Nixon White House itself shared the name of the film.

Deep Throat was the brain child of a hair dresser from Queens (Gerard Damiano) who thought up the film's storyline while driving across the Queensborough Bridge into Manhattan. After witnessing Linda Lovelace's unique ability to perform fellatio, Damiano pitched the idea for the flick to a couple of New York wiseguys who then fronted the $25,000 film budget. Filmed in Miami over a six day period, *Deep Throat* would go on to earn more than $600 million. Unfortunately for Damiano and the cast of the movie, there was no trickle down income from the mob's windfall profit. Damiano's original one-third partnership was bought out for pennies on the dollar and he was told to skedaddle immediately after the film's success. Lovelace was reportedly paid between $1,500—$2,500 for her performance in *Deep Throat* and her co-star, Harry Reems, originally hired to help with the lighting, earned a per diem of only $100. Both actors were burdened with nothing but problems afterward. Lovelace had not only been used by those behind the movie, she felt betrayed by the feminist movement after spending the latter half of her troubled life publicly battling the porn industry. Harry Reems nearly went to jail for his role in the movie and it is believed he was saved from the slammer only when (and because) Jimmy Carter defeated Gerald Ford in the 1976 presidential election.

With all the media attention and government-inspired moral outrage, *Deep Throat* became the proverbial forbidden fruit and the mob was gifted a new Prohibition. But America had proved itself ready to move beyond the sexual rigidity and censorship that had dominated the cultural landscape prior to the film's release. A *New York Times* article proclaimed the film "Porno Chic: after several icons of American celebrity decried censorship and openly attended showings. By the time Judge Tyler rendered his decision to ban the film, *Deep Throat* had become taboo enough to entice the public into a near frenzy; people who'd never had a thought about pornography suddenly had to see it.

In the summer of 1973 I was between high school and college working a summer job humping sheetrock at the Olympic Tower in Manhattan to put aside a few extra coins before I flew off to Minot State College in North Dakota. I didn't know a thing about *Deep Throat*, except that my father and a few of his friends had seen it and seemed to enjoy cracking jokes about it. I was focused on playing football. Fortunately, distractions like VCRs weren't available yet (or like too many kids today obsessed with entertainment technology, I might never have left my bedroom).

Although the bulk of my focus back then was on football, a Freshman English class would forever alter my life (no matter how many detours I would make along the way). Dave Gresham, the smartest guy I know, was my professor. A Renaissance man in the truest sense of the word, Dave had received a Woodrow Wilson scholarship and attended the University of Iowa's Writers Workshop (where he studied, along with fellow classmates John Irving, Andre Dubus and James Crumley, under Kurt Vonnegut and Richard Yates). Dave has designed and built a solar home from the ground up, was a state ranked tennis player and coach at Minot State College and smoked the fish he caught off his sailboat on Lake Sakakawea in some smoking gadget he'd made in his yard. Dave can name birds on sight and continues to rebuild homes, sailboats, etc., to this day. In fact, my last email exchange with Dave found him helping a friend of his make a new mast for a 107 foot boat—out of a hundred foot fir tree. As Dave put it, "with (how's this for bird sightings) ospreys looking down on us and ducks hiding out in his front-yard pond."

Dave and his wonderful wife Linda have also raised a more than exceptional family (two Harvard graduates and one Air Force Academy graduate). Dave was also a great teacher and not to weigh his record down with having influenced a small-timer like myself, it should be noted that he also taught a Pulitzer Prize winning journalist and current head of the Seattle office of the LA Times, Kim Murphy. Kim and I were classmates along with another terrific writer, Michael Vaughn, who was the college paper editor and probably the second smartest guy I ever met. All of us benefited from Dave's ability to polish the already finely tuned (Kim and Mike) while simultaneously grooming the grammatically and academically challenged (myself).

Needless to say, I took every class I could from Dave and it was during my sophomore year when he began a Creative Writing class by reading the opening lines to the George V. Higgins classic, *The Friends of Eddie Coyle*, that I became hooked as an avid reader and a wannabe writer of modern crime fiction. I knew people who talked like the characters Higgins portrayed. I had lived around them most of my life.

By semester's end, Dave had introduced me to Kurt Vonnegut's *Slaughterhouse-Five*, Elmore Leonard's *Glitz* and a host of other writers and their works who would put me on a reading binge that has lasted to this day. Dave had told our class: "Once you see your name in print, you'll always want it there." At the end of the semester he submitted a short story of mine for a college magazine writing award. It received an honorable mention and Dave's prophecy proved correct. A victim of seeing something I had written get published, I indeed wanted more of the same.

After transferring to Hofstra University I won a fiction contest there under author Sam Topperoff's tutelage. Eventually bored with school and too impatient for the dedication writing might require, I took a job cleaning windows, married and started a family. I worked two and three legitimate jobs at a time over the next several years, but the writing bug had been firmly implanted and I would continue trying, on and off, over the next twenty years (always with Dave's encouragement), until I got lucky.

At one point, after moving out of the legitimate workforce into the subculture I write about, while manning the phones in a bookmaking office, I began writing scenes to plays. Although they would never be produced, the dialogue I was engaged in while taking bets was a constant reminder of the world Higgins and Leonard had portrayed so masterfully. It was also a reminder to maybe take another shot at writing a novel.

Before I could put something together worth reading (never mind selling), I stayed with theatre and wrote a few plays about things I was most familiar with: gambling, street finance and irreverence. Three plays of mine were produced off-off Broadway, but I found the theatre required and depended on a lot more than one man's effort. I quickly gave it up to pursue the riches a street life offered to those willing to take risks and hustle.

Fast forward a few more years and a few dozen more detours, including a few divorces, arrests and countless jobs, and the writing bug returned with a vengeance. It was when I first met my wife, Ann Marie. My attempt to impress her as something more than a street smart wannabe resulted in my first published novel, *Eddie's World*. Shortly thereafter Ann Marie and I moved in together. I left the street and the money that went with it behind. The financial transition was a tough one. I had to survive earning a word processing salary, an annual income I had sometimes made inside a few months on the street, but playing it square also meant a peace of mind money can't buy.

It took some time, but eventually I came to realize the fazools (money) wasn't worth the hassle or the risk, and that eating local take-out instead of steaks at The Palm wasn't such a bad tradeoff. I had attained a lifelong goal of getting published and I had found the love of my life.

In October of 2008, Gerard Damiano, the director of *Deep Throat* died of complications from a stroke he'd suffered a few months earlier. He was 80 years old. The less fortunate story of Linda (Lovelace) Boreman ended in April of 2002. After suffering massive internal injuries in a car crash a few weeks earlier, she was removed from life support and died at the age of 53.

Recently Ann Marie and I were discussing how much of a role luck (good or bad) plays in any given life; whether people make their own or it just falls from the sky randomly landing on this or that person; does divine design dictate who gets lucky (or unlucky) at exactly the right time they might need (or deserve) it? It was one of our early morning dialogues that usually starts with a cup of coffee and ends several cups later, somewhere around noon. Although we never came up with a definitive conclusion regarding luck, we agreed we've been the beneficiary of whatever it is and/or however it happens; we've been blessed with good fortune unobtainable on the open market.

Seven novels down the road, all of them originally edited by Peter Skutches (talk about being blessed), I've lucked out again. Ed Gorman, to whom this book is dedicated, recommended *Johnny Porno* to Greg Shepard at Stark House Press and here we are. Greg's enthusiasm, encouragement and support has been more than invigorating for us. *Johnny Porno* has the honor of being Stark House's first venture into publishing original novels.

How lucky can one guy get? It never ceases to amaze me.

—Charlie Stella

For Ed Gorman
Thank You

'TIS BUT THY NAME THAT IS MY ENEMY;
THOU ART THYSELF, THOUGH NOT A MONTAGUE.
WHAT'S MONTAGUE? IT IS NOR HAND, NOR FOOT,
NOR ARM, NOR FACE, NOR ANY OTHER PART
BELONGING TO A MAN. O, BE SOME OTHER NAME!
WHAT'S IN A NAME?

Chapter 1

John Albano used his right thumb to count through a thick wad of five-dollar bills while George Berg listed the reasons weekend receipts were off.

"Friday was supposed to piss down rain, it didn't," Berg said. "Shoulda been good, it wasn't. Maybe they went the regular movies instead, who knows. I had five guys the afternoon I told come back later, two of them didn't bother. I had nineteen end of day. Then yesterday, cloudy all day, a little chilly, that shoulda helped, but there was the Mets-Pirates at Shea and the Giants-Jets up to Connecticut, that preseason fiasco, the Yale bowl. What that cost me, I shoulda went the trotters. I show it three times for a fifty-five count. And today, this rain it looked like again, I showed it six times, the theater, from nine until half an hour ago, I still couldn't bust a hundred. Total's one seventy-two for the weekend, ninety-eight today. That lunatic the bar there in Brooklyn, he's making threats I don't clear two hundred, but what the hell'm I supposed to do they don't come? God help me it's sunny next weekend. They'll all be out the beaches while I'm sweating I don't catch a beating here for not meeting an impossible quota. That happens, we get beach weather next week, I'm thinking I shouldn't even show it. What's the point?"

John looked up from his count, one hundred thirty five-dollar bills so far, and said, "That's your call, George. Just make sure you let them know in Brooklyn if you're not gonna show it. It'll save me time I don't have making the trip out here."

They were standing in front of the Knights of Columbus on East Gate Road in Massapequa, Long Island. It was a cloudy, humid afternoon. A film case holding the porn film rested against John's left leg. He stopped his count to wipe sweat from his forehead with the back of his hand.

"I'm just saying is all," Berg said. "I mean, I was filling the place with fifty, sixty guys a showing there almost nonstop I first got the thing. Now guys are on vacation, it being summer and all, football season around the corner, I'm lucky I'm puttin' gas in my tank for all the work I'm doing."

John was close to finished with his count. Berg was right, the total was low. They wouldn't be happy in Brooklyn when he dropped the money off later. If he ever got there, he was thinking. He had two more stops to make.

"Most guys already seen it," Berg continued. "Last week they asked me skip the opening scene, go straight to the sex."

"I hope you did it for them," John said.

"Yeah, I did, but only because it got them out sooner rather than later. Some a them use the toilet there, I know they're beating themselves off. I have the old lady clean it with Lysol soon's they're gone, but sometimes she brings the kids and they gotta use it. It's disgusting."

John couldn't imagine it, letting your wife clean toilets where a group of sweaty men had watched pornos. He shook the thought off.

"I don't know you remember the crowds when you were just counting heads," Berg said. "It's thinned out considerably. We need an angle, something new to generate interest."

John finished the count. "Eight-sixty," he said, then counted off twenty-four fives and stashed them in Berg's shirt pocket. "Minus one-twenty is seven-forty."

"Peanuts, I know," Berg said. "We need that new angle."

One of the men who'd paid to see the movie approached them. He was a heavyset bald man with thick black glasses. He looked at George first, then John. "Whatever happened the other guy?" he asked.

"What other guy?" John said.

"Tommy Porno," the bald man said. "Guy used to bring the films. He was supposed to get me something. I left him a fifty-dollar deposit last month and he never came back."

"Sorry, pal," John said. "I don't know anything about it."

"And you are?"

John had dropped down to retie his sneaker laces. Annoyed at the question, he gave the bald man a hard stare. "Excuse me?"

"Just asking."

"Okay," Berg said. "You asked. Now leave the man alone."

"The other guy took a fifty," the bald man said. "He was supposed to get me a copy of the movie."

John looked to Berg. "He serious?"

"Maybe that's why he disappeared," Berg said, "he was robbing people."

"I gave him a fifty," the bald man repeated.

"Then I guess you're taking a powder for that fifty," Berg said. "Tommy DeLuca hasn't been around for more than a month now. I'd get over it, I was you."

The bald man motioned at John. "Why I was asking him," he said. "Maybe he knows the guy."

"Got nothing to do with me what you did with Tommy DeLuca," John said. "Sorry for your loss."

The bald man frowned.

"Okay?" George said. "Go get yourself a beer you want. Tell them I said it's on me."

Still upset, the bald man walked away.

"I hope I don't have a nickname," John said.

"You kidding?" Berg said. "That nasty prick from the bar in Brooklyn

used to ask 'is Tommy Porno there yet?' Now it's Johnny Porno he asks for."
John felt his jaw tighten.

"Screw'em," Berg said. "Fuck's in a name?"

"I don't like it, for one thing," John said.

Berg shrugged. "What's his problem anyway, that guy the bar? Comes off like a real asshole."

"Nick Santorra," John said. "You're right, he is an asshole."

"I think Tommy DeLuca liked the name, tell you the truth. Got his rocks off being called that, Tommy Porno. This mope just now, the one DeLuca beat for a fifty? He's probably not the only one. Maybe DeLuca did disappear for stealing."

"He really call me that, Johnny Porno, the guy onna phone?"

Berg shrugged again.

"I got nothing to do with this crap outside of hauling it back and forth weekends," John said. "I never even seen the damn movie."

"You like magic acts you should," Berg said. "See it, I mean. The star, Linda Lovelace, she has some humble tits and all, a crooked tooth or two, but she can swallow a telephone pole. It's something every man should get to see at least once before he dies, know what he's missed."

"That the line of shit you hawk this thing with?"

"That and a line or two about how a guy should bring his wife some night, the ones still go down on the old *bracciole*, so's they see it can be done."

"Jesus Christ."

"Might work, ladies night. Or maybe a couples special."

"You wanna tell this to somebody else?" John said. "I'm not gonna see the movie or bring my wife to see it, I ever get married again."

"Fair enough," Berg said. "I did make a point of telling the mamelukes paying to see it, call it 'Peter Rabbit', the movie. Like it says on the side of the film case there, even though it's spelled wrong."

John was thinking about the pornographic moniker he didn't want. "What's that?"

Berg pointed to the film case. "The name on the case there," he said.

John looked but wasn't seeing it. "What about it?"

Berg waved it off. "Nothing," he said. "Look, you gotta tell your people I can't help it the head counts are down."

"They're not my people, George."

"Sorry, but it's getting old, this movie. We can use something new. That one with the *Ivory Snow* girl'd do good. I haven't seen it yet, but I hear she gets plowed by a Mandingo and then there's some orgy stuff goes on. Weirdoes came to see this one'll pro'bly love that one, too."

"I'm not in the executive loop," John said. "All I do is aggravate myself in traffic all weekend. In the meantime, the count being so low, they'll probably send a guy out here next week, somebody to spy. You won't know who it is, so stay sharp. I can't tell you which day because they won't tell me, but it could be both days."

"As in you-think-I'm-skimming?"

"As in I-like-you-enough-to-warn-you," John said. "They first had me doing it, the head-counting, I turned in numbers without knowing what you guys were claiming. I remember a few guys were caught skimming had to fork over extra the next week. One of them, next time I saw him after his numbers were off, he was drinking his meals through a straw."

"More threats," Berg said. "Great."

"Hey, I'm not threatening anybody."

Berg put both hands up. "Sorry," he said. "It's just another headache I don't need right now, spies."

"Well, don't say I didn't warn you."

"I'm warned, I'm warned," Berg said. He remembered something and perked up. "Hey, you think about my idea?"

"Which idea is that?"

"One I mentioned last week. We get that broad here to do a signing we'll all make a killing." He thumbed over his shoulder at the Knights of Columbus building. "I'll talk to the guy runs this place, grease him a few and see we can't use it, too. We'd fill both places you get Linda Lovelace to sign autographs."

John wrapped a rubber band around the cash he was holding. He folded the wad in half and stuffed it inside his front pants pocket.

"She does something like that, it'll probably be in the city where they can jam the place at ten, fifteen dollars a head," John said. "Linda Lovelace is not gonna come out to Massapequa, George. It's a pipe dream to think so."

"I'm just saying, couldn't your people give her a push?"

"I already said they're not my people."

Berg wasn't listening. "Or one of the costars," he said, "the short one smokes the cigarette while the guy eats her, or the nurse with the big tits. She'd do good, too. Any of the broads in that movie would fill this place. And it's not like they wouldn't earn. We charge the guys a five for an autograph or some shit and let the broads keep a deuce of that. Half a these perverts'd drop a five to watch one a them take a piss."

John stared at Berg a long moment. He sighed at what his life had become. Less than a year ago he was making close to five hundred dollars a week working as a union carpenter. Then he punched out a foreman and he was out of work. He had been working odd jobs to make ends meet ever since. The last six months he'd been driving for a local car service five days a week and was barely able to pay his child support, never mind the rent or anything else. Then a few months ago a fistfight in a bar over a woman he didn't know was married led to a weekend job counting the number of guys paying five bucks a pop to see bootlegged copies of *Deep Throat*. When one of the guys doing the collections was caught skimming from the mob and disappeared, John got the promotion, so to speak. Now he was making fifty bucks per day instead of the twenty-five he made counting heads.

Dropping off and picking up the film reels and collecting head count money was a lot more work and responsibility than counting the number of guys paying to see the movie, but until his employment situation changed for the better, John couldn't turn the work down. Sometimes it became a bit much, though, especially having to humor guys like George Berg.

"Watching them take a piss?" he said. "Where do you get that from?"

"I'm just saying," Berg said. "Guys are into porn, they're mostly perverts."

"Well, don't hold your breath on those autographs. Like I said, the girls doing those movies, Linda Lovelace, whoever else, they aren't coming out here to sign their names."

"Then they should get themselves business managers."

"Right," John said.

"I mean it," Berg said.

"I'll tell you what," John said. "I ever meet Linda Lovelace or any of the other women in the movie, I'll let them know you're available to manage their careers."

"You joke, but I'm serious," Berg said. "Agents, they're called. I could be one."

John said, "Meantime, Willie Mays hit his six hundred sixtieth home run Friday. How come you don't talk about that?"

"Because they lost," Berg said.

"What?"

"They lost. Mets lost."

"Yeah, and? The man hit number six-sixty. Who cares they lost?"

"You bet them you care."

"Excuse me?"

"Put it this way," Berg said. "Next time Mays homers in a game I bet, I hope there're runners on base."

"I gotta go," John said. "See if you can't find some new blood for this movie."

"There are only so many guys live in Massapequa, John. I can't manufacture them."

"That's what they tell me to tell you. Find new blood instead of pissing and moaning."

"Do I piss and moan?"

John didn't answer. He was already thinking about having to deal with the asshole at the bar that took the receipts and recounted the money extra slow and now was calling him Johnny Porno behind his back. The guy had given him grief the first day John started collecting and hadn't stopped since.

"My brother is working on the guys at the UPS depot," Berg said. "That might turn into something. Another guy's been coming says he knows some bus drivers are interested."

"Now you're thinking," John said. "I'll give you a call if I hear who they're sending to watch you."

"Hopefully you don't make the call."

"They could send somebody anyway. They could've done that this weekend. You're skimming and they know it, it's a headache neither of us needs."

John picked up the film case and brought it to his car. He opened the trunk and laid it down faceup. A strip of adhesive tape ran across the center. It read: "Peter Rabit." John saw "Rabbit" was spelled wrong. He slammed the trunk shut, lit a cigarette and got in the car. He pulled the wad of cash from his pants pocket, stashed it in the small gym bag he had stuffed under his seat, then pushed the bag back and started the engine. He turned up the volume on the radio to listen for traffic.

He had two stops to make on the east shore, the drop-off in Brooklyn that would be annoying and take at least two hours, and then he needed to get some sleep. He was scheduled to drive an early-afternoon shift the next day. He also needed to find time for his son, not to mention pay the kid's mother the two weeks child support he still owed.

At thirty-five years of age, with no job prospects on the immediate horizon, he wondered if he'd made a mistake when he listened to his mother's pleas for him not to join the army like his brother. Paul Albano had planned on a military career but was killed in Vietnam eight years ago. John still felt guilty for not enlisting.

His brother was on his mind as John pulled away from the curb. He had to stop at the corner for a red light, at which point the radio station gave the traffic report. He turned up the volume and learned of a three-car accident on the Southern State Parkway.

It was going to be a much longer night than he had anticipated.

■　■　■

Captain Edward Kaprowski, in his second month as captain of the newly formed NYPD Organized Crime Unit of a statewide task force, met with Lieutenant Detective Neil Levin outside the Cadillac dealership on Hillside Avenue. Kaprowski, at thirty-one, was a short, squat man with blonde hair and beady eyes. He tossed the cigarette he'd been smoking at a sewer grating and waited to see if it dropped down. When it did, Kaprowski pointed at a construction dumpster cordoned off with crime scene tape at the end of a long driveway.

"Body was dumped there," he said. "Dead at least five weeks, ripe as the day is long and missing both hands. That said, the guy's wallet with everything in it, minus any money, was in his back pants pocket; driver's license, Social Security card, a few other forms of identification. Thomas Nicholas DeLuca, a.k.a. Tommy Porno. An associate with Eddie Vento's crew. Forensics says the body was dumped there within the last week, which makes no sense they held it so long someplace else."

Levin, working undercover for both Internal Affairs and Kaprowski's Organized Crime task force, was forty-one years old and a twelve-year veteran. He looked at the construction dumpster and said, "His hands were missing?"

"Chopped off," Kaprowski said. "Probably soon's they grabbed him and before they put two behind his ear, the official cause of death."

"Because of a porn film?"

"Because of the money the dopey bastard stole from the mob over a porn film."

"How much?"

"God knows. Didn't have to be much, though. Soon's this hits the papers it'll go a long way to keeping the dummies run that film around for the wiseguys honest."

"The deceased was an example."

"They whack a guy, leave the body so it'll be found, it's the only explanation. The missing hands were obvious enough."

Levin pointed to the construction container. "Why there?"

"Eddie Vento bought his Cadillac there. Coincidence you think? DeLuca had a no-show construction job with somebody close to Vento. Started off as a head-counter, graduated to collecting and probably couldn't resist skimming. Early word is he left markers all over the city. Bookies, mostly. A couple card games the boys sanction, probably a few they don't."

"Forensics gives him a week in the dumpster?"

"Five to six days. Inside a week, they said. You get close enough you can smell it. Some of what they found inside had liquefied. In this heat, the humidity, I'm surprised it wasn't called in sooner, the stink."

Kaprowski led Levin back around the corner. "You live over in Bayside, right?" he asked.

"Off Bell Boulevard, yeah," Levin said. "The only thing left from a short marriage, that house, but I had to take a second mortgage to buy her out."

"How long you married?"

"Two years, six months, ten days, and her lawyer made me pay for every minute."

"Any kids?"

Levin seemed confused. "None. Why?"

"Living with anybody now?"

They had walked past the dealership on Hillside Avenue. Levin suddenly stopped. "No," he said. "You already know my story. What's up?"

"It's called small talk," Kaprowski said. "Most people have something to hide, they give it up in small talk."

"You brought me into this three weeks ago," Levin said. "You're having doubts, feel free to cut me loose. I have better things to do my day off."

Kaprowski started walking again. He waved Levin on.

"Except for me, what they read about inna papers, this unit, we're still virgin," Kaprowski said. "Least as far as corruption goes. That won't last, but for now, at least until the wiseguys figure us out, we're operating free of common knowledge. We're as undercover as undercover gets, which is why I make bullshit small talk, to try and gauge your commitment. I don't want or need people aren't committed to this operation."

"All due respect, Captain, I'm the one in the field of fire on this. Bad enough I'm with Internal Affairs. I turn up dirty cops and I lose the few friends I had. I turn up cops in bed with the mob, those cops can reach out in ways regular cops can't. You want more of a commitment than that I don't know what to tell you."

"I can appreciate your situation, Detective. I do appreciate it. Which is why you can't blow it with IA. You do your job there same as you always do, except now you'll come to me before you go to them. I can't afford there's somebody in IA already on the mob payroll."

"You gonna filter it, that what you're saying?"

"If I feel it needs to be filtered, yeah."

"What about the feds? My understanding of task force is a joint operation."

"It's a joint circle jerk is what it is. How often the feds share with IA in your life?"

"Never."

"Well, we're gonna return the favor and for as long as I can get away with it. I'll keep them in the darkest of Africa before I give them the tip of my dick on this investigation."

They reached another cross street on the avenue. Kaprowski pointed at a construction crew building a new curb along Hillside Avenue.

"Soon's they formed the committee, I had these guys show up in fronna my house."

"Those guys?"

"Chipped curbs," Kaprowski said. "Last week I come home, I still had chipped curbs in fronna my house. Same chipped curb as when I bought the place two years ago. Next morning the crew across the avenue there was rebuilding it, my curb."

He stopped to point at a stocky man wearing a red bandana. "I asked the foreman who authorized it, the fat guy there with the bandana, and he says he was given an address and told to fix the curb. I thought nothing of it, figured it was the city did the work, whatever. Then my wife gets a call from some goomba claims he's a friend of Carmine Correlli, actually says the guy's name over the phone, tells her he hopes the crew they sent did a good job and if she needed anything else done around the house, he noticed we had a crack in our stoop out front, they'd come and fix that, too. No charge."

"When was this?"

"Last week."

"They aren't wasting time."

"My wife called me at work, told me about the call she got, I came home and took a sledgehammer to the new curb. It's still busted. I get a fine from the city I'll hire my own contractor. Otherwise it stays busted. I been haunting this little prick every chance I get since. Got a guy feeding me his work sites so I can show up, give him the runs."

"You know the guy IA is looking into runs interference for Eddie Vento, right?"

"Sean Kelly," Kaprowski said, "the miserable piece of shit. Yeah, I know."

"There was another one, a detective working drug enforcement, Hastings, but he's been forced into retirement. Kelly supposedly helped broker that deal, but we don't know how, which suggests somebody higher up the food chain had to okay it. IA figures Kelly got involved because of the unnecessary attention Hastings was bringing Eddie Vento. Hastings was shaking down card games and bars in the area and apparently got himself punched out in Vento's bar over in Williamsburg. Irony is, now you showed me how the last guy running the film and doing the collecting turned out, it's the guy replaced him knocked Hastings out. Johnny Porno they're calling him."

"Another street name to be proud of," Kaprowski said. "Maybe you should bring him down the morgue, show him the guy he's replacing. He might reconsider the position."

"You think?"

"He knocked a cop out, how's he still on the street?"

"Rumor is Vento had a camera installed because Hastings was shaking down his bartenders. Last thing NYPD needs now is a film of one of its own shaking down a mobbed-up bar."

"Kelly tracking down the fuck film?"

"As of last week, but we haven't gone out yet. We're supposed to have something this week. My guess is it'll be something Vento throws him. Some bullshit arrest can't hurt anybody, but might look like Kelly is doing his job."

Kaprowski was staring down the stocky man with the red bandana. "Some load of shit, that film detail," he said without taking his eyes off the stocky man.

Levin watched and waited to see who blinked first. He smiled when he saw it was the construction worker that turned away from the staring contest.

"It's a second prohibition for the mob, that movie," Kaprowski said. "You'd think after Knapp they'd learn something. The spotlight they gave that commission was nothing more than a dog and pony show."

"Frank Serpico reminded dirty cops to be more careful," Levin said.

"And NYPD did their little dance and went right back to business as usual, which is why I'm running this thing under the radar for as long as I can get away with it. Sooner or later there'll be cops doing what Kelly is doing with Eddie Vento and every scumbag like him. Our best chance to make a real dent is to lay low enough they don't find out in time, they can't duck when we throw our first punch."

"That's pretty ambitious."

"Look, this thing works, this unit, I hope to start an Organized Crime investigative division someday, something independent from the feds."

"Now it sounds like a fantasy."

"Yeah, I know, but otherwise I'm jerking myself off with this unit, and I have better things to do, too."

"I had my yarmulke I'd run down the synagogue, say a prayer or two."

Kaprowski turned to Levin. "You're looking to feel me out you're wasting your time. I'm Polish, my wife's Sicilian and my best friend's a Jew. He's not cheap and my wife is religious. Very much so."

"Fair enough. For the record, though, I'm not religious."

"Me either, although it breaks my mother's heart I'm not. She's still over there, Krakow. Swears her hometown cardinal will become pope some day. Imagine, a Polish pope?"

"That's, like, what, a Jewish president?"

"Close enough," Kaprowski said.

The two men shook hands.

CHAPTER 2

Nancy Kirsk-Albano-Ackerman was still recovering from her orgasm when Louis Kirsk emerged from the bathroom with a towel wrapped around his waist. Nancy was on her back in the bed. Her legs shook one last time as she felt the color drain from her face.

"You okay?" Louis asked.

Nancy took a few deep breaths and reached for her pack of cigarettes on the night table. She looked at Louis, taking in his tall, lean body before looking up into his sparkling blue eyes. She licked her lips as he tied his long dirty-blonde hair in a ponytail with a rubber band. Duane Allman, she sometimes thought of, because of the way Louis looked with beard stubble.

"Your head looked about to explode it was so red," he said.

Nancy fished a cigarette from the pack, lit it with her lighter, then sat up and rolled her eyes.

"Un-fucking-believable," she said. "That was the best, baby. The absolute best."

Louis winked at his ex-wife. "That's what they all say," he said, then watched as her smile disappeared.

The telephone rang. It had been ringing on and off the entire time they were having sex. Louis ignored the phone to glance at his watch. He turned toward the dresser when the towel dropped from his waist. He grabbed his underwear from the dresser, bent at the waist and stepped into them.

Nancy said, "That your girlfriend calling again?" She pulled the sheets up so they covered her knees. "She's certainly a tenacious little bitch."

"She's midwestern is what she is," Louis said. "Thinks she's gonna be an actress someday. She read a biography about Marilyn Monroe and thinks it's easy."

"She even legal?"

Louis was pulling his pants on. He feigned amusement. "Very funny," he said. "You talk to your other ex yet?"

"About what?"

Louis hated when Nancy played dumb for the sake of engaging him. It was getting late and he needed to get her out of the apartment. He also needed to know if her ex-husband would be stopping off at her house with all those five-dollar bills again. She had mentioned a few times over the past two months what a pain in the ass it was to have to shop with fives.

"You know about what," he said as he sat on the bed and pulled his socks on. "That thing he's doing you told me about."

Nancy exhaled a small cloud of smoke. "What thing?"

He leaned forward for his boots, but couldn't reach them and had to get up off the bed. "That fuck movie, the porno, *Deep Throat*. You said John was doing something with it for somebody in Brooklyn and he was making all those trips to the Island and whatnot. The five-dollar bills he keeps paying you with?"

"Oh, that," said Nancy, rolling her eyes again.

Louis rubbed his face from frustration.

"He was a head counter or something," Nancy said. "What he told me anyway. He says that's what they pay him with, the fives, so he passes them on to me."

"Sounds like he's the one doing the collecting, he has all that cash on him. The fuck's a head counter anyway?"

"Something to do with how many people see the movie. He counted them, I guess. Maybe he collects money, too, now, I don't know. What do you care?"

"Maybe when the phone rang before it wasn't my girlfriend."

"Who then, your bookie?"

"Close enough."

Nancy's eyes narrowed. "You borrowed money again?"

"You should be a cop," Louis said. "You'd fit right in. You could guess wrong and keep working backwards."

"Now how much do you owe?"

"None of your business, except your other ex might be able to help me out there. He coming to see you with his child support this weekend or not?"

"Yeah, right. John's behind two weeks as it is."

"Maybe I should be there when he comes."

"He doesn't like you, Louis. You know that."

"And I'm not exactly fond of him, but this is business."

"None of yours, he'll say. Besides, what do I do with my husband? You can't confront John at my house, not with Nathan there. Think about it."

He would have liked to smack her for being sarcastic. Louis was hoping to catch John Albano the day he collected, preferably after he was done so the count would be high.

"When's he come to see his kid?" he asked.

Nancy crushed out her cigarette. "Why?"

"Maybe you're still banging him, too, I wanna know."

"I wouldn't mind if you were jealous, but it shouldn't be over John. It's pretty obvious we hate each other."

"When's he pay for the kid? Which day?"

"Usually Sundays," Nancy said. "When he shows up, but he didn't show up last week. He owes me two weeks now."

"Morning or afternoon? When he shows."

"Used to be mornings, before the weekend stuff he's doing. Now it's whenever. What's this sudden interest in John anyway?"

Louis ignored the question. "He have the money with him when he comes?"

"What? No, I just said. He's late."

"I'm talking about the other money, the cash he collects."

"How do I know? Besides, he isn't going to deal with you about child support. He won't discuss anything that has to do with his son. There's no talking to him about that kid."

"Except you say he isn't paying on time and he don't spend enough time."

"Because he's broke and he's working two jobs," Nancy said. "But don't kid yourself, his son comes first. John would walk away from a million bucks if that kid called."

"He would, huh?"

"He isn't going to discuss child support with you, Louis."

She didn't get it, the dumb fuck. "You're sure of that?"

She leaned toward the night table for the ashtray. "No way," she said. "And thank God he never knew about us when I was married to him. He might've killed you for that."

"He might've tried," Louis said. He finished tying his boot laces and stood up. "Point is, he's got all that cash, he shouldn't be late paying you. He should be flush, the work he does for his new friends."

"John doesn't even like those people, the ones he's working for, and he's barely making it now. He's still working two jobs, even with this thing he does with that movie. By the way, did I tell you I know a woman knows the guy directed it?"

"Who?"

"Some woman gets her hair done where I go. Sharon Dowell. A real piece of work. Loose as they come. In her forties going on fifty, tries to look twenty. Word in the salon's always been she sleeps with gangsters. Looks like she's been around the block a few thousand times, so it might be true."

"I take it you don't like her."

"We say hello. We've talked a few times."

"And she knows the director of the movie?"

"What she says. He was a hairdresser."

"What's he, a fag?"

"Not according to Sharon. More like a swinger."

Louis was interested. "This broad balled him?"

"She's probably balled everybody, but don't get any ideas. She's not your type, Louis, trust me. Too old, for one thing. You like them young as I recall."

Louis stroked the air with a fist.

"And she's bossy," Nancy said. "Very bossy. Apparently she has connections. Maybe from the director guy, I don't know, but the girls at the salon think he's mobbed-up, too."

"Yeah, well, everybody knows somebody," Louis said. "She really screw this director?"

"She sure made it sound like she did. She likes to drop names, though, so who knows. She claims she fucked one of the Vignieris, the one in jail, I think."

"She fucked old man Vignieri, she is connected."

"Who knows. All I know is I was sick of hearing her one day and got her jealous talking about you. I told her you look like Duane Allman. I don't doubt she left a wet spot on her chair after."

"You got a mouth on you, you know that?"

"Please."

"Tell me this much. How'd John find that job in the first place, the movie thing?"

"Something to do with a fight in a bar. I don't know."

"He ever connected? His family, whatever."

Nancy rolled her eyes again. "Please. John's a straight arrow. His mother's brother was involved or something way back and wound up dead, but that was a long time ago."

"Those guys he's working for are connected."

"Like I said, he mentioned something about a fight in a bar. Ask him, you're so interested."

"I wish you would find out how much money he's carrying when he stops by to pay you."

"I ask him something like that and he'll tell me to fuck off. He'll tell you the same thing."

"Can't you call him?"

"If it's that big a deal and you'll stop bugging me I guess I can. He gave me the phone number of the bar where to reach him on weekends. It's in Brooklyn. Williamsburg, I think. John said I should call there if I need him in an emergency."

"What's the name of the place?"

"I don't remember. Something fast, with the word 'fast' in it. I'll give you the number."

"I'll bet six-to-one it's connected, the bar."

"You'd bet on anything."

"And I'd win, too."

"Except your bookie isn't being paid."

Louis stopped what he was doing and stared at her.

"What?" she said.

"I forget," he said, "is this why we divorced, because you can be such a cunt?"

Nancy lit a fresh cigarette. He knew she hated the C-word, but it was his best weapon when she got on him about gambling. Usually the C-word stopped her cold.

"Well?" he said.

"Look, John is always broke, so I don't know what you think will come of being there when he comes to drop off the money he never has," Nancy said. "Like I said, he owes me two weeks now. He drives around in that beat-up Buick and I don't think I've seen him with a new shirt in two years."

"So buy him one."

"Very funny."

The phone rang again. Nancy's face tightened.

Louis yanked the cord from the back of the phone. "There," he said. "Happy now?"

"Excuse me," Nancy muttered. "Excuse me for driving over here, doing your dishes, your laundry, blowing and then fucking you."

"I didn't hear you complaining about that last one while your legs were up in the air."

They stared at each other until Louis glanced at his watch.

"Don't you have to pick up your kid soon?"

"I guess I'm being pushed out the door again," Nancy said. "That last call a warning from the next Marilyn Monroe, little Miss Ohio? Is it her turn to service you now?"

"It was Oklahoma and she was a runner-up."

"Whatever."

"I have things to do, Nan. I'm just reminding you about your son, the one you always claim you need a vacation from, even though he's always at his grandma's. He there now?"

"Fuck you, Louis. He's there a few hours a day a few days a week. And John's mother, the bitch, she's no piece of cake either. I swear that old bag moved to Queens just to haunt me."

"Except it's a good place to dump the brat off when it's convenient, right?"

Nancy slid to the edge of the bed, stood up and headed for the bathroom. "I'm gonna shower," she said. "Asshole."

Louis slapped her on the rump as she passed.

Nancy stopped in her tracks. "That hurt," she said.

Louis winked at her. "You love it," he said.

Nancy tried but couldn't suppress a smile.

Louis liked his ex-wife's perky ass and the fact she was still a looker. She'd had a kid but there was no way to tell from her body. At thirty-five, her stomach was still flat and her breasts had remained firm.

"Talk to the man," he said. "Find out how much money he's collecting for those guys."

"Why do I sense your wheels are turning?"

"Because they are."

"Okay, but John really does hate you."

"He's just jealous is all," Louis said. "Probably knows I still get to nuzzle up to that little landing patch of yours, which I believe I've come to fall in love with again."

"Yeah, well, you might visit it more often."

"I might," said Louis, winking at her again. "Find out how much money your ex collects every week and I just might."

■ ■ ■

It was a few minutes past eleven when John finally stopped at a diner to eat. His stomach had been growling the last two hours and his head had started to ache. He told the hostess he'd sit at the counter and took a seat at the end nearest the kitchen.

It had been a tough night and it was starting to feel like it would never end. After bypassing an accident on the Southern State Parkway by taking the Meadowbrook across the Island instead, John had run into emergency road construction: three lanes forced into one. Traffic had slowed to a crawl. When he finally made it to the LIE, weekenders returning from the Hamptons made it worse.

Then John had caught shit at the bar from the guy he'd like to punch in the face someday. Nick Santorra was a wannabe with an attitude John was sure was one big put-on. Sonny Corleone, John had thought the first time he met him, what Santorra was shooting for with his tough-guy routine.

"The fuck is this?" the punk had asked after recounting the receipt money earlier.

"My stops say it's slowing down," John had told him. "Pretty much everybody has seen the movie already."

"Or maybe your guys are skimming," Santorra said. "Or maybe you are. It's humid enough. Maybe you stopped off and bought yourself a new air conditioner. Maybe I should come out to your car and check the trunk?"

John had stared the guy down then. It was when he had wanted to hit him the most.

"Be my guest," he had said instead. "It's the ten-year-old Buick with the dented fender across the street."

Santorra had turned to smirk at the bartender then. "A wiseass," he'd said. "I tell you what, wiseass. You can do the head counts at your stops next week."

"How'm I gonna do that? I have seven stops. I can't be at all seven at the same time."

Santorra had turned red then. He looked at the slips of paper attached to each stack of money and pointed to George Berg's from Massapequa. "Start with this one," he'd said. "Then go to the next worse."

"He sees me he won't skim," John had said.

"Don't worry about it. We'll send somebody else you don't know. Just in case you're both jerking us off, you and this guy in Massapequa."

John had wanted to laugh in Santorra's face. The guy didn't make sense. He was barking for the sake of making noise. "Whatever," he'd said.

Then he'd left.

By the time he had finished with business in Brooklyn it was way too late to see his son. He'd called from the bar and caught an earful from his ex-wife about being late with the payments and not seeing his son and who the hell did he think he was calling the house so late anyway?

John had hung up on Nancy mid-rant. He'd catch hell for it again the next day when he dropped off the money he owed, but at least the rest of the night was his. He was looking forward to some soup, a cup of coffee and maybe liver and onions when he stopped at the diner on Queens Boulevard.

"Tough night?"

John had been holding his head in both hands and hadn't seen the waitress standing there.

"Sorry," he said. "Something like that."

The waitress smiled. "What'll you have, hon?"

"Soup, anything but chicken soup. Liver and onions after that. And a cup of coffee?"

"Skip the liver. I think it's from the eighteenth century."

John appreciated the tip. "Thanks," he said. "Hamburger deluxe?"

The waitress winked. "Coming right up."

She turned to pour a cup of coffee and John glanced at her backside. He looked away when she turned to set the coffee on the counter. He looked again when she headed for the kitchen and watched her wiggle away until the swinging kitchen doors blocked his view.

He had sat at her station before. Her name tag read Melinda. She looked about his age, give or take a few years; between thirty-three and thirty-six, John guessed. She was a pretty woman with short blonde hair and bright blue eyes. He liked the way she had looked into his eyes when she spoke. He hadn't seen a ring and was wondering what her deal was when there was a commotion behind him at the cashier counter.

John watched it in the mirror's reflection behind the coffee urns. It looked to be an argument over a check. Two men were giving the cashier a hard time. John thought he recognized one of them before a busboy blocked his view.

It got loud fast. John recognized one of the voices, Sonny Corleone himself, Nick Santorra, cursing a blue streak.

"What are the odds?" John whispered.

"Fuck your mother's cunt!" Santorra yelled.

John saw himself cringe in the mirror. He turned his head to watch the action over his left shoulder.

"Please leave," he heard the hostess say. "Forget the check. You're disturbing our customers."

"Fuck your customers!" Santorra yelled.

"Please, sir. Just leave."

And then they were gone.

"Don't you hate assholes like that?"

John turned back around. It was the waitress, Melinda. She set a small dish of coleslaw and a cup of vegetable soup on the counter in front of him.

"I hope his wife is packing her things and running off with the plumber," she said.

"The plumber?"

"Or the kid who delivers their pizza. The gardener, if they have one. The insurance salesman'll do, too. Anybody."

John put his hand out. "I'm John," he said.

She pointed to her name tag. "I'm assuming you can read," she said.

"It's a pretty name," he said. "And, yeah, I do hate assholes like that. More than you could know."

CHAPTER 3

Eddie Vento had both feet up on his desk when Tommy Burns appeared in the office doorway. Vento set aside the *Racing Form* he had opened across his lap and removed his feet from the desk.

"Tommy me boy," he said. "The mick that does the trick."

"Mr. Vento," said Burns, extending his right hand.

Vento stepped around the desk, slapped Burns's hand away and gave him a bear hug, lifting him a few inches off the ground. "You sure your old man isn't Italian?" he said. "They changed the rules, you know. We could add a vowel your last name, get you made now."

Vento gave Burns one last squeeze before releasing him.

"I wish," Burns said, "but the old man was the real deal. Galway to Boston to New York. Knocked up my mother here, hung around long enough to teach me to take a punch and off he ran. He's still alive, it's in Boston. Haven't seen or heard from him since I made my confession a dozen years ago."

Vento slapped Burns on the back before returning to his chair. "He did something right, your old man. I had a dozen guys half as tough as you I'd be one happy guinea."

"I appreciate it, Mr. V. My father, too, I suppose."

Vento opened the second drawer in his desk and removed a stack of twenty-dollar bills secured by a rubber band. He set the money on top of the *Racing Form* and pointed to one of two folding chairs facing the desk. "Sit," he said. "That's a bonus, fifty fresh ones from the Williamsburg Savings Bank."

Burns looked at the stack of cash. "Wasn't a big deal," he said. "Tommy DeLuca left a trail of skanks he was sleeping with after he was flush with what he stole."

"I won't ask where you kept him, but I am curious where you gave him the manicure."

"Hudson Street," Burns said. "One of the lithography joints runs along the entrance to the Holland Tunnel downtown. Guy works in one owed me. Let us up, showed me how to use one of the paper cutters they have. Very clean."

Vento's eyebrows furrowed. "Who's us?"

"Not to worry, family on my mother's side. Was here visiting the week before, was back in Galway the next day."

Vento's concern evaporated as his eyebrows relaxed again. "What can I say? Balls and smart. I really do wish you were Italian."

"The trick was the dumpster," Burns said. "Getting him in the thing. I must've hurled half a dozen times before I got home. Spent the first hour burning my clothes and the next two showering. The dead, Mr. V., they fucking stink."

"So they say," Vento said. He grabbed a bottle of Johnny Walker Black and two shot glasses from a shelf behind his desk. He set the glasses on the desk and poured two drinks.

"You're making your way in this world," he said. "A couple days ago I passed your name along to a friend of mine. Guy might be a boss someday. He's having issues with his wife, asked if you'd have objections to something like that. I told him no. Was I right?"

"He's a friend of yours, say no more."

Both men grabbed a shot glass.

"*Salute*," Vento said.

"*Sláinte*," Burns said.

They touched glasses and downed their drinks. Vento immediately poured refills. He noticed the money still on the desk and pointed to it.

"Take that," he said.

Burns took the cash off the desk and folded it before stashing it inside his right pants pocket.

Vento said, "You might want to count it."

"I wouldn't insult you."

Vento winked at Burns and raised his glass. Burns grabbed his glass and the two men downed their drinks in silence.

"It okay if I smoke?" Burns asked after setting the shot glass back on the desk.

"You gotta ask?"

Burns lit a Camel regular. Vento relit a cigar he'd left in an ashtray.

"I might have something special coming up," he said.

"I'll be around," Burns said.

"Good, because it can't be one of my own. This one brings extra heat."

"Sounds like a badge."

"It is and it has stripes and has to disappear, the time comes. Disappear as in vanish."

"The meantime I'll prepare."

"Do that, because this guy, he goes, he can't be found. Not while I'm around."

Burns took a long drag off his cigarette.

"You ever think to use a filter?" Vento asked.

"Too used to these," Burns said. "Anything else, I wind up sucking harder just to get a taste, give myself a headache."

"This badge," Vento said. "He's dirty so there's a hefty stash somewhere we don't know. You find that on your own, it's yours on top of a fee."

Burns acknowledged the tip with a head nod.

"Meantime, keep your distance from this joint until I call you," Vento said. "Go out the back when you leave from here. It'll make the feds filming the entrance dizzy you don't come back out the front."

"I saw them on my way over," Burns said. "They're in a plumbing van off Hooper Street. They stay out there all night?"

Vento poured himself another shot. "Giving each other hand jobs, probably." He held the bottle up.

Burns declined. "I'm up early for mass tomorrow," he said. "My mother's a stubborn woman. Insists I go with her every Monday."

Vento set the bottle back down, downed the shot he'd poured for himself, and stepped around the desk to hug Burns good-bye. He said, "Don't blow it all on one broad, the money."

"Never," Burns said. "I'd give it to my mother, but then she'd hand it off to the church and I'd have a problem with that, it being blood money."

Vento was feeling the booze. He took an awkward step back and had to grab the desk. "You think the church gives a fuck where their money comes from?"

"Probably not, but I'd know," Burns said. "I still get nightmares from the statues in Holy Family when I went to school there. I even think about them, I see them moving. In my head like. The eyes and whatnot."

"St. Anthony?"

"Huh?"

"You pray to him to find your pecker?"

Burns got it. He forced a chuckle. "Another thing my old man gave me, I'm sure," he said. "Fuckin' Irish curse."

"Well, just let me know when you wanna get it wet, your limp noodle. I'll send a broad over take care of you."

"I'm free tomorrow night. Or is it tonight already?" He looked at his watch and said, "Tonight, I guess."

"You still by the Canarsie market?"

"Ninety-third between Foster and Farragut."

"You alone?"

"I'm having company I will be."

"Okay. Still go for the dark stuff?"

"I do indeed. A little meat on their bones is good, too."

"I'll find somebody," Vento said. "Somebody clean, but wear a hat anyway. Never know with these broads. Some don't know enough to douche, the stink alone'll peel your eyelids."

"It's the way of the modern world," Burns said.

"What's that?"

"Last thing the old man said to me before he scrammed. Told me he was leaving, I started to sniffle and he cuffed me one. 'Don't look at me like that, boyo,' he says. 'Parents split up all the time nowadays. It's the way of the modern world.'"

"He was right, your old man, the way things are today."

Burns said, "And a fuckin' shame it is."

■ ■ ■

Before he went to the bar to sell his last ounce of marijuana, Louis double-checked his gambling figures for the week. He had called in six bets Saturday afternoon and lost five, two of the favorites he'd bet, Cincinnati and Los Angeles, laying two-to-one. Sunday he'd bet the Reds again and lost again. He also lost the other five bets he'd made, but at least those were underdogs and he wouldn't have to pay a premium for laying odds. He would need eleven hundred dollars for one bookie and another six hundred for the new office he'd been calling to shop a better line.

Between the money he owed a loan shark, his betting losses, and living expenses, Louis needed a score and soon. Earlier the bartender at the corner tavern had told him he had a fish on the line, some young kid from the neighborhood looking to deal nickel bags. Louis couldn't cut his weed with any more oregano than he already had, but if the kid was naïve, he could pad the price enough to pay the weekly interest he owed his shylock.

When he was inside the bar, he saw Jimmy the loan shark was already perched on his stool. Louis was three days late on the interest from a two-thousand-dollar street loan. At three points a week, he owed sixty dollars. In four days it would be ninety. He had exactly six dollars in his pocket.

The bartender motioned toward the kid looking to buy marijuana, but there was no way Louis could bypass the loan shark. He signaled the bartender to hold the kid off and went to see the big man.

"I rang your phone enough times," Jimmy said. "You ignoring me?"

"Never," Louis said.

Jimmy was a three-hundred-pounder with broad shoulders and a perpetual scowl on his face; there was no reading what he was thinking.

"You got my money?" he asked.

"Can you give me five minutes?"

"Why, you gonna hold up the joint?"

Louis didn't get it at first and couldn't tell if Jimmy was joking. He forced a chuckle, but the big man wasn't smiling.

Or maybe he was.

"I have a little business to conduct in the bathroom and I'll be right back," Louis said.

Jimmy reached for his drink, a scotch and soda. "Funny," he said with no expression, "a good-looking kid like you, I never took you for a fag."

That one Louis got. He laughed for effect. "Good one," he said. "I'm right back, okay?"

The big man looked at his watch. "Five minutes," he said.

Louis had the bartender introduce him to the kid, who looked no older than seventeen. They used the men's room to conduct business. Normally Louis didn't deal with kids because they couldn't be trusted, but in this case he was more than willing to make an exception. You could only bullshit guys like Jimmy so long before they broke one of your arms.

A few minutes later he returned to the bar and handed off the interest he owed the loan shark. Jimmy saw Louis had some extra cash in his hand and offered to take it.

"So we don't have to go through this again next week," he said. "Sunday nights I like to catch up on my beauty rest."

"And here I am thinking I might be able to pay you off next week," Louis said.

"And how's that gonna happen? You gonna parlay the few bucks you have phoning bets in?"

"It's a secret," Louis said.

Jimmy patted the empty stool next to him. "Then sit here and buy me one so's I don't feel neglected."

Louis had better things to do, but there was no refusing the big man. He sat on the stool, set a ten-dollar bill down and motioned at the bartender.

"Jimmy's with me," he said.

"I'd thank you but I shouldn't a hadda tell you," Jimmy said.

The bartender served Jimmy a scotch and soda before pouring a beer from the tap for Louis. The two men drank in silence while a conversation about blow jobs mid-bar became loud. One drunk preferred the use of hands when getting head. The other claimed it wasn't a blow job if a woman used her hands.

"Personally, I could give a fuck," Jimmy said to Louis. "It's the idea anyway, some broad taking it in the mouth."

Louis wasn't sure what the big man was getting at and the last thing he wanted was to discuss it. He listened as the two drunks continued their argument six stools away.

"She uses her hand, she's jerking you off," the one drunk said. "You could do that yourself."

"Yeah?" the other drunk said. "Can you put it in your mouth at the same time?"

"He's got a point," Jimmy said.

Louis saw it was getting late. He was supposed to pick up his girlfriend and was afraid he'd miss her call sitting there being bored out of his mind. He was about to say he had to leave when Jimmy nudged him with an elbow.

"Speaking of blow jobs," he said, "a friend of a friend of mine, some whale bets ten dimes a day the office on one-eleven, he has a guy looking to buy the car they used in that movie."

"What car in what movie?"

"The blow job thing... somebody's throat?"

"*Deep Throat*," Louis said.

"Whatever. There's a car they use in the thing, an Eldorado something. A Fleetwood, I think. Some Cadillac the guy says he'll go five large above original sticker price for."

Louis hadn't seen the movie, but remembered his ex-wife had mentioned something about the director.

"He can buy one new for less," Louis said. "Caddy's go for what, seven, eight grand maybe. What year's the thing?"

"I don't know," Jimmy said. "He wants it should be the one from the movie. He thinks it'll be worth a lot some day."

Louis was about to mention what his ex-wife had told him, but stopped short and asked a question instead.

"How does he verify something like that?"

"What?"

"That he doesn't get sold a replica off a lot someplace?"

"I guess the paperwork, I don't know."

"Or maybe they get somebody from the movie to do it?"

"What's that?"

"Verify it's the right car."

"Whatever," Jimmy said. "I'll tell you something else, this guy wants the car, my friend says he's got it bad for the broad did the movie. He'd probably throw her an extra grand or two she cleaned his pipes."

Louis saw it was after one o'clock in the morning and slid off the stool. "She probably gets two dozen offers a day for that," he said. He grabbed his change from the bar, except for two dollars for a tip.

"Next time you're late, you're buying me dinner," Jimmy said.

"I'm not sure I could afford it," said Louis, trying to crack a joke.

The big man gave him the blank look again. He blinked twice and made it all the more confusing.

Louis patted Jimmy on the near shoulder. "Thanks," he said. "You gave me a good idea."

"What's that?" Jimmy said.

"If your friend'll really pay two grand for a blow job, somebody should arrange it."

"That'd make you a pimp."

"I can pay your weekly juice, would it make a difference?"

"See you in four days," said Jimmy, before he held up four fingers and repeated himself. "Four."

CHAPTER 4

The humidity still hadn't lifted when John made it home. He climbed the three floors to his apartment and let himself into the one-bedroom sauna, what it felt like, then went straight to the bedroom where he turned the air conditioner on high. He stood in front of it with his eyes closed a few minutes before retreating to the bathroom.

He let the cold water run in the shower while he thought about the bills he had to pay in the morning, but wasn't sure his checking account could cover. He used the toilet and listed the bills off in his head: rent, electric, telephone, life insurance.

John knew he had six hundred to cover the rent, electric, and telephone, but he'd be short on his life insurance. The six-month premium had gone up to eighty dollars. He had ninety-five in cash on him and there might be sixteen left over in the checking. He would get paid from the car service, at least his tips, if he drove tomorrow afternoon, but then he'd have to hustle to an insurance branch that would take payment before they closed or get hit with a late fee.

He tried not to think about it as he stepped under the cool water. He stood there as long as he could take it, then turned the water from cold to hot and tilted his head back to let the spray soothe his scalp.

John was exhausted after another twenty-hour day. He wondered about the waitress and if she was just as tired being on her feet all day as he was sitting in a car. He wondered if she was showering now, too, and what she looked like naked and whether or not they'd be compatible in bed if he ever got that lucky.

When he was relaxed enough, John turned the shower off and stepped out of the tub. He saw his reflection in the mirror hanging from the back of the bathroom door and thought about his unwanted nickname, Johnny Porno. The thought made him frown.

He examined his reflection and noticed he was starting to gain weight. He'd never been close to two hundred pounds before, but was thinking he was already there or damn close to it. He had retained some muscle definition working construction, but there were love handles now he hadn't noticed before. He turned sideways and saw it was worse than he'd thought. A small pouch had started above his waist.

He dried his head, chest and legs, then his arms and hair again as he made his way to the kitchen. He checked the fridge for something to snack on and enjoyed the cool he felt with the door open. There was leftover macaroni his mother had given him, a slice of cold pizza and half of a turkey sandwich.

He decided against eating and made a drink instead. He poured from a bottle of cheap gin, nearly filling a highball glass. He added a few ice cubes from the plastic tray he kept in the freezer. He used flat tonic water from a bottle he'd left open on the counter two days ago; there was hardly any fizz when he mixed the drink.

John sat at the kitchen table and did the math between his checking account and bills on the white margin space along the cover page of the *Daily News*. He added the figures twice each and frowned at the result. He had been right about the leftover sixteen dollars. If he got an advance for driving the next day, he could pay his backed-up child support and the life insurance and still have two, maybe three dollars until Wednesday.

He drank deep from the highball glass. Less than a year ago he could afford to pay for his life and still have a few extra bucks to take his son to a baseball game. Last year he'd had enough to buy the kid the bike with the banana seat he'd asked for.

So far this year all he'd done that was close to special was take his son to the official opening of the World Trade Center back in April. He had wanted to take him to the opening-day game at Yankee Stadium to see the first ever designated-hitter game, but April 6 had been a Friday and the same night he had started his job counting the number of men that showed up to see *Deep Throat* at theaters on Long Island.

In two months the kid would be ten. John felt guilty thinking about his son. Sometimes the guilt was overwhelming. He did his best to think of something else and glanced at the headlines about a plot to kill President Nixon. He read some of the article, saw it was an ex-cop the Secret Service suspected in New Orleans, a guy nicknamed Punchy. John thought about Nick Santorra and thought Punchy might be a good name for him, too.

He took another long drink, refilled the glass with gin, added another ice cube and stood up. He used his free hand to carry one of his two kitchen chairs into the bedroom. He set it down facing the stream of cold air blowing from the air conditioner, sat, closed his eyes and drank deep again.

Tomorrow was another day.

■ ■ ■

Louis fell asleep watching a World War II documentary. Holly woke him at two when she called from the Port Washington train station to tell him she was on her way. She called again a few minutes later to make sure he was still awake and Louis told her he was and that he would be waiting for her at the Woodhaven Boulevard subway stop. Then he put his head back down on the pillow and fell asleep.

He woke again nearly an hour later. He saw the time, threw on some clothes and rushed out to his car. He ran two lights to make up time, but a tow truck pulling a car away from an accident on Metropolitan Avenue cost him five minutes.

He was at least half an hour late when he spotted Holly standing at the curb on Woodhaven Boulevard with her arms folded across her chest. Louis beeped the horn and flashed his lights. Holly didn't acknowledge him. He called to her after making a U-turn at the next light and she barely turned her head.

When he pulled up to the curb, Holly was glaring at him. He leaned across the bench seat and opened the passenger door. She ignored him another few seconds before finally getting in.

"I'm sorry," he said.

He tried to kiss her and was rebuffed when she pulled away.

"I thought I turned the alarm clock on, but it didn't go off," he said. "You waiting long?"

Holly glared harder at him.

"I'm sorry," he repeated.

"I'm out here alone at three-thirty in the morning," she finally said. "And I called you this afternoon."

"I wasn't home."

"Bullshit."

"I wasn't. I was out doing privates."

"Yeah, your ex-wife's probably."

The problem with telling a new girlfriend too much about an ex-wife, even when accusing the ex of being a first-class bitch, was they gathered all that information and stored it. Louis had met Holly a few months ago, but she had already become suspicious of his relationship with Nancy.

"Don't be like that," he said. "I was working, I swear."

Holly had turned in the seat so her back was flush against the door. She was a tall, thin girl with a pretty face, perky rump, long legs, blue eyes and long blonde hair. Model material, Louis had thought the first time he saw her.

"What?" he said. "I said I'm sorry. I overslept."

"I thought the alarm didn't go off?"

"What? Shit, Holly, gimme a break."

Holly faced front again. "You working in the morning?"

"Yeah, but not windows. Something else."

"Can I at least sleep in? I don't have class until the afternoon."

"What, I'm gonna throw you out?"

"I don't know. You didn't answer my call, you didn't bother waking up, I know that much."

It wasn't going to be easy talking her into anything tonight. He might as well give it up and try again tomorrow, Louis was thinking, except he had to be ready at a moment's notice if he intended to rob Nancy's ex-husband of all that cash he was collecting from that porn movie. Louis was hoping to work Holly somewhere in his game plan.

"Look, I'm sorry. I really am, okay?"

"You're saying that a lot tonight."

And he'd keep saying it if it eventually got her to help him. Holly Nordstram was a former runner-up Miss Oklahoma, was from a good family and was a firm believer in hard work and education. In fact, it was Holly's work ethic that first attracted her to Louis. When he showed up to clean the windows at an acting studio where she was attending a workshop and he complained bitterly about the job being neglected, she assumed the neglect was the fault of another window-cleaner. Rather than clearing up the misunderstanding, Louis got her number. That had been three months ago. Now that she'd been living in the big city and probably learning the ropes a lot faster than she ever could in Oklahoma, he was afraid of losing her confidence.

"I say it because I mean it," he told her. "I'm sorry if I'm busy trying to make ends meet, Holly, but I don't have a choice. I wasn't smart like you. I didn't take school seriously. I have to work for a living."

She fell silent. At this point in their relationship Louis knew how to tap into her upper-middle-class guilt. They were nearly back to his apartment when she finally spoke again.

"I'm sorry, too," she said. "I know you work hard. I shouldn't get upset."

Bingo, he was thinking. Maybe the time was right after all. The feminist cause *du jour* had become pornography. Holly and her young, affluent friends were enthusiastically riding the anti-porn bandwagon. He would have to work with her recent musings against pornography and try to convince her that Nancy's ex-husband was somehow connected to the movie *Deep Throat*; that she'd be doing her fellow sisters in feminism a solid by helping him rip John Albano off. Holly and her friends had recently spent an afternoon protesting in front of one of the porn theaters on Forty-second Street.

"It's nothing I'm proud of," he said. "Being another working slob, but it's what I do and I have to make the best of it when there's extra work."

"You're not a slob for working hard, Louis, don't say that."

It wouldn't be easy getting her to go along with a robbery, but Louis had learned a long time ago the way to a woman's heart was with compliments.

"I tell you how pretty you look today?"

"No, but thank you."

"I tell you how much I missed you?"

"No, and I wouldn't believe it because you were sleeping."

He held up a finger. "Unless I was dreaming about you."

"Sure," she said. "Can we stop for some pop?"

"What?"

"Soda. Do you have any in the fridge?"

"Coke, I think. I'm not sure. I'll go get some if I don't. I need to get you to forgive me tonight."

"If you're looking for sex, it won't be that easy."

"I'm always looking for sex with you, honey."

"When it's convenient, it seems."

"Come on, Holly," Louis said. He matched her frown with one of his own, then said, "What if I had a proposition that involves acting?"

Holly made a face.

"I'm talking about helping the cause," he continued. "Your cause against pornography."

Holly seemed skeptical.

Louis turned onto the street where he lived and parked in front of the apartment building. Then he turned to Holly, took her hands in his and explained some of his game plan.

■ ■ ■

Nick Santorra was in a foul mood when he finally made it home. It had been a bad day that turned worse from the moment he left the house a few minutes after noon. First there was the speeding ticket he got on the Cross Island Parkway. Twenty minutes later he got another one on the Belt Parkway. Both tickets had come as a result of Nick's new job chauffeuring Eddie Vento, who happened to be a skipper with the Vignieri crime family and his wife's first cousin's husband. Nick had joined Vento's ranks with the hope of becoming a made man himself one day. After two years of performing gopher work for the mob and having to fork over most of what he earned on his own for the sake of a no-show truck driving job, Nick had finally moved up, the way he viewed the driving job.

Except so far it wasn't all that glamorous, his new position. Today Nick had to pick up his boss's dry cleaning and then chauffeur Vento's wife back and forth to local stores. She was shopping for her daughter's engagement party, something else that would cost Nick another fifty dollars in a couple of weeks.

Then he was stuck at the bar in Williamsburg doing the tally count for the fuck movie he was sick and tired of already. Even though it was the only chance he got to abuse somebody lower on the mob food chain, it was a lot of work counting all that money and having to deal with guys who would steal from their mothers.

After the tally count at the bar and after Vento held a private meeting in the basement with some Irish kid Nick didn't like, he drove the drunken wiseguy to make a few pickups in Queens where he was stuck sitting in the car while mobsters exchanged cheek kisses and bear hugs ten feet away without ever acknowledging his existence. Then Vento insisted on stopping to see one of his girlfriends to get his pipes cleaned and that had taken almost an hour. Afterwards the wiseguy decided he wanted a piece of cheesecake at some diner in Queens and Nick was stuck being his company for that, too.

It was at the diner where the tension bubbled over and Nick lost it, first on a waitress and then with the cashier when a ten-cent charge wasn't removed for a cup of coffee he never drank. Vento gave him shit for it later when they were in the parking lot, telling Nick he couldn't curse like that in a room full of people because it made them look bad.

"What's the matter with you?" Vento had told him. "First of all you don't act like that in a public place. Second, you don't talk like that to some broad unless she's your girlfriend. You wanna act like a tough guy, save it for the street."

Nick had been dumbfounded at the lecture. He'd been trying to impress Vento since he first went to work for him and was sure he'd started to make some headway when he was told he'd be the wiseguy's new driver. Vento's regular driver was serving a two-year sentence for assault. Nick had thought the move from flunky to personal driver was a big deal and had even taken his wife out to celebrate.

He'd since found out the road to becoming a made man was a lot bumpier than he'd originally thought. Being Eddie Vento's personal driver wasn't half as glamorous as Nick had imagined. All he'd done so far was pick up dry cleaning and make shopping runs. He'd become a glorified gopher subject to Eddie Vento's vitriolic temper tantrums and the man could go from calm to insane in two seconds flat. When that happened, there was nothing Nick could say or do to avoid the berating he'd get for putting or not putting on a turn signal.

Nick found himself catching a lot more flack than he'd ever caught before and was starting to wonder if or when it would be worth it because he was still bringing home peanuts in salary for all the aggravation he was getting. He wondered if the driver he was replacing maybe had it better serving out the assault conviction up in Fishkill.

When he finally dropped the wiseguy off, it was close to one o'clock in the morning, but before Vento let Nick go, he had him haul six cartons out of his basement.

It was then the abuse and humiliation had been stretched an extra yard his ego didn't have to spare; when Vento told him what was inside the cartons.

"Posters and panties," the wiseguy had said.

Vento wanted them distributed where they were showing the fuck movie, *Deep Throat*. Nick resented it. He knew the big shots were making big money off the porn flick while guys like him were picking up crumbs for all their work.

"What you're gonna do is take those home and have them signed, the panties and the posters," Vento had said. "Sign them Linda Lovelace and have the guys running the movie sell them off as specialty items. Fi' dollas for the panties and two for the posters. They keep a quarter on whatever they sell. We get the rest."

"Panties?"

"Just make sure the same person signs them all the same way. Or the mopes might figure out they're fugazy."

Now, sitting at the dining room table, his hand cramping from signing poster after poster, Nick felt stupid.

Earlier he'd asked his wife to help, but Angela freaked out when she saw the posters were of Linda Lovelace and that the panties were supposed to be from the porno flick.

"That's disgusting," she had told Nick. "That woman should be in jail and so should you for selling that shit."

Nick hadn't had the energy to fight with her then. He let it go and started signing the posters instead. It was a time-consuming process during which he had to pull the plastic sleeve off each one, unroll it, then sign and re-roll it before slipping the sleeve back on.

It was nearly four o'clock in the morning when Angela awoke to use the bathroom and saw the dining room light was still on. She saw Nick was still working and said, "How long you gonna do this? It's four o'clock in the morning."

"As long as it takes," Nick said. "You could've helped me, you know."

"With that filth? You better get if off the table before the kids wake up."

"You could help me do that at least."

"No thank you, I gotta get up in the morning. I don't have the luxury of sleeping until noon."

"Yeah," Nick said. "Or getting off your ass once you're awake."

Angela flipped him the bird.

Nick considered telling her to go fuck her mother's cunt, the words were right there on the tip of his tongue, but then he thought about the lecture he'd gotten from Eddie Vento and kept his mouth shut.

CHAPTER 5

John was up early when a fuse blew. Without air conditioning the apartment had turned into a sweatbox.

He showered with cold water while a pot of coffee brewed on the stove. He dressed quickly and left the apartment twenty minutes later, his shirt sweat-stained before he was in his car. Rather than waste the morning, he showed up to work early and was lucky when a call for an airport run turned up. John's good fortune continued at the airport, where he caught a return fare into Manhattan he didn't have to report.

He worked steady the rest of the morning into the early afternoon and was able to stop at an insurance office to make the payment on his life insurance policy. He mailed the rest of the bills he'd written checks for and was thinking he might not have to ask for an advance to pay the backed-up child support when the afternoon fares dried up in spite of a few rain showers. Then he had to shell out close to five dollars to fill his gas tank and by three o'clock he was down to thirteen dollars. He owed his ex-wife seventy.

He had another run to LaGuardia for a pickup at four followed by a JFK run at five-thirty. He was still short his child support when it was time to check out for the day at seven o'clock, but John decided he'd pay just one week of what he owed and then catch up on Thursday. He made the trip to Queens after cashing out with just over fifty dollars in his wallet.

He didn't see his son when his ex-wife opened the front door.

"Jack around?" he asked.

Nancy put her right hand out, palm up. John had already counted out thirty-five dollars. He placed the cash in her palm. Nancy scowled at the sight of single dollar bills.

"What's this shit?" she said.

"One week. It's all I have."

Nancy rolled her eyes. "And the singles?"

"Tips, Nan. It's what I get when I'm driving."

"What happened to the fives?"

"You complain about those, too."

"They're easier to work with than singles."

"There's a ten and a five in there."

She rolled her eyes. "When are you gonna get a real job?"

"You mean like yours?"

"Fuck you."

"No thanks."

"You wish."

"Never."

"Asshole."

John took a deep breath. "Jack around or not?"

"He had a sleepover," Nancy said. "If you really gave a shit, you'd already know that."

"I forgot," John said. "I'll be back Thursday with the rest of the money. You have anything planned for then?"

"There's a bazaar in Valley Stream next week you could take him to. Maybe he could spend the night with you for a change."

"That so you can bang your current husband for a change?"

Nancy swung at him with her hand holding the cash. John blocked the smack and the money rained all over the front stoop.

"You fuck-face bastard," she said.

"Nice," John said. "Very classy."

"Go fuck yourself, you loser. Go get in your piece-of-shit car and get lost."

"I guess Nathan isn't home," John said. "You got Louis hiding in there under the kitchen table?"

John knew she'd had an affair with her first husband while John was still married to her. He assumed Louis was still in her life.

Nancy was picking the cash up off the lawn and stoop. John didn't help her.

"You're just jealous because he's twice the man you are," she said. "And he's twice as big where it counts."

She was leaning off the last step on the stoop. He warned her to be careful, but she lost her balance and fell. He couldn't help laughing. Nancy's face turned red.

"I hate you, you cocksucker!"

John motioned toward the street. "A little louder," he said. "They didn't hear you up the block."

"Fuck you!" she screamed.

John held his right hand to his right ear. "What's that?"

"I hate you!"

John spotted one of the single-dollar bills she had missed and pointed to it. "You missed one."

"Go drive your taxi, John. And bring me the money you owe, you deadbeat fuck. He's your son, too."

It had been funny until she called him a deadbeat. It was something he wasn't proud of, the fact he was behind making child support payments. It wasn't the first time and he doubted it would be the last unless things changed soon. She was also right about his job. He hadn't had a real one for more than a year now. The extra work he picked up here and there wasn't cutting it. The weekend gig running a porn movie back and forth from Brooklyn to Long Island and making collections for the idiots behind it was as demeaning as it was lousy pay. The only benefit so far had been it was unreported income. At least he wasn't paying taxes on it.

He returned to his car feeling down. Nancy wasn't a genius but she could be mean. She had scored a blow calling him a deadbeat. He was also upset about forgetting the sleepover. His son had told him and John had forgot. He doubted Nancy would even mention to his son that he'd stopped to see him.

He started the engine and was about to pull away when he heard Nancy call to him. He glanced to his right and there she was with a big smile on her face as she gave him the finger from the top of the stoop.

The woman was comical, he thought.

■　■　■

Louis knew the steady diet of five-dollar bills John Albano had been paying his ex-wife for child support was dirty money that had something to do with the recently banned porno movie *Deep Throat*. The other thing he knew was if the money was dirty, robbing it couldn't be reported.

Although there was the mob to consider, Louis understood how they operated. Once the money was missing, Albano would be the one held responsible. The connected guys Louis dealt with, between gambling and borrowing money, were all consistent when it came to cash. None of them were interested in stories about why you didn't have it when you were supposed to.

The plan was to catch Albano on a Sunday night before he delivered his weekend receipts to the Williamsburg bar. Louis had clocked him three consecutive Sundays. Except for his last three stops, the collection route had been the same. Concerned that he might take an alternative route to stop and see his kid, Louis had grilled Nancy about it the day before. It would help if he could insure her second ex-husband didn't deviate from his routine. Louis had a few ideas about how to rob John Albano, but it would be a lot easier if he had some help.

Holly had been cool to his original plan, but Louis knew he could always depend on Nancy. His ex-wife was shrewd, though, so he would have to do more than promise her a cut of the take. Nancy had already grown bored with her third husband and was still very much in love with Louis. She had only married the geeky musician because of his money. There might even be a small score in her divorce, since the guy she'd married owned the house they lived in now.

The possibilities, when Louis was calm enough to think through his more immediate financial problems, seemed endless.

This week, however, his window-cleaning salary wouldn't come anywhere near covering his gambling nut. He needed to score some grass he could sell fast and then he'd need to take another street loan to pay the two bookies he owed. Louis had no idea how much money Albano collected over the weekend, but however much it was, Louis needed it and he would have to move fast to get it by the end of the week. Otherwise, he didn't know how he'd pay off the close to seventeen hundred dollars he owed two bookies, much less the two grand he still owed Jimmy.

He called in five bets on the trotters at Roosevelt and stood to lose another two hundred dollars he didn't have. He'd already lost sixty dollars on two Saratoga bets earlier in the day, a straight twenty-dollar win and a ten-dollar exacta that didn't come through. Lady Luck had been cruel lately, running ice-cold it seemed. His luck had to change fast or Louis had to rob John Albano sooner rather than later.

■　■　■

Lieutenant Detective Sean Kelly, at thirty-nine years of age, was a sixteen-year veteran and the senior detective in a task force investigation into the illegal distribution of the recently banned porn film *Deep Throat*. Kelly wore sweatpants, a baseball cap and an oversized Led Zeppelin T-shirt as a disguise to throw off any surveillance watching the mobbed-up bar on the first floor of the apartment building he'd entered five minutes earlier. He smirked at the sounds of sex he could hear through an apartment door, then leaned against it, cupping his left ear. He smiled as the woman's yelping grew to a crescendo.

Kelly waited until the man began to grunt before knocking on the door.

"Shit," he heard Eddie Vento say.

Kelly gave it a moment, then knocked again.

"Fuck," Vento said. "Get offa me."

Kelly smiled. He heard light footsteps running away on the other side of the apartment door, then heavier footsteps approaching it. He was about to knock again when the door opened.

"I waited until I thought you were finished," he said.

Eddie Vento, wearing a white wife-beater and light blue boxer underwear, stood in the doorway smirking. "You shouldn't spend all your money on clothes like that," he said. "I didn't know you I might shoot you."

"Can I come in?"

Vento stepped back to let the detective inside.

Kelly passed through the doorway. He heard a toilet flush and turned in time to see a woman pull on a pair of black bikini underwear. She was naked from the waist up. She saw Kelly looking and slammed the bathroom door shut.

Vento had just closed and locked the apartment door. He turned and saw Kelly was staring toward the bathroom. "She works downstairs weekends," he said.

"Pretty girl."

Vento grabbed a half-smoked cigar from an ashtray on the coffee table in front of the couch. "She's a ballbreaker is what she is. Non-fucking-stop, sometimes."

Kelly spotted a black bra on the couch. He picked it up.

Vento finished lighting his cigar and motioned at Kelly with it. "You enjoying yourself?"

Kelly set the bra on the coffee table as he sat on the couch. "Can we talk?"

Vento took a seat in an armchair facing the detective.

"This thing with the movie," Kelly said. "I need to make a bust soon. Now this guy turned up in a Queens dumpster, I need something to show I'm doing my job."

"Can't it wait a few weeks?"

"Not anymore. It's an issue now, this movie. City Hall expects arrests. Leaving the guy without his hands may keep other guys from stealing, but it also made it easy for reporters to learn his business. Today they know a guy was whacked, tomorrow they'll know where he dropped his last load."

The bathroom door opened down the hall. Both men turned toward the sound of footsteps as Bridget Malone entered the room wearing an open pajama top and panties. She stopped a moment to button the top.

"Got a better look now?" she asked Kelly.

"You wanna give us some privacy here?" Vento said. "We're talking business."

"Excuse me," said Bridget with sarcasm. "Can I breathe? Is that okay?"

Vento bit his lower lip. Kelly watched Bridget head into the kitchen.

"She's awful young," he whispered.

"Don't kid yourself," Vento said, "she's been around the block."

"Been around what block?" Bridget said. She was standing with her back to them as she looked through a cabinet.

"Never mind," Vento said. "Get whatever you want and go."

"Fine," Bridget said. "I'll eat my chips in lockup."

She was holding a bag of potato chips. Kelly sniggered as she fingered a chip from the bag to her mouth. She forced a smile and he watched her rump wiggle back down the hall.

"Lockup? Where'd she learn that one?" he asked Vento.

"From sitting in one," Vento said. "She was dating some druggie when she first come to work downstairs. She was with him when he got pinched moving horse. She's no stranger to the system. Like I said, she's been around."

It was uncomfortable information. Kelly turned toward the hallway again.

"She's got a mouth on her like every other broad, but she's alright you look past the front she puts on," Vento said. "She keeps an eye on the old lady upstairs can't do the stairs. Looks in on her a couple times a day, goes to the store and so on. She don't know you is all."

Bridget suddenly returned. "Can I get a soda so I don't choke from thirst?" she asked.

"You could've got that before," Vento said.

"Can I get it now?"

"Make it fast. Me and Mr. Horse have business."

Bridget exaggerated a chuckle. "Mr. Horse?"

Vento glared at her.

"I'll be gone in two minutes," she said. "I have to go upstairs anyway. Mrs. G wanted me to rub her feet."

"Wipe her ass while you're at it. She shit herself the other day, stunk up the stairway."

"Christ, Eddie, she's eighty-six years old."

"Good for her."

"What's your excuse?"

Vento stood up out of the chair.

"I'm going," said Bridget as she darted into the kitchen. "I'll be gone in two minutes."

"You see what I gotta put up with?" Vento said to Kelly.

The detective wasn't smiling. He watched Bridget as she moved around the kitchen.

"Not only this bullshit I gotta listen to," Vento said, "but she wants to go in the business and do a porno." He thumbed over his shoulder. "She thinks it's glamorous."

"Tell him my life story, why don't you?" Bridget said. She pulled the tab on a can of Coke and sipped.

"She's pretty enough," Kelly forced himself to say.

"Thank you," Bridget said. "Like it would make a difference to him, I did a fuck movie."

Vento slapped his hands together in frustration.

"I thought you liked when I talked dirty, Eddie."

Vento turned and glared at her again.

"What?" she said.

"Get lost."

"He's got all these connections, but he won't do anything for me," Bridget told Kelly.

"I said get lost," Vento said.

"I should make my own connections," she said. "I know at least one person who'd love to know what he likes in the sack."

"You're pushing your luck, cunt."

Bridget had started toward the door, then stopped in her tracks, her face flushed red. "Cunt?" she said. "Fuck you, Eddie. Go fuck your wife. Let her talk dirty for you."

Vento was across the room before she could get out of the apartment. The smack knocked her to the floor.

Kelly stood up from his chair. Vento cocked a fist.

"You got anything else you wanna say?" he yelled. "Get it out now so you won't have so far to fall next time."

Bridget was stunned from the smack and didn't feel the tear running down one side of her face. She leaned her back against the wall alongside the door and felt her mouth for blood.

"Get out!" Vento yelled before opening the apartment door.

She flinched at the sound of his voice, then turned to her right and crawled past him to pick up the soda can.

"Leave it," Vento said. "You can get it later."

Bridget crawled out the door. Vento waited until she started to stand, then put his foot on her ass and shoved her out the rest of the way into the hallway. She fell forward onto the floor and lay flat on her stomach. She covered her head with both hands when Vento slammed the door shut behind her.

"I should put her in a porno," he said to Kelly. "She has something in it, she can't shoot off at the mouth."

He returned to the armchair, sat and relit his cigar.

Kelly said, "That don't make you nervous, she threatens to talk like that?"

"No," Vento said. "She knows I'll cut her fuckin' throat she ever does that."

Kelly wasn't so sure.

"Where were we?" Vento said.

"About the investigation," Kelly said. "Now that you're leaving bodies to be found, can you feed me a live one?"

CHAPTER 6

John thought about stopping at the diner to see if Melinda was working, but he didn't want to appear desperate. He went home instead. He'd just stepped inside the building when he was surprised by the old man standing in the hallway with a candle.

Alexis Elias saw the look on John's face and said, "What? I frighten you?"

"Scared the shit out of me is more like it," John said. "What's going on?"

The seventy-year-old native Greek had moved into a first-floor studio apartment six months ago. John had looked out for him since.

"Is too hot," said Elias, his accent still thick forty years after coming to America. "I go outside."

"You need an air conditioner."

The old man made a face. "What good is air conditioner now, genius? No electric."

"For when it's working."

"For what, to pay more bills? I am Greek, we don't need such things. Is hot like furnace inside, we go outside."

"You can come up to my place, you want."

The old man waved the suggestion off. "For what? To catch pneumonia?"

"Whatever," John said. Elias was stubborn. There was no arguing with him. "You should talk to the super," John said. "He sells used air conditioners."

"He doesn't know his elbow from his ass. Move."

John stepped aside. "You gonna be alright?"

"Why not?" Elias said. "I'm strong like bull." He took a few more steps and stopped at the door. "You worked for criminals today?"

Elias didn't approve of John's weekend work and reminded him of it every chance he got.

"Well?" the old man said.

"No, not today."

"Right, weekends you work for them. My mistake."

John folded his arms across his chest.

"What do I care?" Elias said. "You're young and stupid. I try to teach, but you don't listen."

"We done now?"

"Fine, ignore me. We change subject. How is your mother?"

"Fine, but that's none of your business."

"Why not? She is widow too long now. Why you don't invite her here to dinner? I cook for her."

"Because she's my mother and you're a dirty old man."

"Pff," said Elias as he turned to the door.

"Good night, Alex," John said.

"Call me Zorba," Elias said. "I am Zorba."

"Your name is Alex."

"Go play with air conditioner," the old man said as he stepped outside.

John stopped at the super's apartment and learned a burned fuse in the basement had damaged some of the wiring and wouldn't be replaced until the next day.

"And how'm I supposed to sleep tonight?" he asked.

"I'm sorry, there's nothing I can do," the super said. "You're welcome to use the basement if you want. It's a little cooler down there."

"The cellar?" John said. "No thanks. Can you check on the old man before you go to sleep? Elias. Make sure he's okay."

"Zorba?" the super said. "Of course, except I saw him with a woman from around the corner again today. Maybe he goes there again if he can't sleep."

"Right," John said. "Perfect. He's getting laid and I'm worried about him."

"Excuse me?" the super said.

"Nothing."

He headed up the three flights to his apartment. It was pitch-black when he got inside. He cursed when he banged his knee against the corner of the kitchen table as he searched for the junk drawer where he kept a flashlight. He went to pour himself an ice water and realized the refrigerator wasn't working either.

"Christ," he said, then let the sink water run until it was as cold as it would get.

He downed the glass of water, poured another and brought it with him to the bedroom. He stripped out of his clothes, lay on his back and closed his eyes. John was still sweating, but exhaustion eventually took over and he fell asleep.

The telephone woke him at eleven. He was disoriented when he answered and heard somebody cursing.

"Who is this?"

"Nick."

John was still half asleep. "Nick who?"

"You being funny?"

"What?"

"This Johnny Porno?"

John realized it was Nick Santorra. He huffed, then yawned extra long on purpose.

"You think you're cute, right?" Santorra said. "Am I keeping you awake?"

"Yeah, actually," John said. "I was sleeping. You woke me, Punchy."

"Punchy? You'll be punchy you keep jerking me off."

John yawned again.

"Do that again and I'll kick your teeth down your throat," Santorra said. "How's that?"

"I can't help I was sleeping," said John, still smiling.

"Yeah, well, now you're not. You need to come down to the bar tomorrow and pick something up."

"I can't tomorrow. I work."

"You work for us."

"Weekends. Monday to Thursday I drive a car."

"Take a break then."

John didn't respond.

"You there?" Santorra asked.

"I can't get off during the day. Has to be night."

"Yeah, well, make fucking sure you show. It's important."

"What is it?"

"Just be there," Santorra said.

John shook his head when Santorra hung up. The guy was an asshole.

He unplugged the phone so he wouldn't be disturbed again. He tried closing his eyes but the guy had got under his skin one more time. Sleep wouldn't come easy.

■　■　■

Detective Levin met up with Captain Kaprowski at the corner of Flatlands Avenue and East 93rd street. Fire department trucks had just left after putting out a suspicious fire at a local real estate office. Onlookers had yet to disperse.

Kaprowski motioned toward his car, a green Catalina, parked at the curb in front of an Italian bakery further up the avenue.

"What was that about?" Levin asked.

"Blacks trying to move into a white neighborhood," Kaprowski said. "It's not the first time that place was hit. Probably won't be the last. They listed homes and apparently a few black families went to see them. Local yahoos aren't appreciative."

"You'd think this shit only went on in the South."

"Then you'd think wrong," Kaprowski said.

They had reached his car. He pointed at a group of men standing in front of a small bar across the avenue.

"Those clowns probably have something to do with it, the fire," he said. "The bar there, the Peanut, that's been mobbed-up since it opened."

"And here I thought they were concerned citizens," said Levin before they both sat inside the car.

"What do you have on Kelly?" Kaprowski asked.

"He visited Eddie Vento's place a little while ago dressed like a homeless hippie," Levin said. "It's tough to disguise yourself you're over six feet with red hair and freckles. I could give him an A for effort, but that'd be cheating."

"Vento there?"

"I don't know. Kelly didn't go in the bar. He went in the doorway alongside the bar entrance. There are four apartments in the building above it, two on each floor. Vento's wife's on the title for the building. Vento keeps the barmaid he's banging in a one-bedroom on the second floor facing the street. Probably where Kelly went. He went home from there, but I don't know if Vento was there or not. He might still be."

"What good's Kelly without Vento?" Kaprowski asked.

"No good, but IA is stretched thin because of what's going on here in Canarsie, all the stolen cars. Word is there are cops running interference for the boys further up this avenue, the junkyards on Flatlands over towards Pennsylvania Avenue."

"Chop shops."

"What I'm hearing. Not to mention the Fulton Fish Market and what's going on there."

"It's a federal task force handling that, the fish market," Kaprowski said. "There's gotta be more to the cars if Internal Affairs is stretched thin here in Canarsie."

"Has to do with a few MIAs is what I heard," Levin said. "Mob associates that've vanished around stolen cars."

"Okay, that's the Gemini Lounge," Kaprowski said. "Further up Flatlands across Ralph Avenue. The guy owns the Gemini's allegedly the same guy whacked a porn dealer fell out of favor with local goodfellas. Jewish name, the porn dealer, I forget it offhand."

"Who'd've ever known porn was so lethal," Levin said.

"Don't kid yourself. The animals running things on the streets now, they'd kill for an extra ten cents on the dollar. Between all the films they're making and the controversy with the courts, the porn business is booming."

"Something tells me you'd prefer it if Internal Affairs wasn't so focused on the cars."

"I'm not worried about IA, Levin. What they don't know won't hurt us. If you could've placed Kelly with Vento, had something concrete, it'd be one less day wasted is all. Dirty cops are dirty cops. Hopefully we'll bring them all in together, the ones in bed with the mob over stolen cars and guys like Kelly running interference for their porn business."

"And then they'll cut their own deals."

"Probably," Kaprowski said. "But those deals'll bring down a wiseguy or two, which'll bring down another couple and a couple more after that. And probably one or two dirty cops'll kill themselves from being disgraced and I know I won't lose any sleep over the likes of them."

"Okay, then," Levin said.

"Let me know when Kelly starts this investigation for real," Kaprowski said. "I want names, addresses, license plate numbers and blood types, you can get them."

"Blood types?"

Kaprowski was looking at the men in front of the bar.

"Can you drop me back at my car?" Levin asked.

"Where'd you park?"

"Rockaway Parkway. Across the street from Johnny Porno, where he lives."

"I'm impressed," Kaprowski said.

Levin held up a finger. "That's one address," he said. "In case you're counting."

■ ■ ■

"You sober, Billy?" Detective Sean Kelly asked Billy Hastings. "Because if you're not, I'm not gonna waste my time."

Kelly had found Hastings sitting on a bench on Emmons Avenue in Sheepshead Bay. Restaurant traffic across the avenue was heavy as Kelly watched four fairly attractive middle-aged women dressed for action get out of a Buick Electra parked at the divider. Three had dark hair, one was a redhead. The redhead wore a tiger-print short dress with matching heels.

"Big red," Kelly said.

"Huh?" Hastings said.

Kelly watched as the women crossed the avenue and went inside Randazzo's clam bar.

"Guineas on parade," he said. "Except maybe red. She could be one of God's children."

Hastings turned to see what Kelly was talking about, but was too late.

"You sober or not?" Kelly asked him.

"You wanna smell my breath, go 'head," Hastings said. He opened his mouth wide.

Kelly slapped his face.

Hastings jumped up off the bench. "You wanna try that again?" he said. He was showing teeth inches from Kelly's chin.

Kelly took a half step back. "Down, boyo," he said. "It was a play slap, for Jesus sake. No need to lose your lunch."

Hastings had relaxed his mouth but continued staring.

Kelly avoided the eye contact. He looked to his right and saw the red-head was back out of the restaurant. She stopped at the curb to let the one-way traffic pass before crossing to the divider. As she passed under the street light, Kelly could see she had fair skin and freckles.

"Nice," Hastings said. "Very nice."

The Electra was parked on the water side of the divider. The redhead made eye contact with Kelly before opening the door. The two exchanged smiles before she got what she had left behind, closed the door and head-ed back across the avenue. Kelly thought he detected an extra swivel to her hips.

"Fuck face," Hastings said. "Over here."

Kelly turned to Hastings again. "I smacked you, lightly, because you're jerking my chain, Billy. I ask you you're sober, you know what I mean. Pills, the white stuff, whatever it is you shove down your throat or put up your nose. I wanna know you're hearing what I have to say, understanding it. This is important, that you understand, because I'm hearing things from different people about your actions of late and it's making a lot of guys you don't wanna make nervous very nervous. Guys didn't want me to secure your pension inna first place. Old friends of yours. Guys thought maybe you'd crack from the pressure and give one or two of them up. Guys thought, still do, maybe you're better off onna day trip on one of the fish-ing boats behind us. In case they need some extra chum."

Until he was forced into retirement a week ago, Hastings had been an eleven-year veteran detective with the New York Police Department. A dirty cop with a drug habit and a deviant sexual appetite, Hastings had a short temper and an inability to control it. When he was caught on cam-era starting a fight in a connected bar, a fight he eventually lost, Lieutenant Detective Kelly assumed the role of peacemaker and brokered a deal with higher-ups for Hastings to leave the department without losing any of his pension or benefits. Tonight, after hearing a rumor about Hastings buying throwaway handguns, Kelly came to warn him against acting foolish.

Hastings remained silent.

Kelly offered him a cigarette.

"Sure," Hastings said.

Kelly handed him his pack. "The point being," he said, "your temper and tough-guy reputation aside, you're looking for throwaways suggests you haven't calmed the fuck down yet. A genuine fear you're not yet willing to let sleeping dogs lie has stirred up some tension amongst former friend-lies. I did what I could for you, Billy. So did some other people. You were more than lucky to walk away with your pension, the benefits. You could've done worse. A lot worse."

"And I appreciated it," Hastings said. "Told you so then, don't feel it's necessary to repeat myself now."

Kelly took a long drag on his cigarette. He turned and blew the smoke over his left shoulder toward the pier. "That's it?" he said. "You appreciated it? We can all relax now or it's none of our business what comes next in Billy world?"

Hastings grinned.

"I miss something?" Kelly said. "Because the guy some people were afraid you might be looking to take out now you're not on the job anymore, the guy knocked you unconscious, fair and square the way it was told to us, that guy now works for Eddie Vento, is part of his crew, so to speak. Put it in popular street vernacular, the way the guineas say it, he's with somebody. You take him out, they retaliate with a certain film of you in that bar that night, we've all gotta answer for it."

Hastings rubbed his nose.

Kelly said, "You itchy, Billy? You do some coke, maybe?"

"Actually, I'm just wondering what'd happen I was to knee you in the balls for the way you slapped me," Hastings said. "Like Pearl Harbor that was, that smack. Then with the threats and all, you're gonna make me chum and so on. I'm thinking before any of that happens, I could knee you in the nuts, gut you like a fish with the knife in my back pocket, leave your intestines for the chum, they need bait, the fishing boats. I'm thinking your concerned friends should've sent somebody can do more than just talk. You wanna make threats it helps you send somebody with the stones to get it done."

Kelly took a full step back. "Let's not get carried away," he said. "I play-slapped you, Billy. Gutting a man for something like that'd be a gross overreaction."

"Don't piss yourself," Hastings said. "The wife wants to move."

Kelly swallowed hard. "Excuse?"

"Kathleen. She wants to move."

Kelly took a moment and felt somewhat relieved Hastings seemed calm again. "How is Kathy?" he asked.

"Kathleen. Her name's Kathleen."

"She's a pretty girl."

"She's a prized piece of ass all of my concerned friends pro'bly jerked off to a half-dozen times each. She's doing fine, though, my wife. Kathleen's fine."

Kelly put both arms out. "I meant no offense."

"Except for that slap before."

"Would it make you feel better, you slapped me back?" said Kelly through a nervous chuckle. "In the face, though. My nuts aren't what they used to be."

Hastings ignored the offer. "She wants to move away from New York. That's why I collected a few throwaways. She wants to move and I'm thinking it's better I bring something from here to there, rather than buy new from people I don't know wherever the fuck she decides we're gonna live. She wants us to start over someplace new."

"I didn't realize you two were having problems."

"We're not having problems. It's the lost income is all."

Kelly reached into his pants pocket and pulled out a small envelope. "That was the other reason I wanted to see you," he said. "Some of your friends thought maybe this'd help. It isn't much, but it's the sentiment that counts."

Hastings ignored the envelope. "Looking to buy me off, Sean?"

"You need to be more trusting of your own," Kelly said. "Go on, take it."

Hastings didn't move.

"Or I can mail you a money order instead," Kelly said.

Hastings mumbled something, turned around and walked away.

"What's that?" Kelly said.

Hastings kept walking.

"Billy!" Kelly yelled. "Hey, come on, man! Billy!"

"*Fidelis ad Mortem*," Hastings yelled.

"What?" Kelly said. "What was that, Billy? What you say?"

Hastings continued walking. Kelly watched until the ex-cop crossed Emmons Avenue and was heading up Twenty-ninth Street. Then Kelly put the envelope back inside his pants pocket, tossed his cigarette in the street and looked back at the restaurant.

"Fuckin' nut," he said.

CHAPTER 7

Nathan Ackerman was up early to take his stepson to summer camp. He prepared two bowls of Cheerios with skim milk before making a cup of Sanka and perusing the sports pages of the *Daily News*. He saw where the Yankees had lost their second straight game to Kansas City while the Mets had beaten the Dodgers at Shea. A few weeks ago Nathan had picked up a pair of box tickets for a Friday-night Yankees game against the Orioles. It would be Little Jack's third Yankee game of the season, the first two having been a doubleheader back in May when the Bronx Bombers beat the Twins twice.

Yesterday, though, Nathan had learned the Philharmonic would be performing a three-day benefit Mahler program upstate the same weekend. Mahler was Nathan's favorite composer. He hoped Jack's father would take the boy in his place.

He checked the time and saw it was close to eight o'clock. He was about to go looking for his stepson when the boy entered the kitchen carrying his baseball glove.

"Morning," Nathan said.

"Good morning," Jack said.

The boy spotted his cereal, sat in his chair, grabbed his spoon and started to eat.

"Maestro," Nathan said.

Jack looked up from his cereal. "Me?"

"I have a surprise for you. Two surprises, actually."

"What?"

Nathan pulled the Yankees tickets from his pocket. "August thirty-first, Yanks-Orioles," he said. "A back-to-school gift."

The boy's eyes opened wide. "Really?"

"Yes, sir," Nathan said. "The only thing is I can't make it so I want you to ask your dad if he can go."

"Sure," Jack said. "He can take me."

"Good, then."

"Can I see?"

Nathan handed over the tickets. "Third-base field boxes," he said. "You can razz the Oriole players up close. Give a yell when Brooks Robinson gets a hot one and maybe it goes through his legs."

"That guy never makes an error," the boy said. He examined the tickets wide-eyed. "This is so neat. Thank you, Nathan."

"It's my pleasure, sir."

"Why can't you go?"

"Gustav Mahler. Any other composer and I'd cancel, but I love Mahler."

"That the Titan guy?"

Nathan was a Mahler aficionado and had been schooling the boy on classical music between baseball discussions and episodes of the *Partridge Family*.

"Yes," he said, "the Titan guy. We're doing Mahler's First the night of the game in fact."

Jack was reading the small print on the back of the ticket. "This is great," he said. "I can't wait to tell my dad."

"Which you should do as soon as possible so he can make plans," Nathan said. Then he reached out and took the tickets back. "In the meantime, finish eating so I can take you to camp. I'll put these on your dresser in your room, okay?"

The boy was still staring at the tickets.

Nathan pointed to Jack's cereal.

"Oh, right," the boy said, then dipped his spoon back into his cereal bowl.

Nathan enjoyed the boy's enthusiasm and was happy the kid would leave the house feeling good about something. His mother wasn't a morning person, as she described it, and was often nasty when she took her son to camp. It was the reason Nathan often volunteered to take him instead.

The drive to Long Island was quick. Nathan was back a little before ten. He found his wife in the kitchen having her first cup of coffee.

"He could've cleaned his cereal bowl," said Nancy, rather than good morning.

"We were in a rush," Nathan said.

"He make it to camp on time?"

"Barely, but yes."

Nathan joined her at the table. He smiled and received a frown in return.

"You have rehearsals today?" she asked.

"No, actually. I'll play some in the basement a little later, but no rehearsals. I can pick up Jack if you want."

"I'd appreciate it."

Nathan had the day off and was thinking they might go to a movie while Jack was at camp. He asked her, but Nancy waved the suggestion off.

"I don't have time for movies," she said. "I'm going to the doctor's at one, why I'm up so damn early." She stopped to sip her coffee. "And I have a three o'clock appointment at the beautician. Maybe tomorrow if you're free."

"It'll have to be early," Nathan said. "I have rehearsal tomorrow afternoon."

"Well, I can't help that, can I?"

"No," Nathan said. "I suppose not."

Nancy got up from the table to rinse her cup out in the sink. She set it in the drain board afterward, then looked up at the clock on the wall above the kitchen doorway. "I have to shower and fix myself before I leave," she said. "Please don't play until I'm gone. In case the phone rings."

"Right," said Nathan obediently as his wife headed upstairs. He wondered where she really would spend the day and with whom. Their marriage had turned into a sham. He was sure she was seeing someone else and had been playing him for a fool since they were married.

Nancy had first introduced herself at her son's school when Nathan and a few of his Philharmonic colleagues had played a benefit for the music department. She had been pretty and confident and he had been lonely. It was during the Philharmonic season they began dating. He'd been single until then and had saved enough to buy the house they now lived in.

After two-plus years of marriage Nathan was well aware that Nancy Kirsk-Albano had hooked a fish when he proposed to her almost three years ago. Except for his relationship with her son, it had been a mistake to have ever spoken to her.

Divorce was on his mind when the phone rang. He answered and the caller hung up.

■ ■ ■

John woke up and found he was staring at his alarm clock. He'd forgotten to set it before falling to sleep. It was nine-fifteen. He had a few minutes to spare and closed his eyes again. He'd been dreaming, but couldn't recall what, except he was sure that a woman dressed in white was Melinda.

He took a shower and dressed and was about to head down to the local deli for an egg sandwich and coffee when he thought to call his ex-wife and confirm his son's schedule for the rest of the week. Little Jack was attending summer camp Monday through Friday. Some days the kid was home earlier than others. John hoped to spend some time with his son tonight.

The other thing John wanted to do today was find a way around Nick Santorra at the Brooklyn bar. The guy had become unbearable; between his loud mouth, his threats and last night's phone call, it was only a matter of time before the punk pushed the wrong button and John lost control. The repercussions from hitting Santorra wouldn't make his life any easier. Either he found a way to avoid dealing with the loudmouth or he found another weekend job.

He plugged the phone back in and it rang before he picked up the receiver. It was a local builder he had worked construction for in the past. Two of his men had left the builder in the lurch for union work in the city. He offered John ten dollars an hour off the books for the rest of the week. John accepted, then wondered if maybe his luck was changing.

He needed to get to Bay Ridge as soon as possible and forgot about calling Nancy. He made it to the construction site, a row of attached homes a few blocks from Shore Road, within half an hour. He spent the bulk of the day putting up sheetrock with a guy from New Jersey who had relocated to his brother's couch in Brooklyn because of the flooding earlier in the month that had devastated the town of Bound Brook in New Jersey.

The guy's hard luck story reminded John things could be worse.

A few hours passed and it felt good doing physical work again. He saw the homes would still need taping and kitchen cabinet installation and hoped the builder would keep him on. He guessed the job would take at least another few weeks.

His muscles were sore when he finished for the day. He was also voraciously hungry. Except for a buttered roll during a short mid-afternoon break, John hadn't eaten all day. He drove to Coney Island and parked around the corner from Nathan's Famous where he had two frankfurters and French fries.

Afterward, he took a long stroll on the boardwalk and was enjoying the ocean breeze until he remembered he was supposed to stop at the bar in Williamsburg. John cursed himself under his breath when he also remembered his ex-wife and son and the call he hadn't made to them.

He did an about-face and headed back to his car. He'd have to be calm when he dealt with Nick Santorra later. John still didn't know what it was about, his being summoned to the bar.

He inhaled the ocean air before pulling into the light traffic on Surf Avenue. As he drove past Astroland and then the Aquarium on his right, John remembered Santorra's warning the night before.

"Just make sure you show."

John figured he'd have to hear it again when he got there, Santorra getting all full of himself and showing off in front of the other guys at the bar. He didn't understand it, why guys like Eddie Vento kept morons like Santorra around. He wasn't half as tough as he acted and couldn't be very helpful to guys who lived off their reputations. Sooner or later a guy like Santorra would have to deliver on one of his threats and John doubted the big mouth could get it done.

He turned on the radio and listened to the song about something going round in circles. It was sung in question form, asking if something would fly high like a bird up in the sky. It was a catchy tune for a little while, then it became annoying and John changed to an AM all-news station, Ten-Ten WINS.

He turned up the volume when he heard the announcer say, "...a mob rubout in Queens."

A few minutes later John learned it was a story about his weekend predecessor in the porn film distribution business. The body of Tommy DeLuca had been found in a Queens dumpster two days ago missing both hands.

"DeLuca was believed to be an associate of the Vignieri crime family with ties to pornography," the reporter said. "Tonight police are offering a reward to anyone with information...."

John turned the radio off.

■ ■ ■

She had parked on 102nd Street off the corner of Jamaica Avenue a few minutes before three o'clock. At four o'clock Nancy called home to tell Nathan she'd been delayed and wouldn't be home until late. At five o'clock she called Louis's apartment to see if she had missed him outside the apartment building. At five-thirty and again at five-forty-five Nancy tried his apartment buzzer, but no one answered.

At six o'clock she walked around the corner to a pizza parlor on Jamaica Avenue and bought a slice and a soda. She had been having menstrual cramps since she left the house and hadn't eaten anything all day. Nancy had hoped to see Louis again before the bleeding started.

It had been two days since she heard from him and now she was afraid he might've fallen for the young one he'd been chasing lately. Holly her name was, a twenty-something blonde with small tits, a perky ass and long legs. Miss Kansas or Missouri or Arkansas, wherever the hell she was from. Nancy had seen her one time when she had followed Louis to Jones Beach earlier in the summer. The blonde had worn short cutoffs over a bright pink bikini that showed off her long legs. Nancy had been furious at the sight of Louis holding her hand.

The day after spotting them on the beach, Nancy had confronted Louis over the phone. When she asked him where he'd been the day before, Louis had lied about working.

"Really?" she had said.

"Yeah, Nan, I was working. What business is it of yours, anyway? You're married again."

It was something she sometimes regretted, but something she planned to change as soon as she was entitled to half of Nathan's assets. In the meantime, she had to live with Louis having girlfriends, even ones in their early twenties.

She had been crazy for him since they first met at a beach party the night the Pittsburgh Pirates beat the New York Yankees on a ninth-inning home run by the guy with the Polish name. She remembered because Louis had bet the Yankees and couldn't stop cursing about the guy who hit the home run, Mazooski, or something like it, his name was. She had eventually calmed Louis down with a blow job that took her nearly an hour he'd been so distracted by the bet he'd lost.

They started dating the next day and she hadn't been able to get over him since. Her mother had called Louis poison and was probably right, but Nancy couldn't stop herself from needing him. She knew there was no security in a relationship with Louis, emotional or financial, and had been clever enough to seek the latter from someone else. She had seized the opportunity by marrying Nathan Ackerman.

Another half hour passed before Nancy began to seethe. It had been more than three hours and she felt like a fool.

There was a bar on the corner she knew Louis sometimes frequented. She decided to wait for him there. She'd give him one more hour before she left and might even flirt a little with the bartender if he wasn't a skank, or maybe with somebody else, so that word would get back to Louis about how his ex-wife was still a looker and why didn't he tell them about her before.

It was seven-fifteen when Nancy stepped inside the bar. She spotted a pair of toothless wonders, a sixty-year-old lush wearing enough makeup to pass for a clown, and a couple of barely legal young men at the bar. The bartender wasn't bad, a tall, thin, dark-haired guy with blue eyes, so she sat away from the losers and ordered a vodka tonic.

"Louis coming in tonight?" she asked when he set the drink down in front of her.

"Louis the window-cleaner?"

Nancy nodded.

"You a friend of his?"

"Sort of."

"He didn't say," the bartender said. He turned toward the two younger guys at the opposite end of the bar. "Jimmy due in tonight?"

Both young ones shook their heads.

"Who's Jimmy?" Nancy asked.

"Jimmy's a shylock."

"Louis's?"

The bartender shrugged.

Nancy remembered how Louis had implied the phone calls at his apartment might've been from loan sharks. There was that one time when they were still married and he had come home all bloody and bruised and lied about getting jumped. She later learned a pair of goons some loan shark had sent did the damage because he owed five thousand dollars they didn't have. She had gone to the bank the next day for a loan to pay down half his debt before they broke his legs. Apparently he still hadn't grown up or stopped gambling and was as irresponsible as ever. On the other hand, he would need help and that had always been a guarantee that he'd come back to her.

"Anything I can do for you?" the bartender asked.

He was smiling then and Nancy could see that he too was missing teeth. She sipped some more of her drink, set down a dollar tip, and said, "Thanks, no. Just tell him Nan was here."

CHAPTER 8

"There a good reason I shouldn't have you tuned up?" Eddie Vento said. John did his best not to avoid direct eye contact. "The guy's been riding me," he said. "He wouldn't stop."

"The guy is around somebody," Vento said. "Me."

Twenty minutes ago Nick Santorra had started in on John as soon as he'd stepped inside the bar upstairs. John still wasn't sure how long it had taken before it was too much, but then it had happened and now here he was sitting before a wiseguy answering for the single punch he'd thrown.

"I don't know what you want me to say, Mr. Vento," he said. "I apologize."

Vento didn't say anything. He lit a cigar instead.

What had happened was Santorra spotted John and turned to the rest of the guys sitting around the bar and said loud enough so they could all hear him, "And here he is, the late great Johnny Porno, the man too busy to show respect. The one who put all our lives on hold because he's got better things to do. Or maybe he thinks we're all a bunch of schmucks."

"I was working," John had said. "I told you I hadda work."

"See what I mean?" Santorra said. "Fuck all of us and tough shit, too."

"I'm here now."

"Hear that, fellas? He's here now."

John was clenching his teeth trying to compose himself.

"You have some pair of balls," Santorra went on. "Who fuckin' cares you had to work? Not me."

John had remained silent.

"He agrees," Santorra said. "Johnny Porno's got balls."

"My name is Albano. John Albano. And I told you I hadda work."

"Your name is whatever the fuck I call you, jerkoff."

John had felt the muscles in his face tense.

Then Santorra said, "He had to work and bada-boom, bada-bing, fuck all of us."

Santorra's last crack with the dopey sound effect was what had pushed John over the edge, the *bada-boom, bada-bing*.

"Just you," he'd told Santorra.

"Excuse me?"

"Fuck you," John said. "Just you."

Santorra had swallowed hard. His fear showed as he continued acting tougher than he was. He'd put himself in a bad position; either he put up or looked bad. What he did was turn to the other guys in the bar, but they were all waiting to see what happened next, too.

Santorra took a deep breath, wheeled on John and poked him in the chest. "Oh, yeah?" he said. "Fuck you, wiseass."

John took the poke, but had left the trace of a smirk on his face, enough so to show he was way more amused than he was scared. He had already placed the punch in his mind, a quick right cross he'd try to place on the tip of Santorra's jaw.

"Think you're funny?" Santorra said in response to the smirk. He was insulted then and was forced to poke John a second time. First he said, "Take that smirk and go fuck your mother's cunt."

It was then John decked him.

There was a slight commotion immediately after. John was shoved against the wall by a few guys and when they let him go he could see Santorra was still splayed out on the floor, eyes closed. Then Eddie Vento came up from his basement office to see what had happened. John was brought downstairs to explain himself, except there wasn't much he could say.

Santorra had been pushing his buttons since they first met and tonight he'd pushed one too many. It had been tough enough taking his verbal abuse; there was no way he'd let Santorra get physical.

Now Eddie Vento reminded him of mob protocol. "You know there has to be a consequence, right? I can't let a connected guy get banged around like that."

John figured it was best he kept his mouth shut.

"You're from Canarsie, right?" Vento asked.

"It's where I grew up."

"I'm surprised you were never scooped up by one of the crews there. Very mobbed-up, Canarsie is. I have a friend has a strong crew operates out of a bar on Flatlands Avenue, next to a funeral parlor there. I got a guy around me lives there, too. Tough Irish kid lives near the market on Foster Avenue. Name's Tommy Burns. Know him?"

John shook his head. "No," he said.

"Scrappy little mick," Vento said. "And a tough cocksucker, push comes to shove. He's stuck doing freelance cause he's not Italian, but you, on the other hand, you are one of us."

John didn't like where this was heading.

"Something you should think about before you go tagging one of our own like you did upstairs tonight," Vento said. "But, truth be told, the way you took that cop Hastings out, that was a beautiful thing we're still enjoying around here."

John was never more uncomfortable. He did his best not to show it.

"You didn't know he was a cop, did you? The night you decked him, I mean."

"Not until he showed his badge," John said.

"I love it," Vento said.

"And I had no idea the woman was his wife," John said. "That was an honest mistake."

It had been. His car had overheated and John had gone in the bar to make a telephone call. The woman had smiled at him, he had smiled back and then she waved him over when he was finished with his call. He sat at the stool alongside her, a young-looking thirty-year-old with long red hair, green eyes and pale skin. He bought her a drink and was in the process of getting her telephone number when some guy started yelling from across the room. The guy was flashing a badge and was claiming she was his wife. The woman hadn't worn a wedding ring, nor had she mentioned she was there with her husband.

Then when John had tried to walk away, there was no way to avoid what had happened next. The guy had shoved him two or three times before taking a wild swing. John had ducked the punch and hit the guy in self-defense.

"You don't have to explain yourself to me about that," Vento said. "She's not wiseguy pussy, she's free trade. Was his problem, not yours."

John cringed at the way Vento described the cop's wife.

"Was that knockout made me offer you the job," Vento added. "It was also a way to protect you, putting you on my payroll. And it's a good thing you're under my umbrella now, pal. That cop is a last of the Mohican hardons. He wanted a piece of you, my friend. We showed a few friendlies the tape we had, I should show it the six o'clock news, it was so good. They're the ones helped back Hastings down. His buddies convinced him it wasn't worth his pension doing something stupid like shooting you in the back of the head, but the real reason they backed him down was because we had that tape. Clear as day what he did before you dropped him. Waving the badge around, the shoves he gave you. The swing he took before you nailed him. Was a beautiful stroke of luck on our part we'd just installed the camera because he was shaking down a couple a my bartenders every time he needed money for the junk he was shoving up his nose. Imagine? We gotta install our own crime prevention equipment to avoid the leeches on the police force."

John was glad he hadn't known the details behind what had happened that night. He figured he'd been lucky to get out of there without being arrested.

Vento explained how a detective on his payroll had been helpful in cutting the deal whereby the wiseguy refrained from using the tape and Hastings was transferred to another precinct with the understanding he steer clear of the Williamsburg bar and anybody associated with it.

"Like I said," Vento continued, "that was a beautiful thing, what you did to that cop. It's legend in here now."

"I tried to avoid it," John said.

"But he wouldn't let you," Vento said. "What happened upstairs, I understand."

John was suddenly hopeful of escaping grief for knocking out Nick Santorra.

"I see you around, but only in passing," Vento said. "How come you don't hang around the bar?"

"It's not for me," John said. "I have child-support payments and a job driving for a local car service. Things are too tight for me to hang around bars."

"Fair enough," Vento said. "And don't take offense my asking what the fuck you're doing driving car service? You're around here, you can do better than that."

John explained how a fistfight with a union shop steward more than a year ago had cost him his job and how he'd just picked up a private job today and that was why he was so late coming to the bar.

Vento sighed when John finished talking. "You have to excuse the mope you hit," the wiseguy said. "He's got a fire under his ass since he's driving for me. He's my wife's first cousin, a real moron, but he's my responsibility now and I can't let guys take a swing at him like you did tonight, not without they pay a penalty. Looks bad to the other guys, I do that."

John understood it was a possible way out, but that it would probably cost him money he couldn't afford to give away.

"I can see you're a hard working guy and you're obviously good with your hands," Vento continued. "I can always use guys are good with their hands. You don't have to drive cars you don't like it."

"It's not that I enjoy it," John said.

Vento didn't hear him. He said, "Of course there is a downside to swinging at somebody every time they piss you off."

"I can apologize to Nick you want."

"Huh?" Vento said. He looked confused a moment, then waved off the offer. "That'd only make things worse. He'll be embarrassed you apologize. It'll be better you put something in his pocket. Through me, though. Give me, say, I don't know, fifty bucks? I'll see he gets it and that'll be that."

John felt his stomach churning. He'd just worked half a day putting up sheetrock so he could put fifty bucks in Nick Santorra's pocket. It was worse than catching a beating, he thought.

"We got you working with the fuck film, right?" Vento said.

"Yeah," John said. "But I'm not sure how much longer. This construction thing, I might have to work weekends there."

Vento didn't hear him again. "We might have another one soon," he said. He grabbed a folder off his desk and opened it. He pulled two stills of a thin naked woman being escorted by six people in robes. "This thing started on the West Coast is a big hit now. *Behind the Green Door*. The broad they use is a hot item. *Ivory Snow* girl or some shit, what they claim. She's better-looking than the one did the movie we're hustling now, except she gets boned by some jungle bunny. Anyway, we'll be looking to move it here on the East Coast soon enough."

John barely glanced at the pictures before setting them back down.

"How many stops you making now?" Vento asked.

"Seven."

"You can handle more?"

"I guess."

"How about double? The extra stops, you can get to them before you're regular route. Be finished before noon."

"Mr. Vento, I was thinking—"

"And you'd double your end. Plus expenses—tank of gas and a meal. Least another twenty."

John imagined the hundred twenty dollars and kept his mouth shut.

Vento said, "It works out, I can get you a union job. We got people there, I'm sure you know that. A friend of ours runs construction in Manhattan. If not there, we can put you in the fish market or over the docks in Brooklyn. Things work out here, I can see to it you're working steady again. Do the right thing by me, it'll be a no-show. Then you can really earn."

"That's very generous," John said. "Can I think on it?"

"Absolutely," Vento said. "So long's you show respect and don't think on it too long. I don't like making an offer to somebody, they disrespect it by ignoring me."

"I'll let you know," John said.

"It's only right."

"I understand."

"Good then," Vento said. He stood up behind his desk and shook John's hand. Then he reached down and grabbed a poster of some kind and held it open for John. "Nick tell you what you were coming here to pick up today?"

John's eyes narrowed when he saw it was a poster of a woman in a nurse outfit. He squinted trying to see the signature in the bottom right-hand corner.

"Linda Lovelace," Vento said. "It's the broad does the sword-swallowing in the fuck movie. I was thinking we put 'Head Nurse' right below the signature. What do you think?"

"Makes sense, I guess," John said. "That really her signature?"

"As far as the jerkoffs buying it goes it is. We're gonna distribute them to the guys showing the movie and squeeze some extra cash out of the thing before it dies. Receipts are starting to slow up. Business needs a boost."

John was thinking about George in Massapequa and his idea about having Linda Lovelace show up to sign autographs.

"I kind of like it, the 'head nurse' thing," Vento said. "Nick did the signatures. He's not gonna be happy he has to add that, though, not after this. Said his hand was all cramped when he finished. Probably why he's so cranky upstairs before."

John took pleasure at the thought of Santorra having to sign the posters. Then he took a closer look at the handwriting and noticed something wrong. He pointed to it.

"What?" Vento said.

"Lovelace," John said. "He spelled it with an 's.' I'm pretty sure it's a 'c.'"

■ ■ ■

Billy Hastings saw his eyes were bloodshot in the mirror's reflection and splashed cold water on his face. He'd been up nearly forty-eight hours. To supplement his adrenaline as it faded, Billy had used amphetamines, heroin and cocaine. Twelve hours ago, hopped up on a speedball he'd injected under his tongue, Billy had killed a man.

Now that he was crashing, Billy popped the cap from a small vial of cocaine and poured some onto the edge of the bathroom sink. He flushed the toilet to drown out his snorting and the adrenaline-induced gasp that followed. A few seconds later, his energy magically restored, Billy put his stash and equipment away. He returned to the kitchen where his wife was still sitting at the table. Earlier she'd been reading aloud to him from a notebook half filled with her handwritten confessions to several extramarital affairs. Billy motioned at her to continue.

"You sure?" she asked.

"Yeah," Billy said.

Kathleen Hastings used a finger to find her place before she picked up where she had left off.

"'He drove inside the garage and we went up the ramps until he got to his space and then he parked,'" she read. "'He let the car run and put on the radio. Then he lit a joint.'"

Billy sniffled as he pinched the tip of his nose through a tissue. The rush was already fading. He wet his lips and leaned against the refrigerator.

"You sure you're okay?" Kathleen asked.

"Yeah," Billy said. "Go 'head. Then what?"

"'He gave me the joint and I smoked it,'" Kathleen read. "'I held it in my lungs a long time and while I did that he leaned over and felt my breasts.'"

"What were you wearing?"

Kathleen looked up from the notebook. "My green halter."

"No bra, right?"

"No bra."

"Keep reading."

"'I let him kiss me on the mouth and then he untied my halter and kissed my tits. He sucked one of them and then put a hand between my legs.'"

Billy moaned. Hearing her tell the story again excited him. He grabbed himself through his sweatpants.

"Keep going," he said.

"'I had my jeans on and told him it was too hard to take them off in the car and that there were other cars that might pass and see us. He told me I couldn't leave him like that and put my hand between his legs. He made me rub him there until he was hard. Then he opened his pants and pushed my head down.'"

Billy knew his wife's confessions were partial truths, but what was left to his imagination always proved electric. The images of Kathleen with other men had become continuous loops in Billy's head; pure carnal passion caught in a series of snapshots that both enraged and excited him.

The man he'd killed last night had been the first one listed in the same notebook, a thirty-four-year-old building superintendent Kathleen claimed to have met at a bowling alley more than three years ago. Although, over time, Billy had adapted to the sexually deviant lifestyle they currently engaged in, he continued to blame Victor Vasquez for his wife's initial betrayal.

With Vasquez erased from the slate, Billy was anxious to eliminate the other man responsible for dishonoring his pride. First, though, he needed to see the man defiling Kathleen.

"Inside," he told her.

Kathleen pushed her chair back from the table, stood up and walked to their bedroom. Billy followed her up to the doorway, then stopped to watch as she sat on the edge of the bed. She removed her pants first, then underwear.

"Show me," he said.

Kathleen turned on the bed to face him and slowly spread her legs. Billy was touching himself through the sweatpants.

"Do it," he said.

Kathleen closed her eyes and licked her lips as she slowly gyrated her pelvis.

"That's it," Billy said.

Kathleen moaned.

Billy watched a while, then said, "Yeah. Do it."

"Yes," Kathleen said.

"Fuck that guy."

"I am."

Billy licked his lips. "Is it good?"

"Yes."

"Is it?"

Kathleen moaned again, louder this time.

"Who is it?" Billy said.

Kathleen continued moaning.

"Who?" Billy said.

"You know."

"Say his name."

"No."

"Say it."

"You say it."

"Please, baby."

"No."

"Say his name."

Kathleen rolled over, raised her ass and continued gyrating her hips.

Billy was worked up to tears. They began to flow down his cheeks. "Oh, God!" he cried. "Say his name for me. Please!"

"Johnny," she said.

"Johnny who?"

"Johnny Albano."

"Oh, God, baby. Oh, fucking God. What's he... what's he... tell him to fuck you."

"Yes."

"Tell him."

"I will."

Billy was close to orgasm. He slapped the open door with his free hand. "Tell him!"

"Fuck me, Johnny!" Kathleen yelled. "Fuck me!"

A growl erupted from the bottom of Billy's throat as his release began. His hips bucked a few times as he grunted from somewhere deep in his chest. Then he felt light-headed and needed to brace his back against the doorframe.

Kathleen had turned on the bed and was sitting on the edge. She crossed her legs and watched as her husband slid down the bottom half of the door to the floor. He was breathing hard. She waited until his breathing relaxed, then got up off the bed.

"You want pancakes?" she asked.

"Yeah," Billy managed to say.

"Bacon?"

"Yeah."

Kathleen had to step over him. "Don't move," she said as she did so.

Billy watched his wife heading toward the kitchen. "I love you," he told her.

"I know," she said. "I love you, too."

■ ■ ■

John saw there were lights on in the windows of the apartment building where he lived and breathed a sigh of relief. Last night he'd barely slept from the heat and humidity and couldn't imagine another night without air-conditioning.

He parked the Buick across the street, grabbed his cigarettes off the passenger seat and pulled one from the pack before getting out of the car.

Old man Elias was sitting on the stoop smoking a cigarette of his own. John tapped his front pants pocket for his matches as he crossed the street but didn't feel them. He tapped his rear pockets and was about to backtrack to the car when Elias called to him.

"What you are doing, some kind of dance?"

"Huh?" John said. He gave up on the matches and headed back toward the stoop. "Give me a light."

Elias handed him his lit cigarette. John lit his cigarette and returned the one he borrowed.

"You work late, eh?" the old man said.

John knew Elias was fishing. "Something like that."

"Something like what?" he said. "You work late or you don't."

"I had an interview, sort of."

"Sort of. What is sort of?"

The old man wasn't going to let go. John said, "I had an interview to take on more weekend work. That okay with you?"

"For Mafia?"

"Distributing the film."

"Working for Mafia."

"I do it for the money," said John, frustrated for having to go through it again. "I need the work, Alex. I know you don't like to hear that, but I don't have a choice right now."

"Bullshit. Man is free, always has choice. You do this because you are young and stupid, not because of money. Money you can get somewhere else."

John took a long drag on his cigarette.

"And don't call me Alex, I told you." The old man tapped his chest. "I am Zorba."

"You're senile is what I'm starting to think."

Elias waved John off.

"Anyway, I'm not in the mood for an argument now," John said. "I'm tired and I need to get some sleep."

"Stay with Mafia friends and they put you to sleep."

"Right," John said. "Good night." He took a step to his right onto the stoop.

Elias grabbed his foot. "Don't run away from me, idiot. Stay two minutes. Listen."

John stepped back down off the stoop.

"Two things," Elias said.

"What?"

"First, you can get money somewhere else."

"Driving car service? No thanks. I hate it."

"What they are doing for you, these Mafioso? What, they are making you rich? You want to be one of them now?"

There was no avoiding the old man's directness. John leaned against the railing on the stoop.

"So?" the old man said.

"They're giving me extra work," John said. "Doubling my route. They can get me back in the union. I can do that, I wouldn't have to do this other shit."

"Really? They do all this favors for you because why, you're handsome man? You have big one?"

"I get back in the union, I'm not gonna need the weekend work. That's all I'm saying."

The old man pointed a finger. "They give you something, it's not for nothing. What's the matter with you?"

John was thinking back to his conversation with Eddie Vento and the way the man had laid it out. Between the extra stops he was getting and the union pull Vento had dangled like a carrot on a stick, he was seeing some light at the end of what had been a long and dark financial tunnel. Although he'd be expected to hang around the bar and get more involved, if the wiseguy could get him reinstated in the carpenters' union, John would have a lot more of his life back, not to mention the extra money he'd have for a change.

On the other hand, the old man was right, Vento was a wiseguy and John knew better than to get involved with "those people," what his father used to call them.

"What was the other thing?" he asked Elias.

"Your mother has brother was killed by Mafia, no? He wants to be like them and they kill him. You told me this already, why your mother is upset now, what you're doing."

It was something he'd wished he hadn't shared with the old man. John's uncle, his mother's only brother, was involved with a local mob crew when he quit high school. After putting his family through some tough times with a series of arrests, Paolo Zampino disappeared two weeks before the start of a trial for armed robbery. Six months later his body was found in the trunk of a car. Elias had brought the story up more than a few times since John took the weekend job.

"Yeah," John said. "It's true."

"And your mother, her family, they were crushed by this, no? The loss of a son and a brother to those animals."

John looked straight ahead.

Elias wagged a finger. "The people you are working for are no fucking good. They use you and when they don't need you, they throw you away like garbage. Get away from them and stay away. I tell you for your own good."

John knew the old man was right, except his immediate economic situation precluded him from taking the advice.

"I'll quit as soon as I can," he said. "I promise."

"You don't hear what I say."

"I did," said John as he stood up. "I just can't do it now. Not yet."

He left the old man and headed inside. He was halfway up the first flight of stairs when the building went dark.

"God damn it," he said. He put his hands out to protect himself, gave it a few seconds, then gave up and carefully walked back down the stairs and outside onto the stoop.

"No lights?" Elias said.

"Yeah. I can't sleep like this again."

"Go sleep in car."

"Huh?"

"You don't have girlfriend, go sleep in car."

"I'm not sleeping in my car."

"Then go to Momma. You can take me. I can cook breakfast in the morning."

John stepped off the stoop and was headed for the curb. He turned to point a finger at Elias. "Not funny," he said.

The old man stood up. "What? What's wrong with that?"

John ignored him and continued back-stepping across the street. The sound of screeching tires broke the silence. He turned in time to see a red sports car racing across the near corner. John was forced to leap out of the way as the car veered toward him before pulling away at the last moment.

He dove to the ground and rolled against his car. When he got up the sports car was turning off Rockaway Parkway at the far end of the block.

He thought of giving chase but knew it was pointless. The Buick would need half a minute to warm up and was no match for a sports car.

Elias was off the stoop and standing near the curb. "Who was that?" he said.

"Some asshole," John said. "Probably some kid playing with his father's car."

"Don't go looking for him, eh?" Elias said. "Go to Momma's and get some sleep instead."

John started the Buick's engine. He gave it a few seconds to warm up before stepping on the brake, then slipping the transmission into gear.

"I'll see you tomorrow," he told Elias, then pulled away.

He drove half a block at normal speed before he fed the engine gas and sped to the corner to make the right turn in pursuit of the car that had nearly run him over.

CHAPTER 9

"Need a hanky?" Detective Sean Kelly asked Eddie Vento's girlfriend. Bridget Malone had just snorted one too many lines of cocaine and was bleeding from her nose. She hadn't seen Kelly until after she'd wiped her face with the back of her right hand and spotted her arm with blood.

"Shit," she said. "God damn it."

"Here," Kelly said. He handed her his handkerchief. "Use this." She continued wiping her nose with her hand and smeared some across her face.

"Hold on a second," he told her, then guided her head back while he applied the handkerchief to her nose. "Hold it like this. Pinch it a little and tilt your head back. Sit down a second, it'll stop."

He led her to the fender of a car parked at the curb. "Sit," he said.

Bridget spoke through the napkin. "I don't know how this happened," she said. "It just started bleeding."

Kelly knew she was full of shit. He'd been following her since she left the apartment above her boyfriend's bar. First she'd taken a bus to Prospect Park and made a drug connection. Then she'd gone to a bar on Seventh Avenue and sat drinking with a few people closer to her own age. She'd done at least one line in the ladies' room because Kelly had been having a beer at the bar and could see her eyes when she came out.

After learning from Eddie Vento how Bridget Malone had been involved in a heroin bust, Kelly ran her name through department connections but still didn't know if she had cut a deal or not. While it was possible her legal troubles had died along with her boyfriend, it was equally possible Bridget Malone was working off her end of the heroin bust gathering information against her wiseguy boyfriend. The potential risk was too great for Kelly to accept Eddie Vento's cocky assurances.

She had been on her way home and was within a mile of Fast Eddie's bar and her apartment when she stepped into an alley to do another line. Kelly saw her stagger. Then she had to use the wall to keep from falling. It was then he saw she was bleeding and brought her the handkerchief.

"You okay?" he asked her now.

Bridget still had her head back and was holding the handkerchief against her nose. "Yeah," she said. "Thanks."

"I was on my way to see a friend when I thought I recognized you. Eddie's girl, right?"

Bridget removed the top of the handkerchief from her eyes but continued pinching her nose. "Yeah," she said.

"That was a little awkward the other day," Kelly said. "I wish Eddie had kept his temper."

Bridget wiped around her mouth. "Your name again?"

"Eddie calls me Mr. Horse."

"You one of his bookies?"

"Something like that."

"Because those usually show up at the bar on settle-up nights. I don't remember seeing you there."

"We usually meet at a diner."

Bridget tested her nose for bleeding, saw it had stopped and straightened her head. She used the handkerchief to wipe some of the residual blood from her face.

She turned her head and Kelly saw the bruise on the left side of her face from where Eddie Vento had slapped her the other day. He pointed at it. "That hurt?"

"Only if I touch it. Mr. Horse, you said?"

"What Eddie calls me, yeah."

"But that's not your real name."

"That an issue?"

"Only if you're a cop."

Kelly forced a smile. "What makes you say that?"

Bridget didn't answer. She used the car's side view mirror and wiped her face with the handkerchief again. When she was satisfied, she turned to Kelly and held up the bloodied hanky.

"Keep it," he said.

"Thanks."

"You gonna be okay?"

"I'm fine. Like I said, I don't know how it happened."

Kelly chuckled.

"What?" Bridget said.

"Nothing."

The two eyeballed each other, Kelly with a frozen smile on his face and Bridget expressionless until he pulled a pack of cigarettes from his pocket and offered her one.

"No thanks," she said.

Kelly continued staring at her as he lit his cigarette.

"Is there something else?" she asked.

"You should be more careful," Kelly said.

"With Eddie or my nose?"

"Either or," he said.

Bridget waited for more.

Kelly winked, turned and walked away.

■ ■ ■

John had given up his search for the sports car after ten minutes of driving through the neighborhood. Still unsure of how to spend the rest of the night, he headed for Queens on the Belt Parkway. He got off at Cross Bay Boulevard and headed north on Woodhaven to Queens Boulevard. It was close to one o'clock in the morning when he decided against spending the night at his mother's house where he knew the electric would be working and he'd have air conditioning to help him sleep. He headed to the diner where Melinda worked instead.

He spotted her as soon as he pulled into the diner parking lot. She was still wearing her uniform and had stopped to light a cigarette before descending the back stairs. He wondered if she was on her break or ending for the night, then noticed she was wearing sneakers as she started across the lot.

"Don't tell me you're going to another diner now?" he said.

He had pulled up alongside her.

"Excuse me?" she said.

"I'm John," he said. "We met inside a few nights ago. Remember the guys got loud with the cashier?"

She was squinting. She said, "Yeah, I remember you."

"Good. You're still in uniform. You going or coming... Melinda, right?"

She was confused a moment before she realized what he was talking about. "Oh, this," she said. "Yes, Melinda. I'm going. I prefer doing my own laundry, why I'm wearing it home."

"Can I give you a lift?"

She pointed to her car, a white 1970 Valiant, about four cars from the end of the lot. "That's mine," she said.

"Feel like a drink someplace?"

"I'd rather a coffee."

"Another diner?"

"I can always glom some tips."

They took separate cars with John doing the following. It was a ten-minute ride to another diner up near the courts on Queens Boulevard. They parked alongside each other, but John was embarrassed because of his car.

Melinda held up a cigarette for him to light before they went inside.

"Excuse the dents," he said as he struck a match. "It's ugly but it gets me around."

"I never judge a man by his car," Melinda said. "Unless it's a fancy one. Then I just assume the man is a bad one."

"They can't all be bad," he said. "Although I never went for women driving Cadillacs."

He lit a cigarette of his own and the two exchanged smiles. He was feeling himself blush again when she asked what it was he was doing out so late.

"The truth?" he said.

"Unless you feel you have to lie."

"The electric went out in the building where I live. Second night in a row. I was thinking about heading to my mother's place to sleep there, then decided to stop and see if you were still at work."

"I feel honored, but just so you know, you won't be sleeping with me tonight."

John held up both his hands. "The thought hadn't crossed my mind," he said.

"I can take that as an insult, you know."

"It has crossed my mind, but not tonight. Tonight I just wanted to meet you outside your job to make friends."

Melinda was smiling. "Make friends?"

"I'm saying it wrong," John said. "You know what I mean."

She was close to finished with her cigarette and motioned toward his car with it. "So, you do a lot of driving or something?"

"Yeah, you count car service. I drive for a place where I live in Canarsie. No medallion or nothing. Although today and the rest of this week I have construction work."

"You sound like a busy man."

"Except I'm thirty-five and what's that all about, you're probably thinking, my driving for a car service."

"Actually I wasn't thinking about it at all, but since you put it that way..."

"I used to be a carpenter. A union carpenter until I had a problem on the job. I lost my union card and have been doing pickup work ever since, driving and picking up handiwork jobs when I can. The guy I'm working construction for now I've worked for before, a private contractor needs help sometimes. This week I'm putting up sheetrock and hanging door bucks."

"Door bucks, huh? Sounds exciting."

"Now you're making fun of me."

She dropped her cigarette and stepped on it. "No, not at all," she said. "You sound like a hard-working guy."

"When there's work available, yeah. I'm a kind of jack-of-all-trades, I guess."

"And your name's John and that's as good as Jack," Melinda said.

John wasn't sure if she was ribbing him.

"Never apologize for being a working man, hon," she said. "Come on, I'll buy you a cup of joe."

■ ■ ■

She told him about her previous marriage to a New York City cop and how it had turned to shit the day she learned he was shaking down prostitutes for sex. The story had broken the same night she had a college exam that she wound up skipping to avoid the local news teams camped at the curb in front of her house.

"He was screwing prostitutes," Melinda said. "Imagine?"

"He get in trouble?"

"Besides my going to a divorce lawyer the next morning? Yeah, but then he did some kind of plea bargain and only did six months. He did lose his job and pension, but I was the one who suffered. I must've taken two dozen tests for VD afterward. I swear it was when my first gray hairs started showing."

"Where's he now?"

"Who knows and who cares. Florida, I think. He had the nerve to ask me for a temporary loan, what he called it, the day he got out of prison, but I hung up on him."

"Good for you."

"Yeah, except I never felt like such a fool before. Prostitutes, for Christ sake. I had nightmares about venereal diseases the next five years."

"Well, my divorce wasn't as dramatic, but it had to do with cheating, too."

"Hers or yours?"

"Hers, with her first husband, you can believe it."

"I hope I can. I read somewhere that men use that as a pickup line, how their wives cheated on them. Some women like to hear that stuff."

"You?"

"I don't know yet," she said. "Tell me more. How'd you meet?"

"I was doing the drywall in the building where she lived."

"She younger?"

"Same age as me. Thirty-five, but her first husband was a couple years younger."

"And?"

"We started talking one day and I asked her out. One thing led to another, but she never let me in on the situation with her ex or I might've paid a little more attention. She went down to Florida a few days before we were married. She said to see her grandmother. Her mother covered for her, but we spoke over the phone so I didn't question it. She probably started cheating before we were married. That or she never stopped sleeping with her ex."

"She sounds horrible."

"She is, but we have a kid together so there's that between us, too."

"How old?"

"Nine. Gonna be ten soon. Name's John also, but we call him Jack."

"You get to see him?"

"Not as much as I should, but that has more to do with work. I think Nancy, my ex, would let me take him if I ever got my feet on the ground. I don't think she much cares for being a mother."

"Well, I never did finish college so he ruined that, too, for me. I am grateful we didn't have kids, though. He couldn't. I don't know how I would have dealt with the situation if there was a kid involved. Sometimes I wish I'd had one anyway."

"You're still young enough, no?"

"I'm thirty-seven, John."

"I wasn't asking your age."

"In case you were wondering."

"I would've guessed younger."

"Thanks. I'm also a good girl, though, in case you're wondering about that. I don't kiss on first dates, never mind the rest of it."

"That's twice you made that point."

"I'm glad you're counting."

"I'm good until I run out of fingers."

"How often do you see your boy?" she asked.

John lit a fresh cigarette. "Not enough," he said. "Between driving during the week, at least until today, then having to deal with clowns like that asshole in the diner the other night, it doesn't leave much time for recreation."

Melinda was confused. "You knew those jerks?"

"One of them," John said. "The big mouth. He gave me some lip a few hours before I met you the first time. It's a long story."

"Should I hear it?"

"Only if you wanna be bored."

"Nobody wants that, but tell me anyway. How do you know him?"

John had to think of something to say.

"I borrowed money," he lied.

"What do you mean?"

"I was short and he puts it out. I borrowed some."

She leaned forward, both arms on the table. "Are you kidding me? He's a loan shark? That's what that guy was?"

John's face flushed red.

"Jesus, how much did you borrow?"

"Not a lot. Enough, though. Enough so he could get loud when I come up short."

Melinda was trying to gauge whether or not he was telling the truth, then thought why would he lie about it.

"Tell me I didn't scare you off," he said. "I'm not half the screwup I probably sound like."

She was still trying to understand. "Is there a reason you needed the money? A good reason, although I can't imagine any good enough to go to those people for anything."

"My kid," he said. "Child support, rent, his shoes, my shoes. Life, I guess. I didn't have much saved when I was married and what I had she did a good job of costing me in court when we divorced."

"Jesus," Melinda said. "I don't know what to say."

"Say you'll see me again. That'll take some of the sting out of what I can't believe I just told you."

Melinda was suddenly uncomfortable. "You're not some kind of gambler, I hope. They're the people go to loan sharks."

"Trust me, I'm no gambler."

"Hold on a minute," she said. "Let me ask Jill."

"Who's Jill?"

Melinda waved at one of the waitresses across the diner. A tall, thin redhead with freckles and green eyes joined them.

"Well?" Melinda said.

"He's handsome enough," Jill said.

"Yeah, I know that, but what do you think?"

"You promise to treat my best friend like the princess she is?" Jill asked John.

"Yes, ma'am."

"Watch that ma'am bit."

"So?" Melinda said.

"Give him a shot," Jill said. "You can always throw him back."

"Ouch," John said.

Melinda was looking into his eyes. He returned the stare until she pointed to her watch. "Okay, that's it. Jill and I have a lot of gossip to catch up on."

"Do I get a phone number?" he asked.

"Not until I get yours and I can check to make sure you're not living with somebody like a wife you didn't mention."

He jotted his phone number on a piece of napkin. She gave him a wink as he pushed the napkin at her. He blushed one more time.

"Would you look at that, the way he blushes," she said to Jill. "That the cutest thing or what?"

"Okay, then," he said as he slid out of the booth. "It was nice meeting you, Jill."

The two shook hands.

"Melinda," he said, then shook her hand as well.

"Good night, John," she said.

He went to take his wallet out, but she stopped him. "I have this," she said.

He seemed embarrassed at the gesture and quickly left.

CHAPTER 10

"Where'd you get all that money?" Holly asked Louis. She noticed the twenties as soon as he paid for his espresso. "You go to the track again?"

He took a sip of the demitasse and set the cup down. They were sitting at a table in Café Reggio on MacDougal Street in Greenwich Village. They had walked there after Louis picked her up outside the acting studio further west on Bleecker Street. Holly had ordered an Italian ice but couldn't finish it. She'd also seemed distracted and kept glancing toward the street.

"I tell you I was on the island and you assume I was at the track," he said. "They don't even run at Belmont now. They're up in Saratoga."

"And Aqueduct," Holly said. "I know they're there, too. I saw you circling horses in that racing paper at your apartment."

"And Aqueduct, yeah, but not now they aren't. Jesus, can't a guy have a few bucks on him without a third degree?"

What had actually happened was he met a woman in a bar across the street from an OTB in the city. After getting her drunk on vodka tonics, Louis lifted her wallet from her pocketbook. He was decent enough to replace the wallet, but not until he removed five of the six twenties he'd found inside.

"So, where'd you get it, if not at the track?"

"How about what I do for a living, cleaning windows," Louis lied. "I had a private out in Great Neck across from the train station there. Good job, too. I'm hoping it becomes a steady."

Holly was suspicious. "Somebody paid you all that money to clean their windows?"

"It was an apartment building, Holly. I did five apartments and I spent, like, five hours there. What is this anyway, the Inquisition?"

Holly stared at him a long moment before glancing at her watch. "Oh, my God!" she said. "I can't believe you just said that. I have a history test in two days and I haven't studied yet. It's on the Spanish Inquisition."

Louis didn't believe her. "Glad I could help," he said with indifference.

"No, really," Holly said. "I can't stay. I have to get back to the dorm."

"Meaning you can't come home with me?"

"No, Louis, I'm sorry," she said, her face twisted with apparent remorse. "I really can't. I have to study for this."

"Can we at least go for a walk or something? I want to go over a few things. You know, what we talked about."

Holly glanced at her watch again. "Can we make it fast?"

"I guess I don't have a choice."

He left a dollar tip and followed her lead. They walked north along McDougal Street. Holly's dorm was across from the northeast end of the park.

"It's about that guy I told you about," Louis said. "I'm pretty sure he's making a delivery with the film again this weekend."

"I'm not sure it's a good idea trying to take that from him," Holly said. "He's probably involved with the Mafia. That's what they're saying at the college, that it's the Mafia behind the movie."

"And so what if it is?" Louis said. "All the more reason to take this guy down. He's making dirty money from a dirty business. Who's gonna care?"

"Unless you get caught."

"He's not going to catch anybody, this guy. Trust me on this. What he'll probably have to do is run for his life for screwing up with their money. He'll probably leave the state."

"I don't want to be responsible for anybody getting hurt, Louis. I mean, I don't care if he's a bad guy and all, if you take money from him, but I don't want someone to get hurt because of it."

"Yeah, well, try and remember what this guy is pushing out there," Louis said. "The way the women are treated in those movies? He doesn't care about that. None of those guys do. They just use those girls and probably pay them peanuts to make these movies. They make all the money, the guys do, while the women wind up turning tricks in their old age. Think of that before you worry about this guy."

He could tell he'd gotten to her again. Just in time, too, since they were close to her dorm.

"Okay," she said, "but I really have to get back to the dorm and study now."

Or maybe she was preoccupied.

"Sure you're not going to meet somebody? Some guy?"

Holly blushed. "Who? Of course not. Don't be silly."

"Because I don't think I could take that, losing my girl now, after I've given up the track and stopped gambling in general and have started to think about buying a house."

Holly inadvertently looked at her watch one more time. "I hope that's true, Louis. Really, I do."

"It is."

"Good then. Good." She kissed him on the cheek, then hustled across the street toward her dorm.

Once she was gone it bothered Louis the way she had blushed when he asked if she was going to meet somebody. He'd never seen Holly blush before, not like that. He was wondering whether or not he should follow her to the dorm when a tall, thin girl wearing a braless halter and tight bikini bottoms roller-skated to a bench a few feet away. Louis gave her the once over as she adjusted one of her skates with a key.

"Know where I can get some weed?" he asked.

"'Scuse me?" the skater said.

"Pot," Louis said. "Know where I might cop some?"

"Sure. Give me two minutes and I'll take you."

"You're not a cop, are you?"

The skater giggled. "Do I look like one?"

"Have to ask."

"How much you need?"

"What'll fifty get me?"

"A lot more than you need unless you're dealing. Maybe you want to sample it first."

"Sounds fair."

The skater was up off the bench. "Follow me," she said, then stuck out her hand for him and led Louis back west across the park.

■ ■ ■

Angela Santorra wasn't happy about cashing in the last of their kids' savings bonds, but what really pissed her off was having to do it alone because Nick wasn't willing to get up and go with her. He had come home ranting the night before about killing somebody as soon as he got the chance. When she got up to tell him to be quiet already and not wake the kids up she saw the knot on his forehead above his left eye.

"The hell happened to you?" she had said. That was her first mistake.

Nick spent the next half hour raving about it.

"I'll kill the cocksucker for what he did," he'd yelled. "I'll kill him and his ancestors. I'll put two behind his ear and another one through his heart. I'll cut off his balls and feed them to his mother. I'll break every bone in his body."

"Who?" Angela had asked, her second mistake.

"The motherfucker japped me. The guy hit me when I wasn't looking. Took a cheap shot and then he took off before I could do anything. Ran like a rat bastard and now I got this knot on my head and tomorrow my eye'll turn black and it'll look like I caught a beatin', which I didn't, I got japped."

Angela figured Nick had started another fight he'd lost. It had happened before when his ego was wounded and he needed to fictionalize what had happened to feel better about himself. The last time had been at the kiddie rides on Cross Bay Boulevard when he'd cursed a guy half his size and the guy told Nick to go fuck himself. The fight was over as soon as the guy hit Nick in the stomach and he couldn't breathe. He'd dropped to his knees gasping, but Angela had known enough to look the other way and pretend she hadn't seen what had happened. That time Nick's excuse had been that the guy had caught him off guard and kicked him like a girl.

Last night, when he was finished making excuses and death threats, Nick mentioned he needed money for something and that she'd have to cash in the rest of the kids' savings bonds.

"We already cashed in most of those," she had told him. "How much do you need?"

"I don't know. Two hundred."

"Two hundred? Where are we gonna get two hundred dollars from? They don't have that much in bonds. And we'll be cashing them premature so it'll be even less."

"I don't care how much there is, just go and get it tomorrow morning. I have to drop it off in the afternoon."

"Drop what off? What'd you bet and lose now?"

"What's the difference what I did? Just get the money."

"Damn it, Nick. That's all there is. How could you bet that money?"

"I didn't bet. I fucked something up."

"And it cost two hundred dollars?"

"Angela, I'm not in the mood for this, okay? I got a headache from where this piece of shit japped me and now you wanna break my balls about something else I caught shit for."

"What? What was it that cost two hundred dollars?"

The third mistake was asking him what it was he needed the money for.

"You really wanna know?"

"Yes, I do. Please, tell me."

"Those fucking posters I had to sign last night. And the panties. All that shit you couldn't help me with because you were too fucking busy with the kids in the morning. All that crap I had to sign, I made a mistake."

"What kind of a mistake?"

"An expensive one, alright? Just go get the money in the morning and leave me alone."

He had started to yawn then. Angela figured it was best to leave him be and let him sleep it off. Maybe she'd find a way around cashing in the bonds the next day, but when she woke him up and couldn't get him to go to the bank with her, she went ahead and did it herself.

And that was that, the bonds her brothers and sisters had given the kids when they were born were no more. Cashed in prematurely, they were worth one hundred fifty-six dollars. Angela didn't know where they would get the rest of the two hundred Nick had said he needed.

He was still sleeping when she got home. She took the opportunity to go through his pants and wallet to see if he'd been out screwing around again, because if he had, she was bringing that money over to her mother's to hide and Nick and his whores could go straight to hell. It was what her mother had suggested the last time she'd found lipstick on his collar and then smelled the perfume she knew wasn't hers. He'd been with a few other women over the course of their marriage and even before that when she knew he was screwing one of the women at the beauty parlor where she used to get her hair done, but what was the point of complaining. She was his wife and the mother of his kids, and aside from the affairs she knew about, Nick had been an okay husband and a decent enough provider.

She was grateful Nick was Eddie Vento's wife's first cousin, even though he met a lot of women around that bar in Williamsburg and sometimes came home drunk. If she had to weigh the pros and cons of that bar and what went on there, it was definitely more beneficial than not.

Eddie had arranged it so Nick was on the books as a driver in the garment district even though he didn't have the proper license to drive a truck. Angela doubted Nick even knew where the garment district was. He had told her the paychecks were delivered to the bar, which was another reason he had to be there. It's where he went most nights and he didn't like it when she asked him why.

"Business," Nick would say. "Go ask Eddie."

It was a steady paycheck plus they were covered with family insurance that included dental. Angela didn't know how they would afford to live without it. It was something she thought about whenever Nick did something stupid like whatever he'd done with those posters last night for it to cost them two hundred dollars.

When it was time to watch her stories, she turned on the radio in the kitchen and tuned into the Cousin Brucie show. She raised the volume enough so Nick would have to get up to turn it back down. Then she went down to the basement to iron laundry while she watched the small television Nick had brought home for her last Christmas.

She had just tuned into *As The World Turns* when she heard him yelling. The basement door opened and he came halfway down the stairs. His eyes were bloodshot and his hair disheveled.

"You get the money?" he wanted to know.

"There was only one-forty," she lied.

"How much?"

"One-forty."

"What happened to the rest?"

"That's all there was."

"Okay. Alright. I can give Eddie his money and still have enough left over for the gun."

"What gun?" Angela said.

"The one I need to kill somebody."

Angela gasped as Nick turned and walked back up the stairs.

I should've said one-ten, she was thinking.

■ ■ ■

The blonde had spread her legs wide before bending at the waist to drop her head down and look at her audience upside down. Her long hair swept the stage left to right as she gyrated in the awkward position. The crowd, about fifteen men in several small groups spread around an oval stage, applauded. Two Hispanic men sitting close to the center of the stage were drinking two-dollar Budweisers. They whooped it up when the blonde blew them a kiss between her legs.

"Personally, I never understood it," Detective Levin told Detective Steven Brice, "watching some broad shake her cans on a stage like that. I understand her motive, sure, but the guys drooling over her like that, those two there? Makes no sense."

The barmaid, a short, stocky woman with red hair, was wearing a black one-piece jumper that exposed a lot of thigh and cleavage. She placed a fresh napkin down before setting a Heineken on top of it, scooped up the three singles Levin had set down, thanked him, then headed for the register located mid-bar on the back counter.

"I could go for that a lot sooner I could one of them up on the stage," said Levin about the barmaid. He turned on the bar stool and extended his right hand. "Neil Levin. We'll be working together starting tomorrow on the fuck film."

Brice shook Levin's hand and chuckled. "Here I thought I was gonna have to make bullshit conversation again. Happens six times a day at least, some guy picks on me to tell his life story to."

"Don't worry, a few weeks chasing bootlegged copies of a movie and you'll be wishing you were back here," Levin said. He took a sip of beer and set it down on the center of the coaster. He watched a tall man pay for a beer a few stools away and said, "Two bucks a beer. Fuckin' robbery. You should talk to the manager this dump."

The blonde had dropped down to her back, then lifted herself up into a spider crawl. She made her way to the edge of the stage and turned so her crotch was facing the audience. Both Hispanic men reached up to fit dollar bills into the string of her bikini bottom.

"They'd probably go home and jump their wives, except some of these girls are working," Brice said.

At age thirty-three, he had just become a detective with the vice squad.

Although he enjoyed undercover work, Brice had been looking for something more exciting. He had hoped for Drug Enforcement and was disappointed when he was sent to Vice.

"Prostitution in a place like this?" Levin said. "I'm shocked."

"That's the least of it. But we're only supposed to be interested in the hooking going on."

"Management behind it?"

"Probably, but not the stuff goes on inside the place. No percentage for them letting girls get caught hooking in here. Could lose their liquor licenses."

"If anybody gave a fuck."

"It's easy enough they take it outside. There's a motel about two blocks from here. They go in the VIP room and angle it out from there, the girls. Nobody's the wiser. They let a guy sample the goods here, maybe a quick hand job, blow job, whatever, they get them out to the hotel for money that goes directly south, no detours into management's pockets."

"At which time they probably pass a business card off with their home phone and work private ever after," Levin said. "Except the boys behind this operation wouldn't earn off that."

"I'm sure they do that, some of the girls," Brice said. "They're gonna sell it, can't say I blame them."

"A cop with a heart, eh?"

"Better them than the mob."

"Point is," Levin said, "doing this, you're working for the mob. Whoever the genius was put you on this detail, he's doing the guys running this place a favor."

"Maybe he is," said Brice. "I'm just following orders. Hopefully, this new unit we're on together, chasing this film, that'll be more rewarding. In the meantime, it's a job."

"Why it's a good country, America."

Brice seemed annoyed at the comment.

"I'm breaking your shoes," Levin said. "You're a young stud, I can appreciate that, but there's a lot goes on you're still green about. Trust me on that."

Brice nodded and said, "What do you know about the guy running our investigation?"

"Lieutenant Kelly? Not much more than you. He's at it a long time, has roots with Vice that'll make him unbearable you make a suggestion he's not interested in. Guys like that are usually dinosaurs but not always. We'll know soon enough."

"He into this detail?"

"Into it how?"

"He behind it. I've worked for guys just going through the motions, this for instance, makes it hard to stay enthused."

"So I was right, my hunch. You are the ambitious type. Wyatt fuckin' Earp. That's great. Just what I need this stage of my life, close enough to retirement I can taste the pina coladas, an ambitious gunslinger wants to clean up Dodge before his thirtieth birthday."

"I'm thirty-three."

"You look younger."

"I'm not and I'm no hero either. I just don't like wasting my time."

Levin pointed at the blonde. She was touching her toes now, her ass to the audience. "I wouldn't call this wasting my time. At least you get a show."

"What I get is bored," Brice said.

The crowd erupted into a cheer. They both looked up as the blonde stepped off the stage onto one of the tables where a stocky man had tilted his head back. A five-dollar bill lay across his nose. The blonde straddled his head, then lowered herself until she could remove the money with her crotch.

"Now there's talent for you," Levin said. "How long you think it took her to learn that trick?"

"About five seconds, assuming she practiced first. Why I never get wood in here." He listed off the fingers of his left hand. "First, because they're skanks, most of the women they hire here. Second, I see these losers letting one of these women probably been fucked half a dozen times before noon, they let them sit on their face for I don't know what the guy gets out of it, makes me queasy, not horny."

"Any number of cops working the same beat might get propositioned to look the other way, the girls make a side deal," Levin said. "A freebee to go, so to speak."

"They'd be wasting their time," Brice said. "Not interested. Not without a couple dozen steam cleanings through an expensive car wash first. Then maybe a couple months in a monastery, a year or two of clean living, then maybe, I had the urge, I'd maybe let one of them hold my hand. Anything more than that, I'd have to pass."

"So you're not on the take, that it?"

"That's a loaded fucking question. On top of an insinuation I'm working for the mob. You on the take, maybe? Looking to feel me out? That it?"

"Most guys'd be tempted is all," Levin said. "A place like this, a guy could knock off a piece in lieu of being bored all day."

Brice turned on his stool again. "First off, I wouldn't pay for it. Second, I wouldn't jeopardize my fuckin' job."

"I meant no offense," Levin said. He stuck his hand out, but the crowd cheered again, louder this time. Both men turned to see the string bikini bottom come off.

"That even legal?" Levin said.

One of the bikini bottom straps had broken free. The blonde, smiling now, was covering herself with it as she back-stepped toward the curtain.

"No, but it's an accident happens at least a couple times a day," Brice said.

"Least since I'm coming here."

"You gentlemen like anything else?" the barmaid asked.

"I'm good," Levin said.

"Me, too," Brice said.

They watched until the blonde disappeared behind the curtain. The crowd gave a round of applause before settling down again.

Levin said, "How long's that, you're coming to this place?"

"Two weeks," Brice said. "Here and another joint over in Queens. I rotate the days. Builds up their confidence they see me different days. They talk to me, the bartenders. This one passed me a name the other day, one of the girls she shills for. I usually stay for one girl, give her the allocated number of bills for tip money, have a couple beers and leave. That way they think I'm into one girl instead I'm a cop looking to bust somebody."

"Who's your girl today?"

"Not on yet. Black beauty, though. Very pretty."

"You gonna put a bill on your nose like that slob before?"

"I'm not that brave. I'm afraid something might jump off, make me blind."

Levin glanced at his watch. "I just wanted to say hello. You're free later, I'm buying. Get a six pack where I live for the price of two in here. What time you quit?"

"Noon, but I'm heading up to Connecticut, see family."

Levin extended his right hand again. "Okay, then I guess I'll see you tomorrow."

Brice accepted the handshake. "Tomorrow," he said.

Another cheer erupted from the crowd as a tall, thin redhead with small breasts carried a mop and pail across the stage. She stopped to shake her ass to the baseline in Betty Wright's "Clean Up Woman," then proceeded to center stage.

"This should be good," Levin said.

"Only if you got a strong stomach," Brice said.

Levin looked up and saw the redhead slowly licking her lips as she straddled the mop. "You know what?" he said. "Suddenly I don't wanna find out."

CHAPTER 11

He had a new coworker today, a big Russian, but the guy moved slowly, was sloppy, and wasn't much for conversation. John did his best to avoid the guy when it was time to do the taping, especially after catching a whiff of the man's breath.

He had come to work without getting much sleep the night before, but he was feeling better about his prospects today. There was the chance of getting his union card back for one thing, and the extra stops on the weekend would bring in much-needed cash.

He wasn't sure when he'd be able to get over to the diner to see Melinda again and thought about calling to ask for her schedule, but decided against it. He had made some progress the night before and didn't want to ruin it.

It was close to two when he took a lunch break. He picked up a ham and Swiss on rye sandwich, a small bag of potato chips, a diet iced tea and a *New York Post* from a nearby deli. He ate in the tiny yard behind the job site under a tarpaulin he used to cover two stacks of cinder blocks. He glanced at the cover of the newspaper while he chewed on a big bite of his sandwich and saw the headline was about some guy named Kissinger being named Secretary of State.

John flipped to the sports pages and glanced at the baseball results. The Yankees had lost their second straight to Kansas City, the Mets had beaten the Dodgers, and John's second favorite team, because they had been his brother's favorite, the Giants, had beaten the Expos.

He turned the page and read a small article about the preseason blowout at the Yale Bowl the weekend before. He moved on to the horse racing pages and read through the horse names.

He spotted a horse in the eighth race on the Roosevelt Card named Son of Nancy, an odds on favorite.

"Maybe if you were a long shot and I had two bucks to my name," he said.

John finished looking through the paper about the same time he was finished with his potato chips. He had a few hours of work left for the day. Then he'd have to start thinking about what he'd tell Eddie Vento. The wiseguy had told him he could think about the job offer, but not too long. The pros and cons weren't as black and white as he'd like them to be. Playing it safe, what his mother, old man Elias and probably Melinda would suggest, might mean playing it poor for the foreseeable future.

If the builder he was working for today didn't have anything next week, John would still need the weekend gig, at least until he found something else. Turning down Eddie Vento might cost him more than he could afford to lose.

It was three o'clock when he remembered to call his ex-wife. He would make plans to see his son when he dropped off the balance of the child support he owed. Maybe he could pick up Yankees tickets if they were home the following week or take the kid to the bazaar Nancy had mentioned. He checked the schedule in the newspaper he'd bought at lunch and saw the Dodgers were at Shea to play the Mets tomorrow night and the Giants Friday through Sunday. The Yankees were out of town.

Little Jack was a Yankees fan. If John bought the tickets enough in advance, so long as it wasn't a Saturday or Sunday, he should be able to take his son to see his favorite team. Maybe one of the games during the week before school started.

When he was finished with work John called Nancy to check with her before he bought tickets he wouldn't be able to use. His son answered on the second ring.

"Hey, big guy," John said. "It's Daddy."

"Hi, Dad," his son said. "We've been trying to call you."

John knew his son meant his ex-wife had been trying to call and that it probably wasn't going to be pleasant when she got on the line. He did his best to avoid that conversation by keeping his son engaged. "Why, did anything happen?"

"Nathan got me baseball tickets," Little Jack said. "For going back to school, but he can't make it and wanted to know if you could take me."

"What day's the game, Jack? So long as it isn't a weekend, I can."

"Friday, August thirty-first at seven o'clock."

John had to distribute the film Friday, but could do it in the afternoon. "It's a night game, sure. I can do that."

"Really?"

"I sure will, yeah. Did you thank Nathan?"

"Yeah, I said thanks."

"Good. How was camp today?"

"Okay. I told everybody about the game. They're playing the Orioles."

"Baltimore, huh? They have good pitching on that team."

"Yeah, I know."

"And Brooks Robinson and Boog Powell."

"I don't care, the Yankees will win anyway."

"Okay, I hope so."

"You coming over?"

John could picture his ex-wife looming over their son waiting for his answer. He didn't like putting the kid in the middle of their business and told his son to put her on.

"But you're coming over, right?"

"I sure am," John said. "And I'll take you for Carvel after. How's that?"

"Great!" his son said.

"Okay, then, put your mother on."

"Okay, Dad, love you. Here's Mom."

John waited for her to speak. When she didn't, he said, "Nan?"

"What?"

She had probably been on the line all along, most likely listening on another phone.

"I'll be over after I eat."

"You bringing money?"

"Yes."

There was a click, a momentary pause, then a dial tone. The bitch had hung up.

■ ■ ■

Louis slept with Myra, the roller skater he'd met in Washington Square park Tuesday night, after she hooked him up with an ounce of Panama Red through a dealer friend of hers in the West Village. Myra worked mornings at a button factory on Houston Street Monday through Wednesday and waited tables at an East Village diner weekends. In her spare time, usually while roller-skating in one of the south Manhattan parks, she brokered pot deals for her neighborhood friends in the business.

After copping the ounce last night, she had brought Louis home to her studio apartment off Tompkins Square Park in the East Village. There they drank two bottles of sangria, shared an order of potato perogi, then sampled his pot and screwed until they passed out. When Louis woke up the next day, it was in the early afternoon and Myra was gone. He called the window-cleaning office to say he had had an emergency and hadn't been able to call earlier. He told them he would be back in the morning but might need additional time off Friday and the following week. He would keep in touch.

After hanging up the phone, he felt an itch between his legs. He was scratching at it through his underwear when the lock turned in the apartment door.

Myra was back from her morning job. She carried a small white paper bag with steam rising from the top.

"Bagels," she said.

"You got coffee?"

"Two light and sweet."

"I'm gonna need more than two."

"Oh, the other one was for me. I can run down and get some more if you want."

"Hold on and I'll go with you after I shower."

The apartment was tiny. She sat on the edge of the sofa bed and set the bag on the floor. "You awake long?"

Louis had moved from the sofa bed to one of two folding chairs. He leaned over, opened the bag and pulled out a bagel, then one of the coffees. He set the bagel in his lap and popped the lid on the coffee.

"Thanks," he said before sipping.

"Sure," Myra said.

Louis noticed she had gone out wearing the same outfit as last night minus the roller skates. She removed the halter before unwrapping her bagel and taking a bite. A glob of cream cheese dropped from the bagel onto her left breast. Louis pointed to it.

"Wanna lick it off?" she said.

"Not until I'm awake," he said.

She winked and he noticed another blot of cream cheese had formed at the corner of her mouth. He couldn't look at it while he sipped his coffee.

"I have the rest of the day if you wanna hang," she said.

"Actually I gotta take care of a few things."

"Fuck and run, huh?"

"What?"

She slapped one of his legs. "Just kidding," she said.

The cream cheese was still there. He pointed to it and she smeared it across her cheek with the back of her hand.

"Use a napkin," he said, then handed her one.

Myra wiped her face a few times with the napkin, then dropped it behind her onto the bed.

She was a slob. Louis wondered how he hadn't noticed it last night.

He felt another itch between his legs and started to wonder if maybe he'd picked up something sleeping with her. His heart started to race when he thought he spotted something on the string of her bikini bottom.

"Hold on a second," he told her. "Lean forward."

Myra had just taken another bite of her bagel. A second glob of cream cheese dropped, this time onto her stomach just above her bikini.

"Hey, lucky me," she said. "You're definitely gonna have to lick that one off."

Louis felt his coffee coming up at the sight of two tiny specs crawling along the bikini string. He pushed away from her and stepped inside the tiny bathroom.

"What's wrong?" she asked.

Louis retched, but nothing came up.

"Babe?"

He spit the bile that had formed in his mouth.

"Hey, you okay?"

He dry-heaved again. This time his ribs hurt.

"You sick?"

He spit a few more times until he was sure nothing would come up. When he was back out of the bathroom, Myra was licking one of her fingers after wiping the cream cheese off her stomach.

"You got crabs," he told her.

"What?"

"You gave me crabs."

"What are you talking about?"

Louis pulled at her bikini bottom. "Check," he said. "I just saw two on your suit. The string there."

Myra pulled the bottom off. Louis pointed at her crotch. "Probably came out of the jungle you have. Shave the damn thing. Trim it at least."

Myra was looking down at her triangle of pubic hair. "Maybe you gave them to me," she said defensively.

"I didn't give you shit," Louis said. "I didn't have any." He was looking for signs of the insects on himself now.

"It's no big deal if there are any," she said. "They make creams for it. I've had them before."

Louis was half amazed, half crazed. "You had them before?"

"A few times. It's no big deal."

"What's wrong with you?"

"What do you mean by that?"

"You're nuts."

"Fuck you, man. You're the one is nuts."

Louis dressed, gathered his things, including what was left of the Panama Red, and left.

"At least close the fucking door!" he heard Myra yell behind him.

■ ■ ■

"We can use the recorder or you can go fuck yourself," Captain Kaprowski told the special agent. "I don't like feds, never mind trust them. You're lucky I didn't shoot your ass you flashed that badge. It's the first thing came to mind when I saw it."

Special Agent Darrel Stebenow, at thirty-six years of age, was an eight-year veteran of the Federal Bureau of Investigation. Against Bureau rules of jurisdiction, conflict of interest, and confidentiality, Stebenow had come to Kaprowski for help. Determined to retire as soon as the federal informant he was overseeing safely concluded her obligation to the government, he had brought incriminating evidence against himself in an attempt to validate his sincerity.

"I brought surveillance tapes should be proof enough I'm not here representing the Bureau," he said. "You prefer we record this, fine. This is about a witness in over her head. A woman railroaded into something might get her killed for no other reason than she's expendable in the eyes of an over-ambitious federal prosecutor sees himself president someday."

Kaprowski showed no emotion as he leaned forward to hit the RECORD button. "Okay then," he said. "The particulars first."

Stebenow gave his name, rank within the bureau, date of birth, Social Security number, address and a full confession about seeking Kaprowski at his home in regards to federal informant Bridget Malone. He also mentioned copies of surveillance tapes he'd secured from a federal informant having to do with a federal investigation. A short Q and A followed, during which Stebenow answered whatever questions the police captain felt were relevant to ask. When they were finished, Kaprowski turned the recorder off.

"Up front I'll tell you this much," he told the special agent. "I can't and won't jeopardize my investigation for your informant. She's in the crosshairs, you're that concerned, you're gonna retire anyway, maybe you two should hop a jet someplace remote enough nobody bothers looking for you."

Stebenow produced a set of cassette tapes. "Here's what I mentioned before. You can put the recorder back on if you'd like. These are from a federal wire in an apartment above Eddie Vento's bar in Williamsburg. Our informant lives there rent-free. Bridget Malone is one of three girlfriends we know Vento has, but she's also the one gets the most attention. She works as a bartender in Fast Eddie's, Vento's bar on the first floor of the same apartment building. Just for the record, you can burn me with those tapes worse than with anything we recorded five minutes ago. Those're federal property."

Kaprowski rubbed his chin.

"Look, we're both after the same bad guy here," Stebenow said. "Eddie Vento goes away, maybe he gives some of his friends up, no doubt the world's a better place. I'm not asking you to blow your investigation. I am asking for extra attention to the plight of the informant. If you should pick something up, for instance, you deem intrinsic to her protection, I'd appreciate a heads up. Me, not the Bureau. Of course I'll do the same. Chances are I'll probably come to you first anyway."

Kaprowski toyed with the cassettes as he mulled over what the special agent had said. Then he set the tapes down.

"You leave here, I never wanna see you again unless I call you first."

"Understood," Stebenow said.

"And I'm gonna wanna sit on this, what you brought me here today. I'm gonna wanna sit on it a few days at least."

"Is there someone I can contact besides yourself in the event of an emergency?"

Kaprowski didn't answer.

"I'm the one's gonna burn when this is all over," Stebenow said. "Just my coming here forfeits my career. The tapes, they're brought to the Bureau's attention, those can put me away."

Kaprowski was staring into Stebenow's eyes then. Neither man flinched. Kaprowski said, "Unless they sent you here on purpose, the Bureau."

Stebenow pointed to the tapes. "Why I brought those, in case that's what you thought. Give them a listen."

"Then I'd be complicit."

"Then give them to someone else to listen to. Give them a line of shit where you got them."

Kaprowski rubbed his chin again. "You need to use the bathroom before you go?"

"No, but thanks for asking."

Kaprowski stood up from behind his desk and led the way back up to the kitchen where he stopped to point at the sink.

"Water?" he said.

"No thanks," Stebenow said.

Kaprowski headed through the dining and living rooms to a small vestibule at the front of the house. He opened the front door, then the screen door.

"I appreciate this," said Stebenow before he stepped outside. He turned to say good-bye and offer his hand, then flinched when the door closed in his face.

CHAPTER 12

Detectives Brice, Levin and Kelly had met for breakfast at a diner on Astoria Boulevard a few minutes before nine o'clock in the morning. Brice and Kelly sat on one side of the booth; Levin on the other. Each had ordered a western omelet with home fries, buttered toast and coffee. They ate without speaking. Kelly finished first. Brice next. Levin was still picking at his omelet when Brice pointed to a magazine he'd brought with him.

"There's an article in here about *Deep Throat*," he said. "They're showing it all over the country now. I saw it myself yesterday in Connecticut."

"So much for visiting family," Levin said.

"Huh?" Kelly said.

"I saw it with my brother," Brice said. "Point is, the film is a hot item now they banned it. Article says the same thing. Wiseguys have contracts working with theater owners all over the place, everything under the table. Guys are making a fortune. They can't get a theater, they use schools, warehouses. Churches, they find a pastor desperate enough."

"Best thing they did for the wiseguys behind that movie was ban it," Levin said. "They're probably doing twice the volume they were before."

Brice tapped the magazine. "They're doing better'n that," he said. "It's a major score for the mob, this film."

"Just like Prohibition," Levin said. "Mob's best friends, politicians."

"You guys seen it yet?" Brice asked.

Levin was the oldest at age forty-one. He removed his glasses and leaned across the table to see the magazine. "The movie or the article?" he asked. "No, to either, though. I only read the *Racing Form* and I can't afford the movies."

"I have," Kelly said.

"What'd you think?" Brice asked.

"It's better than the old stag things they had, but she's no Rita Hayworth, the broad they used."

"I'm talking about what she did, the deep throat thing."

"It was impressive. The girl is gifted."

"That's one way to put it," Levin said.

"Being all of six inches, though," Kelly added, "I never had to think about what she was working with in that movie."

"He say six or three?" Levin asked Brice.

"Ask your wife," Kelly said.

"Hey, I'm divorced," Levin said. "Be my guest."

"Anyway," Kelly continued, "the guy was hung." He held two fingers apart and added, "Thick, too. Like this."

Brice finished his coffee and moved the cup to the near edge of the table for a refill.

"Meantime," he said, "I'll bet she got spit for making that thing, a couple grand or something."

"They told her she'd be a star someday," Levin said.

"I heard it was twelve hundred," Kelly said. "And that ain't so bad a day's pay for a couple blow jobs. She'd have to give a couple hundred she was working the streets."

"Compared to what the wiseguys make off it when all is said and done?" Brice said. "Couple hundred grand, I bet this movie makes. At least that."

"Now you're talking out your ass," Kelly said. "Maybe a hundred grand and a big maybe at that."

"You talking legit or under the table, because they're gonna make it both ways," Levin said.

Brice pointed to the article again. "They already are."

"Except that's not the only act in town," Kelly said. "Take a look-see the papers. There's still plenty other fuck films a guy can see without going through the trouble it takes to see that one."

Levin motioned at Brice. "The kid is right," he said. "Once the court banned it, they turned it into gold for the mob. They have leeches been working overtime figuring ways to bleed whatever they can from it."

"I'm not saying they're losing off it, the wiseguys, that's for sure," said Kelly a little defensively. "And you're right, between the legal showings around the country since it's banned in New York and what they're doing with bootleg copies, it's been a score they made with that movie, but it's not the only movie on the block. There's a dozen flicks they advertise the *Daily News* and the *Post* every day."

Levin finally finished eating. He pushed his plate away and pressed his back flush against the booth's backrest. "That wasn't half bad," he said.

Brice said, "I read where the guy made it, the director, the one wrote it, whatever, he used to be a hairdresser."

"Imagine?" Levin said. "Guy like that with his hands all over your wife's hair?"

"Me, I liked the other broad they used, not the star," Kelly said. "The short one. She wasn't so bad-looking. Had a little mileage on her, but she was a lot better than the skank did the magic act."

"You like her as what, best supporting?" Levin said.

"Yeah, why not?" Kelly said. "I like her because she's short can give me a stand-up blow job. I'm talking looks. The star, Linda Lovelace, she had them crooked teeth turned me off. And that goofy fuckin' actor, the one played the doctor, where they hell they find that schmuck?"

"Man's hung, he's one blessed schmuck," Levin said.

"I thought you didn't see it?" Brice said.

Levin thumbed at Kelly. "He just said the guy was hung. I don't watch pornos. I have enough insecurity without seeing some guy hung enough he can choke a horse."

Kelly winked at Brice. "Circumcision, his people are crazy for it."

"At least my people aren't cursed at birth," Levin said.

Kelly flipped him the bird. "I guess it's making some extra scratch now the courts banned it, but I didn't think much of it. All the controversy's just an excuse to watch a fuck film, you ask me. Respectable people are talking about it, the talk shows at night, so now it's okay to go see a porno. *Deep Throat*. Catchy title, I guess. Her thing is down her throat."

Levin winked at Brice. "What thing's that?" he asked.

"Huh? Her tickler, what they called it in the movie. I don't know. Fuck's the difference?"

Brice and Levin laughed, then Levin said, "Since that *Times* article the beginning of the year everybody and their mother cares. They all wanna see that movie now, including out the suburbs, why we're stuck on this thing, because it's already hit the gossip trails and is getting back to the parishes. It's starting to piss off the church on Bingo nights. Guys are out jerking off to this broad and her sword-swallowing routine and nobody shows up the Bingo."

"The Bingo nights?" Kelly said. "What, are you wearing your hat too tight?"

"Which is another waste of our precious time, you ask me," Levin said. "This chasing a porno. You see the paper the other day, Monday? Some building super caught a shotgun in the chest the back of some park in Canarsie. His wife found him. She was right there with him, a couple yards away in their car."

"Married and they went to a park to do it?" Brice asked.

"The hell do I know? Maybe to spice it up. Point is that's real crime, this chasing a porno is bullshit."

"Levin can't help himself," Kelly said to Brice. "College boy gave up Homicide for the easy life and now he feels guilty for it."

"I'm just saying," Levin said.

"Levin's right," Brice said. "We're on this *Deep Throat* thing so's to make the judge put the kibosh on it look good is all. Him and the mayor and the rest of the country we're supposed to be setting an example for."

"Tyler his name was," Levin said, "the judge."

"What a joke, set an example," Kelly said.

"Has to do with the war, you ask me," Levin said. "Everything we did over there is a disaster. Soon's we pull out, the Communists we were supposed to stop will walk right into South Vietnam. Between getting our asses kicked in the war and this Watergate mess, I figure the government figures the country needs something else to focus on. Replace the abortion the war's been and what this Watergate thing is becoming with something supposed to protect our morality. *Deep Throat* it is."

Brice moved his magazine from the table to the bench seat alongside him. "With all the other bullshit goes on in this city, the drugs and whatnot, here we are chasing a fuck film, doesn't make any sense to me," he said. "Wiseguys'd paid off the right set of politicians, they'd put it to rest already."

"That isn't gonna happen," Levin said. "There's more money in it being illegal. Everything's under the table this way, including our overtime."

Kelly shot Levin a dirty look as a short, thick waitress stopped at the table and refilled their coffees.

"Thanks, hon," Brice said. He saw Levin staring at her ass as she walked away and tried to look interested, too.

"This morning we got a tip on a guy out to Massapequa on the Island," said Kelly, getting their attention back.

"What, 's he showing the film in his basement?" Levin said.

"He's showing it somewhere, what some neighbor a his said, she's the one called it in."

"What's that about?" Brice said. "He charge guys come to his house? He's gotta have another place to show it."

"He does," Kelly said, "except we don't know where yet. Like it says in your article there, either they use some theater, the VFW, something like that, Knights of Columbus, or they find a warehouse someplace. Then they charge a premium, couple bucks more than they get for legit movies."

"Not to mention the guy found in a dumpster this week," Levin said. "Tommy DeLuca. Tommy Porno to be exact."

"Guy they chopped his mitts off," Kelly said. "Was running the film around Long Island for somebody. Question is who."

"Maybe our boy in Massapequa knows," Levin said.

"Why we're going there," Kelly said. "To find out. But now I hear there are guys in Jersey making posters, signing them Linda Lovelace and charging the morons an extra deuce a piece for them. You believe it?"

Kelly took another sip of coffee, then covered his mouth with both hands and belched when he was done. "God bless," he said, then pushed his plate away and slid out of the booth.

"So let's go see this guy," he said.

"Massapequa?" Levin said.

"It's where he lives."

"We got a warrant?"

"Not yet. We're just gonna feel him out."

"What about the cream puffs in Nassau? Can't the cops there look into the shit on their own doorstep?"

Brice looked up at Kelly and motioned toward Levin. "He's pissed it's on the Southern State," he said. "The track is on the Cross Island."

"Belmont's closed now, youngster," Levin said. "They're up to Saratoga for the summer meet and what I'm pissed at is I gotta be in the same car with you two after you both ate eggs."

"Leave the window open," Kelly said. "Air'll do you good."

■ ■ ■

Kathleen Hastings had just come back from the gym and was anxious to take a shower when she heard her husband talking to himself in the basement. Billy had left the door open at the top of the stairs. Concerned he'd started another day using amphetamines, she headed down the basement to check on him. She stopped when she heard the washing machine was running. Then she heard Billy speaking Latin.

"*Fidelis ad Mortem, Fidelis ad Mortem, Fidelis ad Mortem,*" he was saying over and over. "*Fidelis ad Mortem.*"

Kathleen called to him before continuing down the stairway.

"*Fidelis ad Mortem,*" Billy said.

"It's me," she said.

"What?" Billy said. "I'm busy."

She reached the bottom of the stairs and was in the den Billy had finished paneling last year. She saw he was sitting at his workbench at the opposite end of the room. She saw the light was on in the laundry room and asked him if he was doing the wash.

"Just some things I wanted," he said.

It was odd, she thought. Billy never did laundry.

"What were you saying before?"

"Huh?"

Frustrated with his being evasive, Kathleen set her hands on her hips.

"The police motto from when I was in the academy," he said. "*Fidelis ad Mortem.*" He winked at her. "Faithful until death."

Kathleen didn't like the way he looked. "You do anything?" she asked. "Pills, I mean."

"Not a one."

"Anything else?"

"Nope."

She didn't believe him. Since he'd been forced to retire, Billy had been abusing the drugs he used and was lying on a regular basis. The downtime he'd been spending around the house had started to concern her as well. Billy needed to find a new job or she would have to. Lately, though, especially the last two weeks, he'd been pestering her to add more details to the notebook he seemed obsessed with lately.

"Okay, you tell me," he said.

"Tell you what?"

"There anything else?"

"What are you talking about?"

"How was your workout?"

"Good, but I need to shower."

"Any good-looking young men watching you?"

"No."

"Can I watch you? In the shower, I mean."

"No. Then I want to soak in the tub for a while. You need to look for a job."

"I do?"

"Yes."

"What if I already went looking?"

"Where?"

"That place on the Island I told you about."

"You think you got it?"

"I don't know. I don't know if they know. I'm probably overqualified."

"You told them you were on the job?"

"Had to. Came from a guy I used to work with. He told them first."

Kathleen shifted her weight onto one leg. "They know what happened?"

Billy had been cleaning his .38 Smith & Wesson Special before Kathleen came home. He turned and picked the weapon up. "The guy interviewed me said he heard I got jammed up," he said. "He didn't ask what for and I didn't tell him why. Okay?"

"I don't mean to push you, but we're going to need income soon and if you can't find something fast I should be looking."

He set the .38 back down. "We're okay," he said.

"You could've told me. That night at the bar, I mean. How was I supposed to know?"

"Jesus Christ," he said. "Again with the bar? Forget that night already. Doesn't do any good to bring it up."

"It's just I feel guilty. I never would've... well... I just wish you could've told me is all."

He put a hand on the .38.

"Don't you have to give that back?"

"No," he said. "This one's mine."

They both remained silent until Billy turned to her again.

"Why'd you go downstairs that night?" she asked.

"Business," he said, "but if I couldn't tell you then, why would I tell you now? It was business. Leave it at that."

"Is it why you quit?"

"No."

"Then you should've let it go, what happened at the bar. You shouldn't've gone crazy."

"Yeah, right, sure. And let those clowns have a laugh at my expense? Some cop's wife flirting with some guy with the cop on the premises. Fuck that."

It had to do with the night John Albano knocked him out in Eddie Vento's bar. Billy had left her at the bar while he went to talk with Vento. Kathleen had mistaken his leaving her as a cue for one of their sex games.

They had often stopped in unfamiliar bars where she might flirt with strange men while Billy watched from a distance. It excited him to do so. The more engaged the stranger became, the more Kathleen flirted, the more intense was Billy's excitement.

That night she had picked a man that had come in to use the pay phone, John Albano, except that night had been different. Billy knew the bar and had gone there to talk to someone in the basement. When he returned, he went crazy and things got out of hand before Kathleen knew it.

Then, two weeks ago, he'd been forced to resign. Kathleen had become concerned about their finances.

"What are we going to do about money?" she asked.

"We're fine," he said. "I told you we're fine."

"How so?"

"Don't make me go into it now."

"I was hoping we could go away this winter," she said. "It's been more than a year."

"We went away last winter, or doesn't Florida count?"

"Florida is boring."

"We'll go away when I have another job."

"When you gonna look?"

"I'm out less than two weeks, you're gonna break my balls?"

"You're out of work three months. That desk job wasn't work, even you said so. A few days and it'll be two weeks you haven't gotten paid."

Billy made a gun with his right hand and shot himself in the head.

"Fine," Kathleen said. "Make jokes."

"It's no joke, your ballbreaking lately."

"Then I'll go back to work. I told you I would. I don't mind working."

"Not yet."

"We're gonna need the money."

"I said we're fine."

"I'm worried, Billy."

"I'll take care of it," he said. "We'll be fine."

"I need to re-up at the gym this week."

"So rejoin," Billy said. "Just leave me alone about it already."

Kathleen suddenly felt guilty for nagging him. She had read where men suddenly out of work went through a blue period and needed support.

"Hey," she said before she turned around and reached back to slap her ass. "If you want it to stay like this, I have to go to the gym."

"I want it to stay like that," he told her, "but right now I have to go out." He stood up from the workbench, slipped the .38 into a small satchel and headed for the stairs. "I'll bring back bagels for later."

"Give me a kiss first."

"No."

"Why not?"

"Because you'll give me a hard-on and then I'll be late."

"So?"

"I'll see you later."

Kathleen watched him go up the stairs. The spin cycle on the washing machine suddenly stopped. She waited a moment and listened to his footsteps. When she heard the back door open, then close, Kathleen crossed the basement toward the laundry room. She opened the washer lid and gasped when she saw the water was tinged red.

CHAPTER 13

"What's the problem, Nathan?" Nancy said. "What's so important you're hanging around this morning?"

He'd already taken Little Jack to camp and had stopped at the bagel place to pick up the cinnamon raisin she liked. He'd even brewed a fresh pot of coffee for when she came down and now she was still in a huffy mood, except today was different; today Nathan was no longer willing to ignore her attitude or pass it off to her not being a morning person.

It was about her never being home in the afternoon and he told her so.

"Since when do I have to answer to you?" Nancy said.

"Does that mean you won't tell me?"

"It means what it means," she said. She avoided his eyes and looked into her coffee before sipping it.

"Then I think we should talk about us," he said.

"What's wrong with us?"

"There isn't any us. It's you. It's all you."

"You saying I'm selfish, Nathan? Is that it?"

"You are, but it's more than that. I think you know that."

She stared him down then. "Now you're going to tell me what I think?"

"No," he said. "I have a pretty good idea what you think, but I'm putting an end to it."

Nancy seemed amused. "Really?"

"You're making a fool of me. I don't know with whom and I don't care. Either it stops or it's over. We're over."

Nancy rolled her eyes. "Now you're making a fool of yourself," she said. "Accusations like that."

Nathan didn't respond.

Nancy got up to refill her cup.

"Is it about sex?" she asked. "Because I told you I'm afraid of getting pregnant again. The doctors told me it wasn't safe for me to get pregnant anymore. I told you that."

"I don't believe that."

"Excuse me?"

"Sex is only a part of the problem, Nancy. I think you know there's more."

"I'm expecting my period any day now. Would a hand job make you happy? If that's what you want we can go upstairs now and I'll do it. I won't do the other. You know I won't."

"Don't talk like that," he said. "Not to me."

She feigned a chuckle. "I don't know how else to say it."

"It's insulting."

"Why, because you play for the Philharmonic? I'll bet the other men in that orchestra know what one is and probably talk like that all the time."

"It's the pretext of your conversation that's insulting."

"The what?"

"Don't skirt the issue. It's not about a hand job. It's about us. Do you want to stay married or not?"

"Well, I did when I woke up this morning, but now I'm not so sure. Not if I have to account for every second of the day. Not if I have to wake up to this every morning."

She couldn't help herself, Nathan was thinking. She was a cheat and cheats lied. She had been lying since the first day they met and all through their marriage. Worse, he had been willing to go along with the lie for the sake of having someone. He'd blinded himself for the sake of company and now that he couldn't live with the lie anymore he was forced to have this conversation and probably another few before he went to a lawyer and started divorce proceedings. He changed the subject rather than pursue what was hopeless.

"You should at least be more considerate of your son," he said. "At least give him some attention."

"I guess we're finished discussing us," she said.

"Be more considerate to the boy."

"He's my son, Nathan, not yours."

"Yes, he is."

Nancy slammed the cup down on the table, splashing most of the coffee onto the floor. "And what the hell do you know about being a mother?" she yelled. "And who the hell are you to tell me how to be one?"

Nathan wiped the coffee spill with paper napkins.

"He has a father, too, for your information," Nancy said. "I don't see him doing his share. He barely pays for his son."

"The boy loves his father and his father is strapped for cash. You should try and be more considerate of him, too."

"And on that note, fuck you and fuck him and fuck everybody else," Nancy said. She was up from the table now. She went to the sink and dropped her cup in it, cracking the handle. "I should be more considerate of everybody but myself. Is that it? I should stay home and play wife and mother and let everybody else do whatever the hell they want and I shouldn't complain or God forbid do anything about it like try and get my hair done or go to the doctor or shopping for a pair of shoes I like because then I'm being too selfish. Meanwhile you go away with that orchestra, traveling all over the place, concerts in Boston, Chicago, Los Angeles, and how the hell do I know you're not screwing some bimbo in your hotel rooms? How do I know you're not having a good old time yourself? Tell me that."

Nathan finished wiping down the floor and table. He pointed to the coffeepot. "You want the rest of that?"

Nancy looked from his face to the pot.

"Do you?" he asked again.

Her eyes narrowed. Then she stormed out of the kitchen, through the living room and up the stairs.

"I guess not," he said.

■ ■ ■

Louis returned to work but was still itching. The doctor had prescribed a salve for the crabs the roller-skating skank had given him. It had eased some of the itching last night, but this morning he was late getting up and had rushed out of the apartment without reapplying the medicine. It was close to ten o'clock when he gave Nancy a call on the off chance she'd be awake early and was surprised when she answered the phone.

"Who is it?" she answered.

"Nan?"

"Louis?"

"Yeah, it's me. What are you doing up so early?"

"Why'd you call then, to wake me up if I wasn't?"

She had an edge to her voice Louis couldn't afford to ignore. He'd have to find some extra time for her today. The problem would be the rash, although he was pretty sure he could work around that if he had to.

"I took a shot," he said. "What you doing today?"

"Yeah, well, I was looking for you two days ago, but you never showed up to your apartment. I had a free afternoon and thought we might make the best of it. Too bad you weren't interested then."

He ignored her sarcasm. "You free today?"

"I don't know. I think Nathan is going to leave me."

"So?"

"I know, but I'm not sure it's long enough yet. I mean, how much I'd get in the divorce."

"You break his balls enough, he'll probably give it all away to escape."

"That supposed to be a compliment?"

"Lighten up. Can't a guy joke?"

"Ha, ha, ha," said Nancy with extra sarcasm.

He could envision her rolling her eyes and had to suppress the urge to hang up on her.

"Did you find out John's schedule yet?"

"He came last night."

"What do you mean?"

"He came last night."

"You were supposed to let me know."

"And how would I do that if you're never around. Like I said, I went looking for you and you never came home. Didn't they tell you at the bar? I was there the other night."

"I haven't been," Louis said. "You find out how much gelt he's carrying?"

"No. What was I supposed to do, ask? I don't know. He's supposed to come again Sunday, but he doesn't always do what he's supposed to. He's like all my other exes, I guess."

He could reach through the line and smack her, he was thinking. Instead, he rubbed his face in frustration.

"You free today or what?" he said.

"Why?"

"Because I'm horny."

"Why don't I believe you?"

Because you're a ballbreaking bitch, he thought.

"I don't know," he said. "Aren't you?"

"Aren't I what?"

"I don't have time for games today, Nan. You want to get together or what?"

There was a pause on the line.

"I'm hanging up in two seconds," he said.

"What time?"

"Two hours. I'm on my way home now."

"Okay, noon," she said.

"See you later."

She had started to say something else when Louis hung up. He was shaking his head when he saw a brand new red Cadillac Fleetwood Eldorado at a traffic light. The showroom sticker was still glued to the rear passenger window. It reminded him of what Jimmy the loan shark had said at the bar about some guy who had wanted the one used in the porn movie and what Nancy had mentioned about some hairdresser involved with the movie. The director, he thought; either him or one of the actors.

The guy who wanted the movie memorabilia, the way Jimmy had painted him, sounded like a sucker waiting to be taken. If Nancy's connection panned out and he could get the director to maybe sign the paperwork, there might be a score to be made.

He had to see the damn movie already. Then, if he had to improvise, he would know what to look for on the used car lots.

It was something else to talk about with Nancy rather than listening to her same old beefs about them not spending enough time together. The woman could wear anybody down. Louis was surprised it had taken her latest husband this long to give up.

■ ■ ■

John was still feeling good when he woke up for work in the morning. Even though Nancy had been a royal bitch when he dropped off the money he owed, he was able to spend some quality time with his son. He especially got a kick out of watching his boy try to eat his way through the banana barge he'd bought him at the Carvel, the way the kid had smeared the chocolate syrup all over his face and on his chin.

He could still feel the hug he'd exchanged with Little Jack before he left. John became emotional thinking about his son. It had become part of the process; whenever he spent time with the boy, a heavy dose of guilt followed upon dropping him off with his mother.

John didn't see the old man when he left the apartment and wondered if Alexis Elias had found himself another date the night before. John smiled thinking about how many women the seventy-year-old had at least chatted up since the two men first met. He could think of six off the top of his head, three who lived in the building, one of them still married.

He stopped to light a cigarette at the curb. This morning he was determined to ask the builder if there would be any work the following week. It was best he knew sooner rather than later whether or not he could turn down Eddie Vento. It would come down to whether or not he had to drive car service again. If he did, he was going to take his chances working for Vento. If not and the builder had more work for him, John was going to turn Vento down.

He was hoping for the best when he crossed the street to his car and spotted the flat rear tire. He glanced at his watch and saw he didn't have much time to change it. Then he saw the other rear tire was flat as well and he knew it wasn't a coincidence.

CHAPTER 14

"I thought you guys worked in pairs?" George Berg said.

The detectives had formed a semicircle at the bottom of the stoop. All three presented their badges. Berg had just stepped out of the house and was still holding onto the screen door. He gradually let the door go and it closed behind him.

"It's a special task force," Kelly said. "I'm Kelly." He stood between Brice and Levin. He motioned at each with his head. "Detectives Brice and Levin."

"What's a task force?" Berg said.

"A shit storm, you get caught in it," Brice said.

Berg looked confused. "What's it about?"

"A dirty movie," Kelly said.

"Dirty how?"

The detectives looked at one another.

"What?" Berg said.

"Dirty like the kind perverts spank their monkey to," Kelly said. "Except this one made headlines when the court declared it illegal. This one carries more than a smack on the wrist."

"*Deep Throat*," Levin said. "No doubt you never heard of it."

"Never," Berg said. "*Deep* what?"

"*Throat*," Levin said. "As in giving a flagpole a blow job."

Berg squinted. "A flagpole?"

"You rehearse this routine?" Kelly said. "Because we have routines we rehearse, too. One is when we cuff your hands behind your back."

"Another is when we take you to a warehouse and beat you until we're tired," Levin said.

Kelly glared at Levin.

"You do know about the guy they found in a Queens dumpster, right?" Brice said. "Tommy DeLuca his name was."

"Chopped his hands off," Levin said. "Probably for stealing from the mob, but he was hustling the same movie we think you're showing."

Berg forced a laugh. "Buddy," he said, "I wish I had a clue what you're talking about, but I don't. None whatsoever."

"You're not gonna talk to us, we could always spread a rumor you are," Levin said. "The guys killed DeLuca might get antsy, think the wrong thing and fit you for a dumpster, too."

Kelly's eyes narrowed. He turned to Brice. "Take Levin for a walk around the block a minute."

"Huh?" Brice said.

"Take Levin for a walk."

Detectives Brice and Levin stepped away from the stoop. They walked out to the curb and then toward Brice's car parked at the far corner. Kelly watched until they were out of view from the stoop.

Berg said, "The fuck was his problem?"

Kelly motioned toward the door. "Come on," he said, "I gotta piss like a racehorse."

■ ■ ■

The builder didn't have work the next week and probably wouldn't for another two weeks at least, he told John. There were problems with a union delegate about using scabs. He'd been threatened over the phone the night before. The bonus, the builder had said, was there wouldn't be any work after today because he'd had to give in and hire union help for Friday, even though he didn't expect the guy the union would send would be worth fifty cents an hour, never mind the fourteen-dollar-an-hour scale he'd have to pay.

John wondered if the builder's union problems had anything to do with the two flat tires. He thanked the man for looking out for him and told him he should call if something changed. He finished out the day and had to wonder if his luck had already turned back in the wrong direction.

He put a call in to the car service and told them he was available the next day if they needed him.

"The hell you think you're doing us a favor?" the dispatcher said. "You come around when you feel like it, tell us you can't work when you find something better. What are we supposed to do, check with you first?"

There was no point in arguing with the guy. Dispatchers could be assholes when it came to flexing the little power they could wield during the course of a day. Most of them were decent enough, but every once in a while you ran into one that got his rocks off treating drivers like dirt and John wasn't in the mood for it then. He told the guy to go fuck himself and regretted it two seconds later when the guy said, "Okay, buddy, fine, I'll do that. And you make sure to give me a call again next time you need work."

Then the dispatcher had hung up and John was left feeling stupid for letting the guy get under his skin.

It reminded him of how he'd handled Nick Santorra. Thoughts of that near disaster reminded him of the flat tires again. There was something petty about slashing tires he couldn't separate from the loudmouth at the bar.

Or it could be some union muscle cracking down on scabs working a construction site they were looking to shake down. Maybe one of them had followed him from the job and slashed the tires to teach him a lesson. John decided there was no point in making himself crazy trying to figure it out. There were other, more pressing issues to worry about, like whether or not to work for Eddie Vento and maybe turn his life around, at least financially. It wasn't as easy a decision as it seemed. There were serious downsides working for a wiseguy.

He called his mother from a pay phone and couldn't tell her his bad news about losing more construction work. He avoided discussing his weekend work and learned she had made a novena for later the same night. John's only brother would have been thirty-eight this year. The career marine was killed during the first major offensive of the war at Ia Drang. Paul Albano had been thirty years old at the time of his death.

John felt bad telling his mother he couldn't attend the novena and then lied about why. Although he understood religion was how his mother continued to cope with the loss of her son, that Paul had moved on to a better place, John couldn't forgive a God that would let his only brother die.

He promised his mother he'd say a prayer for his brother, kissed her through the phone and headed home. He reexamined his car when he got there and decided to leave the tires the way they were until the morning. Whether the vandalism was personal or it had to do with his being a scab, John wasn't about to give whoever had done it a second shot so easily.

What he did was pick up a container of Chinese food and a six pack of beer before he went up to his apartment. Old man Elias still wasn't around, but John wasn't in the mood for company then anyway. He'd check in with the old man in the morning, just to make sure he was okay. Without anyplace to go, John realized he'd be able to sleep in tomorrow. It was a bittersweet irony he'd have to do something about soon.

■ ■ ■

Nancy was sitting up in Louis's bed chain-smoking while he talked on the phone in the next room. She had removed her blouse and pants when she first got there, telling him she was glad he had called and that she needed to get fucked before her period started. The phone rang and he told her it was his doctor calling about the rash. He waved her into the bedroom and turned up the air conditioner to drown out his conversation. That had been thirty-five minutes ago.

Now she was chilly. She pulled the sheets up to cover her legs and glanced at her watch. In five minutes she was going in there and whoever he was talking to was going to know about it. Four minutes later Louis walked in the bedroom holding a beer.

"You want?" he asked.

"No," she said. "It took you long enough."

"It was my doctor."

"Right. So, what he have to say?"

"I have a rash."

"You said. What kind of rash?"

"A bad one. I can't have sex for a few days."

Nancy's face tightened. "Are you kidding me?"

He sat on the edge of the bed. "Afraid not," he said. "It's a bad jock itch and it'll spread if I'm not careful."

Nancy reached for him. He leaned away.

"Let me see," she said.

"Just leave it," Louis said. "I had to shave my hair. Looks weird."

"You shaved your balls?"

"Had to."

She reached for him again. "I wanna see. Show me."

"No, damn it. Leave it alone." He got up off the bed.

"You sure it's not VD or something? I'll call and ask, you know, so don't lie."

"It's not VD," he said. "It's a rash."

"No sex? Great. Thanks, Louis. It's a perfect day now. First Nathan gives me shit about making a fool of him and now I can't even do it."

Louis thumbed over his shoulder. "You could always stop back at the bar and get fucked there, you want."

Nancy put both hands up. "Don't even think about it, Louis, giving me shit too now. I came here to get fucked. I came here the other day for the same thing, but you never came home. I'm gonna have my period any minute and all you ever do is call me for favors and now you have some mysterious rash."

"Can you get your ex to show up Sunday?"

Nancy couldn't believe it the way he could go from one thing to another as if she wasn't in the room. It was all about him. It had always been that way. She should know better and she did but here she was anyway.

"Well?" he said.

She closed her eyes and huffed. "I told you, he came by last night."

"He coming Sunday, Nan? That's what I just asked."

"To see his son, yeah, I think so. Why?"

"None of your business. How's that?"

"Fuck you, Louis. You better be careful with John. He's not a total idiot."

"Yeah, well, I'm not the one driving car service," Louis said. "He's doing that he's no Einstein. And don't go mentioning me to him, either."

"I never say anything to John about you. He hates you."

Louis finished his beer and sat back on the bed. He put a hand out and rubbed Nancy's legs through the sheets.

"I'm sorry about today," he said. "I would've liked going a few rounds myself."

"Except for your phone calls," she said. "Now it's supposed to be your doctor. Like I believe that one."

"That wasn't my girlfriend," Louis said.

"I hate her."

"I know."

"Good."

"Let me ask you something else?"

"About John? Why don't I give you his number and you can ask him?"

"Not about him, no. You mentioned something the other day about the guy did the movie, *Deep Throat*, you know somebody knows him or something."

"I already told you, a woman at the beauty parlor. What about her? She's older than me, in case you're wondering."

Louis sighed. She couldn't help herself with the jealousy.

"Well?" she said.

"I was gonna ask you how she knows the guy did the movie."

"I told you. He used to do her hair. That's what he was, the director, before he became one, a hairdresser."

"She know this guy or what?"

"Why?"

Louis rubbed his face to keep from slapping hers. "I'm just asking you a question, Nan, okay? Lay off the interrogation."

"She used to get her hair done by the guy," Nancy said. "Was probably banging him, too. She banged everybody else."

"She have a name?"

"Why, you want to join the parade now, too?"

"Jesus Christ, can you answer a fucking question without being a jealous bitch about it? No, I don't wanna bang her. I wanna get in touch with the guy did the movie."

"Her name's Sharon Dowell," Nancy said. "I don't have her number. I can probably get it from the beauty parlor."

"The one you go to in Great Neck?"

"Yes. Is this really about contacting the movie guy?"

"I said it was."

"I want you to myself, Louis. At least for a day or two."

"I know that, but you gotta lighten up sometimes. I'm not the whoremaster you think."

"She's not going to stay with you," she said. "Your young one. Not for long. She'll get bored."

"I know that. I don't care. We're not serious anyway."

"What about me? You serious with me?"

"It's been how many years now?"

"We were married in nineteen-sixty."

"And screwing two years before that."

"Dating, Louis. It's called dating."

"Whatever. And here we are, still dating."

"Now we're screwing. We were supposed to be."

"Well, what does that tell you? I think it's serious."

Nancy stared at him a long moment.

"What?" Louis said.

"I may lose Nathan," Nancy said.

"You told me. So?"

Nancy knew he was right about Nathan. She had never loved him to begin with, not really. Still, there was security in the marriage she could never have with Louis.

"You could be a little more sympathetic," she said.

"How's that?"

She pushed the sheets off with her feet. "You could take care of me for a change."

"It'll cost you," he whispered.

Nancy barely heard him above the hum of the air conditioner. "What?" she said as she pulled her panties down.

"Nothing," Louis said.

Nancy kicked the underwear off her right foot and bit her lower lip as Louis slid across the bed, then between her legs to get into position. At least she was getting this today, she thought. After the morning she'd had, it was a lot better than nothing.

CHAPTER 15

Moon over Miami was playing on one of the local channels. Instead of taking her usual long walk up to the park, around it and back, Melinda Cogan ordered Chinese food for dinner and relaxed in front of her television set. It still saddened her that Betty Grable had died less than two months ago. The blonde bombshell, especially in the one-piece pose, her head glancing over her right shoulder with those million-dollar legs; that body with that face and hair was the total package.

Being a romantic, Melinda was a sucker for stories about true love trumping all.

It was something she had to maintain control of, being a romantic. It hadn't worked out for her so far. Melinda's only marriage had been an epic disaster. The only relationship she'd had afterwards was a two-month fling with a lawyer she'd met at the diner a few years ago. The lawyer, as it turned out, had been married.

That one had really stung. The guy had a furnished apartment she thought was his home but was really a fuck pad, what she'd been told men called such hideaways.

Melinda had been a fool for that guy the same way she'd been one for her husband. Sometimes she hated herself for being so gullible, which was why she was determined to play it extra safe with the new guy she'd met at the diner, although there was something honest about him and the way he had told her so much of himself. It was as if he was warning her not to expect too much because he was an honest working slob.

At least she hoped he was honest. She could deal without the frills if he was.

She decided to call him when the Betty Grable movie was over and the credits began rolling. John Albano answered on the second ring.

"Hello?"

"John?"

"Speaking."

"It's Melinda."

"Hey, how are you?"

She liked the enthusiasm in his voice. "Good, and you?" she said.

"Okay, I guess. Better, now you called. I think I had a dream about you."

"You think? I hope it was a good one?"

"I think it was. I know I woke up happy."

"Okay, well, I'm not touching that."

"Fair enough. What's up?"

"I just finished watching a Betty Grable movie and I was thinking of you so I called."

"Thinking of me is good. It's not the same as a dream, but I'll take it. Which movie?"

She smiled on her end of the line, hopeful he wasn't playing along. "You know her movies?"

"Some of them," he said, not very convincingly. "Which one was it?"

"*Moon over Miami*."

"With Don Ameche, right?"

"I'm impressed."

She was, too. It meant there was a chance he wasn't another sports fanatic.

"I think the running back for the Colts when they beat the Giants in the overtime game was a distant cousin or something. Same name, anyway."

"Really?" she said, not even trying to sound interested.

"I guess you don't like sports," he said.

"I don't dislike them. Baseball I can handle. Sometimes."

She didn't want their first date to be a Mets game. Her last date back in early April had taken her to Shea Stadium and it had been so cold she shivered through eight innings before he finally noticed and they left.

"How about we go to a game?" John asked.

"Or maybe we start over and I call you back."

"What's that?"

"Nothing," she said. "Let me ask you this, do you read much?"

It was her second criterion for a man. If they read it meant there was a chance they weren't Neanderthals like her ex-husband, a guy who took pride in saying he never read a book that didn't have pictures.

"Once in a while," he said. "Last book I read was *The Friends of Eddie Coyle*. That was a good one."

Melinda didn't know the book but thought it was good he was a reader.

"The movie just came out back in June, I think," he said. "Robert Mitchum and Peter Boyle."

Or maybe he just saw the movie.

"Have you seen it yet?" she asked.

"No, wanna go? Unless you wanna read the book first. I have it here, if you want."

Melinda smiled again. "Sure, John, that sounds great," she said. "And let's go see the movie, too."

■ ■ ■

"What do you really think?" Detective Brice asked Detective Levin.

"He was scared enough," Levin said. "But Berg held his water, there's no denying that. Looks well schooled to me."

"So what are we doing here tipping him off?"

"You were wondering about that, too, huh?"

They were discussing their very brief interrogation of George Berg earlier in the day. Levin had parked alongside Forest Park after dropping Kelly off a few minutes earlier. He was sweating from the humidity. He turned on the front seat to reach into the back and roll the rear windows down. The unmarked Plymouth Fury didn't have air-conditioning.

Brice said, "I mean we're out here to investigate what's going on weekends, what the hell are we doing stirring things up the middle of the week? This guy, he's involved, he's gonna show the movie now?"

"I'd like to know where the tip came from," Levin said. "George Berg obviously isn't showing it at his house. How the hell would one of the neighbors know anything unless they were going to see the thing themselves?"

"I could see that," Brice said. "Some people are envious that way. They see somebody has something going, making a few extra bucks, they get jealous and call it in."

"You know that from experience?" Levin said.

"Kind of, yeah. My old man used to move swag off the docks out of our basement. Pillowcases, sheets, T-shirts, underwear, like that. Somebody on the block was envious gave him up."

"He get in trouble?"

Brice waved it off. "He greased the cop rang the bell. Gave him a package of T-shirts or something. Wife-beaters, I think they were."

"New York's finest," Levin said.

Brice lit a cigarette. "The other thing, don't Nassau cops have a vice squad?"

"Why they call us a task force, my son."

"It's bullshit," Brice said. "Big waste of time dicking around out here like this. Berg probably stopped at the first pay phone on his way home and called our hassling him in. He'll probably spend the weekend playing cards in his basement and drive whichever neighbor gave him up crazy."

Levin's eyebrows furrowed. "You believe that crock?"

"What?"

"Look, this mope Berg was showing the film alright," Levin said, "so why didn't we catch him in the act? Sit on him Saturday morning and see who brings him the movie, where he goes next and so on. It's bullshit. This entire detail is bullshit. There's gotta be a more efficient way to nail the wiseguys behind porn than hanging around guys like George Berg."

"What are you saying?"

"Think about it."

"You're humoring me."

"Well, think about it."

"Think about what? Maybe Kelly's got a plan."

The kid wasn't getting it, Levin realized. "You're too philosophical," he said.

"It's my one year in college," Brice said. "Three C's and a D."

"They let you take four gym classes?"

"No, but listen to this," Brice said. He lifted his ass off the seat and farted.

"You're an infant," Levin said.

"It's the eggs," Brice said. "God bless America, my old man used to say."

The smell was overwhelming. Levin got out of the car.

Brice let his window down. "This mean I get to drive now?"

■ ■ ■

Nancy was gone before seven-thirty. Louis used the White Pages to look up the name she had given him, Sharon Dowell, but now he wasn't sure how to spell it. There were two listings. He tried the second number first.

"Hello," a man answered.

"May I please speak to Sharon?"

"Who's calling?"

"Tom," Louis said. "I work at the beauty parlor."

"What beauty parlor?"

Louis didn't know the name of the place.

"Yes, where Sharon gets her hair done," he said. "Do you know when she'll be back?"

"This some kind of joke? My mother's in the hospital."

"I must have the wrong number."

The guy called him an asshole before hanging up.

Louis tried the second number. This time a woman answered.

"Mrs. Dowell?" Louis said. "Sharon?"

"Who's this?"

"I'm calling for a friend of yours from the beauty parlor. Nancy Ackerman."

"Ackerman?"

"You might know her as Albano. Nancy Albano."

"I know a Nancy from the salon where I go, but I'm not sure I know her last name. What's this about?"

"I'm her ex-husband. My name is Louis and I'm calling to ask a favor."

"You the first or the second ex? If I have the right Nancy, I mean."

"The first," said Louis through a forced chuckle. "I'm Louis."

"The one she always talks about, okay. You're the stud with the ponytail."

"Thanks, but I doubt I qualify as a stud. Actually, Nancy had mentioned something about your knowing the guy who directed the porn movie *Deep Throat*. Something about he used to be your hairdresser or something."

"Jerry Damiano," Sharon said. "Yeah, he was. He used a different name in the film credits. Gerry Gerard, I think it was. He's even in the movie, plays a fag in one scene."

"A fag?"

"He just talks like one. Trust me, he's straight."

"So, you know him pretty well?"

"Well enough. Why?"

"I was wondering if I could maybe meet him."

"You want a part in one of his movies? You must be a hung stud, you want that."

"No, not that. Just some information is all. And maybe a business proposition."

"I haven't seen him in a while, but I'm sure I can get in touch with somebody knows where he is. What's it about?"

"A car."

"A what?"

"Just something I want to propose to the man. Can you hook me up with him?"

"Yeah, sure. Why not?"

"That would be great."

"There something in it for me, Louis? I don't accept checks."

"Hey, whatever you want."

"A date for now, but you can't tell your ex. I don't need the aggravation."

Louis winked at himself in the mirror. "Say when."

"When."

"Excuse me?"

"When," Sharon said, "but we'll have to meet someplace. I'm expecting someone."

"Someone who?"

"Does it make a difference?"

"No, not really, except it's pretty late already."

"We have about three hours."

"You sure?"

"I'm not gonna beg you, honey."

"You might not even like me."

"You're the guy your ex describes, if she's the right ex, I'm sure I will, although I have a few years on you."

Louis made a face.

"Not to worry," she said. "I'm not ancient. I'm no throwaway."

Louis pulled the receiver away a second time before he asked where it was they should meet.

CHAPTER 16

Lieutenant Detective Sean Kelly was wearing his sweatpants, baseball cap and the Led Zeppelin T-shirt again today. He acknowledged the bartender with a nod on his way to the pay phone near the stairs in the back of Fast Eddie's. He picked up the receiver and waited until the bartender motioned toward the stairway with his head. Kelly returned the nod before heading down the stairs to Eddie Vento's office.

He found the wiseguy sitting behind his desk scribbling on a *Racing Form*.

Vento pointed to the chair facing his desk. "Sit," he said, then waited until Kelly was in the chair and added, "How goes it, constable?"

"Slow and steady," said Kelly through a yawn. He spotted a stack of pictures on the corner of Vento's desk and picked one up. "Cute girl," he said. "Who is she?"

"That's the *Ivory Snow* girl," Vento said. He set the *Racing Form* off to one side of the desk. "Those are stills from that other movie, *Behind the Green Door*."

Kelly was taking his time flipping through the pictures. "It is? What's she doing driving a car?"

"I asked the same thing until I saw the movie. Part of the story line, what there is of one before all the screwing."

Kelly yawned again before setting the pictures down.

Vento pointed at them and said, "Personally, I think that one, the broad at least, is a lot better'n the thing we're peddling. This *Ivory Snow* girl angle they're pushing, it's gonna sell. Marilyn Chambers is a lot better-lookin' than Linda Lovelace. A lot better. So's the movie, the way it's shot and without that dopey comedy they did with the doctor in *Deep Throat*. This one, they even got a football player made a cameo. The guy played for Oakland, broke Namath's jaw." Vento looked over a promo sheet with the cast to *Behind the Green Door*. "Ben Davidson," he said.

"That was Ike Lassiter broke Namath's jaw, but Davidson always gets the credit," Kelly said.

"Whatever. He's in the movie, too."

"Doing porn?"

"No, just a cameo, but the girl and the sex is a lot better in this thing. The flip side is the ape they got plowing her. Some gorilla they found inna jungle someplace."

Kelly picked up the pictures again.

"I guess we had the better gimmick, though, what Lovelace could do with a pole down her throat," Vento said. "That and all the attention it got."

"I hope somebody shot this bone after they made the movie," Kelly said. He was holding a still of the actor Johnny Keyes wearing an exotic necklace.

"The hell do I care?" Vento said. "The broads do these movies, they let anything inside them. Personally, I don't mind if she's banging a shine. Live and let live, I say, but some of these broads, the raunchy ones, they do things with animals, real animals, dogs and whatnot. What I heard about our star, what she did before *Deep Throat*. Imagine?"

"No worse than this," Kelly said. He was still holding the still of Johnny Keyes.

Vento lit a cigar. "What's the problem you had to see me?"

Kelly set the picture on the edge of Vento's desk. "Couple things, actually. One is this guy on Long Island we visited today. Whatta you wanna do with him?"

"He give you anything?"

"*Nada*," Kelly said. "He was stand-up, if that's what you were worried about. Played dumb as a stump."

"And?"

"I still need somebody," Kelly said. "I gotta have something now we talked to the guy. Who can you give me?"

"Maybe a new guy I have. I don't know yet. Let me think about it. Not one of the films, though, you can forget that. They're too valuable."

"What about this other one with the spear-chucker?"

Vento shook his head no. "Word is we made a move on the two guys out West made it, brothers or some shit they are. It's too valuable to turn over now."

"It's not like we'd keep it. I process it into evidence and take it back a week or two later."

"A week or two it could be earning."

"You guys didn't bleed enough out of this stuff yet?"

Vento pointed a thumb up at the ceiling. "The beast at the top is forever hungry, my friend. There's never enough it comes to two things this life, pussy or money, and the beast, he'll always take money before pussy."

"And on that note," said Kelly, opening his palm to Vento. "I believe I'm the one in need."

Vento leaned over to open the bottom drawer of his desk. He pulled out a strongbox, unlocked and opened it, then grabbed a thin stack of paper-clipped twenty-dollar bills and tossed it on the desk.

"And the other thing you had to discuss?" he said.

"Your girlfriend," Kelly said.

"Which girlfriend?"

"The one I walked into the other night."

"The one lives here?"

"She has my hanky."

"Excuse me?"

"I had to lend it to her to plug the blood was flowing out her nose like a hose," Kelly said. "She'd just snorted herself into a near OD."

"Stupid cunt."

"I think you're taking chances with that one."

"What do you mean?"

"The way she shoots off at the mouth, for one thing. She mentioned something about me being a cop for another."

"Excuse me?"

"Implied maybe's a better word. Implied."

"Maybe it's your red fucking hair, the freckles. You should try getting some sun. Gat a tan, something."

"And then there's the junk," Kelly said. "That's a deadly combination in my book, 'specially push comes to shove."

"Meaning?"

"Junkies, Eddie, you can't trust them. Not ever."

"Unless you know something I don't, I'm not worried about her."

"Maybe you should be."

"You got something to say, spit it the fuck out."

Kelly put a hand up. "I'm just being careful here."

Vento gave it a moment, then said, "Duly noted. Now I have a question. Any more word on our friend the shakedown artist?"

"Hastings? Retired."

"Good," Vento said. He pointed to the cash on the desk. "Don't spend it too fast," he said. "Things are drying up on this movie. At least on the Island they are."

"You'll have to do something on this Massapequa thing," Kelly said. "I need something before Saturday or my guys will start wondering things they shouldn't."

"I'll call," Vento said. "Hastings really retired?"

"Forced off is the word," said Kelly, suddenly uncomfortable discussing it. He squirmed some in his chair. "Got smart and listened for a change. Stepped out before he lost his pension, but that was more our doing, that balancing act. Not that it makes him any less of a psycho." He motioned toward the film stills. "I get a screening some day or what?"

Vento pointed to the cash Kelly was still holding. "You could probably get the actress to do a live show for what you're holding there. I doubt she got much more'n that anyway."

"The one screwed the ape? I'd rather jerk off."

"Yeah, you probably would," Vento said.

■ ■ ■

"Would you look at what the cat dragged in?" said Sharon Dowell to the big man that had just walked in the bar. He was at least six foot, three hundred pounds. His shoulders were broad enough to block sight of the doorway behind him.

"Sharon?" he said.

She'd been sitting at the end of the bar waiting for the guy she'd spoken to on the phone earlier. "You better remember my name," she said, then took a long drag on her Pall Mall.

The big man approached her and Sharon craned her neck to offer him her cheek. He kissed her before sitting on the empty stool to her right.

"I haven't seen you in forever," she said. "Where you been?"

"College," the big man said.

"Geez, I didn't know. When?"

"Couple, three years ago."

"Where?"

The big man pointed at the ceiling with his left thumb. "Fishkill," he said, then waved to get the bartender's attention. "She's with me," he said. "Whatever she's having and a Rob Roy."

"Rob Roy?" Sharon said. "When's the last time I heard somebody order one of those?"

"I can pace myself this way," the big man said. He pulled a pack of Marlboros from his shirt pocket. "How've you been?"

"I can't complain. I shouldn't anyway. I had that settlement a few years back, that keeps me afloat."

The big man set a twenty on the bar. "What settlement's that?" he asked.

Sharon extended her right arm across the bar. "Got hit by a bus the summer of sixty-eight," she said. "Shattered my elbow all to hell. See how I can't straighten it? That's as far as it goes. Lost a percentage of its use for life. That plus the fact the bus driver had a few. Didn't even know he hit me, the drunk. Said he thought it was some kids threw something at the bus made the thump. A dozen witnesses forced them to settle."

The big man had just lit his cigarette. "How much you get?" he asked while holding the smoke in his lungs.

"A good enough piece of change. Enough so's I don't have to sling dishes anymore, but it gets damp outside, especially it's cold, the thing swells up to a balloon. Hurts like hell."

"Sorry to hear it."

Sharon pointed at him. "First time we met, you probably don't remember, was the steakhouse in Canarsie."

The bartender set both drinks on the bar. The big man pushed the twenty at him, then turned to Sharon and winked. "Rockaway Parkway, sure," he said. "I remember. Brothers it was called. You was with Benny Luchessi back then, right?"

"Before he was married, yeah."

"Well, good for you, you're not waitressing anymore," he said, then raised his drink in a toast. "*Salute.*"

Sharon picked up her Tom Collins. They touched glasses. "Cheers," she said.

Both took sips of their drinks.

"So, what are you doing here tonight?" the big man asked. "You with somebody?"

"Waiting on somebody," Sharon said. "Somebody half my age, I think. Imagine?"

"Hey, good for you."

"Well, I'm not so sure about that. It doesn't do what they say for the ego, being with somebody so young. Might impress the ones keeping score, but it never fools the players."

The big man nudged her with his elbow. "So, what, I would've showed up a little earlier, I had a shot? It's not nice to tease old fellas like myself."

Sharon set a hand on his huge shoulder. "I thought guys your age could keep it up, Jimmy...."

They shared a chuckle.

"Well, he don't show, this teenager you're waiting on, I'll give you a lift," Jimmy said. "Maybe you invite me in."

"You still driving those big cars you used to like?"

"What else I'm gonna do, my size? Elektra, the Ninety-eights, Bonnevilles. I stay away from the Caddys because of the attention, but I'm too big for anything smaller."

Sharon sighed. "I used to love the back of Benny's Fleetwood, I have to say. It was like being in your own apartment."

Jimmy laughed again.

"Speaking of Fleetwoods," Sharon said. "The kid I'm waiting on is interested in the one they used in that porno they're making all the fuss about. Says he knows somebody knows somebody else wants to buy the thing."

The big man squinted.

Sharon sipped her drink again. "Truth is, he's only coming around tonight to pursue it, that car. I know the guy directed the movie."

"No kidding?"

"An old fling from way back, but the kid, the one I'm waiting on... "—she stopped to glance at her watch—"he's already late, he's pro'bly looking to score off the car somehow."

"What's his name, this kid?"

"Louis. I'm not sure his last name. Kisk maybe. Or Kirsk, something like that."

"He by chance got a ponytail?"

"From what I hear," she said. "I actually haven't met him yet. Supposedly blonde. A real hunk, too, is what I was told."

The big man laughed.

"What's funny?"

"He meeting you here?"

Sharon glanced at her watch again. "Should've already."

Jimmy got up off the stool, drew on his cigarette, then motioned her toward the back. "Let's step out for some air," he said.

"Air? It's muggy out."

"I got something I wanna run by you."

■ ■ ■

Nick made three passes on the street where John Albano lived before he felt it was safe enough to park. The Buick was still in the spot where it had been the night before and both rear tires were still flat. Too bad, he thought. He would've enjoyed slashing a new set of tires.

He checked the rearview mirror and saw the bruise on his head. The knot had started to recede a little, but the bruise was still turning colors. It would probably take a full week before it faded. He remembered how the guys in the bar had given him shit after he'd been knocked out. The humiliation had only just started after they splashed cold water on his face.

Now, except for an occasional car stopping for the traffic light on the corner, the street where John Albano lived was mostly quiet. Nick remembered there was a bus stop directly across the street from Albano's building. He drove past the Buick one last time before parking at the opposite end of the block. He lit a cigarette and sat low behind the steering wheel until a bus finally passed.

Nick walked the length of the block to the passenger side of the Buick's front tires and kneeled down as if to tie his shoes. He took a quick look both ways on the sidewalk, took the stiletto out and pressed the release to expose the blade. He jabbed the tire along the dirty whitewall and listened for the hissing sound as the air escaped. He jabbed the tire again on the opposite end, then did it a few more times before the front end of the Buick began to descend.

He walked to the front of the car and glanced at the driver-side tire. He peered over his shoulder and could see lights on in the apartment building where Albano lived. Last night he had double-parked alongside the car to do his work. Tonight he felt more exposed and decided to leave the one tire facing the street untouched.

He could always come back another night.

CHAPTER 17

John was up early Friday morning. He shaved and showered while his coffee brewed. Afterward he sat down to a breakfast of toast with peanut butter and coffee. He listened to Sports Radio 66 and learned both New York teams had won the night before.

John was feeling good about Melinda's phone call and that she'd mentioned she had been thinking of him. He'd flirted with her and was pleasantly surprised when she flirted right back. He also remembered how she hadn't seemed too keen on going to a baseball game. They had settled for a movie instead, *The Friends of Eddie Coyle*. He had told her he'd lend her the book the movie was based on and found it in the kitchen.

John took the book with him when he left. He could drop it off at the diner for Melinda at some point during the day after he replaced the two tires that had been slashed. He looked at the car from the stoop and saw how the right front end appeared to droop. He crossed the street and saw the right front tire was flat.

It took three hours and sixty-five dollars, half of the cost of which he had promised to pay the next week, before a local garage had him back on the road with three retread tires. It was another financial hit he couldn't afford. Between losing his construction and driving work, John was beginning to appreciate the job offer Eddie Vento had made.

He drove straight to the bar in Williamsburg and promised himself he'd be smarter about Nick Santorra if the punk goaded him again. He said hello to the few faces he recognized and sat at the near hook of the bar closest to the street windows. He spotted Santorra sitting at one of the tables in the back reading a newspaper.

"Mr. Vento in?" John asked the bartender, Eugene.

"Not until later," Eugene said. "No trouble today, okay?"

"Not from me."

"You want anything?"

John knew he should leave, but couldn't resist playing a hunch. "Coffee," he said.

Eugene headed for the coffeepot at the far end of the bar. John winked when Santorra looked up from his newspaper.

Eugene brought the coffee back and then waved John off when he tried to pay.

"Thanks," John said.

He sat staring at Santorra while he drank his coffee. He was close to leaving when another guy in Eddie Vento's crew introduced himself and asked how it was going.

"Not so good," said John louder than necessary. "Some punk slashed my tires the last two nights. Somebody without balls. I almost feel sorry for him, guy's gotta run around the middle of the night like that."

He could tell Santorra was listening because the wannabe's face had turned red, a sure sign of his guilt, John thought. Eugene saw what John was up to and reminded him about not causing trouble.

"Promise," said John, crossing his heart. He turned his attention to his new friend, the one who had just introduced himself. "Thing of it is," he said, "that kind of bullshit, giving somebody flats works both ways. Any asshole can do it. Or they can hire some kids to do it."

Santorra had apparently heard enough. He got up to use the men's room, slamming the door shut behind him.

John glanced at his watch, acted surprised at the time and said he had to get going. He left a message for Eddie Vento that he would be back later. Then he tried to leave Eugene a tip but was stopped again.

"Forget it," Eugene said.

"Thanks again," John said.

Eugene turned away at the same time Santorra came back out of the bathroom. "You think he remembered to flush?" John said.

Eugene stopped, turned around again, and said, "You can't help yourself, can you?"

John winked at Eugene and got out of there.

■　■　■

He imagined using the butter on her young perky ass the way Marlon Brando had used it on the French girl in the movie and how it would taste to lick some of it before he used the rest to enter her. She would hurt at first but then the butter would lubricate her and she would meet his thrusts with her own and eventually they would collapse on the bed and he'd never let her leave his apartment, at least not for the rest of the day and maybe through the night.

It was what Professor Joseph Jacobs couldn't stop thinking after they had watched *Last Tango in Paris* together in his living room on the projector he'd borrowed from the university.

"My favorite scene was that first one," Holly said. "When he ravaged her. It was sooooo exhilarating. My God."

Jacobs wanted to ask her if she was as wet as he was hard. Too nervous to do so, he handed her the joint he'd been smoking, then went into the kitchen to hide his erection.

Holly had seemed to be excited, too, but he wasn't taking any chances.

He'd had a problem once before with a student he thought was ready and willing and it had nearly cost him his tenure. Jacobs wasn't about to go down that road again, not without this one making the first move.

"I don't see this as porno," she said from the living room.

He was trying to push his erection so it faced down and wouldn't show through his sweatpants.

"It's not like the smut they show on Forty-second Street," she added. "I don't think Brando would've done a porno."

She had argued vehemently against pornography in his sociology class when the topic was brought up. Jacobs had taken a more liberal view of the issue and when Holly showed up at his office to discuss the topic of her term paper, he asked her if she had ever seen the controversial film starring Marlon Brando. Holly said she hadn't.

"Perhaps you should someday," he'd told her.

"I'm not sure I'd want to," she had said.

"You really can't argue against something without knowing the facts. Some people consider Last Tango art. Others call it pornography. And some say it's a dirty old man's way of getting laid, although I doubt that's an issue for Marlon Brando."

"What do you think?" she had asked. "Really."

"I think it's always up to the observer," he'd told her. "For me it's between art and erotica, but it's definitely not porn. I don't see it as that."

Holly had waited for more.

He said, "It's not like you'd go blind from seeing it."

"I guess not. But how would I go about it? I'm not comfortable going to a theater on Forty-second Street."

"It's not in those theaters, not Last Tango. Respectable people are seeing it."

"Because of Marlon Brando?"

"Probably. Look, the school has a film department. A quite famous one, actually. I can ask, if you're interested."

"Really?"

"Sure. If you're serious. I wouldn't want to bother anyone if you're not."

"No, I'll watch it."

"Good, then. I'll see what I can do."

That had been a week ago. Jacobs borrowed a copy of the film the department head had access to and brought it home along with a projector. He told Holly about it the night before when they went for a long walk through the Village and this morning she showed up bright and early to view it with him.

He had become infatuated with her since the first morning she showed up for his summer class on modern society wearing white shorts and a tight T-shirt. Holly was flat-chested compared to the buxom women he was usually attracted to, but her blonde hair and blue eyes and wholesome look gave her an ingénue edge he couldn't ignore.

She was taking two courses over the summer and his was her favorite, she had told him. She had also mentioned having a boyfriend she'd met before the spring semester ended, but that it might've been an infatuation more than anything serious.

And now she was saying she liked the scene where Brando had rough sex with the French girl.

"See?" he told her from the kitchen. "Some people look at it as a rape scene and you found it exhilarating."

"It was," Holly said. He could hear her getting up and then she was standing in the doorway between the two rooms. "I mean, she obviously liked it. She went along with it. She didn't stop him."

"A man could get in a lot of trouble saying exactly the same thing," Jacobs said. "She liked it? Think about it."

"I guess," Holly said. "Some of the women I've met said they saw it and didn't appreciate the way the girl accepted what he did to her. They claim that's just the male ego. Something to do with a man's fantasy about rape."

Jacobs turned to her and saw she was leaning against the kitchen wall. "And maybe that's because they prejudged it," he said. "Sometimes it's just six of one, half a dozen of another. What's that Sly and the Family Stone line, 'Different strokes for different folks'?"

"I guess," she said.

She had showed up this morning wearing shorts again and he had hardly been able to keep from looking at her legs the entire length of the movie. The light blue halter she wore had clung to her small breasts until he turned on the air-conditioning and woke her nipples up. They were still perky he noticed when he turned to face her again.

"I've had a fascination with older men, too," she said. "A few times since high school."

Was she telling him it was okay for him to make a move? He smiled in case she was and then she blushed; a good sign, he thought.

"Maybe she needed to go through that, the girl in the movie," Holly said.

He was hard as a rock and couldn't stand it much longer.

"You ever do that?" she asked. "With butter, I mean."

He felt a tingle and had to turn away from her.

"It was pretty wild," she said.

"Yeah, it was."

"I know it's supposed to hurt."

"Anal sex? I guess. Probably why they used the butter."

Holly blushed again. "Don't people use Vaseline or K-Y Jelly or something like that?"

"If they have it. If not, I guess butter's the next best thing."

Holly jammed her hands inside her shorts pockets then, tugging the front waist down a little. "Can I ask you a question?" she said.

Jacobs's eyes had moved to her waist in anticipation of maybe seeing the start of her pubic patch. He forced himself to look up at her face again. "Sure."

"Promise you won't be embarrassed?"

She wants it, he thought. This is it. "Sure," he said.

"Promise?" she said.

He could barely speak. "Promise," he managed to say.

Holly's hands were out of her pockets. "Have you ever..."

He was too excited to let her finish. The words were out of his mouth before he could stop. "I want to fuck you so bad, Holly."

Her eyes opened wide. He thought she might scream, but then she looked down and her face registered disgust a moment before she turned away and walked out of the apartment.

Jacobs yelled her name but couldn't move from where he was standing. He looked down and saw he was holding himself inside his sweatpants.

"Oh, fuck," he said. "Oh, shit."

■ ■ ■

The air smelled foul when John first returned to his car after leaving the bar. He lit a cigarette, but it was too hot to smoke. The humidity had gone up a notch; so had the temperature. Ten-Ten WINS put it at eighty-six with ninety-five percent humidity. The streets were steamy.

He waited less than two minutes before Nick Santorra was out of the bar checking on his year-old blue Pontiac Lemans. John wrote down the tag numbers as Santorra walked around the car and checked all four tires. Next Santorra ran his hand along the finish and was on his way back to the bar when John pulled away from the curb. He beeped to get Santorra's attention, then waved as he drove past the bar.

A look of anguish appeared on Santorra's face.

"How's it feel?" said John at the rearview mirror. He watched as Santorra stepped out into the middle of the street staring after him.

Thirty minutes later John dropped the novel off for Melinda at the diner in Queens on his way to see his son. The upside to his weekday unemployment was the opportunity to spend the afternoon with Little Jack. Sometimes sharing a hamburger at a diner was enough to carry him to the next visit. He hoped his boy felt the same way.

He had just under twenty-five dollars in his wallet, all of it owed, but he'd have cash again tomorrow. At least he could take the kid out for dinner.

He had arranged with Nancy for their son to be home from camp after lunch and was surprised to find Nathan instead of his ex-wife at the house.

"The little man around?" John asked.

Nathan Ackerman opened the door and waved John inside. "Sure is," he said. "And he's anxious to see you."

John was met with a big hug from his son. He picked his boy up and kissed him on the cheek.

"Coffee, John?" Nathan asked.

"I don't wanna put you out."

"Nonsense, I'll put up a pot."

Nathan was gone before John could stop him.

"We have the whole day?" Little Jack asked.

"Until you get bored with me," John said.

His son's face lit up in a smile.

They spent the next half hour in the kitchen. John having coffee and his son showing off the baseball tickets Nathan refused to take any money for.

"It's my pleasure," Nathan said. "Besides, I got them from somebody myself. Didn't cost a dime."

"You're a good guy," John said. "I'm not sure you'd tell me if they did cost you, but there's something to a man paying his own freight, 'specially it comes to his son."

"I was afraid you'd say that," Nathan said. "Because you're a good man yourself, but I did get them for free. In the meantime, I have to practice my flute."

"I thought you played the bass?"

"He's joking," his son said.

It had to do with an argument one night between Nathan and Nancy. Nancy had told him to "go play your flute." Ignoring the sexual connotations, Nathan had used the phrase as a private joke with which to bond with his stepson.

Nathan ruffled Little Jack's hair and wished them both a good time. He was on his way upstairs when John wondered for the fifth or sixth time since he had first met Nathan Ackerman what the hell he was doing with Nancy.

■   ■   ■

The first few weeks after the incident in Eddie Vento's bar Billy Hastings listened to friends on the force and stayed clear of John Albano. Rather than seeking immediate revenge, Billy used department resources to gather information and quickly learned the details of Albano's life.

The out-of-work construction worker had been brought up in Canarsie,

Brooklyn, had moved to Sheepshead Bay after marrying a divorced woman from Queens, then moved back to Canarsie when they divorced two years later. Albano had a nine-year-old son that lived with his ex-wife, who had remarried and returned to Queens. Billy also learned where Albano lived, the make of the car he owned and where his mother had recently moved to in Queens to be close to her grandson.

Two men had haunted Billy's psyche. He was quick to move on the first after he was forced to resign from the police department. Having already dispatched Victor Vasquez, Billy turned his attention on John Albano. First he needed to catch up on Albano's daily routines and habits. Wearing a disguise that included a wig, fake mustache and thick glasses, Billy drove to Canarsie and parked across the street from the apartment building where Albano lived. He spent half an hour sitting and observing the people traffic in the area until he was forced to move when an old man seemed to be staring at him from the stoop. Billy moved further up the block and parked alongside a fire hydrant. He waited more than an hour before the old man left the stoop and then Albano finally appeared.

Billy circled the block and parked off a near corner this time. He watched from behind a *Daily News* he made believe he was reading as Albano discovered his Buick had flat tires. After a trip to a nearby gas station where the Buick was refitted with tires, Albano drove to Eddie Vento's bar in Williamsburg.

Nearly half an hour passed before Albano was out of the bar. Then he sat in the Buick with the engine running a few minutes before he pulled away. Billy followed the Buick to the Ozone Park address in Queens where Albano's ex-wife and son lived with her current husband, a Jewish guy named Ackerman. Billy made himself comfortable as he waited in his car parked up the block from where Albano would have to pass when he left on the one-way street.

CHAPTER 18

Louis was waiting for Nancy outside the bar on Jamaica Avenue. He appeared anxious. When she asked him what was wrong, he said there was something he needed to discuss, something important. Nancy could only imagine what it was this time.

He guided her inside the bar with the excuse he had to make a phone call. Nancy waited at a table while he used the pay phone in the back. She recognized two of the men sitting at the bar and the bartender from when she had stopped there earlier in the week. The bartender nodded before asking her what she'd like to drink. Nancy told him a white wine spritzer. She glanced over her shoulder and saw Louis had huddled inside the phone booth with the receiver to his ear. She lit a cigarette while she waited.

A few minutes later Louis grabbed his beer and the white wine spritzer off the bar. He brought them to the table, handed Nancy her drink, and said, "Cheers."

Nancy touched his Budweiser bottle with the edge of her wineglass. "What's it about?" she said. "What are we doing in here?"

"I figured we might as well have a drink since we can't have sex," Louis said.

"Bullshit," Nancy said. "What is it? Really, Louis."

A big, well-dressed heavy man carrying a sports jacket folded over his right arm walked in the bar. Louis waved at him, then asked Nancy for fifty dollars.

"Fifty? I don't have fifty. I barely have twenty."

"Then give me whatever you have," Louis said. "I owe this guy and I'm late."

"Jesus Christ," Nancy said. She looked through her purse, found an extra twenty and three more of the fives John must have given her. She gave Louis thirty-five dollars and lied about the rest.

Louis took the money to the bar where the big man was sitting. Nancy could hear Louis apologizing. She saw the big man lean over to look at her. She was frightened and turned away.

She lit a cigarette, then watched in the mirror behind the bar as the bartender handed the big man a short stack of small white envelopes. The big man looked through the envelopes before folding them into a pants pocket.

A few minutes later the big man left and Louis rejoined Nancy at the table.

"Who was that?"

"A guy I owed."

"A loan shark?"

"Something like that."

"He looked scary."

"He is."

"What's his name?"

"You really need to know?"

"Jesus, Louis, how are we supposed to pay for our drinks now? I only have a few singles left."

"It's okay. They'll put it on my tab."

"You run a bar tab? No wonder you're always broke."

"I'm always broke because things don't happen the way they're supposed to. The Mets and Yankees last night for instance. They both win on a night I bet them to lose."

"You haven't learned a thing, have you?"

"A few things," he said. "They haven't paid off yet is all. This guy just put me on to something, probably to pay him off, but it might help."

"And what's that?"

"Something to do with a car."

She knew something was wrong when he'd called her early this morning. It was an awkward moment with Nathan sitting there reading a magazine, but Nancy had managed to get her message to Louis by saying she'd call him back.

"You sure?" Louis had told her over the phone. "Say yes or I'll call right back. I swear it."

"Yes, I'll call you back," Nancy had told him.

And so she showed up today and there he was waiting for her on the street acting fidgety about something and so far it had cost her thirty-five dollars.

"A car?" she said now. "What about it?"

"Forget that for now," Louis said. "I need a favor."

"And what was the thirty-five I just gave you, a gift?"

"A real favor," Louis said. "I mean it, Nan. It's serious."

"What is it?"

Louis made her wait until he lit a cigarette.

"I'm in trouble," he said. "Serious trouble."

■ ■ ■

Nancy's reaction to the loan shark was what Louis had hoped for. He'd brought her to the bar so she'd see Jimmy and realize what he was up against. He had asked the big man to give her a hard stare as a favor, and when Jimmy leaned over to look at Nancy, Louis could tell she was scared shitless. He figured it was the best way to keep his ex-wife on edge. So long as she thought he was in danger, Louis could count on her help.

The other thing he had discussed with Jimmy was the car from the porn movie. Last night he'd serviced a woman who personally knew the director. Sharon Dowell was a horny broad who seemed willing to help in his quest to contact the director of *Deep Throat*. They had gone to a short-stay motel near JFK after meeting at the bar. He'd been more than an hour late, but she'd waited him out. The entire investment had cost him less than twenty dollars in cash and less than three hours time.

Louis had appreciated her, all business and minimal aggravation. She was certainly experienced and had immediately recognized his rash for what it was.

"It's not something I haven't seen before," she'd told him. "That's too bad for you because I'm pretty good with my mouth, I do say so myself. Let's you concentrate on me for tonight and then we'll save the goodies for when your doctor gives you a green light."

He'd done the deed and she'd made a few phone calls right there in front of him and hopefully in another day or two she'd call him back with something he could act on.

If Sharon Dowell could get him a meeting with this Damiano guy, Louis might be able to broker a deal for the Cadillac. Jimmy had a buyer waiting in the wings, one of those collector nuts with deep pockets. All he needed was a meeting or even a phone call, or maybe a piece of paper with the guy's signature.

Now he was thinking about more immediate issues. In addition to the vig he owed Jimmy, Louis needed to front two bookies enough so they didn't send an army out looking for him. Until he could rob John Albano of his collection cash there was only one other place he could go for money.

Why he'd called Nancy as soon as he woke up this morning. She'd given him shit at first the way she always did, but there was no way she'd pass up a chance for sex. Once he took care of her it might be a record, the three times he went down on a muff in two days, except Nancy would count for two so it might require an asterisk like they were talking about giving Hank Aaron if or when he broke Babe Ruth's record.

Sunday night the bookmaking offices would close out for the week and Louis was still late with money owed to two offices. Hopefully Jimmy had scared Nancy enough for her to help out.

Now that he'd told her he was in trouble, serious trouble, it was time to ask.

Nancy beat him to the punch. "How much?" she said.

"Five grand."

"Five thousand?"

"Yes."

"And where the hell am I going to get that?"

"How much can you get?"

Nancy's face tightened. "You selfish bastard," she said.

"I wouldn't ask if I didn't need it."

"Yeah, you would, only you know I wouldn't give it to you, not to gamble."

"This isn't to gamble. It's to keep my legs in one piece."

"God damn you, Louis."

"I'm sorry, babe, but I'm up against it here. I mean it. You saw that guy. Jimmy's no jerkoff. He wants his money and I have to pay him."

"And what happens the next time you gamble and lose?"

"I'm done gambling, I swear it. No more after this."

"I wish I could believe you."

"This time you can."

"I don't have five thousand dollars to give you."

"I have to give him something."

"I can get a thousand. Maybe twelve hundred."

Louis grabbed his head with both hands.

"It's all I have," Nancy said.

"It's not enough."

"How much do you owe them?"

"I told you, five grand."

"Jesus Christ."

"How about half? I could probably work something out with him for half."

"I don't have it. I told you I don't."

Louis sensed it was time to bluff. "Alright, you know what? Forget it. This is my headache anyway. I shouldn't involve you, you're right."

Nancy was near tears.

"I listened to some asshole and I should've known better," he continued. "It's my fault and my problem. I'll handle it."

"How?"

Step two, he was thinking; blow her off. "Don't worry about it," he said.

"No, I want to know. What will they do to you?"

"That's my problem. Forget about it."

"Louis, damn it! Don't do this to me."

She reached across the table and grabbed both his hands.

"Don't worry," Louis said. "I'll handle it."

Nancy's eyes had started to tear. "You son of a bitch," she whispered. "Not without me."

Game, set, match.

■ ■ ◾

John had bought his son a baseball game for his ninth birthday last year. They were in the middle of a game with Little Jack and the Yankees leading 6-1 against the Mets when they heard Nancy's footsteps on the stairs.

"You couldn't take him out someplace?" she said.

"He wanted to play the game," John said.

"Yeah," the boy said. "I wanted to play a series."

Nancy looked at John. "You don't feel uncomfortable?"

"Not until you showed up."

"Very funny."

John turned to his son. "Let's go have a catch," he said. "Why don't you get your glove, bat and ball. I'll throw you some pitches, you want."

"Okay," said Little Jack, but he was clearly upset.

Nancy started to say something. John put a finger to his lips for her to wait. She did, but not for long. As soon as the basement door closed upstairs, she lit into him.

"My husband is upstairs and you invite yourself in?" she said. "Don't you have any shame?"

"I knocked on the door and Nathan was nice enough to invite me inside," John said.

"And you go ahead? You're not embarrassed to be in another man's house?"

"You're amazing, Nan, you know that?"

"You ever think Nathan and I would like some privacy?"

"How do you manage something like privacy, Nan? I mean, you're never home, right?"

"Fuck you."

"No thanks, I keep telling you."

"Where are you taking him?"

"I just said, for a catch."

"And then?"

"We'll get something to eat. Why?"

"I need him home by seven."

"Why seven?"

"Don't argue with me, John, I have my reasons."

John took a deep breath. "Fine," he said.

"And I'll need my money on time this week. I can use an advance if you have it."

"I don't have it."

"Why'd I bother asking?"

"You can't help yourself."

"Fuck you," she said. "Fa-uck you."

John shook his head as he walked past her and headed up the stairs.

■ ■ ■

Eddie Vento didn't need anyone to chauffeur him around tonight. Nick was grateful for the break. He headed home early with the intention of clearing out his garage. After what had happened at the bar earlier in the day, he would sleep a lot easier knowing his car was locked inside rather than on the street.

He was close to home when he spotted a big Polack he knew Eddie Vento sometimes used to collect street loans. The Polack was standing outside a bar on Cross Bay Boulevard. Nick pulled to the curb and beeped the horn to get the big man's attention.

Stanislaus Bartosz, a six-foot-eight, 245-pound hulk, had a scar running down the right side of his face and was missing both upper front teeth. A twice-convicted felon, Bartosz took his time making his way to the Pontiac.

Nick saw the big man was squinting to see. He leaned toward the passenger window and waved. "It's me!" he yelled. "Nick Santorra."

The big man stopped in his tracks. Nick put the car in park and got out. "It's me," he repeated. "Nick. Nick Santorra. Eddie's guy."

It took the big man another few seconds to recognize Santorra. He made his way to the curb when he did.

"How the hell you been?" Nick asked.

"Never mind me," Bartosz said. "Fuck happened your face?"

"Why I was looking for you," Nick said. "I got something, you're interested."

"A guy can always use some extra scratch," the big man said. "Sure. What is it?"

"Something private," Nick told the big man. "Something stays between us. Let's walk around the corner, discuss it."

Nick was home twenty minutes later and quickly saw the problem with clearing out his garage was all the crap that had accumulated since they first bought the house. There was no way he could get all the junk out of the way to make room enough for the car, not without throwing out half the stuff in there.

He had to settle for leaving the car in the driveway. He examined the knot above his right eye again in the rearview mirror and saw it was turning yellow around the edges. It would take another few days before the discoloration completely faded. His in-laws were coming Sunday morning.

Nick would have to make up a bullshit story nobody would believe. It pissed him off just thinking about the looks he'd get.

When they were ready to eat, Nick learned Angela had cooked baked ziti for dinner. He told her to freeze it for another night; he would barbecue instead. At least that way he could keep an eye on the car.

He lit candles to keep the gnats and mosquitoes away while they ate dinner in the backyard. Afterward, Nick went to the basement to sign the new boxes of *Deep Throat* posters. He was careful getting the spelling right this time, except for once when he'd started to daydream about shooting John Albano.

CHAPTER 19

It was still humid out when Detective Levin returned home at the end of his workday. A set of surveillance tapes waiting for review had been left in his mailbox. Levin set them on the kitchen table, grabbed a beer from the refrigerator and began unbuttoning his shirt as he headed for the air conditioner. He turned it on high, removed the rest of his clothes, and finished his beer before using the bathroom.

He stood under a hot shower a full five minutes, his face taking the water full force until he turned and let it massage the back of his neck. It was how he preferred to relax, a hot shower followed with a cold beer in a cool room. He looked forward to sitting on his couch with his feet up.

He wrapped a towel around his waist when he was finished in the bathroom, then went to the kitchen for a second beer and frowned when he saw the tapes.

"Shit," he said.

Levin grabbed another beer and brought the tapes into the living room. He smirked at the dates on the labels.

"A month old," he said. "Lotta good these'll do."

He set up the recorder on the cocktail table, popped one of the tapes in, picked up his beer and a notepad and sat on the couch. He set his feet up on the edge of the cocktail table, leaned forward, pressed PLAY, and sat back again.

An unfamiliar voice narrated the first conversation:

The following recording is from Tuesday, July third, nineteen-seventy-three, between Edward Vento and Bridget Malone, a weekend barmaid at Fast Eddie's in Williamsburg. The following was recorded in the apartment above the aforementioned bar.

Malone: You okay?

Vento: Fine, yeah.

Malone: Want another hit?

Vento: No. Whattaya wanna kill me?

[The sound of someone inhaling.]

Vento: You're gonna kill your brain cells you don't take a break with that shit.

[The sound of someone exhaling.]

Vento: I'm serious. You should learn to go a little easy with that crap.

Malone: I don't do it every day.

Vento: You do it every time you're with me.

Malone: Want some coke instead?

Vento: What I just say? Leave it alone for half an hour.
[The sound of rustling.]
Malone: A cigarette okay?
Vento: Yeah, gimme one.

"Regular health freak," Levin said.

Malone: Who's the new guy comes in weekends?
Vento: What new guy?
Malone: The one your idiot nephew's always giving shit. The one counts
the perverts who see the movie.
Vento: Oh, Albano. John Albano. Why?
Malone: Just curious. He's a new face.
Vento: He's the guy knocked the cop out. Eugene said one punch.

Levin wrote "Hastings."

Malone: Your nephew keeps giving him shit.
Vento: He's not my nephew, the dip-shit. He's my wife's first cousin.
Malone: He's got a big mouth on him, your nephew. Calls the new guy
Johnny Porno.
Vento: He's not my nephew.

Levin wrote the name "Johnny Porno" on his notepad. He stopped the
tape and referred to notes he'd taken off another tape, then drew a line
connecting June 14 to July 3.
He hit the PLAY button.

Malone: I was thinking maybe I should talk to him.
Vento: Talk to who?
Malone: Johnny Porno. He must have connections there, your nephew
calls him that.
Vento: He's not my fuckin' nephew and the guy, Albano his name is,
John Albano, is a fuckin' head counter is all he is. What is it with you
and this porn shit?
Malone: You're supposed to hook me up, remember?
Vento: Hook you up. Nice. Ever think I don't want some broad I'm
banging fucking the perverts they use in stag films? Those guys'd fuck
farm animals you paid them enough.
Malone: You said you'd talk to the guy.
Vento: Rothenburg? Yeah, well, he's dead.
Malone: How?

"Murdered," Levin said.

Vento: Whattaya mean how? What's the difference?

Malone: He was supposed to help me, you said.

Vento: If you really wanted to do it, yeah, he was the guy. There are others, don't worry. There are plenty leeches out there looking for broads
dopey enough to think it's glamorous sucking dick on film.

Malone: Maybe it has to do with earning a living, Eddie. I don't wanna
live off bar tips the rest of my life. You said you'd help me with this.
When?

Vento: When I say so. Until then don't talk like some skank.

Malone: I'm not a skank.

Vento: No, you're not. You're still a good-looking broad. You could get
somewhere, marry somebody with that, but you wanna make a fuck
film. Makes no sense. You were my daughter I'd kill you first.

"Father of the year," Levin said.

Vento: Anyway, guys like Rothenburg'd ruin you before you knew what
happened. You don't need that shit in your life.

Malone: Except I don't wanna bartend the rest of my life.

Vento: Yeah, you said. You're twenny-three years old. You got plenny
time to fuck up your life. *Vada lento.* Go slow.

Malone: Sure, go slow. What do you care? Ten years'll go by and I'll still
be working the bar downstairs.

Vento: *Ashpetta,* please.

Malone: I want something more from life than this, Eddie.

Vento: Who doesn't?

Malone: You see where Betty Grable died yesterday?

Vento: Now you wanna be Betty Grable?

Malone: At least she had a life. If I die tomorrow, what did I ever have?

Vento: Speaking of tomorrow, can you let me enjoy what's left of this
fuckin' day? Bad enough the holiday's the middle of the week this year.
[A pause on the tape that lasts nearly a minute.]

Malone: You gonna be with wifey tomorrow?

Vento: Don't remind me. Yeah, with her and her sister and our kids and
the other kids and everybody else I can't stand. I hate this fuckin' barbecue bullshit. I'll wanna shoot myself by noon, so gimme a break tonight
with what you want. Least until the weekend, gimme a break.

Levin listened to the rest of the tape and the next one. He hoped Detective Sean Kelly's name would come up but it never did. There were two

more tapes he could review in the morning if he woke up early enough, but for now he was too tired.

Tomorrow they would spend an entire day performing useless surveillance arranged by Kelly. He would use the opportunity to try and enlighten Detective Brice to their situation without revealing his own investigation. Levin liked Brice and didn't want the kid entrapped in the net Internal Affairs had been weaving around Sean Kelly the last few months. It was Levin's last thought before he fell fast asleep on his couch.

■ ■ ■

"That Jackie Brown guy, he's headed for a fall," Melinda said. "Dealing guns like that, at his age?"

John looked up from his coffee and smiled. She'd obviously started reading the novel he'd left for her.

"What do you think?" he asked.

"I like it," she said. "I read the first chapter during my break. I'm enjoying it."

"Good. I'm curious to see what they do with the movie."

Melinda pointed to his coffee. "Eating light tonight?"

"Please. I'm still digesting a Big Mac I had with my son about an hour ago."

"Well, I'll top you off in the meantime," she said, then refilled his cup and set the pot back on the warmer. "Let me know if you need Tums or something."

He watched her work the next half hour. They exchanged glances between her taking care of the customers at the counter. When there was a lull in the action, he waved her over.

"You ever work the tables?"

"Once in a while," she said. "I prefer the counter. It's a better turnover. People eat at the counter usually don't spend much time doing it."

"Ever have trouble?"

"All kinds. Comes with the territory, but it usually doesn't go very far. All these diners, the owners make sure local cops get enough free coffee to keep them looking out."

John noticed the time and told her he had to run.

"See what I mean about the counter?" she said. "You coming back?"

"You want me to?"

"I wouldn't ask if I didn't."

"Then I'll be back."

"Okay, then. I'll see you later."

He went to leave a tip.

"Don't you dare," she said.

"Okay," he said, "but the next coffee is on me."

He drove back to the bar in Williamsburg to meet with Eddie Vento. The wiseguy was on his way out when John got there. They walked to Vento's Cadillac Coupe DeVille where John noticed Nick Santorra wasn't sitting behind the steering wheel.

"So?" Vento said.

"I'm in for the extra stops," John said. "But I can't commit to anything more than that yet."

"Meaning what?"

"Hanging around the bar," John said. "I can't do it."

"When will you know when you can? Should I hold my breath?"

"I can't say," John said. "I don't know."

"Not the answer I was hoping for," Vento said. "It's good you showed up told me to my face, though. I can respect that."

"I do appreciate the offer."

"You do, huh? Should I throw a fuckin' parade?"

John wasn't sure what the wiseguy meant. He thought it best to not ask and stood silent as Vento sat behind the wheel of the Cadillac.

"There anything else?" he asked John.

"Just thanks, I guess."

"You're not sure?"

"Thank you."

"Jesus Christ," Vento said. Then he put the Cadillac into gear and drove away.

It was an uncomfortable moment. John wasn't sure if he should be relieved or worried.

CHAPTER 20

The Walther was still under the spare tire in the trunk. Billy had followed Albano to the Ackerman home and watched from half a block away. At any point he could've taken the gun, walked to the house, rung the doorbell and shot the man.

He didn't.

He continued following Albano instead; first to a diner on Queens Boulevard where Albano sat at the counter and had a cup of coffee while he chatted with a waitress.

Later, after Albano paid for his coffee, he was on his way again. Billy kept his distance, but not so far that he might lose sight of the Buick. The trip to Williamsburg took twenty-five minutes. Billy waited off the corner on Hooper Street, close enough to where Fast Eddie's was located to see Albano park alongside a fire hydrant near the bar.

After a few minutes he was feeling tired. He did a line of cocaine. The adrenaline rush was strong and made him fidgety. A car door slammed up ahead and Billy saw Albano was standing alongside Eddie Vento's Cadillac. The two men had a short conversation that ended abruptly when the big car pulled away from the curb.

A minute later Albano was back in the Buick heading along the reverse route they'd just taken coming from Queens. Billy pursued the Buick a little closer before he noticed a set of taillights in his rearview mirror. Albano was moving faster this time, catching the synchronized traffic lights without fail. Billy pulled to the curb and let the car he suspected was following him pass. He waited a moment and pulled back into traffic, this time tailing the banged-up Chevy Impala. He lost sight of Albano at the next light and didn't see the Buick again until it pulled into the diner parking lot on Queens Boulevard. The Impala pulled into the same lot.

Billy parked along the curb and waited a few minutes. When he saw the Buick heading out the exit at the other end of the lot, the Impala followed it. Billy waited until both cars were out of the lot before pursuing them. A few minutes later he realized Albano was following the white car directly ahead of the Buick while being tailed by the Impala. Whatever was going on, Billy doubted any of the other drivers knew what it was.

A short time later Albano pulled into a driveway directly behind the white car. The Impala parked further up the same block.

Albano was out of his car. He followed the waitress to the front door of the house and then they were inside.

"The girlfriend," Billy said. "What a nice surprise."

■   ■   ■

They were on her couch, Melinda on top. Things were getting heated fast. She was grinding against him. His hands moved down her back to cup her ass. She moaned when he slipped one hand under her skirt. She could feel herself coming, then pushed herself up and off him.

John looked up and saw she had moved to the end of the couch. She was breathing hard with both her hands raised.

"Sorry," she gasped. "I had to stop."

"Why?"

"I can't."

"Why not?"

"I can't, John, please."

"You okay?"

"Too okay, yes. I want to, trust me, but I can't. I shouldn't. I won't. Not this soon. I'm sorry, really."

She got up off the couch and headed for the kitchen. "I'm getting cold water for myself. You want?"

"Please," he said.

He heard her chuckle. "I really am sorry," she said.

He was hard and had thought it would happen after thinking it wouldn't, not for a while yet. He did his best to lose his erection, but it wasn't easy.

A minute later Melinda did an exaggerated hop and skip into the living room with his glass of water. She was smiling as she sang, "'Morning friend, we recommend, blue plate number two.'"

"That supposed to relax me?"

"Yes."

"It's from some movie, right?"

"Guess which and I won't be able to deny you."

"Something with Betty Grable."

"Close, but this ain't horseshoes."

"Ever hear of close enough for jazz?"

"*Moon over Miami*," Melinda said. "I had to say it so you wouldn't guess."

"I wouldn't have."

Melinda sat in an armchair across from the couch. "You're a great kisser and I was way too worked up way too soon," she said. "I'd hate myself in the morning whether you did or not. Then I'd take it out on you. It's better this way, trust me."

"Okay," he said, unconvincingly.

"So, what are your plans for the weekend?"

There was no way he was telling her about the job he'd just agreed to stay with a couple of hours ago, but John did tell her he was busy until Sunday night.

"Can you get off early enough to see the movie?" Melinda asked. "Or we could go Monday."

"I can try for Sunday night but can't guarantee it. We could always go for drinks and a late snack."

"Drinks to loosen me up?"

"If that's what it takes."

"Clever boy."

"Or we could be adults and just go for it now."

"I'd love to, John, believe me."

He patted the couch alongside him.

"But I think you'd better go."

"Huh?" he said.

"Please," she said. She motioned toward the door.

He got up and walked around the coffee table. He stopped at the door. "Kiss good night first?"

Melinda bit her lips. "No way," she said. "Go."

■ ■ ■

After convincing Nancy to front him one thousand dollars to cover his gambling nut, Louis spent the rest of his Friday scouting locations for the robbery he planned to commit Sunday. There were seven stops he'd clocked along John Albano's route. He had focused on the last three in order to guarantee the most bounty, Massapequa, Rockville Centre and Valley Stream, the only stops Albano sometimes took out of order.

Louis still had no idea what kind of cash he might net, but he did know he'd have a bunch of porno film reels. He wouldn't be able to get rid of the film in New York for fear of the mob behind it, but selling them off on his way south would provide some extra cash for the road trip.

He was thinking about Florida on his way back to the apartment. He'd been there twice, once to Disney World with Nancy on their honeymoon and another time right after their divorce, to Miami, where he went to purchase marijuana from a Cuban connection he'd made in Manhattan.

Florida was also where Louis first learned to hotwire a car. After he'd made his pot deal in Miami, Louis had decided he liked the warm weather and the women in their bikinis on South Beach enough to stay there awhile. He had rented an apartment on Collins Avenue and lived large until the money dried up. When he was forced to find new income, a friend told him about a chop shop in Ft. Lauderdale that provided tutoring on how to steal cars to anyone eager enough to risk the consequences of getting caught.

Louis moved to Ft. Lauderdale and spent the next six months boosting cars. Mostly, he took them from parking lots, but for high-ticket sports items like Porsches and Corvettes, Louis would take them off the streets or go into private driveways.

He eventually stopped when Nancy called him from New York with news that she was pregnant and getting married again.

"To who?" Louis had asked her.

"You don't know him," Nancy had said. "What's the difference? You don't care. You live down there now."

It was the first time Louis was jealous over his ex-wife. "What's his name?" he'd asked.

"John Albano," she'd told him.

"Never heard of him."

"How would you?"

"I don't know. Come down here before you do it."

"What? Don't be crazy. I can't."

"Yeah, you can. If you love me you will."

"I can't, I'm engaged now."

"Come down or you'll never see me again."

"I'll never see you again anyway."

"You will, I promise. Come down now and I promise I'll move back up after you're married."

"And what good'll that do me?"

"Take it or leave it."

"What do you mean, take it or leave it? How can you say that to me? I hate you, god damn it."

Louis had hung up on her that day, but his plan eventually worked. Panicked he might turn her away for remarrying, Nancy flew down a few days before her wedding and the two carried on a three-day affair before she returned to New York. Two years later, after his partner in a stolen-car and pot-dealing ring was arrested, Louis didn't stick around to see if he'd be given up. He flew to Chicago instead, where he stole a car out of the long-term airport parking lot and drove to New York.

His affairs with Nancy had been on-again, off-again, ever since. As much as she was hooked on him, he needed her, too. Although she had argued against his plan, Louis knew he could count on Nancy. He enticed her with a promise to start over; they would take the money and run.

He'd still need a backup plan, however, just in case. Louis was starting to think the bazaar Nancy had mentioned in Valley Stream was the place to make his move. He'd even come up with an idea of how to put Albano in position to be robbed. It wouldn't hurt to have Holly help him with some of the details.

He gave her a call and was annoyed when her line was busy. He turned on the television to watch the late, late show, but was asleep before the first commercial.

CHAPTER 21

John was still frustrated when he left Melinda and wasn't paying attention when a big man standing near his car asked him for a light.

"Huh?" said John, looking up too late to avoid the punch.

He felt the air rush from his lungs a moment before he folded at the waist. The second punch, one to the back of the head, dazed him enough so he didn't feel his forehead hit sidewalk when he fell forward.

Melinda was kneeling alongside him a few minutes later. She helped him back inside the house and sat him on a kitchen chair. His forehead was scraped where it had made contact with the cement. Melinda held a damp dish towel against the bruise.

"The hell happened?" he asked.

"I don't know but I looked up and saw one guy holding a gun on another guy and there you were lying on the ground and I screamed. By the time I got outside, the guy with the gun and the big guy were gone. Who were they?"

"I have no idea. I never seen the guy hit me before. All I know is he nailed me in the stomach and I couldn't breathe. Then you were there."

"What about the other guy, the one with the gun?"

"Never saw him."

"Who could it be? What for?"

"Maybe some guy looking to rob somebody, I was the lucky one."

"Should we call the police?"

John felt for his wallet. "They didn't take anything."

"That guy had a gun, though."

"I'd rather not get the police involved," he said, then leaned forward. "Back a my head hurts. You got aspirin?"

Melinda went to the bathroom, brought back two aspirin, filled a glass with cold water and handed them to John.

"I think I should call the police," she said. She felt around the back of his head and he flinched. "Sorry," she said.

"Hurts back there."

"You've got a little lump."

"Sure it's little?"

"From what I felt. You probably have a slight concussion. Did he hit you with something?"

John finished half the glass of water before shaking his head no. "I don't know, but I don't wanna involve the police. I just need to get home and get some sleep before tomorrow. I have a busy day."

"You can stay here you want."

"You mean all I hadda do was get jumped?" he said.

"You still won't get anything," she said, "but you can stay. You probably shouldn't drive like that anyway."

He winked at her. "I'll manage," he said. "Just knowing you made the offer."

There was no traffic when he left a few minutes later. He wondered if Nick Santorra had sent the goon or if he was the most unlucky guy in the world. Before he knew it, John had pulled into a gas station to look through a public telephone book for Santorra's address.

A few minutes later, his headache hurting a lot worse than it had been earlier, he was driving through Howard Beach. He made one pass by the ranch home and saw where a line of bushes ran the length of the driveway dividing Nick Santorra's property from the neighbor on his left. The Pontiac was parked up close to the garage door in the driveway.

Earlier in the day his son had gotten a whistle from a candy machine and it reminded John of a story his brother had told him before he joined the Marines. Paul Albano had worked part-time at a local gas station during his junior and senior years of high school. After a teacher failed him for cutting class, a mechanic at the garage told him how to vandalize a car without damaging it.

"Duct-tape a whistle to the bottom of his tailpipe," the mechanic had said. "All it does is make noise, but it'll drive your teacher crazy."

It was a silly, harmless prank, but John had borrowed the whistle from his son to give it a try. It gave him pleasure to think about Nick Santorra trying to figure out the noise his car would be making the following day.

He parked half a block up from Santorra's house and walked quickly and quietly back to the driveway. He used the bushes as a shield. The pain in his head throbbed as he dropped to all fours and crept toward the car. The house across the street posed the greatest threat, but the lights were off. John worked with speed, using duct tape to secure the whistle to the bottom of the tailpipe about a foot from the end so it wasn't easy to spot. Then he crawled back out from under the Pontiac and hustled back to his car.

When he finally made it home, there was no sign of Elias on the stoop again. Dizzy from what he suspected was a minor concussion at the least, John gingerly knocked on the old man's apartment door to double-check on his friend. There was no answer. Too woozy to inquire with the super, John headed up to his apartment.

He skipped his gin and tonic, turned on the air conditioner and stripped. He lay on his back and closed his eyes. He let the air conditioner's hum ease him into a dream about Melinda and how close they had come to consummating their relationship. He could hear her moan when he grabbed her ass. He felt himself getting excited and thought he heard himself grunt a moment before he woke up in a cold sweat.

John could feel a tingle below his waist. When he looked he saw the sheet was wet. Between the prank with the whistle and the wet dream, John wondered if he was going through a second adolescence.

■ ■ ■

Billy shot Stanislaus Bartosz in the back as the big man was getting out of the car. He'd just parked on an abandoned strip of road intersecting Fountain Avenue in Brooklyn. The putrid smell from the sanitation dump was overwhelming. Billy lit a fresh cigarette before getting out of the car and finishing off Bartosz with two bullets behind the big man's right ear.

Earlier he'd been forced to pull his weapon and a replica of his old detective badge to keep the ape from beating John Albano to death, what it looked like might happen. Bartosz had caught Albano off guard with a solid punch to the solar plexus, then nailed him with a jackhammer right that sent the windless man face-first to kiss the concrete.

Billy had spotted Bartosz's tail to the house in Queens and was sure the big man was there to do some damage when he saw Bartosz waiting near Albano's Buick. The rest was easy. Bartosz had to respect both the badge and the gun.

Billy had made him sit up front. They rode in silence until Billy turned onto Linden Boulevard. Then Bartosz had wanted to know where they were going.

"Have a talk," Billy told him.

"About what?"

"About what you were doing beating on the man back where your car is."

"What's it to you?"

"Whether or not I charge you with assault. How's that for starters?"

The big man had seemed to sulk.

"What?" Billy asked.

"It's embarrassing."

"You can tell me or spend the night in lockup."

Billy had turned left off Linden Boulevard onto Eldert Lane. Bartosz said, "The fuck we going?"

"Come on, fella, I got better things to do tonight myself. What was the beef? The broad he was with your sister or what?"

"Where we going?"

"I told you, for a talk. Or I can swing back to Linden, take you to the Seventy-fifth Precinct. Up to you, except personally I don't recommend it, spending the night with however many smelly coons they have waiting for transport in the pen there tonight. Worst time inna world to go through lockup's the summer. Something tells me you already know that."

"She was my ex," Bartosz had said then.

"Your ex what? Good-looking broad like that was letting you plow her? Why don't I believe it?"

"Believe what you want."

Billy found the area he'd been looking for, a dirt road that led to a hill behind a clump of trees. He stopped, put the car in park but left it running.

"Okay," he'd said then. "You can go now."

Bartosz did a double-take at the area. "You fucking kidding me?" he'd said. "It's the fuckin' jungle over here. I don't know where I am."

"Brooklyn," Billy said. "Fourth largest city in the world."

"The fuck I'm supposed to get back to my car from here?"

"I look like I care?"

"You really gonna make me get out here?"

Billy had turned his gun on the big man then. "Or I could shoot you," he'd said. "Then push you out, let the rats have a three-day feast, the size of your carcass."

The big man had opened the door and swung one leg out. He had to push himself the rest of the way using the door frame and the back of the seat for leverage. He had just planted his second foot on the ground when Billy shot him. The force of the bullet sent the big man sprawling forward. With the door open, the smell from the Fountain Avenue garbage dump was too strong to ignore. Billy had lit a cigarette to offset the fetid odor. He'd taken a few drags while Bartosz moaned a few feet from the car. When Billy felt he could hold his breath long enough, he got out of the car, walked around the back and approached the big man from the right. He leaned over and fired two shots behind the big man's right ear.

That had been earlier. Now Billy drove past the building on Rockaway Parkway in Canarsie where John Albano lived. Billy was searching for Albano's car, but couldn't find the Buick. He circled the block twice as he contemplated parking, going up the stairs, knocking on Albano's apartment door and getting it over with already. He could kill him right there and still get home in time to have Kathleen read him a story.

He started to yawn again and pulled to the curb. He had parked a full block away from Albano's building. He could use another jolt, but was out of cocaine. He knew of two places he could get some, one back in Queens on Cross Bay Boulevard and the other further west on the Belt Parkway near Coney Island.

Billy yawned one more time before he decided he needed the jolt tonight more than he needed to kill John Albano. Then he pulled away from the curb, turned left on Rockaway Parkway and headed for the Belt. He was thinking he might pick up a jelly apple for Kathleen in Coney Island. Or some saltwater taffy. She had a sweet tooth and liked that stuff, too.

CHAPTER 22

"He did what?" Louis asked.

He had answered the phone in a daze and wasn't sure he had heard Holly right. Something about a guy exposing himself and then going to her dorm. Louis looked at his watch and saw it was two o'clock in the morning.

Now she was crying.

"What happened?" he said. "Calm down and tell me from the beginning."

Holly told him what had happened and that she didn't know what to do. She admitted to being infatuated with her professor, but she had been conflicted about having sex with him so long as she was still attending one of his classes.

"In other words, if you weren't in his class you would've banged him," Louis said. "Very nice."

"I'm trying to be honest," she said. "Yes, I think so. But then he did that, held himself like that in his kitchen... and what he said to me... now I don't know what to do."

She was sniffling again. Louis saw an opening and took it. "And now you come to me for advice. The student comes to the window cleaner because her professor turns out to be like most men, just interested in a piece of ass."

"Don't say that. I feel bad enough."

"You're a smart girl, Holly. Probably a lot smarter than I'll ever be, but sometimes you're naïve to no end. Your professor isn't interested in you the way you'd like to think. He's interesting in getting laid."

Holly was crying again.

"Hey, it's your life," he said. "You're the one has to make the decisions."

"I can't turn him in," she said. "I can't do that. I was just as responsible as he was."

"Because you're pretty and he couldn't control himself?"

"Because I'm at fault, too. I wanted to be there. I went about it the wrong way, but it's just as much my fault. He could lose his tenure."

Louis grinned on his end of the phone. "And now it doesn't even bother you to hurt me, telling me all this. Thanks a lot. It's the first time you've called me in a few days, you didn't bother returning my calls and now you tell me how you wanted to screw some other guy. Great. Thanks, Holly. Sleep tight."

He hung up the phone and looked at the television. The credits were rolling from the Hercules movie he'd been watching earlier. The phone rang again. He let it ring a few times before deciding to answer.

"I'm sorry if I hurt you," Holly said.

"Yeah, well, why the hell you calling me anyway?"

"I'm sorry," Holly said. "I'm so sorry."

She sobbed some more before she was able to control herself.

"I feel like an idiot," she said.

"You're not an idiot. You're young is all."

"I'm sorry I hurt you, Louis. I am."

"You're damn straight I'm hurt," he said with a smirk on his face.

"I'm a dope."

"You really want my advice?"

"Yes. I do. Please."

"Don't file charges. Don't go to his boss. Let the guy wiggle. I'm sure he's all fucked up about it anyway."

"He's been trying to talk to me all day."

"He's probably afraid he lost his job."

"I can't do that. I wouldn't."

"It'd be just as bad for you if you did. There's that to consider. He can't see that, though. He's probably scared shitless. Not that he shouldn't be, the fucking pervert."

"I wish I hadn't gone there."

"Here I am fighting your war against porn and you go and watch one with your professor. How's that for ironic?"

"It wasn't porn, Louis. *Last Tango* isn't porn."

"Except it gave your professor a hard-on he couldn't control."

He faced the mirror over his dresser, curled his free hand and stroked the air with it. "I'll bet he's nailed a couple dozen kids from his classes. How old you say he was?"

"I didn't say. He's in his forties, maybe fifty."

"And you like him. Enough so you would've slept with him."

"I don't know anymore," she said. "The way he looked, what he said. I don't know."

"Well, there's not much I can do," Louis said. "And I have to get some sleep. I have things to do tomorrow and Sunday that require I'm alert."

"Can I see you?"

"Why, so you can cry about your professor some more? No thanks."

"Please, Louis."

"I don't have time. Not this weekend."

"I can help you."

"I don't see how. Not while you're all broken up over your perverted professor."

"Please?"

Louis didn't answer.

"Please, Louis?"

"I don't know," he said dismissively. "Let me think about it. I'll call you tomorrow."

"Will you?"

"I'll call. I'm not making any guarantees, though."

"I don't want to be here this weekend. Not at the dorm."

"You come here, you'll be alone most the weekend anyway. I have that thing to do."

"I don't care. I just don't want to be here."

"I'll let you know in the morning."

"Promise you'll call."

"Hey, I'm not the one ignores phone calls."

"I'm sorry about that. Please call me."

"I'll see. Good night, Holly."

"Good night."

He hung up, turned to the mirror and mimicked Holly's pleading. "'Promise you'll call,'" he said. "'Please, Louis.'"

The phone rang again. He knew it was Holly. He picked it up without answering.

"I still care about you," she said. "I want you to know that."

He hung up again.

"Where do they grow people that stupid?" he asked his reflection.

■　■　■

Special Agent Stebenow was wearing gym shorts, a Miami Dolphins T-shirt and carrying his sneakers in one hand as he crossed the sand toward the water's edge. He had been following Bridget Malone since she left the apartment above Fast Eddie's a few hours ago. Twenty minutes earlier Bridget and two girlfriends she met in Park Slope had spread a towel on the sand near the water. A few minutes later the girlfriends left Bridget to join a group of young couples sitting around a small fire near the fishing dock. Stebenow watched as Bridget stripped out of her clothes and couldn't tell if she was wearing a bikini or her underwear when she ran off toward the surf.

There was a full moon. Stebenow noticed at least two other couples on blankets close to the water as he made his way from the boardwalk to the surf. The sand was cool against his feet.

He could see Bridget body surfing toward the shore when he made it to her blanket. He observed how neatly the blanket had been spread on the sand and how a towel was folded under a small radio. A pair of cut-off shorts and a sweatshirt lay on the towel alongside a beach bag.

Stebenow looked up and saw Bridget trying to balance herself against the tug of the receding water around her feet. She stepped out of the surf and jogged a few feet before she saw him. She smiled as she drew closer. He could see through her white panties and bra. When he spotted her triangle of dark pubic hair, he turned away.

"Agent Stebenow?" Bridget said. "I almost didn't recognize you without your sunglasses."

"It's too dark for those now," he said. "Speaking of which, isn't it a little dangerous swimming this late?"

He grabbed the towel from the beach bag and held it out to her without looking.

"Dangerous how?" she said. "You mean sharks or black men?"

Stebenow pointed at her face. "That's a nasty bruise."

"Yeah, well, sometimes Eddie can get nasty."

"You okay?"

"You really care?"

"Yes."

"Can I take that for a sexual advance?"

"No."

"Because I'm white?"

"No, because I'm married."

"Separated."

"I'm not divorced."

Bridget finished drying her legs and stepped inside the cut-off shorts.

"Did you get it on tape?" Stebenow asked.

"No."

"Why not?"

"Because I wasn't expecting it," Bridget said. She removed her bra and Stebenow turned away again. "The tape was full from the night before. I didn't get a chance to change it. I'd look a lot worse if he caught me doing that."

"You don't have to take being hit."

Bridget pulled the sweatshirt over her head. "And here I thought you'd appreciate the extra drama."

"We want to put him away. Nobody wants to see anything happen to you."

"I might believe you, but I know that prosecutor could care less. He'd be fine if I were killed so long as it was on tape."

Stebenow read the script on the sweatshirt. "Mrs. Jay's Beer Garden."

"In Asbury Park. I went there to see a friend play drums. He's in a new band."

"Somebody your own age?"

"That bothers you, huh, Eddie and me?"

"On so many levels you can't imagine."

"You could always save me from him. It be a first for me, a black man. How 'bout you? Ever been with a white girl before?"

Stebenow ignored the question. "Can you take a walk?"

Bridget squatted down over the beach bag. She pulled a cassette from a pocket inside the bag and held it out.

"Don't you want this first?"

Stebenow pocketed the tape. "I wish you were a little more careful," he said.

Bridget giggled, waved to her friends and then yelled she'd be right back. She followed Stebenow to the boardwalk, across it and down the ramp to the sidewalk and his car. He unlocked her door and held it open.

"Thank you," she said before getting in.

He walked around the back of the car and could see she had turned the rearview mirror to look at herself. He got in and waited until she was finished before readjusting the mirror.

"You need to keep a fresh tape in the recorder," he told her. "Just in case he does something like that again."

She took his right hand and held it against her bruised cheek.

He looked away from her. "Does it hurt?"

"I think you could make it better," she said.

She moved his hand across her mouth and kissed it.

Stebenow slowly pulled his hand away.

"I wouldn't tell if you wanted to have sex with me," Bridget said. "I'm of age. It would be of my own free will."

"I'm married, Bridget."

"Yeah, so?"

Stebenow opened his window.

"You're too much," Bridget said. "You're like the one square cop I ever met."

"You meet many cops, do you?"

"That one visited Eddie would've pushed my head into his lap already, we were ever this close."

"Which one was that?"

"I don't know his name. Eddie calls him Mr. Horse. I'm supposed to believe he's a bookie but I know he's not."

"And how's that?"

"Red hair, freckles? He isn't an Irish cop, I'm a nun."

"Kelly," Stebenow said. "He is a cop, so be careful. Be extra careful. He might be watching you for Eddie."

"You know that, why don't you bust him?"

"He's peripheral to the investigation. He'll go down when the time comes, but he's not our focus. Eddie is."

"Well, he showed up the other night while I was on my way home, the Irish cop. He let me borrow his hanky."

Stebenow lit a cigarette. "What was that about?"

"I was bleeding from the nose."

"Snorting?"

"Once in a while your nose bleeds. It's no big deal."

"Aside from the fact, like I said, he might've been tailing you, there are health issues like ruining your nasal passages."

"I'm not an addict, what Eddie thinks."

"You're bleeding from the nose you're well on your way."

She reached for his cigarette. He let her take it from his mouth. She took a long drag.

"This porn thing isn't working," she said. "It repulses him when I talk about it and he isn't going to tell me any names besides the one he already did. That Rothenburg guy."

"That name helped," Stebenow said.

"Well, he isn't going any further than that. I keep pushing him, but this is what I got, a slap across the face."

"If you could get him on tape with Kelly, Mr. Horse, that might bring this to a close a lot sooner."

"The guy came over out of the blue the other day. Eddie never mentioned him to me."

"My point being, if the tapes are always fresh, you have the thing ready... he might've said something the other day you didn't hear."

"That's a lot more dangerous than you think," Bridget said.

"I understand that."

"I don't think you do."

"You going back tonight?"

"It's where I live," Bridget said. "So long as he pays the rent, it's where I live."

She had an edge to her voice. He apologized about pushing her with the tapes, then added, "It's just the sooner we have something concrete, the sooner you're off the hook. I'd like to see that, believe it or not, you being out of this."

She had been snagged in a heroin deal two years earlier and had agreed to testify against her former boyfriend to avoid a prison sentence. When her boyfriend died in jail, Bridget was forced into a deal with the government gathering evidence against her boss, Eddie Vento.

"He plays cards tonight," she said. "If he doesn't go straight home, he'll be back around six. He'll be drunk and horny, but that's good for you because it's the only time he name drops, when he's drunk. He'll want me to talk dirty to him, too, in case they haven't let you listen to the tapes yet."

"I'm sorry," Stebenow said. "I mean it."

"Right," she said.

She went to get out of the car and Stebenow stopped her.

"What?" she said.

He pulled his wallet from his back pocket, fingered a ten out and handed it to her.

"Sure you don't want a blow job?" she asked with venom.

"Be careful," he told her.

Bridget forced a phony grin, lost it just as fast and then got out of the car. Stebenow watched her walk back up the ramp toward the boardwalk. He waited a full minute after she disappeared before driving off.

CHAPTER 23

Nancy couldn't believe she was doing it, walking back into her bank to take another thousand dollars out of her safe-deposit box for Louis. It was money she had managed to squirrel away during her marriage to Nathan; excess grocery money as well as some of the child support she didn't really need. She removed the contents of the box, two envelopes of cash and some jewelry, before she counted out ten one-hundred-dollar bills. She recounted what she had left and wrote the figure on one of the envelopes—$6,200.00.

Lately, she'd thought about hocking the engagement ring John had given her. The one-carat pear-shaped diamond had been appraised for one thousand dollars two years ago, less than half of the value of the ring Nathan had given her. She had already lied about John's ring, telling Louis her second ex must have stolen it. Louis couldn't know what she had stashed in the safe-deposit box because then he'd ask for it.

The diamond Nathan had given her made her rethink rushing a divorce too soon. She had been living good and no longer had to work since marrying Nathan. There was financial security and enough independence to maintain her affair with Louis. She had health insurance coverage that included dental, and should Nathan die, there was mortgage insurance to pay for the house and a life insurance policy that would keep her out of work for ten or more years.

While it was true Nancy didn't love Nathan and probably never could, and that she still loved Louis, it was equally true there was no way she could depend on Louis. Even if what he had told her the other night was true and they would soon have enough to start over, was there really a chance in hell it would work?

She knew the answer without having to think about it. Louis would always be Louis. He would bet when he wanted to bet and he would fool around when somebody new caught his eye. Truth be told, if push ever came to shove, Nancy could count on being the one shoved.

Still, the dichotomy wasn't something Nancy could do anything about; she resented Nathan for all his decency and loved Louis for all his indecency.

And here she was bailing him out one more time.

Tomorrow she would use her only child to help Louis rob the boy's father.

■ ■ ■

Nathan was up early Saturday morning to babysit his stepson while Nancy went grocery shopping, to the bank and the butcher. He cooked bacon and eggs for breakfast and afterward pitched wiffle balls in the backyard. Nathan got a kick out of Little Jack's announcing each batter in the Yankee lineup before making believe he was stepping into the batter's box at Yankee Stadium.

"Now batting," Little Jack would say, "number seven, Mickey Mantle." Nathan threw a few dozen pitches before the kid needed to use the bathroom. He used the opportunity to call an attorney to confirm an appointment he had made the day before. He had just hung the phone up when Nancy returned carrying a shopping bag filled with fresh meat from the butcher.

"There's more in the car," she said.

Nathan retrieved the rest of the groceries, thanked his stepson for holding the door open and set the bags on the table.

Nancy told Little Jack to play in the basement for a few minutes while she talked to Nathan. The boy headed downstairs. Nathan sat at the table.

"I know you mean well being friends with Jack's father," she said. "And I appreciate all you do for my son, but what you did the other day, letting him in, making him coffee, upset me."

"I don't see why."

"I know you don't and that's just as upsetting."

"Why?"

"Because you're my husband," she said. "And John takes advantage when he knows he has allies."

"Did you ever stop and think I do it for your son?"

"I know that. I understand you mean well, but that only encourages his father."

"Encourages him how? To do what?"

"To be late paying his child support, for one thing."

"Oh, big deal. He's having a rough patch. You're too hard on him for that. We're not desperate for the money."

"That's not the issue, Nathan. And you just proved my point. There you go defending him again."

"I'm not defending anybody. I'm just saying you should pay more attention to the boy than worry about his father or the money he owes. Big deal. Every kid needs a father, Nancy. Little Jack needs his. He loves him and your constantly knocking your ex in front of your son isn't right."

She rolled her eyes. "And you're still defending him. You invite him in the house and make him coffee and let him downstairs to play with Jack and he never has the money he owes or spends enough time with his son."

I just wish you were a little more considerate about me in all this."

Nathan sighed. She had almost managed to make him feel guilty until that last comment about being more considerate of her. She was the most selfish woman he'd ever met.

"You shouldn't keep the man from seeing his son," he said. "That boy loves his father."

"Maybe if he proved himself for a change, if John did, I wouldn't feel this way, but your siding with him now just makes it all the more frustrating."

Nathan didn't understand what she was getting at. "Prove himself how? For what?"

"To me and his son," Nancy said.

Nathan waited for more.

"Oh, what's the point?" she said.

"What?"

"Not now. I can't deal with this anymore today. We'll talk about this later."

He had no idea what she was talking about and was grateful when she walked out of the house.

■ ■ ■

The phone woke John at eleven o'clock. He saw double when he looked at the clock. He closed his eyes tight and counted to five before opening them again. When he did, his vision was still blurry, but the double vision was gone.

He answered on the fourth ring.

"It's me," Melinda said. "You okay?"

"A little groggy, but yeah."

"How's your head?"

"Hurts, but not as bad as last night."

"I couldn't sleep all night," she said. "I was worried sick after you left. I should've gone with you."

"You should've made the offer. I would've liked that."

"Don't make me feel more guilty than I already do."

John saw the time and knew he had to get moving. "I have to be on the road soon," he said. "Can I call you later?"

"You better."

"I will."

She kissed him through the phone.

"That what I think it was?"

"Yes."

"You use your tongue?"

"Don't push your luck."

He kissed her back.

"That's better," she said.

"I'll call you later," he said.

"Don't forget."

"Bye."

"Bye."

He hung up before swinging his legs off the bed. Then he stood up too fast and had to sit back down. His head was swimming. He got up again, a lot slower this time, then headed for the bathroom to turn on the shower and start his day. He popped three aspirin, downing them with a glass of water. He drank another glass before he spotted the bruise on his forehead in the mirror above the sink. A small scab had formed. The wound reminded him of Nick Santorra one more time.

"Fuck," he said, then stepped into the tub and let the hot water do its work.

■ ■ ■

Angela was busy putting away the groceries when Nick asked her for a cup of coffee. He'd been waiting on a call from Stanislaus Bartosz, but so far the phone hadn't rung. It was a little after eleven o'clock and he would need to leave the house before one, Nick told his wife.

"Eddie's sending me on something solo," he added. "About time, right?"

"Alone? That's good, right?"

"Yeah, it is. You get the bagels?"

"On the counter."

Nick spotted the brown paper bag on the kitchen counter and retrieved it. He set it on the table, opened the refrigerator and grabbed the cream cheese.

"Means he's giving me more responsibility," he said. "Could mean I'm close to earning my stripe."

"That's good, too."

Nick was bummed from her lack of enthusiasm. She had never paid close enough attention to understand street talk.

"I get a stripe, I become somebody," he said.

"Great," she said.

"It means I get made," he said. "I'll be a made man."

She was putting a box of cereal on a high shelf in the cupboard. She turned to him and smiled when she was through. "I know that's good," she said. "That's like the movie, right, *The Godfather*?"

Nick stared hard at his wife.

"What?" she said.

Moron, he thought. "Nothing," he said.

The couple had coffee together when she was finished with the groceries. Angela complained about an upcoming barbecue on Staten Island they had to attend because her sister had come to their Fourth of July party the month before. Nick wasn't much interested. He noticed the time and said he had to hurry.

"You want me to make you something?" Angela asked.

"Since when do I take lunch?"

"I'm just asking. I can if you want. I bought fresh mortadella. I can put vinegar on the Italian bread the way you like."

Nick had a change of heart. "You know what? That sounds pretty good. Yeah, why not?"

She got up from the table to make the sandwich. "Oh, and before I forget, the car was making a strange sound before. I couldn't hear it when I slowed down, but it was loud when I was driving on Cross Bay Boulevard."

Nick felt his stomach drop. "What kind of sound?"

"I don't know, loud. Loud and high. I don't know how else to describe it."

"That motherfucker."

"Nick, please."

"Cocksucker."

"Nick!"

"Where is it, the car?"

"Out front."

"I told you to put it in the driveway for now. Didn't I tell you that? Where'd you find it, you went out this morning?"

Angela was taking cold cuts out of the refrigerator. "In the driveway," she said. "I thought you were going out so I left it out front. Why? What's the big deal all of a sudden?"

"Some piece of shit I think is looking to fuck with me."

"Nick, your language, please."

"Oh, fuck my language already. You smell anything in the car? Anything strange the way it drove?"

"No, it drove fine. I didn't smell a thing."

He crushed out his cigarette and got up from the chair. "I'll be right back," he said. He headed for the door when Angela shouted at him.

"Nick!"

"What!"

"You want lettuce and tomato?"

"Yeah."

"Cheese?"

"Provolone?"

"Yeah."

"Yeah."

"And the vinegar?"

He had the door opened. "What?"

"Vinegar?"

"Yeah!"

"Okay, go ahead."

"Jesus Christ," he said before rushing out to the curb to examine the Pontiac.

CHAPTER 24

They were sitting in Detective Brice's yellow Ford Mustang Mach I. It was a few minutes before noon. The sun was strong. Detective Levin shielded his eyes from the glare.

"Who's this guy?" he asked.

"We'll know after we call it in," Brice said. He wrote down the Buick's license tags on his *Daily News*.

Levin wiped sweat from his forehead with the back of his free hand. He held a can of Coke in the other. "It gets any hotter, you'll have to use some gas and turn on the air conditioner," he said.

Brice flipped down his sun visor. "It's no good for the engine to run the AC sitting here like this," he said. "Besides, you could always take off the shirt you're wearing over a T-shirt."

"The T-shirt absorbs the sweat or I'd get stains like you."

Brice repositioned the sun visor and glanced at the sweat stain under his right arm.

"That's five cars so far," Levin said.

"And Berg was out to meet every one of them," Brice said. "Change of plans, I guess."

"I wonder it has anything to do with that big, fat warning we gave him the other day."

"You're still on that kick, huh?"

"Where's Kelly?"

"Said he'd be here."

"Except he isn't."

"You still out tomorrow?"

"For my cousin's wedding," Levin said.

"Since when do Jews marry on a Sunday?"

"He's marrying a shiksa," Levin said. He saw Brice was eyeing him. "One of yours," Levin added. "A gentile. They always get married on weekends. Sundays if they're cheap."

Brice turned to watch the Buick again. "I'm not looking forward to this tomorrow, being alone with Kelly. He holds my age against me."

"Overbearing is he?"

"He's alright when you're around, with me, I mean, but that's because he doesn't like you."

"Why they call us the chosen people," Levin said.

Brice was still watching the Buick. He pointed to it when it pulled away from the curb in front of George Berg's house.

"Whoever it was, the car can use some bodywork," he said.

They had been parked since nine o'clock in the morning. Levin finished his soda and put the empty can in a paper bag.

"Really," he said. "Either turn the air on a few minutes or I gotta go for a walk to try and cool myself off."

"In this heat?" Brice said.

"I'll walk in the shade."

"Good luck."

"That mean you won't turn it on?"

"I told you, it's not good for the car running the air conditioner while it's idling."

"That what Mach One means, you can't run the air conditioner?"

Brice turned to Levin. "That degree you got, it's in ballbreaking, right?"

Levin sighed, opened the door and got out. He stretched his arms over his head, yawned and stretched again. When he turned in the direction of George Berg's house, he could see the owner waving to him from his stoop.

"Nice work," Brice said.

Levin squatted down alongside the passenger window. "He probably spotted us two minutes after we got here."

"Yeah, well, now it's official."

Levin winked before standing up out of his squat. "I'm going for a walk."

"While I do my job," Brice said. "That's great."

"I stay here we'll both be jerking ourselves off," Levin said. "I'm gonna find a bathroom where I can do it in private."

■ ■ ■

They were in bed after having sex first thing in the morning. Billy had been out late the night before and Kathleen had woken up horny. She whispered a dirty story in his ear about a hand job she'd given one of the football players when she was in high school, making up most of it until Billy was hard and then she climbed on top of him. They slept again afterward and didn't wake up until it was close to noon.

Billy put up a pot of coffee. He was finished with his first cup when Kathleen joined him in the kitchen. She put four slices of bread in the toaster and set out a stick of butter on a plate while Billy retrieved the mail and newspaper from the stoop. She had the toast buttered when he returned. They sat across from one another at the table and sipped their coffees.

After a while Kathleen pointed at his newspaper with her butter knife. "Anything interesting?"

"Not really," Billy said. He was paging through the *New York Post*, scanning the articles it looked like.

"What time you get in last night?"

"Pretty late. After two, I think."

"Closer to three."

He looked up from the newspaper. "Then what you ask for?"

Kathleen was surprised at his tone. When she looked up, Billy was glaring at her.

"There's nothing new in the world," he said. "Lots and lots of bullshit is all."

She nervously dipped one end of a piece of toast into her coffee and took a bite. She wiped her mouth with a napkin before looking up at him again.

"Maybe we should call a realtor," she said.

It was something she had been thinking about, selling their house and starting over someplace else. Now that he wasn't a cop anymore, they had options.

"Sure," Billy said, "except I have something to do later."

"When?"

"Around three."

"Then I should call soon. At least to get an idea of the market value."

"I already know that. One-twenty, tops, this neighborhood. Probably more like one-five or one flat."

"You looked into it?"

"Not directly, no. I have an idea, though."

"One-twenty would give us close to a hundred to buy someplace else," Kathleen said. "We could get a lot more for our money outside New York."

Billy nodded but wasn't paying attention. He seemed to be reading something.

"I'd still like to get an estimate," Kathleen said. "You think they'd come today? I'd have to clean up some."

"They aren't gonna care if the dishes are done, Kathleen."

"I don't want somebody coming in with the place a mess."

She was waiting for his attention, but Billy was focused on whatever he was reading.

"Billy?"

"It's not a mess," he said. "If we're just looking for an appraisal, you don't need to scrub the joint."

It bothered her that he was so preoccupied. She knew he wasn't looking for a job. It was something else and it made her uneasy.

"Or we could borrow off it until you find work," she said.

"Re-mortgage? I'd rather not go that route."

"Then I should work."

"No."

"I'm getting bored anyway. I'm at the gym five days a week, mostly from boredom. I need something to do. I might as well get paid for it."

Billy stared at her again.

"You're bored, are you?" he said.

"I'm just saying."

"Just saying what?"

"I can help with the bills."

"And then you wouldn't be bored."

"What?"

"Maybe you just need to get out and about," he said. "A change of scenery, make your day more exciting."

"I didn't say that."

"No, you didn't, did you?"

Billy was back to staring at her. This time she felt a chill.

"You're not working," he said. "Not ever."

Kathleen looked away.

"Money's fine," he said. "Stop worrying about it."

She picked up her coffee and sipped again. She had been suspicious of Billy's whereabouts the last few times he left the house. He used to tell her he couldn't say where he was going because of his undercover work, but now that he was a civilian again she had hoped the secrecy would end and it hadn't.

"I've been thinking about someplace warm," she said. "To live, I mean. Someplace where it doesn't snow."

"But not Florida, right?"

"No, definitely not Florida."

He folded the newspaper in half and leaned both elbows on the table. "Where then? Where warm?"

"I don't know. California? Arizona? New Mexico, maybe."

"Somewhere west, huh?"

"Why not?"

"Might be okay," Billy said. "Certainly lots of hard bodies out there, young guys looking to pick up good-looking divorcees off the beaches in California."

Either he was picking a fight or providing the outline for a new sex story. Sometimes he did that, suggested something that turned him on and then she'd have to fictionalize it so he could get off.

She wasn't in the mood, though, and pointed to the newspaper he'd been reading. "You done with that?"

Billy pushed the *Post* across the table.

Kathleen unfolded it, licked her right thumb and index fingers to turn the first page.

"I'll bet they'd love that, the lifeguards on a beach out there," Billy said.

"Seeing that red patch of yours through the white bikini I like."

He had become a voyeur over time. First it was through her retelling her sexual past that had turned him on. Then he asked her to act out what she had done with other men, sometimes using vibrators and sometimes, like the other day, using nothing at all. Over time, whether real or imagined, it became obvious that it was the image of his wife being turned on that excited Billy most.

She was still looking through the newspaper when she saw a name she recognized, Victor Vasquez. She picked up the paper and brought it closer to read the article.

"What's up?" Billy asked.

Kathleen didn't hear him. She read about a funeral mass taking place at a church near Starrett City in Brooklyn. Victor Vasquez, devoted husband and father of three girls, had been killed a few days ago in a park in Canarsie.

Kathleen had been involved with Vasquez for a short time three years earlier. It was the first affair she had confessed to Billy and was also the first she'd recorded in the notebook.

"What?" Billy asked.

"Somebody killed Victor Vasquez."

"Your Victor Vasquez?"

Kathleen looked up. "Yes."

"Don't look at me," Billy said. "I didn't do it."

She was searching for a sign that he was lying or telling the truth, but couldn't find one.

Then Billy said, "And if I did? Would you leave me, Kathleen? Would you betray me ... again?"

She wasn't sure anymore so she didn't answer.

"Did you?" she asked instead.

"You want that other slice of toast?" Billy said.

CHAPTER 25

Elias was sipping coffee on the stoop when John ran into him on his way out of the building. He tried to duck past him but the old man put a hand out to stop him.

"Good morning, Mr. Criminal," Elias said.

"Mister MIA," John said. "Where you been?"

"What this is, MIA?"

"Missing in action. Everybody thought you got married."

Elias hadn't been looking at John. He sipped his coffee, saw the bruise on John's forehead and pointed to it.

"What happened?"

"I fell."

"Bullshit."

"I did."

The old man motioned toward the street. "I see car outside last night. Looks like somebody watching here, this building."

"Maybe it was a guy waiting for his date."

"Maybe he's waiting for you."

"Yeah, what makes you think that?"

The two men stared at each other until Elias waved John off.

"You okay?" John asked.

"How do I look?"

"Like you didn't get laid last night."

"I didn't, but is beside the point. Maybe this is Mafia friends waiting for you. You don't know it's not."

John sighed. "You're seeing things," he said. "I hear you're spending a lot of time around the corner."

"She's nice lady, but crazy. Madame Hortense, eh?"

"Who?"

"You should read more."

"Soon's I find the time."

Elias waved him off. "Pff," he said.

"See you later," John said.

The old man bowed. "I thank you for the warning."

Elias headed inside the building; John went to his car. The seven extra stops were mostly on the south shore of Long Island with five located between Freeport and Bayshore and the other two north off the Southern State Parkway in Uniondale and Hicksville. Although some of the new stops were Saturday showings only, coordinating them with his regulars located on the north shore proved to be a challenge.

He had arranged his route according to the first showing at each location. He made his first few stops without a problem, picking up the extra film reels at stop four. Then traffic slowed him down before one of his regular stops in West Islip and he was fifteen minutes late to the garage on Union Boulevard. When he showed the men waiting there the movie paraphernalia he had brought, three autographed posters of Linda Lovelace and two pair of the panties were sold on the spot.

John had been told to stop at George Berg's house instead of the Knights of Columbus. Although he wouldn't be leaving the film, the stop was supposed to throw off police surveillance. He'd been nervous the police were watching Berg. The last thing he needed was an arrest he couldn't afford.

Once he had started his route, he remained focused on the reward; he stood to double his weekend pay. He stopped at Berg's house and played the game with one eye on the time.

"I guess you didn't get Linda Lovelace to make the drive with you today, huh?" Berg said.

"Would you believe me if I told you I have a shitload of autographed posters in the trunk?"

"I'd believe it if I saw them. And then I'd be pissed for not getting any royalties on the idea. The hell happened your forehead?"

"I fell."

"Head first?"

"George, gimme a break here."

"Sorry," Berg said.

"I also have signed panties," John told him. "And I'll give you a little inside info, just because I like you and hate to see you get upset over our inability to do business this weekend."

"What's that?" Berg asked. "It's not really her signature?"

John looked in both directions before winking at Berg. "But you never heard that from me," he said.

Berg motioned with his head for John to look up the street. "Yellow Mustang about halfway up the block," he said. "There're two of them in it, two of the three came here the other day, knocked on my door, wanted to know if I knew anybody peddling a porno. The other one didn't show yet had the balls the other day to walk inside my house, use the toilet. He even took a soda from the fridge before he left."

"Sounds like a warning to me," John said. "Or they wouldn't've knocked, right?"

"Somebody's getting greased. Except today I'm the fall guy. No movie, no money."

"Word is there's another one about to hit the market. You can run a double feature."

"What, she make a sequel already?"

"Something from the Coast they're bootlegging here now. *Behind the Green Door?*"

"The *Ivory Snow* girl," Berg said. "She's a cutie alright."

"She is?"

"Marilyn Chambers. You haven't seen her?"

"I don't have time to watch movies, George. Maybe some day when I'm retired."

"I hear that."

"Okay, I guess I'll see you next week again."

"Hopefully under better circumstances."

John shook Berg's hand, pulled away from the curb and glanced up at the rearview mirror. He saw the yellow Mustang hadn't moved. He glanced at his watch and saw he'd burned an extra five minutes he didn't have to spare.

■ ■ ■

Bridget jammed a worn paperback novel under the front end of the projector to adjust the height of the picture on her living room wall. She had set the projector on the end table beside her couch while Eddie Vento, his feet up on the cocktail table, snored on the opposite end of the couch. Half an hour ago, they had watched the new film he said his crew would be pushing, *Behind the Green Door*, but when the scene with the black guy began, Vento made her turn the projector off.

Last night he'd come back to the apartment drunk after playing cards through the night and wouldn't talk. Bridget had let him sleep until noon, but now he was grumpy with a hangover. She needed to get him out of the way for a few minutes while she changed the tape in the recorder hidden under the couch.

She flipped a switch and the projector whirred to life. Vento woke from the noise and quickly covered his eyes from the flashing spots on the living room wall.

"Again?" he said.

"This is the other one," she said. "I wanna show you something."

Vento removed his legs from the table and leaned forward with his right hand still shading his eyes as the music began.

"Show me what?" he said.

"How much better-looking I am than this woman."

The music from the movie started.

"Turn it down," Vento said. "God damn noise."

Bridget turned the volume down. Vento started for the bathroom.

"Wait, don't go yet," she said. "Watch."

Vento was halfway across the living room. "Watch my ass," he said.

Bridget stopped the projector.

"You could've waited," she said. "It would've taken you all of two seconds."

"What?" he yelled.

She was about to repeat herself when she heard him peeing. "At least close the door," she said. "Asshole," she whispered.

She quickly retrieved the recorder from under the couch and replaced the used tape with a blank one. She rushed back to the projector and slid the tape in the end-table drawer.

Vento was drying his face when he returned a few minutes later. Bridget turned on the projector again, then turned up the volume. The music from the start of *Deep Throat* began.

"Turn that fucking thing off," he said. "I know she's a dog. Nobody cares. She can swallow a telephone pole."

"Maybe it takes practice," she said.

Vento sat on the couch again. He stared at Bridget until she turned the projector off.

"I know I can make money doing that," she said. "All I need is the connections. I wouldn't mind driving that car she had in the movie, that Cadillac."

"Trust me," Vento said, "it wasn't hers."

"I'll bet she can afford one."

"Not in this life."

"Bullshit."

"Fine, bullshit. You know everything. Go make some coffee."

"In a minute. You're telling me she's not making money?"

"I'm telling you it's not half what you think, if that much. And the car belongs to the guy made the movie, the director. If not him, it's somebody works with him. The guys made that movie, backed it, didn't go for spit."

"You know him, the guy made it?"

"Which one, the director or the guy backed it?"

"Either."

"Yeah, I know the guy backed it. He already moved his operation down there where they made the thing, Florida."

Bridget set her hands on her hips. "And?"

"And what?" Vento said. "Enough with you and these movies already. I'm tired of hearing it."

"Thanks a lot, Eddie. First you make promises and then you ignore me."

"Promises about what?"

"The movies. You know the guy who made that movie or not?"

"What guy?"

"The one with the car."

"Jesus Christ, I just said. I know of him. I know who he's around. I know the guy backed it, him and his sons."

"Well?"

"I thought you needed to know I might tell you."

"Great. You know what it all sounds like to me? Bullshit, that's what."

"Sorry you don't approve."

"What I shouldn't approve of is this ... us ... you, Eddie. I'm gonna be an old maid, maybe I should find me a sucker instead of being one for you."

Vento motioned at her to come to him. "Don't go off half cocked," he said. "Take it easy with this. I'm tryin' to look out for you here."

Bridget was standing in front of him. He reached for her, but she stepped back. "I mean it," she said. "What's the point. I ask you for something and you blow me off. Thanks, but no thanks."

"And maybe I'm trying to save you from a life you don't know about," Vento said. "You'd do a lot better married to some guy someday."

"If you really know somebody can help me, then do it. How's that? Otherwise, I'm done with being your *gumarra*. I can tend bar anywhere."

Vento rubbed his head with both hands. "Alright, fine," he said. "I'll make the call, but you go make the coffee, please already." He huffed, picked up the phone and dialed a number.

Bridget stood staring at him from across the room with her arms folded. Vento looked her off when someone answered on the other end of the line. She waited until she heard him talking before heading to the kitchen to make his coffee.

CHAPTER 26

Detective Kelly was more than two hours late, but had brought them corned beef and pastrami sandwiches, coleslaw, pickles, French fries and sodas.

"How many've showed so far?" he asked.

Levin bit into a pastrami on rye smothered with mustard he had spread from a Gulden's packet.

"Six," said Brice, using a plastic fork to spread coleslaw on his sandwich.

"You get the tags?" Kelly said.

"We gonna bother to run them?" Levin asked.

"What's that supposed to mean?"

"The warning we gave this guy," Brice said.

Kelly bit into a pickle. "You guys have a beef?"

Levin was about to take another bite of his sandwich. "You want the sandwich back?"

"Don't be a wiseass," Kelly said. "I'm serious, what's the problem here?"

"It seems kind of silly, us sitting out here all day after we approached the guy a few days ago," Brice said. "And the guys pulling up, the way he's meeting them out there, it's probably a show anyway."

"Not to mention me having to park back at the deli a few blocks away if we're letting him know we're here."

"I just parked there myself," Kelly said. "Walk'll do you good, but neither of you shouldn't trouble yourselves thinking so hard. Not that I need to share it with you two, but there's a clever method behind the madness. Not to mention the easy-as-pie overtime."

Levin took a drink from his soda. "Except this way we never even get to see the movie," he said. "I was looking forward to it."

Kelly glanced over his shoulder to shoot Levin a dirty look.

"Don't mind him," Brice told Kelly. "He's got his balls twisted for having to blow tomorrow's overtime on some wedding."

Kelly huffed. "He should show a little appreciation is what he should do."

"You were saying?" Levin said.

"You talking to me?" Kelly said.

"Something about the clever method and the madness."

"You're enjoying yourself trying to push my buttons. That's good."

"So's this sandwich," said Brice, trying to change the subject. "Where'd you get them?"

"Grabstein's."

"The place in Canarsie?"

Kelly didn't answer Brice. He turned on his seat to look into Levin's eyes. "Out with it, you have a problem."

"The guy there wash his hands before he handled the meat?" Levin said.

Kelly was still staring Levin down. "Fuck you," he said.

"Jesus Christ, lighten up," Brice said.

"He charge you?" Levin asked Kelly. "Sometimes they don't they see a badge. You show him yours?"

"You think I'm dirty? That what this is about?"

"Maybe," Levin said. "Except guys on the take know enough to share with their partners."

"Fuck your mother," Kelly said.

"Then I'd have to fuck yours and I'm not sure I'd want to."

Kelly showed teeth. "How about I break your fucking jaw?"

"That'd take too much time," Levin said. "I'd have to fall asleep first."

Kelly thumbed toward the curb. "You wanna take a walk and see?"

"Oh, oh, oh!" Brice yelled. "What the fuck already. Give it a break, both of you. I'm supposed to be the immature one here."

Levin and Kelly were still locked in a stare-down. Brice saw it and nudged Kelly so the senior detective had to turn to face him.

"What?" Kelly said.

"I think it's too hot today and it's getting to the both a yous," Brice said. "So why don't one of you go home and the other stay in the back and take a nap maybe. How's that sound?"

"That mean you prefer I leave?" Kelly said.

"We'll have time to smooch tomorrow. Mr. Happy back there is off."

"You volunteering for a double tonight?"

"I'm not," Levin said.

"I didn't ask you," Kelly said.

"In case you were wondering."

Kelly pointed a threatening finger at Levin. "One day you're gonna push and there won't be anybody around to stop something from happening."

"You mean like breaking my fucking jaw?"

"Yeah."

"But then I wouldn't be able to eat these wonderful lunches."

"No, I guess you wouldn't," he said. "Kike asshole."

Levin rewrapped the other half of his sandwich and set it on the seat alongside him. "And on that note, I'm gonna leave early," he said. "My stomach don't feel so good anyway. I think it's bad, the meat."

"That the pastrami?" Kelly said. "Yeah, well, I spit on that one."

"Jesus Christ," Brice said. "Don't say shit like that when people are eating."

Levin was out of the car. He walked around to the driver's side and winked at Brice. "See you when I see you," he said. He raised his right hand and wiggled his fingers at Kelly. "Tootles."

"Fuck you," Kelly said.

Levin winked at Brice again and left.

"I hate that fucking guy sometimes," Kelly said. "College-boy cocksucker thinks he's so fuckin' smart."

Brice glanced at his watch, then saw Levin skipping across the street. "You know what? He just might be."

"Fuck him," Kelly said. He reached over the seat and grabbed the other half of Levin's sandwich. "Three dollars," he said. "I ain't wasting it."

■ ■ ■

Levin had just turned the corner when a car pulled up alongside him at the curb. He glanced to his right and saw a black man behind the wheel. Levin thought the man looked official and kept walking.

A few steps later the driver tapped the horn.

"Detective?" he called.

Levin ignored him. The driver pulled up a few feet ahead of Levin and parked. This time Levin stopped. The driver extended his left arm out the window and presented his badge.

"Special Agent Stebenow," he said. "We need to talk."

Levin thought he recognized the man's voice. "What about?"

"Sean Kelly."

"Who's that?"

Stebenow turned the engine off and got out of the car. "I know you're with Internal Affairs and I'm not looking to blow your cover," he said. "I'm concerned for a witness of ours. I'm afraid your guy has maybe figured out who it is."

Levin looked up and down the block.

"We can take a drive if you want," Stebenow said.

"You have air-conditioning?"

"Sure," Stebenow said.

Levin walked around the back of the car.

"Stopping me like that, out in the open. That supposed to be a threat?" asked Levin once he was in the car.

"It's not like that," Stebenow said.

Levin pointed at the dashboard. "Air conditioner."

Stebenow brought up the windows before turning the air-conditioning on.

"You make the sign of the cross before when you said that, about not being here to blow my cover?" Levin said.

"I'm not jerking your chain," Stebenow said. "I have concerns, aside from my official capacity."

"You're a humanist, that it?"

"I believe I have a witness whose life is in danger."

"Don't we all?"

Stebenow turned the corner and pulled to the curb. "We have to go the full fifteen rounds on this?"

"This when you count to three?" Levin said.

The two men stared at one another until Stebenow closed his eyes. When he opened them Levin was still staring. Stebenow checked his side view mirror, then pulled away from the curb.

"It's a woman," he said.

"What's her name?"

"I can't say."

"There you go," Levin said. He pointed to a delicatessen off the corner. "You can let me out there."

"Hold on a minute. Hear me out."

"If you're looking to share information, you're gonna have to offer something up front. I'm not going first."

"You could have my ass in a sling for my approaching you," Stebenow said. "I'm out of my jurisdiction. I know that."

"So, what, you're just the trusting type?"

Stebenow parked again, this time turning the engine off. "I don't have anything for you," he said. "Nothing I can share beyond a fear of Kelly."

Levin waited for more.

"I think he's onto our witness," Stebenow said. "I think he might be watching her."

"I'm supposed to be more sympathetic now?"

"I'm being honest. I think Kelly is watching the girl."

"And you need me to verify it."

"It isn't about the case, trust me on this. I'm afraid for her life."

"You hear yourself?" Levin said.

"It isn't the case."

Levin motioned toward the delicatessen with his head. "Buy me a soda," he said.

Both men got out of the car. They walked to the corner and crossed the street. Stebenow followed Levin inside. Both men stopped under the breeze from the air conditioner.

"That feels good," Levin said.

He walked to an aluminum garbage pail filled with ice, reached an arm in and pulled a can of soda out. Stebenow grabbed a container of orange juice from an open refrigerator.

Levin had his wallet out before Stebenow. He paid for both drinks. "You owe me," he said.

They stepped outside where Levin popped the soda top and drank deep from the can. Stebenow pinched open the container and sipped at the juice.

There was a bench alongside a rack of newspapers. Levin sat on one end, Stebenow on the other end.

"It's Vento's girlfriend," the special agent said, "the one from his bar. There. Now you can have me canned, you want."

"And?"

"She's working off a drug bust. It was her boyfriend, but she was helping. They played tapes for her of him with another woman and she agreed to deal him away. He died inside. Natural causes, you can believe it. Somebody in the DEA was a friend of the federal prosecutor and when they found out she was involved with Eddie Vento, they put the hammer to her. 'Turn informant or get used to munching muff the next dozen years.' You know the deal. They laid it on thick, actually told her how big black bubble-butted butch-dykes like skinny white girls inside the joint. Scared her half to death, so she went to work for us."

"She was helping her boyfriend deal drugs, then dealt him away, she's not some babe in the woods."

"No, she's not. And chances are she'll fuck up the rest of her life down the road anyway, but this is one I'm not comfortable watching go down."

"As in there've been others."

"A couple, yeah."

"Maybe you're in the wrong line of work," Levin said. He took another deep drink from his can of soda.

"I'm definitely in the wrong line of work," Stebenow said, "but until I'm out, I can't watch another witness go down, not like this."

"I'm not fond of plea deals either, but that shit is out of my hands. I've come to accept it."

"And when they die, the witnesses? You ever have that?"

"Personally, no, but there are plenty dirty cops ate a bullet once they were nailed. You should know better."

"You know anything about my witness?"

"Nothing," Levin said. "If Kelly is tailing somebody for Vento, he's not discussing it where we can pick it up on a wire."

"He probably wouldn't. It's the girl Vento keeps in the apartment above his bar. She also bartends a few days a week."

"She have a name?"

"Bridget Malone."

"Malone? That's somewhat familiar. Don't forget, though, I get to listen to OC surveillance two months after the fact. Best case scenario, one month. Whatever's going on behind closed doors with Kelly and Vento, we don't know."

"Could you put somebody on him for this?"

"I'm not the top cop in my outfit. Talk to the guy is."

Stebenow frowned.

"You're talking a favor then, and a twenty-four-hour one, the surveillance," Levin said. "How'm I supposed to pull that off?"

"What if I offered my time?"

"And when you get spotted?"

"I might not."

Levin laughed. "And when you get spotted?"

"Look, the girl, she's got her own problems, don't get me wrong, but this time she's out of her league. She doesn't deserve to die."

"Most of the dopes get caught up with the mob never do," Levin said. "And then they find themselves in the middle of it and they make deals and put their trust in a system that could care less about them. Your federal prosecutor probably can't wait to run for mayor. Your SAC probably can't wait to become director. Guys like you can't wait to become SACs."

"And guys like you?" Stebenow said.

"I can't wait to retire," Levin said. He finished his soda and tossed the can in a small trash pail under the bench. "I was Catholic, I'd make the sign of the cross."

Stebenow waited for Levin's attention. "Will you look out for her?" he asked when he had it.

"I won't jeopardize my investigation or my job," Levin said. "I'll do what I can outside of that, but it won't be much. Don't forget I'm with Kelly most of the time. Unless you want I should ask him."

Stebenow went to the newspaper stand and wrote his phone number on the cover of a *Daily News*. "That's where you can reach me," he said.

"Okay," Levin said. "And you'll get my number if I ever use yours."

Stebenow headed back to his car. Levin watched until the special agent had crossed the street, then fished some change from his pocket, left it on the outdoor counter and grabbed the newspaper off the stand.

CHAPTER 27

The realtor said he would come before he finished for the day, somewhere between four and five. Kathleen straightened up around the house. She scrubbed the floor, cleaned the windows, then put out a vase of fresh flowers.

Billy spent most of the time in the basement before heading out without telling her where.

More secrets.

The Vasquez murder still bothered Kathleen. She looked through newspapers from earlier in the week and found the story in Monday's paper. Vasquez had been killed late Sunday night in Seaview Park. His wife, who was waiting in their car while he stepped out to do his business, found the body.

Kathleen knew the park from one of her trysts with Vasquez, one of a few she'd never mentioned to Billy. It was their second time together, when Billy was working nights. Vasquez had taken her to the park where they had sex in his car.

When she confessed the affair to Billy, she had only mentioned the first of their encounters and even then she had made up some of the story. Billy made her write it down in a spiral notebook along with several other accounts of her sexual history. Some she embellished, others she omitted. Reading from the notebook eventually replaced foreplay for Billy.

Still, she was sure she'd never told Billy about her and Vasquez in the park. She decided to check her notebook. She went to her closet where she kept it hidden on the top shelf under a row of shoe boxes.

Originally, he'd tricked her into the confession, making her jealous with a phony one of his own about having sex with an assistant district attorney. Kathleen's need to hurt him back was why she had told him about Vasquez, but she never regretted it until now. Their sex life had intensified. Later Billy's voyeurism encouraged her being with other men. Ultimately her physical pleasure was more intense with Billy, but the rituals he seemed to require were becoming uncomfortable.

Kathleen did love Billy and she knew he loved her; there was that between them, but as she positioned a folding chair in front of her open closet she remembered the first few lines of her written confession.

I met Victor Vasquez at a bowling alley one night while you were working late. I wore my tight white pants and saw him checking me out. We smiled at each other and later he bought me a drink at the bar there.

Kathleen had been too scared to give Billy a phony name and now she wondered if she should have. She hoped she was wrong as she brought the notebook down off the closet shelf. Then she opened the cover and saw the confession had been torn out.

■ ■ ■

It was a lot of work, but John was close to finished distributing the film a few minutes after four o'clock. Fitting the new stops before his regulars, he finished up his route on Merrick Boulevard in Valley Stream. It was a familiar stretch of road he knew from when he had shopped for a new car the year he was married to Nancy. They had visited Buick, Chrysler and Chevrolet dealerships there back before he'd realized the mistake he'd made marrying her.

Now he dropped off the film at a warehouse and used a pay phone to call Melinda.

"Hey, it's me," he said when she answered.

"John?"

"Yeah."

"Where are you?"

"Long Island, just finishing up."

"Where on the Island?"

"Valley Stream."

"That's close. How's your head?"

"Fine. It's fine." It nearly was; the headache barely bothered him.

"Feel like dinner?" Melinda asked.

"Sure. Should I pick you up?"

"Just come by. I'll cook."

"Really?"

"I can cook, John."

"I'll be there in half an hour."

"Steak okay?"

"Anything's fine."

"Great. See you in a few."

He hung up, realized he was excited just talking to her again and felt like a kid for it. John hadn't dated in more than six months. It was more than a year since he'd been intimate with a woman.

Things were looking up, he thought, at least in the short term.

Tomorrow would be another story as far as work went. Each stop would take longer than today. He'd have to count and recount the money, repeat the speech about anonymous head-counters who might've been there to make sure the counts were accurate and then he'd be traveling with a lot of cash back to the bar in Brooklyn. He was guessing he'd have close to ten thousand dollars.

As he drove away from the warehouse, John wondered if Nick Santorra had found the whistle yet. He knew it was childish, but he couldn't help smiling imagining the punk tearing his car apart.

He stopped at a liquor store near Melinda's place and picked up a bottle of red wine. He spotted a florist shop on his way out and crossed the street to buy a small bouquet of carnations. He presented them both when she answered her door wearing a white frilly blouse and tight hip-huggers.

"Ms. Cogan?" he said.

She ignored the gifts and gently touched the bruise on his forehead. "Should I make it better?"

"Yes."

Melinda lightly kissed the bruise, then made her way down to his lips. She was looking into his eyes when she took the flowers. John was still holding the wine when she pressed against him and their kissing became more involved. They barely made it through the kitchen before they started shedding their clothes.

■ ■ ■

It was getting more uncomfortable by the minute sitting in the Mustang all cramped up for hours on end in the relentless heat. Brice tried to stretch his legs and could feel they had gone numb. It took him a few minutes to get the blood flowing enough to get out of the car.

"I'm going for a walk," he told Kelly.

Kelly looked at his watch. "Don't get lost," he said.

Brice was starting to think a lot more about what Levin had been hinting at since they began this investigation. Kelly appeared to have an agenda all his own, and although Brice couldn't complain about the overtime or the ease of the work, he didn't like being taken for a fool.

He thought about calling Levin from a pay phone to ask him directly whether or not Kelly was dirty, but decided to wait the day out. Kelly seemed determined to sit surveillance at Berg's house, even though it didn't seem to make any sense. Brice decided to see his way through it before making up his own mind.

It was five-thirty when he returned to the car. He cursed under his breath when he saw Kelly had moved from the passenger seat to behind the steering wheel. Uncomfortable with anyone sitting in his seat, Brice said he'd take the wheel again.

"Afraid I might touch something I shouldn't?" Kelly said.

"Something like that," Brice said.

Kelly got out of the car and walked around the front. He stopped to stretch before getting back in on the passenger side. Brice had to readjust his seat.

"Excuse me for having longer legs than you," Kelly said.

"Why you should've stayed on your side," Brice said.

"You take this car too serious, kid."

"I love this car."

"Yeah, I know. Maybe you should use it to get laid."

Brice looked at his watch. "Maybe I do," he said.

"I hope so. It's not healthy a kid your age isn't chasing gash. Car like this, you should have your way with the young ones. Unless you're one of those whacko car buffs gets wood looking at racing magazines."

Brice turned to Kelly, thought about what his lover would say and couldn't help but smirk.

"You find me amusing, do you?" Kelly said.

Brice said, "We gonna be here much longer?"

"Another half hour or so. That okay with you?"

"Dandy."

The two sat in silence another twenty minutes before a blue Pontiac pulled up in front of George Berg's house.

"Here we go," Kelly said.

"Here we go what?"

"This guy here. He's the one with the films."

"He is? How do we know that?"

"Informants."

"What informants?"

"Mine," said Kelly as he got out of the car.

CHAPTER 28

Even if she didn't help him rip off John Albano the next day, Holly could still help Louis get away. It was one reason to let her cry on his shoulder today. It was what he was thinking when he parked near her dorm on LaGuardia Place.

The worst that might happen was a welcome afternoon fuck. Louis was tired of waiting for the rash to go away and had been teased beyond reason by both Sharon Dowell and his ex-wife. Holly wasn't all that good in bed, nowhere near Nancy, but she seemed to give a little more effort when she was feeling guilty.

He met up with her at the dorm on University Place and could tell she had been crying. They started walking toward Washington Square Park when Louis remembered that was where Myra claimed she trolled for customers on her roller skates. He took Holly by the hand and turned her in the opposite direction.

"I'm not sure I should even be here," he told her. "I feel kind of stupid, tell you the truth."

"I'm grateful you came," said Holly, squeezing his hand. "Really, I am. I was afraid to leave my room. He hasn't stopped calling. I was afraid he'd be outside when I left."

"Except you dumped me for the guy."

"Don't be angry with me, Louis, please. I made a mistake."

"Because he turned out to be a pervert? Wasn't for that, you'd be with him right now."

"I was stupid about him. I didn't realize it at the time."

They walked in silence until they reached Houston Street. Louis guided her west toward Sixth Avenue.

"And don't think I don't know you wouldn't have been interested in him unless you were bored with me," he said.

"It was a mistake," Holly repeated.

Louis put on the drama and sighed. "I thought about it, what you said on the phone, and I think he should pay, this perverted fuck."

"I'd rather just forget it," Holly said. "It's too embarrassing."

"He probably counts on that."

"I don't care."

He was thinking there might be a few bucks in blackmailing the professor. At least it was worth a try.

"He probably does this to a dozen girls a year," Louis said. "Gets them up to his apartment like that. He probably scores with most of them, too."

"I don't want to think about it. Please, Louis."

"Who was it? At least tell me that. The guy you left me standing in the park alone for the other night? That one?"

She blushed before shaking her head and Louis knew he had guessed right.

"He really a history teacher? What'd you say it was again, the Inquisition you had to study for?"

"I lied," Holly said. "Sociology, he teaches that."

"What's his name?"

"Please forget it," Holly said. "I'm glad you came. I feel a lot better you're here now."

"So will that pervert feel better if you don't do anything."

"What can I do? I'll look just as bad as him. It's too embarrassing."

"There are other ways he can pay, Holly."

She stopped walking. "What are you talking about?"

"Money."

"I don't want any."

"So give it to your organization. That'd teach him."

"No, I'm not doing that. It's blackmail."

Louis took her hand again. They continued walking until they reached Sixth Avenue.

"Can I go home with you tonight?" she asked.

"I'm not sure we should do that."

"Please?"

He didn't really want her spending the night at his place. He decided to downplay the idea. "It still doesn't feel right," he said. "Not after this. Not so soon."

Holly sniffled. "You must hate me now."

"I could never hate you. I think I love you. I think I did, but you have to admit I have a right to think things over. You did dump me."

"I don't want to go back to the dorm tonight," she said.

"I can back the guy off. At least let me do that."

"I don't want to involve you, Louis. This was my fault."

"He shouldn't get away with it. I'll just tell him to leave you alone, to stay the fuck away."

Holly went silent.

"It isn't easy knowing the girl you might've been in love with dumped you for some smooth-talking college prick, never mind he almost raped her."

Holly sniffled again.

"A guy is supposed to walk away from that without an ounce of satisfaction? Not this guy."

Holly avoided his eyes.

"Alright," Louis said, "have it your way."

He started to walk away, but she grabbed one of his hands. "You promise not to hit him? He didn't touch me, I swear."

Louis made her wait for his answer.

"I don't want you to get in trouble," she said.

"I promise I won't hit him," Louis said.

"You mean it?"

"There's no winning with you, is there?"

He started to turn away again when Holly pulled him back in the direction of the dorm.

■　■　■

Kelly examined the four reels of film they found in the trunk of the Pontiac. He held one up and turned to the driver.

"What's this?" he asked.

The driver shook his head. "Beats me," he said.

"Loops," Brice said.

"What's a loop?"

"A short. An eight-to-ten minute film they use in the sex joints in the city. The ones where the slime balls drop a quarter in the slot and jerk off."

"How you know so much about it?" Kelly said.

"They gave a class on the various forms of pornography when I transferred in," Brice said. "They covered the loop thing."

Kelly turned to the driver again. "Where's the movie?"

"What movie?"

"Don't jerk my chain, asshole."

"I don't know nothing about a movie."

Brice looked to George Berg to see if he was smiling.

Kelly frisked the driver behind the car. The trunk was open.

Brice read from the driver's license: "Nicholas Michael Santorra. What are you doing out here, Nicholas?"

"Stopping to see a guy for a friend," Santorra said.

"George here the guy you're stopping to see or the friend?"

"I know a guy he knows," Berg said.

"And the mutual friend's name is?" Brice asked.

Santorra shook his head. "I forget," he said.

"Me, too," Berg said.

Kelly had unwound one of the reels of film and was holding it up to the light. "Two broads," he said. "All they do is kiss. They don't even take their clothes off." He turned to Santorra. "They all like this?"

"I have no idea," Santorra said. "I didn't even know they were in there."

"Yeah, right," Kelly said. He turned to Berg. "This what you were waiting for all day?"

"I don't know anything about that stuff," Berg said.

"You're full of shit," Kelly said. "The both of you are."

Brice rolled his eyes. He couldn't believe this was what he had wasted two days waiting for. He thought about Levin again and how he was probably enjoying a nice cool drink in an air-conditioned bar somewhere.

"Am I under arrest?" Santorra asked.

"Shut the fuck up," Kelly said.

"Am I?" Berg said.

Kelly gathered the four reels of film together and headed back toward Brice's car.

"Detective?" Berg said to Brice.

Brice tossed Santorra's wallet inside the trunk.

"Brice!" Kelly yelled.

"Can we go?" Santorra asked. "I don't want to be accused of fleeing the scene."

Brice gave Santorra a hard stare.

"Detective?" Berg repeated.

Brice ignored Berg and headed back to his car.

CHAPTER 29

They had gone at it a few times before they both collapsed and fell asleep. When John woke up, it was from his stomach growling. He saw it was a few minutes before eight o'clock and nudged Melinda from her sleep.

"Hey," she said, "I was dreaming."

"Sorry," John said. "It's getting late. We should order something or go out."

"Dinner?"

"I'm pretty hungry."

"I can make something," she said through a yawn. "Oh, excuse me."

"I remember something about steaks, but we should probably order out now."

She pulled the covers off. "Let me wash up first."

John waited for her to finish in the bathroom, then used it himself while she brewed a fresh pot of coffee. They had agreed on Chinese. She was calling the order in when he joined her in the kitchen.

Melinda wore an open terry cloth robe. John was in his boxers. She poured the coffee at the table and sat across from him.

"This was a first for me," she said. "I'm serious."

"Me, too," John said. "I mean going more than once so soon after. I usually need a couple of hours to recover."

He sipped his coffee.

"You can stay the night if you'd like," she said.

"I don't have a change of clothes."

"I can wash those."

"That'd be great. It'll give me a head start in the morning."

"To go to work, which is no longer driving for a car service, but might still be a construction job you had this week, but you never really told me yet."

John looked at her a moment, trying to phrase what he was about to say so she wouldn't ask anything else about his job. "A different form of driving," he finally said.

"Except you had to think about it first. Why's that?"

So much for careful phrasing, he thought.

"Uh-oh," Melinda said. "I'd rather know up front, John, before we're anymore involved than we already are."

He was embarrassed to tell her, yet he knew he had to. Melinda wasn't the type of woman to ignore lies. He sipped his coffee, but couldn't speak.

"John?" she said. "What's it about?"

There it was. He took a deep breath, looked into her eyes and told her. He could tell she was upset by her expressions. The doorbell rang and she closed her robe to answer it. He saw it was the food delivery and passed her a five-dollar bill.

After retrieving their meal from the delivery man, Melinda set the table. They ate in silence. John wondered if she would ask him to leave when they were finished. He wouldn't blame her if she did. She was clearing the table when he asked her what she thought.

"Does it have to do with what happened outside the other night when you were jumped?"

"What? Oh, no, no way. I don't know what that was about."

"Because there was a guy there with a gun that stopped it, except we don't know what happened after that, do we?"

"I have no idea what that was about. I swear."

"Well, then I think you made a mistake."

"Yeah, and?"

"You lied to me."

"About borrowing money. I apologize."

"I don't like liars, John. I hate them."

He waited. After a pause, Melinda asked, "Is there anything else you lied about?"

"No."

There was a long pause of silence before Melinda said, "You need to get yourself out of this."

"How?"

"Get a new job, for one thing. As soon as possible."

"It's not that easy. I can't walk away before I have something to replace the money I'm making now."

"Suppose it takes a while before you find one?"

"Then I'll have to wait. I have responsibilities I can't ignore."

"Suppose it takes a year?"

"It won't."

"Suppose it does."

"Then it'll take a year. I don't have other options right now. I have to make a living."

Melinda bit into an egg roll.

"I guess you'll hold it against me," he said.

"Your poor judgment or what you're doing on weekends?"

John didn't answer.

Melinda said, "I don't think we can go forward like this."

"We can try."

"I think you're a good guy. Maybe one of the really good ones, but I also think you should've run away from those people instead of going to work for them."

"I did that and I wouldn't have met you."

"That's not close to being funny."

"It wasn't meant to be."

"I guess I'm disappointed," she said. "I don't have a right to be, but I am. I hate to see a good guy get dragged down and I certainly wouldn't want to get dragged down with him. Then again, we're not there yet, so...."

She was being vague. He needed clarity. "So what comes next? You throw me out, you let me stay, what?"

"Tonight? You can stay if you want. I'll have to think about us some more, though, I won't lie to you about that. I don't want to get involved with somebody destined for jail or an early death."

"Nobody is going to kill me," John said. "And I have no intention of going to jail."

"You get caught driving those films around with all that money you'll have tomorrow, it won't make a difference what your intentions are. I mean, those people...."

John knew her concerns were genuine, but he had bills to pay and a kid to support. He couldn't leave the one job without another.

"Maybe I should go," he said.

"Yeah," Melinda said. "I think maybe you should."

■   ■   ■

Billy Hastings had decided against the sound suppressor and left it in the basement. He still had the .38 he had used to kill two men and had to get rid of it. He pulled off the parkway a few hundred yards short of the first bridge past the Rockaway Parkway exit and spent a few minutes covering the gun with black electric tape. When it was fully covered and then some, he got out of the car, walked to the crest of the bridge and let the gun drop into the middle of Spring Creek.

Five minutes later he drove to the Cross Bay Boulevard exit, made one left turn, then drove a few lights before he could make a U-turn and head back toward the exit for the Belt Parkway heading west.

This time he got off at the exit and drove the length of Rockaway Parkway until he passed the building where John Albano lived. The old man he had spotted sitting on the stoop a few nights ago was there again now. Billy looked away from the geezer as he turned the near corner.

The apartment building was close to the last stop on the L train on Rockaway Parkway. The firehouse and the Sixty-ninth Police Precinct were also nearby. Billy had served his first two years on the force at the Sixty-ninth. The area was mostly commercial with a lot of local traffic bottlenecked between Flatlands Avenue and the train station on Glenwood Road. Billy parked a few blocks off the main drag and walked back toward Rockaway Parkway. He had disguised himself with a blonde wig, fake eyeglasses and an exaggerated limp. Police experience had taught him how most people avoided looking into handicapped people's eyes.

He stopped for a slice of pizza and a soda and could see Albano's building on the next block from where he stood outside the pizza parlor. His mind wandered to an image of Kathleen with Albano entering the same building; Albano's hands around her waist as they climbed the stairs to his apartment. Billy imagined them kissing inside the apartment doorway before Albano guided her into the bedroom. He imagined them shedding their clothes and then the look on Kathleen's face as Albano positioned himself between her legs.

Fire engine horns blared from inside the firehouse and interrupted Billy's daydream. A single fireman stood in the middle of Rockaway Parkway to halt traffic while the engines pulled out of the garage. Billy was impressed with how fast they were on their way. Vehicular street traffic had been halted less than a minute.

He walked in the same direction the fire engines had gone, stopping once to bend over and tap the gun he was carrying in an ankle holster. Today it was his weapon of choice, a Walther PPK. Five years ago he had killed a perp from across Kings Highway with a single shot to the forehead using the same gun. It was what he thought about as he headed toward John Albano's address; if it became too inconvenient getting up close, he could always shoot from a safer distance.

He was close to the building when he saw the old man was no longer sitting on the stoop.

CHAPTER 30

The car had been making noise all day and now it was driving Nick crazy. He pulled into a gas station on Sunrise Highway and asked the attendant there to check out the sound his car was making. The attendant said the mechanic was busy and that he couldn't leave the pumps unattended.

"I can't leave the thing here overnight," Nick told him. "How the hell would I get home?"

"What kind of noise is it?" the attendant asked.

"A high-pitch sound. I don't get it until I hit thirty miles an hour or so. It's loud on the highway. Someone might've fucked with my engine, put sugar in the tank or something. I don't know, I'm not a mechanic."

"If you want we can put it on a lift and take a quick look, but I can't drive it. I'm on the pumps."

"Alright," Nick told him. "Can I use your phone in the meantime? I gotta make a few calls."

"Sure, go ahead. I'll put the car up."

"In the office?" Nick said.

"Yeah," the mechanic said. He waited until Nick was out of earshot and added, "You're welcome."

Nick called Fast Eddie's and left the station number for someone to call back. Ten minutes later the phone rang. He picked it up before it disturbed the mechanic.

"It's me," he answered.

"Yeah?" Eddie Vento said.

"I got stopped," Nick told him.

"And?"

"Just like you said. They took the loop reels and left. Nothing after that."

"Good."

"Although I gotta tell you, it wasn't easy not slapping one of those cops in the face. He had a big mouth."

"Yeah, well, that would've gone over great, you hitting some cop. Aside from the fact they would've redid your face for you, it would've given me a headache I don't need."

"Why I stayed calm."

There was a pause where Nick was sure Vento huffed.

"That it?" Vento said.

"Yeah. I had to stop at a gas station—"

The line went dead. Vento had hung up.

"Fuck you, too," Nick said.

He went out to the garage where the mechanic was pointing up at something at the bottom rear of the car. The attendant was laughing.

"The fuck is so funny?" Nick said.

"That," the mechanic said.

Nick stepped closer but couldn't make out what it was taped to the bottom of the tailpipe.

"What is it?" he said.

"Why you heard a noise," the attendant said.

"This a quiz game?" Nick said.

"It's a whistle," the mechanic said. "Somebody taped one to your muffler tailpipe."

"That son of a bitch," Nick said.

"No harm done. We just have to take it off."

"Then do it," Nick said. "I don't have all fuckin' day to amuse you two."

He watched as his car was lowered enough so the whistle could be removed. "You want it?" the attendant asked after taking it off.

"Yeah," Nick said.

A few minutes later, after giving the attendant two dollars and getting a dirty look as if the guy had spent half the day rebuilding an engine, Nick was on his way home. He considered driving straight to Brooklyn and returning the favor by taping the same whistle to John Albano's tailpipe, there would be some justice in that, but Nick preferred doing something to the Buick that would cost Albano a lot more than two dollars.

The first thing that came to mind was a windshield, maybe both. It was illegal to drive a car with a broken windshield so Albano would have to have them repaired. When that happened, Nick was thinking he could either pour a couple pounds of sugar in the Buick's gas tank or just wait until the windshields were repaired before breaking the glass again.

There were a few things he could do to keep John Albano behind the eight ball. Then he remembered Stanislaus Bartosz and Nick pulled to the curb to call the Polack and find out what the fuck had happened, if anything, the night before. He tried the bar where he'd spotted Bartosz on Cross Bay Boulevard and was stunned when he learned the bad news.

"The big guy's dead," the bartender said. "Some kids found him near Fountain Avenue. It's on the news."

Nick was stunned. Bartosz was a genuine tough guy. Nick couldn't imagine somebody like Albano getting the drop on him.

Unless it was somebody else, he wondered.

He got back in the car and lit a cigarette. He smoked it to the filter before he decided Bartosz's death had to have been mob-related. The Polack must've had a beef with somebody, maybe a wiseguy since his body was found near Fountain Avenue. The area had a reputation for being a mob dumping ground.

Feeling a little more relieved, Nick returned to daydreaming about fucking with John Albano's wallet. Albano would have to skim off the top to pay for car repairs. Nick could bring it to Eddie Vento's attention and offer to take care of the problem himself. It would be a double bonus to make his bones whacking somebody he hated.

Nick spent most of the rest of his drive home daydreaming about killing Albano. The rest of the time he was thinking about the ceremony when he would become a made man. Then, instead of taking shit from Eddie Vento, he could give it to somebody else.

■   ■   ■

"What is it you want?" the professor had asked.

Louis could tell the man was scared. "I'm not here to register for one of your classes," he said.

The professor looked confused.

"Has to do with how you can't keep it in your pants," Louis said. "I'm here for some money."

The professor swallowed hard. "How much?"

"What've you got?"

"On me? Not much."

"Then you'd better find some, because I'm not leaving here without something makes Holly feel better about herself."

Holly had rung the bell and then answered when the professor asked who it was. Louis had gone in when the door was buzzed and left her waiting outside. The professor had turned pale when he saw Louis at his apartment door.

"Look," he said. "I already went and borrowed a few dollars this morning. I tried to call Holly all day and wanted to settle this before it got out of hand."

"You apologize?"

"No, not yet. She wouldn't let me."

Louis rubbed two fingers together. "Show her some love."

"The money?"

"Why you're a professor."

"I guess I don't have a choice."

"You should've thought of that before you grabbed your sausage."

"I can't explain how that happened," the professor said. "All I can say is I'm sorry."

Louis put his hand out and the professor handed him the five one-hundred dollar bills. He pocketed three of the five bills on his way down the stairs and showed Holly the other two in the vestibule. She told him she didn't want the money. He kissed her on the forehead.

That had been earlier. Now he was on his way home after taking Holly back to the dorm and promising her he'd reconsider their situation overnight. He had told her he'd get back to her sometime tomorrow after she had taken her best shot at getting him to take her home. The way he saw it, Louis had done her a favor waiting until his rash was completely gone before screwing her again anyway. Not that he told her about the crabs he'd picked up not too far from her dorm, but he knew that putting her off was the smart play and that if he was going to need her again it would be the next day when he robbed Albano.

Tonight he preferred spending the night alone.

And if he didn't need Holly, he'd never see or talk to her again. It wasn't like she was any great shakes in bed anyway.

■ ■ ■

Levin had just finished listening to the last set of surveillance tapes when Brice showed up at his front door. It was a few minutes after ten o'clock. Levin stashed the tapes under a pillow and the recorder under the couch but didn't notice he'd left a notepad he'd been using on the coffee table.

He turned on the television and found preseason football highlights before answering the bell.

Brice looked exhausted. Levin showed him into the kitchen and handed him a cold beer from the refrigerator. They returned to the living room where Levin made sure to sit on the couch. Brice sat in an armchair facing the couch.

"Everything okay?" Levin asked.

"This investigation is bullshit," Brice said.

"Yeah, so?"

"You think Kelly's on the take?"

"That's a heavy accusation. What do you think?"

"I didn't accuse," Brice said. "I asked. And I asked you first."

"Fair enough. It's not easy being the one to throw the first stone. I'm not enthused about working with him, I'll tell you that much."

"It's a bullshit stakeout."

"Yep."

"Doesn't that mean something?"

"Maybe. Maybe not."

Brice lit a cigarette. "I thought you were pushing it pretty hard with him. Looked like the two of you would've gone at it I wasn't there."

"That was a pissing contest, kid. Nothing more than that."

"It seemed like more."

"Trust me," Levin said.

"Well, I wouldn't want to go down with him if he is dirty. I don't like the idea of being made a fool of, either."

"Could be he's keeping things to himself because he doesn't want us involved."

"He ever offer you money?"

"Today was the first time he's ever offered anything, that lunch he bought us."

Brice set his beer down to rub his face with both hands.

"You're thinking too much," Levin said.

"He's dirty, it's with the mob," Brice said.

"They're the ones pushing the film."

"That's the other thing, that film. I mean, really, who gives a shit? Not me."

"Probably not Kelly either, but you can always take it up with the honorable Whitman Knapp or Mayor Lindsey, or our beloved commissioner, Mr. Murphy, you can get a few minutes with him. Chasing this dopey film is policy right now. Bullshit policy, but policy. From the White House to the Gracie Mansion, *Deep Throat* is supposed to be deep-sixed."

"Then Kelly's jerking us off," Brice said. "The way he's pursuing it."

Levin took a sip of beer.

"What're we supposed to do?" Brice asked. "Assuming he's dirty, I mean."

"There's only a few things you can do. Ask for a transfer, a piece of the action, if there is any, or shut up and ignore the man. Do what he says within reason and if it doesn't feel right, get a stomach ache."

"Like you did today."

"I'll guarantee you the rest of my day was better'n yours."

"There's nothing else?" Brice said. "What about the license plates we took down? I ran those." He pulled his wallet out, thumbed through it until he found a piece of paper and read from it. "Logan, Greco, Isolano, Cohen, Bloom, Albano and then the guy we stopped, Santorra."

"Johnny Porno," Levin said.

"Who?"

"Albano."

"Oh, yeah, well, Kelly seemed most interested in him, too, that name afterward."

"Maybe he's the sacrificial lamb. A guy Kelly can justify himself with, this detail, if he needs to bring somebody in."

"Then he is dirty."

"If, I said. If he needs to bring somebody in."

"This is bullshit," Brice said. "Either he is or he isn't." He guzzled what was left of his beer.

"I'll get you another one," Levin said.

Brice sat on the couch. As he did so he noticed a notebook on the end table. He saw Kelly's name scribbled alongside a date and then a line from that date to another. He tried to read the next name, but couldn't make it out. He picked up the notebook when Levin returned with a fresh beer.

"What's this?" Brice said.

Levin handed off the beer and took the notebook.

"It's personal," he said.

"What, you dating Kelly or something?"

"That'd be personal, too."

"Holy shit, Levin. If you're Internal Affairs, let me in on the joke."

Levin brought the notebook to his bedroom. He shut the door behind him when he returned.

"Well?" Brice said.

"Maybe you wanna calm your jets," Levin said. "You're the new kid on the block. I look into something, nobody'll question it. I forget to tell Kelly, he'll throw one of his fits, but that's all he'll do. You do it and he'll bounce you."

"You think the guy is dirty or not?"

"He might be, but that's all I'm willing to say and it's way more than you better say. I don't particularly like Kelly. Fact I think he's a scumbag. But if he's clean I don't wanna see him ruined by rumor."

"Jesus Christ, you don't make it easy. The hell do I do?"

"I'd think twice about doing anything. Prostitution, gambling, fuck films, they're all harmless vices. Ever hear that before? You do anything to Kelly you'll be selling your soul for the wrong price. If Kelly's dirty and he may well be, let Internal Affairs handle it. It's what they're there for."

"Fine. What about Albano? You think he'll give us something if he thinks he's going down?"

"I don't know, maybe. Maybe he walks away. I'm not sure we can approach him yet. Not if Kelly's got an eye on him. I think it best for now we just play the game the way Kelly wants." He motioned back toward the bedroom. "What we do on our own, we keep to ourselves. At least for now we do."

Brice took a long swig from the beer bottle, then another, killing it. He set the empty down on the coffee table and noticed a football magazine was opened to the New York Jets schedule. "I'm starting to wish I had a hobby," he said.

CHAPTER 31

The night he was knocked out in the bar Billy hadn't told his wife he was stopping there on business. Their original plan was to have drinks in a West Village place Kathleen had found in a swingers magazine. The Happy Couples lounge had advertised soft and hard swing nights, the former being introductory for newcomers to the lifestyle and the latter for more experienced couples. Billy had agreed to arrange a soft swing where he would watch Kathleen engage in foreplay with another couple.

They had stopped at the Williamsburg bar for him to sell information he had glommed off a drug dealer he'd shaken down earlier in the week. An Hispanic illegal was putting out street loans from a bodega close to Vento's bar.

The wiseguy had acted indifferently to the information about the bodega and said, "What's that got to do with me, some spic is putting out money?"

"You could tax the guy for protection money or put him to work soliciting loans for you," Billy had said. "Or you could take him for what he is, competition."

"Those people do that shit with their own kind," Vento had said. "They charge them five, up to ten percent, depending on the turnaround. My customers wouldn't go to some bodega unless they were looking to beat the guy. I'm not worried about it."

"The guy is up the block and you're not worried?"

"Not at all."

It had frustrated Billy that the wiseguy wasn't biting. "Maybe I should work for him," he had said.

"Now you're talking out your ass," Vento had said.

"You think so, huh?"

"I also think you should lay off my bartenders when you're looking for lunch money," Vento said. "That badge can get you in as much trouble as you can make with it."

"That a threat?"

Vento hadn't answered.

Billy left the wiseguy's office and had gone upstairs where he saw John Albano getting cozy with Kathleen. The way Vento's men seemed to be enjoying it, Billy had felt he had to act. The fact Albano had tried to back down wasn't enough, not with all those goombahs in the same room. Later he would learn from a friend with the Organized Crime squad that Vento had installed cameras in the ceiling at either end of the bar and the entire fiasco had been caught on film.

Billy knew then he didn't have long before he'd be forced to resign. Colleagues on the police force had warned him against retributions. So long as Eddie Vento had a tape of police misconduct in a bar under surveillance, those within the wiseguy's circle were not to be harassed in any way, shape or form. Billy also knew that guys like Sean Kelly were more interested in protecting their own dirty money than helping a fellow cop.

That had been before. Since he'd become a civilian again, Billy figured he could do whatever he wanted.

Earlier this evening he'd driven to Canarsie and parked on the same street where he'd nearly run John Albano over almost a week ago. Without the old man blocking the stoop, Billy had walked inside the building, then up the stairs to where Albano lived. A few seconds later he was inside the apartment.

Except for a mostly empty refrigerator with some questionable leftovers, the apartment was neater than Billy had expected. Albano used a hamper to store his laundry and kept his sink clear of dirty dishes. The floors were also clean. Billy was extra impressed when he saw the bed was made.

He spent four hours waiting in Albano's apartment after his initial walkthrough. Billy was conscious of pacing the floor and spent most of the time sitting on a folding chair he'd found in the bedroom. It was close to ten o'clock when he finally gave up. Albano's murder would have to wait yet another day.

Half an hour later Billy pulled into his driveway and noticed the lights were out. He peeked through one of the garage-door windows and saw Kathleen's Karmann Ghia was missing. Then he went inside the house, turned on the kitchen light, and saw the note taped to the refrigerator door.

■ ■ ■

After learning about the dirty detective on Eddie Vento's payroll, Special Agent Stebenow became fearful for informant Bridget Malone's life. Two years earlier, in a Philadelphia investigation against the mob there, a thirty-three year old father of four informant was used as bait when his name was purposely released to the local media as a witness for the prosecution in a local mob trial.

Bernard Dillon was executed outside his South Philadelphia home the same night his name was made public. A clerical error was offered as the excuse for the release of his name, except Stebenow knew it was bullshit. When the surveillance cameras that had been positioned across the street from Dillon's home failed to capture his murder, the case was closed and the federal prosecutor moved on to another. Four kids had lost a father in the collateral damage of the overzealous prosecution.

Dillon's needless death had haunted Stebenow ever since. Tonight, after a protracted argument with his wife over her unwillingness to see him since their separation, he told her he was quitting the bureau at the end of the month.

"And how do you expect to live?" she'd said. "You're going to have to help me until I'm working again."

"I'm going to teach again."

"You're crazy. That's a big cut in salary. Wouldn't you be better off transferring within the Bureau?"

"We already talked about this. No."

"I think you're making a mistake."

"I can't do this anymore."

"And I can't stand to hear about it anymore."

Stebenow smirked on his end of the line. It had become his wife's mantra, complaining about his inability to cope with his job. Tonight she'd seemed more mean-spirited than usual.

"I don't want to fight about it," he'd told her.

"You're the one called me."

"I was looking for support."

"Then you called the wrong person," his wife had said before hanging up.

That had been an hour before he left his apartment. Tonight Stebenow was determined to keep Bridget Malone from suffering a fate similar to that of Bernard Dillon. Tonight he was following the man he believed posed the greatest threat to her safety, NYPD Lieutenant Detective Sean Kelly.

Cautious of being spotted by the Internal Affairs detectives investigating Kelly, Stebenow began his surveillance from a car parked up the street from the bar he'd followed Bridget Malone and two of her girlfriends to earlier the same day. The three women sat at one of a few outdoor tables bounded by a rope and chain fence.

According to Bridget, Kelly had met her a few days ago after she'd spent time at the same bar. Assuming most people were creatures of habit, the special agent was guessing Kelly had already trailed her to the bar and would do so again. Less than two hours into his surveillance, his hunch proved right.

Kelly showed up wearing a New York Yankees baseball cap, a multicolored Woodstock T-shirt, gray sweatpants and high-top sneakers. He took a seat on a bench outside a pizza parlor directly across the street from the bar. The dirty cop used a newspaper to shield his face.

Stebenow couldn't push his luck too long; Internal Affairs surveillance might spot him. If Bridget didn't leave before long, he'd have to get her attention and make sure she returned to her apartment. A few minutes before midnight he was forced to move faster than he'd imagined.

■ ■ ■

Detective Sean Kelly had called in a favor with an Irish street gang from Manhattan earlier in the day and was waiting for it to arrive as he nursed his second Coke in less than half an hour. He'd followed Bridget Malone earlier in the week from her apartment to the bar across the street and had figured she'd be there again when she wasn't working at Fast Eddie's.

Kelly could retire in just a few more years and he wasn't about to let some cocaine addict porno-queen wannabe take him down, not when he was so close.

The man he was waiting for finally showed a few minutes before midnight. Billy Quinn was a short, pug-nosed brawler with a prison scar across his forehead. He was missing several teeth and had already been drinking.

Kelly moved his conversation away from the pizza parlor to the curb. He stood behind a parked van to hide from view.

"You got something?" he asked Quinn.

"A shiv," said Quinn with a strong brogue. He opened his right hand to show Kelly.

"It's the table in the middle, so you'll have to haul ass once you do it. Subway's up the block around the corner to the left. You can duck in there or keep running, whatever you prefer, just don't head back this way. That mug you got isn't going to be hard to forget."

Quinn pulled a stocking from his pants pocket. "What this is for," he said. "It's on and off before they know what all."

Quinn turned to look across the street.

"Keep looking here at me," Kelly said. "It's the one with the dark hair. She's with the two blondes."

"What's her name?"

"Bridget, why?"

"Because I'll call to her right before so she turns and makes it easy."

He swiped his right thumb across his throat.

"Jesus Christ, telegraph it why don'tcha," Kelly said.

"Don't worry, I know what I'm about," Quinn said. "Or maybe you wanna give it a go?"

Kelly ignored the thug. "Give me until I'm at the end of the street behind you," he said. "I'll start walking in a second. Soon's I reach the corner I'll lift my arms up over my head like I'm yawning. That's when you move."

"Got it."

"You sure?"

"I just fuckin' said so, yeah?"

"Yeah, I guess you did," Kelly said.

He started walking and was halfway up the street when he saw a black guy get out of a car parked across the street. Something about the guy wasn't right. They made eye contact and Kelly quickly looked away. A few steps later he did a quick pirouette, as if he'd forgotten something and Kelly saw the black guy was waving to the women at Bridget's table. Then the guy stopped and turned toward Kelly again.

"Fuck," said Kelly a moment before he turned around again and started walking. He was fifty feet from the end of the block when he decided to raise his right arm up. He didn't look back until he made it to the corner. When he did, it was because the gunshot surprised him.

■　■　■

"Kelly's the one said it isn't natural you're not chasing women?" Mark Liston asked. He tapped the ash off his cigarette into the ashtray he held on his right thigh and took a long drag.

"Healthy," Brice said. "Kelly said it isn't healthy I'm not chasing gash."

"Gash?"

"What he calls it. Said I should be using the car to get laid unless I was one of those car buffs gets wood looking at racing magazines."

"We should do it on the hood of the car and send him a picture," Liston said. "Which do you think would make him gag first, that we're men or because I'm black?"

"Both," Brice said. "At least at first. After a while, though, I think it'd be you."

"The honky. Probably cheats on his wife with prostitutes, your boss."

"Probably, except I doubt he pays them."

Liston rubbed Brice's neck with his right hand. "What about Levin?" he asked. "You seem to like him."

"He's alright, I think," Brice said, "except he's being careful and I can't figure why. He's been around long enough to know whether Kelly is dirty or not, but he won't come out and say it. It's like he wants me to decide for myself."

"Maybe he's doing you a favor."

"What he said about him taking the flack if Kelly finds out he's looking into things without keeping him informed. Levin also knows something about the guy Kelly seemed interested in, Johnny Porno."

"Where do they get their names?"

"I don't know, but they are catchy."

Liston ran his hand up through Brice's hair. Brice leaned his head back and enjoyed the moment.

"Maybe Levin is protecting you."

"Maybe."

Brice leaned back into the neck massage.

"And you're sure Kelly is dirty."

"Pretty sure. And if he is, I'm not safe."

"You mean us?"

"I mean me."

"Because you don't count us or because you want to be chief of police some day?"

"Yeah, right. I'll settle for my twenty and a pension." Brice leaned over to check the time. "What time is it?" He saw and said, "Shit. I gotta go."

"Why not sleep in and leave in the morning?"

"Because if I oversleep it's not like I can catch up in half an hour. Stamford is an hour out doing seventy without traffic on ninety-five."

Brice was out of the bed and heading for the bathroom. Liston crushed his cigarette in the ashtray, set it on the night table, and got up to gather Brice's clothes. It was a few minutes before midnight. They had spent less than two hours together.

The toilet flushed and another minute passed before Brice returned from the bathroom. Liston handed Brice his pants.

"Be careful with your boss," he said. "I don't like the way he sounds. You trust Levin, stay close to him."

Brice was putting on his shirt. "I'm not sure I trust either of them," he said. "Levin's definitely more tolerant, but I'm not anywhere near willing to test him with this."

"I hate when you put it that way. It isn't this, Steven. It's us."

"Not to them."

"You don't know that yet."

"And I'm not willing to find out."

The two men kissed on the lips before Brice headed out of the bedroom with Liston following. They stopped at the door and kissed again, embracing one another this time.

"Be careful," Liston said.

"I will," Brice said.

"Love you."

"Love you, too."

Brice headed down the hallway toward the elevators while Liston watched from the doorway. Brice pressed the button for the elevator and turned to look back at his lover. The two men stared at one another until Brice smiled. Then the elevator doors opened and he stepped inside the car.

CHAPTER 32

He was up early to make sure the car was okay and found old man Elias waiting for him on the stoop.

"Don't tell me you just got home," John said.

"Alright, I don't tell you."

John remembered he owed the gas station money. "Can you lend me a few bucks?" he asked.

"How much?"

"Thirty'd probably do it."

"How's forty?"

"I don't need forty."

"Take it anyway."

"I'll have it for you tonight."

"Did I ask when you'd have it?"

"I appreciate it."

Elias had his wallet out. He pulled two twenties from inside. John saw the old man had left himself a few singles.

"You sure you'll be alright? Don't short yourself for me."

"Take it," said Elias, waving the money.

"Thanks," John said. He took the cash, pocketed it and headed across the street to his car.

"Hold on," Elias said.

John stopped to listen.

"I see somebody around here again. Somebody looking for you, I think."

"Somebody who?" John said.

"I know his name I tell you. I don't know." The old man touched his chest. "I feel it, eh? Somebody drives by, is looking. Couple of times now. I see him. He sees me."

"I have no idea," John said.

Elias tapped his forehead. "Be careful," he said. "Your head, eh?"

"I will," John said.

"Make sure."

John drove to the gas station, paid the balance he owed for the tires and filled his tank. He was determined to get an early start and went to Williamsburg to have breakfast around the corner from the bar. He would verify the Saturday counts as soon as Eugene opened the bar, then start on the new stops Vento had said he could finish before noon.

He thought about what had happened the night before, how things had started so great and then turned to crap so fast he still couldn't believe it.

One minute he was making love with a woman he genuinely felt for and an hour or two later it was over and he was on his way home alone.

Melinda was on his mind when he walked in the bar a few minutes after nine and saw Nick Santorra was wearing the whistle around his neck. John ignored the man and picked up the Saturday head count from the bartender. He was shocked when he saw the totals. If Sunday was anything close to Saturday, he would be carrying close to thirteen thousand dollars at the end of the day. The amount made him uncomfortable.

He left the bar before nine-thirty and used the BQE through Queens to the Grand Central Parkway. There was a Mets home game against the Giants that would generate traffic around the stadium later in the afternoon, but it was city-bound traffic returning from the Hamptons that would create problems later in the day.

It was a fast drive to the south shore where he collected from the new stops first. The films and cash were waiting at each location when he got there. He was finished before one o'clock. Then he started on his regular route and had to backtrack to the north shore.

The Meadowbrook Parkway was crowded heading towards Jones beach. John was grateful he was heading in the opposite direction. He thought about Nick Santorra and the whistle he had worn at the bar. Was it a threat of things to come? Was Santorra behind the assault the other night? It was more than possible, considering Santorra couldn't handle his own dirty work. Fifty bucks to a guy desperate enough was all it would take to dole out a beating. Considering the situation, John figured Santorra had hired a goon to do the job he couldn't do himself.

John also figured he'd have to be extra careful with the Buick when he parked it the next few nights. He was thinking he might pay the gas station where he'd bought the retread tires a few extra bucks to let him park there the next week or two.

He brought the windows all the way down and enjoyed the breeze as he took the exit for the Long Island Expressway. It was another hot, humid day. Although the weather forecast didn't include rain, it felt as if a thunderstorm was imminent.

John passed a station wagon filled with kids wearing baseball uniforms and thought of his son. He remembered how enthused his boy had been about going to the Yankees game later in the month. He would have to bring a camera and take some pictures. It was to be the last year the Yankees played at the stadium before renovations began. He knew Little Jack would appreciate the history when he was older.

He made it to Kings Park with a few minutes to spare. He took Kings Park Boulevard to Old Dock Road and found the warehouse where he'd dropped the film off the day before. A group of men were exiting the warehouse doors in the rear. John pulled up behind a box truck parked in the loading dock. He saw three men carrying posters and then another man examining a pair of the white panties. He wondered if Nick Santorra had spelled Linda Lovelace's name right on those.

A few minutes later, after finding his way through the loading dock, John spotted the guy in charge. Chris Cowans was disconnecting the projector while another man sold posters at the table where refreshments had been served. John saw there was beer, soda, potato chips, peanuts and sandwiches and wondered if Eddie Vento had a piece of the concession as well.

"Johnny Porno, right?" Cowans asked.

"The name's Albano," John said. "John Albano."

"Sorry," Cowans said. "The guy on the phone said...."

"What time you start?"

"Early. First showing was ten. Then another at noon. Yesterday we had five, though. Was a good night."

"They hitting you for the concession?"

Cowans motioned at the table. "Just the beverages," he said. "We have to buy from some distributor in Valley Stream. It's a few cents more than I could probably get it here, but we're making out alright."

"Good for you," John said.

Cowans handed John two stacks of cash bound with rubber bands. "We called in seven-fifty yesterday and had another two hundred today. Total should be nine-fifty."

John removed the rubber band from the larger bundle and began counting.

"Help yourself to whatever you want from the concession," Cowans said.

"Thanks. I might grab a soda."

"We sold a few posters, too. And two pair of the panties."

John stopped counting. "Give me a minute here," he said.

"Sorry."

"It's alright," John said. He continued counting.

■   ■   ■

Nathan had never met John Albano's mother before last night when he dropped his stepson off and this morning he wanted to call her to see how the kid was doing, but felt it wasn't his place, not since he'd left Nancy the night before.

It was an ugly fight Nancy had started in front of her son, and when Nathan lost his temper and called her a bitch, he'd felt rotten the kid had heard him. It had to do with the way she had been badmouthing the kid's father from the night before, claiming he was selfish and didn't care about his son or anybody else and that she was sick and tired of everyone coming to his defense when she was the one responsible for everything and everybody.

It was all nonsense, but Nathan felt guilty about maybe setting her off in the first place the afternoon she came home and found her ex-husband playing with his son in the basement. Maybe if he hadn't let the kid's father in she would've spared the boy some of her verbal poison.

There was no telling what her story was anymore. Nancy seemed to be playing a new angle since he first mentioned he might go to a lawyer. Nathan wasn't sure if it was an act or desperation. Nancy had grown accustomed to her lifestyle and wouldn't adjust well to change in a more practical direction.

When she brought it up the day before, how he better not think just because he divorced her she would move out of the house, Nathan had told her she could stay until he sold it.

"And then half is mine," she had declared.

"After the mortgage is paid," he'd told her.

"You pay that," she'd said. "I want half the value."

"It doesn't work like that."

"We'll see what my lawyer says."

"Fine," he had told her, "but the more we spend on lawyers, the less there'll be for either of us. And there's Jack to consider, too. You don't want to uproot him while some lawyer takes the lion's share of whatever there is."

"Don't you dare bring up my son to me," Nancy had raged. "That boy is no concern of yours. You try to spoil him to get him to like you, but he's my son. You're no different than his father. You do the fun things and I have to be the parent."

It was then Nathan lost it. "That's not true and you know it," he'd yelled. "His father is a good man. He does what he can and all you do is make it impossible for him."

Then she tried to make a bet with him Nathan still didn't understand. Something about how John wouldn't even respond if she called and told him his kid was in trouble, serious trouble, like if he was abducted or some nonsense.

Nathan had looked at her as if she were crazy. Then she put her hand out with her pinky extended like some twelve-year-old and said, "Make a bet, you're so sure. Come on, bet me."

He thought she had lost her mind and told her so.

"Oh, yeah?" she said. "I'm telling you right now if I called him up tomorrow while he's doing whatever he does all day with that dirty film and the people at that bar, John wouldn't even consider coming here to see what was wrong."

"You're wrong," Nathan had told her. "One-hundred-percent wrong."

"If I called and said Jack was kidnapped he wouldn't do a thing, that's how much he cares about his son."

Nathan had felt his face flush red. He pointed a threatening finger at her and spoke through clenched teeth as low as he could so the boy didn't hear him.

"You selfish bitch," he'd said. "Don't you ever say something like that again where your son could hear you. Show some decency. For God's sake, show some decency."

Nancy had been shocked at his outburst and had taken a few steps back. At least he thought so until she started in all over again. Then Nathan saw she wouldn't shut up unless he left. He asked if she was staying home or going out and did she want him to drop her son off at her ex-mother-in-law's.

"You know what?" Nancy had said. "Yes, I do. Take him there and today I'm going out for myself for a change and maybe tomorrow we'll see how much of a father John is after all."

Nathan didn't know what she had meant, but he was anxious to get the kid out of hearing distance as soon as possible. First he brought his stepson to McDonald's and tried to get him to talk about the Yankees, but Little Jack was clearly upset at his mother's tirade earlier. The boy wouldn't speak.

Then Nathan brought his stepson to John's mother and felt terrible when he had to shake hands with the boy before he left. He still didn't know if he'd ever see him again.

CHAPTER 33

The phone woke Louis a few minutes after nine in the morning. He had thought it would be Nancy and was surprised to hear Sharon Dowell's voice.

"Hey, Jerry was just up here for his birthday a couple few weeks ago," she said.

Louis was thinking. "Jerry who?" he said.

"Jerry Deep Throat, that's who."

"Jerry the director?"

"Yeah, we just missed him, but I have someone trying to track him down. Somebody close to the family."

"Great."

"I should know more in another day or so, maybe sooner."

"Great."

"And guess what else?"

"What?"

"The woman I spoke with knows of a place on the Island where they're showing the film."

"Where on the Island?"

"It's invitation only, but I'm sure I can get us in."

Louis flinched at her choice of the word "us."

"That's great," he said. "When?"

"I'll let you know soon as I find out."

"That's great, Sharon. I can't thank you enough."

"Sure you can, stud."

Louis forced a chuckle. "You have a dirty mind."

"I'll call you soon as I hear something."

"I appreciate it."

"Okay. You take care of yourself. That rash, I mean."

"Will do."

Louis hung up and was about to head down to the deli for coffee and a roll when the phone rang again. He assumed it was Sharon calling back and said, "Forget something?"

"I want to be there for you today," Holly said.

Louis was caught off guard.

"Louis?" she said.

"Holly?"

"I mean it," she said. "I want to be there for you today."

"Really?"

"Yes."

"What time is it?"

"Nine. Nine-fifteen."

"It's early."

"I'll bring bagels if you want."

"I don't know, Holly. I haven't had time to think. I appreciate your change in attitude, but... I don't know."

"You were there for me and I want to be there for you," she said. "I know today is important."

It couldn't hurt, he thought. "Okay," he said. "If you mean it."

"I do. Yes."

"Okay."

"I'll bring bagels?"

"Sure."

"Great. I'll leave in two minutes."

"Wear something sexy."

"Really?" she said enthusiastically.

"Yeah," Louis said. "I miss looking at you."

He hung up and examined his reflection in the television screen. He turned to his right, left, then back right again. He was losing definition. He'd have to start working out again if he was going to keep his edge.

Last night, after he'd planned on a quiet night alone to think things through, Nancy had showed up half in the bag wanting reassurance about their future. He fed her coffee until she was sober enough to repeat today's game plan without hesitation. It wasn't easy. Once she was completely sober, Nancy grew concerned something might go wrong and that she'd be left high and dry. Louis had to swear on his life that the money from the robbery would provide them a new future.

He turned on the television looking for a sports report to check on the night games he had bet the day before. He won three of the five, but the interest on the losses would leave him close to even on the day. His figures with the offices remained in the red.

He went down to the corner deli for his coffee and a newspaper. When he was back in the apartment Louis looked at the probable pitchers for Sunday and circled his picks. He wouldn't be able to call in his bets until the offices opened at noon. He reclined on the couch and took a short nap.

It was close to eleven when the door buzzer woke him.

"It's me," Holly's voice said through the intercom.

Louis buzzed her inside the lobby. He realized he would have to call Nancy from an outside line and unplugged his phone line. A minute later he answered Holly's knock and did a double take when he saw what she was wearing: tight bell-bottom hip-huggers, a tight white halter and open-toed sandals.

"Jesus Christ," he said, "you're beautiful."

Holly blushed as she held up a white paper bag. "Bagels."

He let her inside the apartment, kissing her on the cheek as she passed. The door closed behind them and she turned to kiss him on the mouth. It was a long, passionate kiss that instantly excited Louis. He remembered he was pressed for time and had to stop himself from getting into it.

"What you get?" he asked.

"Two coffees, made just now so they're fresh," Holly said.

Louis took the bag into the living room. They both sat on the couch. Holly put a leg up across his lap.

"I can't," he said. "Believe me, I'd love to. Especially the way you look right now. You're fucking gorgeous."

She pouted as she withdrew her leg from his lap. "Bummer," she said. "Later?"

"Absolutely."

"Promise."

"I promise."

They had their bagels and coffee before Louis took a shower and Holly watched the news. It was close to eleven-thirty when he told her he had to run out for cigarettes. Then he called Nancy from a pay phone on Jamaica Avenue. She answered with a yawn after three rings.

"You're just getting up?" he said.

"Yeah, I have a headache. It'll go away soon as I have some coffee."

"You didn't put up a pot yet?"

"I just woke up. You just did that, woke me."

His teeth clenched listening to her yawn.

"You need to get moving and pick up the kid," he said.

"I know. I also need a shower and coffee."

"Well, it's eleven-thirty already. You think you could move your ass before you blow this thing?"

"Don't you start on me now," Nancy said. "You fed me so much coffee last night I couldn't sleep. And you didn't even take care of me. And don't think I don't know why."

A train was passing on the el running along Jamaica Avenue. "Shit," Louis said.

"What?"

"Nothing, it's a train," he said. "I couldn't hear you. I couldn't do anything last night and I already took care of you the other day."

"Well, I offered to take care of you."

He cupped his free hand over the receiver. "What?"

"I said I offered...."

He waited for the train to pass.

"Hello?" Nancy said.

"I'm here," Louis said. "I told you not while I got this rash. A couple more days and I'll plow you like an open field."

"Promises, promises," she said flirtatiously, then added, "And what are you doing calling me from a pay phone? I can hear the train. I thought you were home?"

"I'm obviously not, right?"

"You better not be with that bitch today, Louis. I'm warning you."

"I dumped her already. I told you that."

"Yeah, you told me that more than once as I recall."

He wondered if she had rolled her eyes. He asked her if she had the phone number of the bar in Brooklyn.

"In my purse," Nancy said.

"Make sure, because without that this is all for nothing."

"I said I have it, Louis. Stop being a nudge. I expect that from Nathan, not you."

"He really gone?"

"He wasn't here when I came home and he's not here now, so, yes, I guess he's really gone. Probably to his sister's."

"Good."

"Although I still think it would've been better if he were here. I could've called him first."

"It'll be better this way," Louis said. "You can call him after you call John. It'll look better all around."

"I don't know, Nathan seemed suspicious when I hinted at it yesterday. He's not a dope."

"We went through this last night. He's no rocket scientist, okay? Just make sure you have everything you need when you leave the house. And make sure you get John inside that tent. All the way inside. Do exactly what we discussed. This is our future, Nan. Don't blow it."

"Suddenly it's my fault if something goes wrong," she said. "You concentrate on what you have to do and don't worry about me. I'll be there and so will my kid and his father."

"Okay. Let me know after you call the bar."

"I will."

"And make sure you have dimes for the pay phone."

"Tell me you love me."

"What?"

"Tell me."

Louis huffed. "I love you," he said.

"I love you, too."

"Okay, talk to you later."

"Kiss me."

"What?"

"Gimme a kiss over the phone."

"That's stupid."

"Do it, please."

Louis kissed her through the phone. Nancy returned the kiss.

"Okay," she said.

Louis hung up.

Holly was in the bathroom when he got back to the apartment. He sipped what was left of his coffee before reattaching the phone line to shop betting lines. He was about to pick the receiver up to dial when the phone rang. Louis didn't know what to do. If it was Nancy he was in for an argument he didn't need. The phone rang again and he answered with an attitude just in case it was her.

"Yeah?" he said.

"You ever intend to pay what you owe?" a voice Louis recognized asked. It was a clerk from one of the bookmaking offices he owed.

"This Max?" Louis asked.

"Yeah. What's it gonna be?"

"I'll have your money Wednesday."

"You owe two weeks now."

"I know. I got jammed up."

"That's what you said last week. What you always say."

"I know. I'm sorry. I'll have it this week, I promise."

"You're cut off until then. You know that, right?"

"Fuck," Louis mouthed. "Yeah, fine," he said.

"Don't let me find out you're betting somewhere else."

"I won't."

"Make sure. We wanna jerk ourselves off, we don't need your help."

"Right."

The caller hung up. Louis did the same. He pulled the line out of the phone again. If he was going to bet today, he'd have to do it with another office and a lot closer to game time. There would be no shopping lines.

He turned when Holly called to him from inside the bathroom. "Who was that?" she asked.

"Just some guy. You gonna be long?"

He heard the toilet flush, then the sink running.

"I'll be out in a sec," she said.

Louis hid the phone line. Holly stepped out of the bathroom naked from the waist up.

"Jesus Christ," said Louis at the sight of her pert little breasts. "You don't make it easy, kid. I have a busy day."

She was holding the two strings that tied the halter in back. She turned around and asked him for help.

"Sure," he said. "Although I gotta tell you it's not easy not raping you right now."

"Louis!" she said.

"What?"

She kissed him on the mouth. "I can't wait to get back here later."

"You know what?" he said. "Me either."

■ ■ ■

A few minutes after her husband left the house Saturday afternoon, Kathleen packed a suitcase, grabbed the emergency thousand dollars the couple kept hidden in a coffee can in a kitchen cabinet and left a note taped to the refrigerator door that read:

I'll call you.

—K

It had to do with her increasing certainty that Billy had killed Victor Vasquez. Kathleen knew Billy had to have been guilty of something for the department to force his resignation, but that had been police business and had nothing to do with her. Although she was willing to live with his losing his job, living with a murderer was something else.

She had taken a room in a local motel with the intention of letting a few days pass before she called her husband, but today she couldn't stop worrying. Lately Billy scared her. She had heard of incidents where cops committed murder-suicide after losing their jobs, and as much as she loved him, she wasn't willing to die with him. If Billy had killed Victor Vasquez, he might kill her, too.

She spent the rest of Saturday in the motel room, having food delivered from a nearby diner when she was hungry. She had tried watching television to pass the time but couldn't focus. When she finally called the house again, it was a few minutes after five o'clock.

"Tell me what you did," Billy had answered.

"Billy?"

"I knew it'd be you. Tell me."

"I didn't do anything. I'm alone. I want to talk."

"I have an appointment, Kathleen. An important appointment."

"Give me five minutes. We need to talk."

"What about?"

"Victor Vasquez."

"What about him?"

"Did you kill him?"

A pause had followed.

"Billy?"

"This conversation being taped?" he'd asked.

"How could you ask that?"

"I'll ask it again, you really want me to."

"I'm not taping you, Billy," she had told him. "Don't be ridiculous."

"I don't feel comfortable talking on phones anymore, Kathleen. Things get taken out of context over phones."

"I'm not coming home until I know you didn't do it."

"I already told you I didn't."

"I don't know if I believe you."

"I really was on my way out," Billy had said. "Did I mention I have an important appointment."

"Billy?"

"I don't know why you'd ask me something like that," Billy had said before he hung up.

Kathleen had held onto the receiver a long time after the call. She'd felt paralyzed with fear and then she was angry for letting things get so out of control. Their conversation had kept her up most of the night. It continued to haunt her today.

Billy had made a point of saying he had an important appointment. Kathleen feared it had something to do with John Albano. Lately Billy had been forcing her to repeat Albano's name before and during sex. He'd done the same thing with Victor Vasquez's name prior to his murder.

Kathleen was sure Billy had murdered Victor Vasquez. She felt sick but was too scared to move. It was noon before she finally got out of bed.

CHAPTER 34

The Buick made the turn onto Main Street in Northport and was slowing down when Nick Santorra pulled out of the gas station less than a block away. He had been waiting for John Albano to make the Northport stop since one-thirty.

He had borrowed a two-year-old brown and beige Chevy Monte Carlo from Mike DiBella at the bar. Nick had claimed he had a family emergency and that his wife had taken their car. He kept his eyes focused ahead as he slowly reached for the ball peen hammer he had slid under the driver's seat earlier.

Nick placed the hammer between his legs as Albano parked at the curb and got out of the Buick carrying a small gym bag. There was a large office building at the corner. Albano walked around the corner toward the loading dock. Nick glanced at the time and saw it was two-thirty.

He figured he had ten, maybe fifteen minutes before Albano would return. He drove past the Buick and made a U-turn at the next corner. He took his time driving back, slowing down to stop alongside a fire hydrant half a block from the office building in case Albano had forgotten something and returned to his car prematurely.

Nick double-checked the people traffic on both sides of the street. Except for one kid playing stoopball, there were mostly older people passing on Main Street. He pulled on the red baseball cap he'd taken from his son and jerked down on the front brim. The cap was too tight and hurt his forehead where the bump he'd received from Albano was still showing. He cursed from the pain, then grabbed the hammer, wrapped it with a towel and slid out of the Monte Carlo.

He had left himself three possible escape routes: a left or right at the immediate corner, or the most direct route back to the highway, a straight drive back down Main Street. There were several lights he'd have to negotiate, but there were other cross streets he could use in the event he was chased.

He took one last look at the people traffic on Main Street before approaching the Buick. He had brought the towel to muffle the sound and intended to break both windshields and at least one of the passenger windows. As he reached out over the hood of the Buick, the towel came loose and slipped off the end of the hammer.

"Shit," he said.

He reached for the towel but the wind blew it off the hood.

Nick glanced over his right shoulder, then brought the hammer down hard. The noise stunned him; it was like a gunshot. A giant spider web formed from the middle of the windshield, but the glass didn't break. Panicked at the sound the hammer had made, he ignored the other windows and ran back to the Monte Carlo. He started the engine, checked his side view mirror for traffic, then raced away from the curb.

As he turned right at the corner, Nick saw the kid that had been playing stoopball staring at him. He drove another few blocks before turning left for Main Street. It should've been one block over, but wasn't there. He turned right at the next corner and drove another block before turning left once more.

"Fuck," he yelled when he couldn't find his way back.

■ ■ ■

Her former mother-in-law was in rare form when Nancy picked up Little Jack a few minutes before three o'clock. The boy had just run out to the car when Marie Albano waved Nancy closer to her front door to give her a piece of her mind.

"You should quit saying nasty things about John in front of his son," the old lady said. "It's not right. Some day that boy will figure it out, what you're doing."

"Why don't you mind your own business?" Nancy had told her.

They had never gotten along, even before Nancy married John, but Marie Albano was Little Jack's favorite grandparent. Nancy figured it was because of the way the old lady doted on her only grandchild. Nancy's mother had remarried several years ago and was living in Florida. She sent birthday and holiday cards when she remembered, but hardly ever called.

"You're not fooling anybody," Marie Albano had said. "No wonder Nathan left you. Good for him."

Nancy had flipped the old lady the bird.

She had arranged to drop Little Jack off at a house in Lynbrook where one of his classmates was having a pool party that started at three o'clock. Nancy had wrapped a model airplane as a gift.

Louis wanted her at the bazaar no later than five o'clock, but she was already running late. It was close to three when she stopped at an ice cream parlor on Merrick Boulevard in Valley Stream. Six tables with umbrellas dotted the area alongside a small parking lot. Nancy ordered her son a vanilla malted while he talked with two kids sitting with their mother at one of three occupied tables. Nancy waited, paid for the malted, then asked the woman watching her kids if she'd mind watching Little Jack while she made a few phone calls.

She used a pay phone alongside the wall of the ice cream parlor facing the small parking lot and called the bar in Williamsburg. Nancy feigned panic when someone answered.

"Is John Albano there?"

"Excuse me?"

"Is John there? John Albano. This is his ex-wife. It's an emergency. I think our son was kidnapped."

"Jesus, lady, you sure?"

"I don't know. He was there and some guy took him I think. I can't find him."

"I'll get him the message. Where are you?"

"I'm not home. Let me give you this number but I don't know if I'll be here when he calls."

She gave the pay phone number.

"Alright, lady, I'll find him."

"Thank you," Nancy said. "Please, hurry."

Then she hung up, rolled her eyes and looked at her watch. She was supposed to call Louis at another pay phone, but decided to call Nathan first. She had to look up her sister-in-law's phone number in her address book before she dialed.

"It's me," she said when Nathan answered.

"Nancy?"

"I just said."

"What are you calling here for?"

"To let you know I did it."

"Did what?"

"Called John's bluff. Now we'll see how much he cares about his son."

"What are you talking about?"

"What I told you yesterday. What I wanted to bet you yesterday but you were too cheap."

"Excuse me?"

"I told him Little Jack was abducted."

"What!"

"That's right. A few minutes ago and now it'll be all day before he gets back to me. His son will be sleeping in bed before we hear from his father."

"You told the man his son was kidnapped? What's wrong with you?"

"Don't be a sucker all your life, Nathan. It's the only way to prove to you I was right."

"You can't do that to a person. He'll be frantic."

"I'll win the bet is all that'll happen."

"Call him back and tell him what you did," Nathan said. "Don't make the man suffer."

"You see what I mean, how you are? He's more important than me. Why don't you call him?"

"I will. Give me his number."

"Oh, you're such a dope sometimes."

The operator interrupted the call for another dime. Nancy deposited two nickels and said, "You still there?"

"You have to call John and tell him what you did," Nathan said. "Please, Nancy."

"Jesus Christ, Nathan, why can't you side with me on this? Just once, why don't you?"

"Because it's crazy. I don't know why you did it, but it's wrong."

"Maybe I did it for us," Nancy said. "Ever think about that? To see if you would side with me for a change instead of defending John all the time. Maybe I wanted to see if you'd care about me for a change."

There was silence on the other end of the line.

"Nathan?" she said.

"You're full of shit," he said. "I don't know what this is about, but I know when you're full of shit. I hope you didn't do something you'll regret. For your son's sake, I hope you didn't."

"Oh, fuck you," Nancy said.

She slammed the receiver down hard and had to walk off her anger before going back to the phone to make the call to Louis. She went through her purse to find another dime while Little Jack sat with the woman and her kids.

It took her a few minutes before Nancy found a dime and when she did it was between two five-dollar bills. The cash reminded her about John and that he'd be getting robbed by Louis sometime after she made the call. It made her stomach queasy to think she would be responsible if anything bad happened.

She glanced at her watch and realized she had wasted too much time thinking about it. Either she went ahead with Louis on this and they had something to start over with or he'd cut her off once and for all and find somebody else. It was a big move, he had told her, but one they could build off of once they had the money.

Nancy dropped the dime into the coin slot and dialed Louis's number. He answered on the first ring.

CHAPTER 35

"He had a red hat and jeans and something was hanging around his neck," the kid had told John. "Then he got in a brown car and drove that way, down that street." The kid pointed at the cross street alongside the office building. "This towel was wrapped around the hammer."

He knew who it was as soon as the kid mentioned something was hanging around his neck, but now he had the towel, too, a souvenir he'd like to ram down Nick Santorra's throat.

John wrapped his right hand with the towel and lightly pressed on the windshield to see if it would give. It was loose but wouldn't break through. He sat behind the wheel and could see enough of the road to keep driving. He fished a single dollar bill from his pants pocket and handed it to the kid.

"Thanks," he'd told the boy.

That had been a few hours ago. Now he was barely able to see above the spider web of cracked glass and had three more stops.

It was getting close to six o'clock when he made it to Rockville Center, his next to last stop. They were showing the film in the basement of a karate school on Sunrise Highway. The guy in charge had decided to give another showing when he saw John was late. There were ten customers watching the movie.

"How much longer?" John asked.

"She just did the deep-throat thing," the guy in charge said. "About forty minutes, I guess, but a guy Eugene called and said you should call the bar when you got here."

"Alright," John said. "You got a phone I can use?"

He was brought upstairs to the karate school office. He used the phone there and called the bar. He was put on hold when somebody strange answered the phone. John figured it was one of the bus boys.

A few seconds passed before Eugene was on the line. He said something that nearly stopped John's heart. Then his heart was racing and he couldn't stop asking questions. Eugene shouted at him to calm down and write down the phone number he was giving him. John did as he was told.

"She call the police?" John asked.

"She didn't say," Eugene said.

"Jesus Christ. She call back?"

"Not yet."

"Tell her to stay put if she calls again."

"Of course."

"And do me a favor and call this number in case she's there," John said. He gave Eugene his ex-wife's home phone number.

"You want us to send somebody your last stop?" Eugene asked.

"Yeah, please," John said. "It's Valley Stream."

"Okay," Eugene said.

John hung up and immediately dialed the number Eugene had given him. The line rang five times before Nancy answered.

"It's me," John said.

"Jesus Christ, you took your time about it."

"Where's Jack?"

"I don't know. I think somebody took him."

"What do you mean, you think? Where are you?"

"The bazaar I wanted you to take him to on Merrick Boulevard."

"You call the cops?"

"No, I'm afraid to. He went in a big tent and hasn't come out yet. I'm watching out front."

"What?"

"Just come, John, okay? I'm scared shitless out here. I'm afraid to leave to make the call."

"Didn't you ask someone for help?"

"I can't, god damn it! Just come, okay? We're on Merrick Boulevard off Liberty, the bazaar in the park there. Hurry!"

John nearly dropped the phone when she hung up. He raced down the stairs where he was told there was still twenty-five minutes left in the movie.

John wasn't hearing it. He didn't bother counting the tally and stashed the money in the gym bag already stuffed with cash from his other stops. He was in the car a few minutes later, jumping the light at Sunrise Highway as he sped east toward Valley Stream.

He was thinking nothing made sense as he weaved in and out of traffic and finally had to slow down when he spotted a police cruiser on the opposite side of Sunrise Highway. Nancy had claimed she couldn't call the police, yet she had made the call to the bar. Or had he heard her right?

He couldn't think straight. He glanced up at the rearview mirror to make sure the police cruiser was still on the other side of the highway divider, then floored the gas pedal and went back to weaving around cars moving way too slow.

■ ■ ■

Today Louis had worn his ponytail tied up under a hat. He'd also had Holly draw pictures on his legs with a ballpoint pen that looked like tattoos from a distance. He wore an oversized long-sleeve shirt and high-top sneakers. A slim-jim was tucked down the back of his shorts.

Nancy had called the bar a few hours ago and was supposed to be outside the bazaar at five o'clock but wasn't there yet. Assuming she dropped the kid off at the pool party, what she had said she would do, it might add another ten, fifteen minutes to her time before she was in position to meet Albano whenever he showed up. Allowing for an extra few minutes, she was still half an hour late.

Louis had already parked close enough to the bazaar so he could spot John Albano's car when it pulled up to the bazaar entrance facing Merrick Boulevard. The trick would be keeping each woman from seeing the other. He had Holly lay down on the back seat just in case Nancy spotted his car. After fifteen minutes with no sign of his ex-wife, Louis became concerned Nancy had screwed something up. It was another ten minutes before he finally saw her in his rearview mirror.

Nancy paced back and forth underneath the welcome sign to the bazaar while Louis grew concerned Albano wasn't going to show. Suddenly he saw Nancy step back closer to the entrance, her arms waving toward the street. Then he could hear Albano's car before he could see it. He watched as the Buick stopped for a red light, then edged its way through the light and pulled up to the curb.

Louis thought he could see the windshield was shattered. Then Albano was out of the car and running around the front end toward the bazaar entrance. Louis grinned when he saw Albano wasn't carrying anything. His grin widened when he saw Nancy waving her ex-husband toward the big tent.

"Finally," he said.

"Everything okay?" Holly asked.

"Yeah," he said. "Let's go. You're driving."

He had already scoped out the bazaar and knew the big tent was deep and wide with several rows of individual games of chance. In the farthest corner from the mouth of the tent was the goldfish toss. There was an exit behind the goldfish stand that led to a parking lot. Nancy was supposed to bring her ex to the goldfish toss, then out into the lot before she told him it was just a bet. Louis would only need a few minutes to boost the car and get out of there.

He ran toward the Buick as soon as Albano disappeared inside the tent. He spotted the gym bag at the base of the passenger seat and crowded up close to the door to hide his using the slim-jim. Ten seconds later Louis had the door open and immediately went to work on the ignition system. It took him less than a minute to start the car. Then Holly backed up alongside him in his car.

His plan was to take the money somewhere safe and hide until he knew Nancy had held her water. John Albano would have his hands full with the guys he worked for. The mob would assume the robbery was an inside job.

"Drive up a couple blocks and pull up to the curb," he told Holly. "I'll pull up behind you with this and then I'll take over."

Holly nodded and pulled away. Louis followed her in Albano's Buick. One red light and thirty seconds later he checked and double-checked his side and rearview mirror before he grabbed the bag and got out. He'd left the Buick locked with the engine running.

Back in his car with Holly, Louis drove one block before he turned off Merrick Boulevard and used side streets to Conduit Boulevard.

"Where's the money?" she asked.

"That bag at your feet looks about right," Louis said.

Holly unzipped the top and peeked inside. "Wow, Louis," she said. "There's a lot of money in here."

"Good," he said. He looked to her and saw she was smiling. "See. That wasn't so bad, was it?"

"Actually, it was pretty exciting," she said.

"That's my girl," Louis said. He was already thinking they might make a good team.

CHAPTER 36

A restless night had convinced Brice he should confront Levin about the notebook and what was or wasn't going on with Kelly. As he turned off Twenty-ninth Avenue onto Bell Boulevard, he spotted Levin talking with a blonde-haired man.

He pulled up alongside a fire hydrant and thought he'd be sick after he recognized the guy from an ethics course given at the police academy by detectives with Internal Affairs. Brice waited until the two men turned their backs and walked away before whipping the Mustang into a U-turn and running the light at the corner.

He drove to Massapequa and parked up the block from George Berg's house before nine-thirty. Brice didn't know what time Kelly would show up and was still nervous about Levin.

The hours passed slowly as it turned into another hot, humid day sitting in the Mustang. Brice couldn't relax and spent most of his time making himself crazy wondering what the hell was going on and whether or not it would involve him.

It was close to one o'clock before Kelly finally showed. The lieutenant detective seemed in a good mood as he started a one-way conversation about the Watergate thing in Washington before switching to the Yankees' five-game losing streak. Kelly didn't stop talking until Brice had to leave to take a piss.

When he returned to his car, Brice saw that Kelly was sitting behind the wheel again. It annoyed him today more so than it had the day before. He would've beefed about it again, except Kelly moved to the passenger seat without being prompted.

A long stretch of nothing but the heat and boredom followed until Kelly went for sandwiches and Brice tried to nap. George Berg hadn't even stepped outside his house. There was no more denying the investigation was bogus and might have been all along. They had been racking up overtime, most of it doing nothing and all of it authorized by Kelly.

By four-thirty Brice's shirt had been soaked with sweat. He took it off and Kelly complained about the T-shirt he wore, calling it a guinea wifebeater.

"I'm not a guinea," Brice had said. "I'm not even Italian."

"Good for you," Kelly said. "Those fucking people. Worse'n niggers."

Brice waited for the rest of Kelly's ranting and was surprised when there wasn't any. A relatively peaceful half hour passed and then Kelly finally said, "Looks like nothing's happening here."

Brice nearly said what he was thinking: No shit, Sherlock.

"Drop you at your car or what?" he said instead.

"I was thinking we'd go for a beer," Kelly said. "Maybe shoot the shit some."

Brice shook his head. "No can do," he said. "Got a date. Married broad hasn't had it inna while."

"You're fucking married women are you?" said Kelly with a disbelieving smirk.

"She's separated," Brice said. "Still waiting on a divorce."

Kelly chuckled.

"What?" Brice said.

"I was beginning to wonder about you, that's all. Glad to hear it, you're dipping your stick somewhere."

Brice swallowed hard.

"Well, I guess you can drop me off then," Kelly said.

Brice kept to himself during the drive to the local deli they'd been using as a parking landmark. Concerned Kelly was already aware of his sexuality, Brice wondered if it was common knowledge. Then, after dropping Kelly off and driving more than halfway home, he spotted something on the passenger seat, a crisp fifty-dollar bill.

"Shit," he said through clenched teeth. "God damn shit."

■　■　■

John felt light-headed; his son was safe, but his life had spiraled out of control. The Buick was gone and with it the mob's money and thirteen bootlegged movie reels.

After getting Nancy's phone call about his son being abducted, John had lost all sense of reality. The adrenaline rush parents feel when one of their own is in danger had consumed him. By the time Nancy told him the truth, that it had been some kind of a bet she had made with her current husband, it was too late.

She had tried to explain it away, telling him he should be happy she'd lost the bet because it meant he wasn't the worst father in the world.

"What?" he remembered saying to her.

She had explained it again, the next time as if winning her bet was some kind of consolation.

"Where's my son!" he'd yelled loud enough to draw attention from some of the bazaar crowd.

"Calm down," Nancy had said. "He's fine."

"Where is he?"

"He's at his pool party. He's fine."

"And you made me come here for what?"

"Nathan said I shouldn't have and I'm sorry I did now that you proved me wrong, but I was sick and tired of him always taking your side and you always being late with the child support and nobody cares a fucking thing about me anymore. Not even Little Jack."

He couldn't look at her then. "Jesus Christ," he had said. "How... why? What's wrong with you?"

Then he had started to leave when she grabbed his arm.

"I'm sorry," she said, tears starting to form in her eyes. "I shouldn't have done this to you, but I needed to prove I was right for once. To Nathan, John. He left me."

"No wonder," he said, brushing her grip off his arm and proceeding back through the tent and then out to the front where he saw his life was over, just like that, in an instant. The Buick and the money were gone.

Afterwards John was sitting on the front seat of Nancy's car, half in, half out. The door was open and Nancy was standing there looking up and down the street, apologizing for doing this to him. All he could think of was the money. Five minutes ago he had feared for his son's life and now he was back to worrying about money.

"Somebody must have stolen it," said Nancy about the car. "Kids, probably. Out joyriding or something. You have to report it."

He had been thinking he should call the bar, but knew that if he did they would send half the crew out looking for him, because nobody, especially Eddie Vento, was going to believe for a second he had been robbed, not on the first weekend his routes had been doubled and he was carrying around all that extra cash.

"John?"

"It's mob money."

"What?"

"You heard me. How'm I supposed to report that? Whoever took the car has the money."

Nancy swallowed hard. "How much?"

John was thinking it had been Nick Santorra and that there was no way he'd recover the money. After breaking his windshield, the wannabe had followed him, and when the opportunity arose, Santorra had grabbed the money.

Now he would have to take off someplace and hide because of some idiotic bet his ex-wife had made. He thought about his son and how Little Jack was probably in danger too now because the mob was going to get that money back come hell or high water. It was something else for him to worry about.

"Jesus Christ!" he yelled. "Jesus fucking Christ!"

"How much was it?" Nancy asked. "Couldn't be that much, you were driving around with it."

John shot her a hard glare.

"What?" she said. "Couldn't your mother help? I mean, if it's a big deal and all. Couldn't you get it from her?"

John didn't hear her. He was imagining Nick Santorra laughing it up. He couldn't get beyond what Santorra had accomplished, first giving his car flats, then having him jumped, then breaking his windshield and topping it off by robbing him.

"John?"

He glared at Nancy. He wished she wasn't there. "What?" he snapped.

"Couldn't you ask your mother?"

"What?"

"Your mother," said Nancy, frustrated with his lack of attention. "Couldn't you ask her for the money?"

"No," he said.

"Why not?"

"Because it doesn't involve her."

"You're her son, right? She'd do anything for you."

"What?"

"I'm just trying to help."

John wasn't hearing her.

"Maybe we should look for the car instead of sitting here," Nancy said. "I'll drive you if you want. You said the windshield was broken, right?"

"He followed me," he said.

"Who? Who followed you?"

He looked up at his ex-wife and couldn't remember her name.

"John?" she said.

"A guy," he said. "A guy had it in for me."

"Who? If you know, you can go there. Take my car. Just drop me off to pick up Jack, then go. We'll take a cab home."

He felt in a daze. "Okay," he said.

She handed him the keys.

CHAPTER 37

"You put on any more weight, Jimmy, I'm not sure I'll be able to reach it next time," Sharon Dowell said. "I'll need an oxygen tube to get anywhere's close."

She was sitting on the couch with her legs up on an ottoman. Except for a pair of underwear, she was naked underneath her robe. She had been smoking a Virginia Slims cigarette. She took a last drag before crushing it out in an ashtray already crowded with crumpled cigarette butts.

"I'm serious," she said. "That stomach pressing down on my head. It's not easy going down on you. My neck hurts now."

Jimmy was standing in her bathroom doorway. He had just pulled up his XXXL boxer underwear. He looked from Sharon to his watch and said, "You talk to the kid?"

Sharon moved the ashtray from her lap to the end table. "This morning."

"And?"

"I laid it on thick. Told him it was Jerry's birthday a few weeks ago. It was."

Jimmy pulled his XXL polo shirt over his head. He struggled finding one of the arm holes. "Who's Jerry?"

"The guy directed the movie," Sharon said.

"Oh. I'm wondering we're better off keeping the number low or not. Guys like Louis, con artists at heart, sometimes they smell a sting."

"Lowballing it's one way to go, sure, but guys like Louis are always looking for the big score," Sharon said. "Lowballing might discourage him."

"And we don't wanna do that."

"You said you'd have a car. That still a go?"

"Yeah," Jimmy said. He was pulling on his pants now. "There's a line waiting on Louis. He owes guys all over."

"Car's gotta look the same as the one in the movie."

"Guy over in Canarsie said he had one, Fleetwood Eldorado. They got a ring there, some crew working with a guy named DeMeo, they're rippin' off cars like kids takin' bubblegum from a grocery store."

Sharon yawned.

"Guy says he'll bring it over late tonight, early tomorrow."

"Then I'll get Louis to come over and take a look at it," she said. "It'll help he didn't see the movie, though, he don't know exactly what it looks like. I tried baiting him with that, seeing the movie. I don't think he's much interested."

"You got the kid hopped up on the director angle, it won't make a difference he saw the movie or not. Just don't let him get too close. The paint the guy uses might not be dry."

"So long's he don't wanna meet Jerry. Last I heard, the poor guy's hiding from all the court crap."

Jimmy sat in an armchair facing the couch to put his shoes on. "It don't work, my friend from Canarsie comes picks the car up the next day, brings it back."

"You're not paying him for it?"

"Guy owes me a favor."

"You probably should air those out, your shoes."

Jimmy finished tying his shoes, cleared his throat and then stood up.

Sharon said, "I have to give the guy anything, he brings the car tonight?"

"I'll leave you something, but you could always blow him, keep it for yourself."

"Fat and funny."

"It wasn't a joke."

The two stared at each other until Jimmy finally smiled.

"Yeah, it was," he said.

"Maybe it's the years since," Sharon said. "After Benny was married I wasn't picky enough."

Jimmy winked again.

"Well, it's up to you now," Sharon said.

"I got him going pretty good with this car. Told him the guy wants to buy it gets wood from the idea. Said he can't wait to sniff the seat where the broad sat behind the wheel."

"Louis'll like that," Sharon said.

Jimmy grabbed his sports jacket from the back of a dining room chair. He pulled his wallet from his pants, pulled out two twenty dollar bills and dropped them on the table.

"Get some cold cuts," he said. "The other twenty's for the guy brings the car."

"And if I do blow him?" Sharon said.

"I'll tell you what," Jimmy said. "Guy tells me he liked it, I'll owe you."

■ ■ ■

Nick had been lost more than twenty minutes before he remembered the road atlas Mike DiBella had told him he kept under the front passenger seat of the Monte Carlo. He had taken a peek at it before leaving Williamsburg to get a general idea of where Northport was in relation to the LIE, and although Nick found the town easily enough, once it was time to get out of there the escape routes he had planned all turned to shit.

The adrenaline rush he'd felt after breaking John Albano's windshield had become genuine panic when he first realized he was lost. After driving in circles in and around Northport and then winding up on Malcolms Landing for a third straight time, Nick had started to sweat.

He parked alongside a fire hydrant, grabbed the road atlas and found the page with Northport. He glanced to his right and saw the water that was the Long Island Sound, then looked back at the map and realized he had driven in the exact opposite direction of the LIE. He kept the atlas open and drove street by street, purposely circumnavigating the hot spot on Main Street where it was still possible, he feared, to run into John Albano. A few minutes later, he'd found Bayview Avenue and eventually Route 25A.

It was a while before Nick was familiar enough with his surroundings to relax. He was headed east on the LIE and thinking he should play up the family emergency he'd told back at the bar and maybe spend some free time making it look good. There were a few theaters he knew of in Queens and on Long Island where he wouldn't be spotted and decided on Green Acres in Valley Stream.

He was relatively calm again when he remembered yesterday's dry run for Eddie Vento to John Albano's Massapequa stop. It had pissed him off to be used like that. Nick didn't appreciate being a stand-in for Albano or a shill for the police. Between running Vento's family around like a chauffeur and having to eat the punch he'd taken from Albano, and then having to play make-believe for the cops, Nick was feeling more like a gopher than a guy on his way up. It certainly wasn't helping his ego to know the fifty dollars he'd fronted Stanislaus Bartosz had been wasted on a dead man.

It was close to five o'clock when he pulled into the theater parking lot on Sunrise Highway. He had a cigarette to further relax his nerves. He strolled outside the theater to look at the movie posters lining one of the walls and was curious when he spotted the kid from *The Andy Griffith Show* on one of the posters. Opie, he remembered the kid's name was.

Nick went inside the theater to check the times and saw there was a 5:30 showing of *American Graffiti*. He bought a ticket, a bucket of popcorn laced with butter and an oversized Coke. He took a seat in the rear of the theater and began munching on the greasy popcorn. He was still wondering about Opie and whatever had happened to him after *The Andy Griffith Show* when he spilled some popcorn onto his chest and realized he was still wearing the whistle.

Then Nick remembered the kid that had been playing stoopball across the street from John Albano's Buick and he was nervous all over again.

CHAPTER 38

Stebenow surprised Levin when he sat across from him in a booth of the mostly empty Mount Olympus Diner on Hoyt Avenue in Astoria, Queens. He waited for the waitress to leave after taking Levin's order before he removed a cassette tape from his jacket pocket and set it on the middle of the table.

"I got tapes coming out my ass," Levin said. "I hope you don't think I'm listening to that one, too."

"Just run-of-the-mill wannabe speak," Special Agent Stebenow said. "Half a dozen rank-and-file punks trying to sound like their favorite wiseguy. Consider it another good-faith gesture."

Levin looked from the tape to Stebenow and back. "It was you," he said. "On a couple tapes delivered to my place. That was you. I get them the same way from Organized Crime. I just assumed ... you working with somebody else on this? Somebody from NYPD?"

Stebenow crossed his heart. "No," he said.

Levin was staring into the special agent's eyes. "Go 'head," he said. "I'm listening."

"Kelly sent somebody to kill my witness. Some punk off the boat affiliated with the Westies, the Irish crew running Hell's Kitchen. Billy Quinn. He's got a record in Ireland and a short sheet here. I stopped him with a warning shot. We have him, but he won't talk. He had a shiv and was heading straight for where Bridget was sitting two seconds after Kelly left the scene. I tailed her last night. So was Kelly tailing her. If I wasn't there she'd be dead."

"You got him, get him to give up Kelly."

"Never happen. He knows enough to sit it out."

"And?" Levin said.

"How close are you to taking Kelly down?"

"What makes you think I'm in charge?"

"You have an idea. Tell me."

"I don't have an idea. And I couldn't tell you if I did."

Stebenow motioned at the tape.

"Yeah, so?" Levin said. "The hell's that do for me, you're willing to lose your job and maybe get prosecuted? I'm not."

"Look, the Bureau won't bring her in," Stebenow said. "I made her stay at a motel last night, but that won't help her if Vento's on to her."

"If it was Eddie Vento last night you wouldn't have saved her," Levin said. "Your witness'd be dead. Vento wouldn't send amateurs and he wouldn't risk a knifing."

"Your guy is onto my witness, and if he wasn't working for Eddie Vento last night, all she was was lucky. The other thing is he saw me. He saw me turn and look at him. I spotted the move for what it was and had my weapon out before his guy made it across the street."

"You tell the girl about Kelly?"

"I didn't have to. She knew he was a cop. You wouldn't need a degree to figure that out."

"Why aren't your guys moving on this?"

"Pro'bly the same reason you guys didn't. Or were you there last night and I'm just retelling this for my health?"

"Go easy, my friend. I wasn't there last night. You do anything official with the guy you grabbed?"

"He's at a safe house for now."

"He's at a safe house why?"

"Because we can get away with holding him longer than you. She's out of danger so long's he's there. This way he doesn't get a call to his attorney. Soon as he does that she's dead."

Levin was incredulous. "What the hell do you hold him on?"

"He was coming at me with the knife. It's good enough for now."

"For how long?"

"I don't know, probably not much longer. And like I said, soon as he's out, he gets word back to Kelly and Vento, they'll make sure they don't miss the next time."

"He talks, this guy you have, we can all move on Kelly."

"Who would give up Vento thirty seconds after we cuffed him," Stebenow said. "But this kid isn't gonna talk."

"I don't know what to tell you," Levin said. "Can't you convince your people?"

"The Bureau isn't going to move because Bridget hasn't delivered enough to nail Vento yet. We think she's close. He nearly spilled something about a porn guy they whacked in Canarsie last month. That was supposed to be her hook, that she wants in on the movie business to become a porn star. Vento was supposed to make the connections, but Kelly obviously had something made him act before we could."

"How much more do they need, the Bureau?"

"I raised a few flags, but nobody cares about this kid. She gets whacked they'll try and nail Vento for that. She's nobody to the Bureau or the prosecutors."

Levin looked Stebenow in the eyes. "I'm gonna ask you something and I want a straight answer."

"Shoot."

"You banging this broad?"

Stebenow rolled his eyes. "No," he said. "No."

Levin was still staring. Stebenow didn't flinch. He pointed to the tape. "The only thing on that worth hearing," he said. "Vento mentions something about Kelly not trusting druggies. Called it 'big mouth syndrome' when they get high."

"Druggies in general or her?"

"What happened last night is a little more than an implication it was her." Levin sipped his coffee. "Bridget Malone'll get less sympathy from Internal Affairs than she gets from you guys."

Stebenow waved the comment off. "How close are you to taking him down?"

"It was up to me, he'd've been doing time already, but it's not up to me."

"I need this guy off the street," Stebenow said. He toyed with the sugar dispenser while Levin sipped his coffee again. "What would make things move on your end?" he asked.

"A direct order from the brass upstairs," Levin said. "Nothing less. I can't make believe I know what happened yesterday. Think about it. How do I document it on your end?"

"When are you on him again?"

"Tomorrow. Why?"

"Is it okay if I contact you? I'll leave a message under the name Casper."

"The friendly ghost? Nobody'd figure that one out. Are you kidding me?"

"Call my number when you get the message."

"When or if?"

Stebenow was anxious. "I don't know yet," he said, "but I'll leave that message soon as I do."

Levin bit his lower lip. Stebenow got out of there.

■ ■ ■

Levin was on his second cigarette before the two-year-old green Catalina drove through the lot and parked at the curb in front of the diner. Levin got in and handed Kaprowski the tape Stebenow had turned over.

"And this is?" asked Kaprowski, holding the tape up.

"A gift from a fed wants us to bring Kelly down," Levin said. "Tape's his bona fides. Proves he's not jerking our chain, except his was the voice on the last set of tapes I listened to, so I'm thinking you already know this and maybe you're jerkin' my chain."

"Excuse me?" Kaprowski said.

"This guy working with us or not?"

"That's a bold fuckin' question, detective. Answered the wrong way it could bring down an entire operation."

Levin took a moment. "You won't answer my question," he said, "which I'll assume you can't. Am I right about that?"

"First hand knowledge of a renegade federal agent is dangerous stuff."

"And that's as close to an answer as I'll get, eh?"

"As good as it gets," Kaprowski said. "Now, you buy it, his motivation?"

"Yeah, I do. I think he's worried about the girl. Says Kelly already tried to take her out."

"He banging her?"

"I don't know. I asked, he said no, but who knows."

"Fuckin' Kelly," Kaprowski said. "I'd like to be the one cuffs him, this finally goes down."

"You'll have to wait in line," Levin said. "Prick's mine."

Kaprowski offered Levin a Marlboro.

"No thanks," Levin said.

Kaprowski lit his cigarette. "That former head of the painters' union was clipped a few months back? Three of the five families had claims on him. That's showing sparks now."

"The guy they got outside some apartment building in Whitestone, I remember. Was back in May, so why now?"

"Sometimes the shit these guys stir takes time to brew. Point is, I don't want a dirty cop preempting a bigger bust."

"Except Kelly will feed you Eddie Vento."

"And Vento may or may not clam up. He does, that'll be the end of that. Today he's yapping over the phone about a dozen missing movies. The name you gave me last week, Vento's got people out looking for him, Johnny Porno."

"Why's that?"

"We don't know yet. We will soon enough. Ties into Kelly, we'll do your special agent friend the favor he wants. We get Vento to roll, that'd be the real victory. Vento makes a deal keeps him on the street we can nail a few union delegates his friends have in their pockets. Vento feeds us one or two delegates, they'll roll on whoever they're kicking back to. Union boys are used to bullying their wives but are soft it comes to jail time. They think for a minute they'll go away, they'll cough up every wiseguy they know."

"I told the fed with the tapes we couldn't do anything."

"And you were right. We can't. Not without having Kelly dead to rights."

"I didn't believe him I'd say turn him over to his own. Let them handle it."

"That'd only move things in a direction we don't want," Kaprowski said. "Besides, you do believe him, right?"

"I do. I think he wants out. I think he wants to save this woman. Maybe to save himself."

"Yeah, well, he can always go to confession," Kaprowski said. "You watching Kelly today? Maybe you should."

"I'm reviewing tapes for Internal Affairs at some point, but I can probably swing it later tonight."

"IA is a cover you can't blow so make sure you do what they ask," Kaprowski said. "If this agent is so concerned about his witness, he's the one should keep an overnight vigil."

"You're sounding a lot more conflicted than you did a few days ago."

"Maybe it wasn't a woman this agent was trying to protect I wouldn't be. Go home and listen to your tapes. You hear anything you think I should know, call."

"Great. That'll leave me time for a beer and a cat nap."

"Oh, please," Kaprowski said. He turned to Levin and rubbed two fingers together. "Know what that is?"

"Polish mating call?"

"Don't push your luck. I only look this cheery from an earlier bowel movement."

"Pleasant image. Thanks."

"As good as it gets," Kaprowski said.

CHAPTER 39

Louis took the Belt Parkway west. When they drove past the Cross Bay Boulevard exit, Holly turned in her seat.

"Isn't that where you live?" she asked.

"It's where I get off to go home, but we're not going there."

"Where we going?"

"I'm not sure yet. Staten Island maybe. Maybe Jersey."

"Why?"

"It'll be safer. Just in case."

"In case what?"

It was her first show of fear.

"Why risk it and find out?" Louis said.

He was thinking ahead of a potential disaster; if Nancy broke down and ratted him out, for instance. Louis wouldn't return to his apartment until he knew for sure. He would call work in the morning and remind them about his emergency the other day. He'd ask for the rest of the week off and hope they'd forward his check when he knew where he was going.

Holly still didn't know that Nancy had been involved, but Louis couldn't be sure his ex-wife hadn't seen his girlfriend. If she had, Nancy might blow a gasket and give him up; a woman scorned was a dangerous animal.

They were close to the exit for the Verrazano Narrows Bridge when Louis decided to get out of New York.

"I don't think I've ever been to Staten Island," Holly said.

"You don't know?"

"I always meant to take a ferry ride, but haven't got around to it yet."

"Only cost a nickel to ride that ferry," Louis said. "Staten Island was like going to the country when I was a kid. My uncle had a bungalow there. It's starting to get crowded now. Pretty soon it'll be as bad as Brooklyn."

He glanced at the bag of money between her legs, checking on it to make sure it was still there and hadn't flown out the window or something. It was starting to make him nervous, all that cash.

"We're gonna have to lay low for a while," he said. "With the money, I mean. And you can't talk about it with anyone."

"Of course not," Holly said. "I would never."

They drove in silence through Staten Island to the Goethals Bridge exit on the expressway. Louis was thinking they'd go down to the Jersey shore someplace and stay at a hotel there a few days. Holly would give him shit about taking off from school, but he could always put her on a bus or train back to the city.

"I guess we're going to New Jersey," she said when they were mid-span across the bridge.

"You ever been to the shore?" Louis said.

"Nope."

"Wildwood? Atlantic City?"

"Nope."

"Maybe we'll go there. They're talking about allowing gambling there some day, Atlantic City."

"I have class in the morning."

"Skip it."

"I'm not sure I should."

"Your class with the perverted professor?"

"Yeah. It's going to be weird until finals next week. I'm going to feel awkward."

"I doubt you'll need to worry about anything in that class," Louis said. "He'll probably give you an A whether you show up or not."

"I have my other class in the afternoon. That one I shouldn't skip."

"Not even once?"

Holly shook her head no.

Louis didn't see her. "Huh?"

"I guess," she said. "But I'll have to be back Tuesday for acting class."

"Consider it done. Meantime, though, I'm gonna cover you with all that cash after we count it."

"Cool," Holly said.

"Yeah," Louis said. "It is, isn't it?"

■ ■ ■

John stopped at the pool party to see his son. He gave him a hug and a kiss and was on his way. A few minutes later he spotted the Buick on Merrick Boulevard and parked behind it.

The engine was still running, which meant it had been hot-wired by whoever had taken it. The gym bag was gone, of course, and the doors were locked. John saw there was a pay phone and used it to call the bar.

"Fast Eddie's," Eugene answered.

"It's John. Nick Santorra there?"

"Hey, John, how'd you make out? You find the kid?"

The question caught him off guard. The missing money was all he could think about.

"Yeah," John said. "He's okay, thanks. Was on the rides at a bazaar. Santorra there?"

"A bazaar?" Eugene said. "Fuckin' kids."

"Nick there?"

"No, not yet."

John realized he couldn't mention the missing money. "Okay," he said. "I'll call back."

"Right," Eugene said.

John hung up and tried to focus. In another hour or two Eddie Vento would start to wonder where the hell he was. Then they would remember the emergency call Nancy had made about his kid. They would call some of the guys John had stopped to collect from earlier and it would start to look bad. No later than tomorrow morning he would be the worst kind of fugitive, one from the mob.

He had to get the Buick off Merrick Boulevard before it was towed. Then he had to get Nancy's car back to her. He drove to a gas station a few blocks away and told one of the mechanics about the Buick. He gave the guy a five-dollar bill and drove him where it remained idling at the curb on Merrick Boulevard. The mechanic used a slim-jim to unlock the door.

John drove the Buick back to the gas station with the mechanic following in Nancy's Dodge. He used the phone at the station to call Nancy, but nobody answered at the house.

He asked the mechanic if he could leave the Dodge there until someone could pick it up later. The guy hesitated until John handed him another five-dollar bill. He tried calling Nancy back, but there was still no answer. He wasn't sure if he should call Melinda, but decided he had to. She answered on the first ring.

"I'm in a spot," he told her.

"John?"

"Yeah, sorry. It's me."

"You okay?"

"No, not really. I was robbed. My car was. I just got it back but they took the money I was carrying."

"What money?" she said, then must have realized what he was talking about. "Oh, God, John!" she gasped. "Oh, God."

■ ■ ■

She'd watched the first four innings of the Yankee game before she fell asleep on the couch. The phone woke her. It was John and he'd been robbed, he told her. She listened to an abbreviated story of what had happened and grew more nervous by the second. She agreed to meet him in Valley Stream. When she got there John was waiting alongside his car.

The first thing Melinda noticed when she parked in front of the Buick was the windshield. It had been shattered.

"What happened?" she asked.

"I think that was the setup," John said. "Happened in Northport. I think the guy robbed me did that first, the windshield. Then at the bazaar I got out of the car without thinking. I left the bag with the money and when I came out the car was gone. I found it a few blocks from here. They left it running with the doors locked."

Melinda made him retell the story starting with the call from his ex-wife. When he finished telling her the details she was suspicious, but not of John.

"Your ex-wife called and told you your son was abducted?"

"She's a moron," John said. "She did it to prove a point to her husband. Claims he always defends me. It had to do with him letting me in their house and making me a cup of coffee. She's nuts. Apparently he figured it out too and left her."

"She told you she made a bet and you believe her?"

"It's what she said. It's crazy, but so's she."

"You sure she isn't involved?"

"What?"

"Your ex, John. You sure she isn't part of it? I mean, it's pretty crazy what she did, calling you like that, claiming your son was abducted."

"She called the bar first. They're the ones told me."

"The bar where the money has to go," Melinda said. "Doesn't that make you look even worse now?"

"Was the only way for her to get in touch with me. I gave her the number in case of an emergency when I first started working weekends."

"Something isn't right," Melinda said. "I can't see a mother doing something like that. It's vicious, John, and it's calculated."

"Nancy doesn't know Santorra. This was him, I know it."

"The guy you had trouble with?"

"Yeah, the guy robbed me. Same guy got loud in your diner. He's the one broke the windshield. He probably sent the guy who hit me in front of your house."

Melinda wasn't buying it. Something wasn't right about his ex-wife and the story he'd just told.

"You sure they don't know each other, your ex and this other guy?" she said.

"What? No way."

"You're sure?"

"Positive."

"Maybe it wasn't him."

"Had to be."

"Maybe it wasn't."

"It wasn't Nancy," John said. "There's no way. She's not smart enough."

"Unless she wasn't depending on her smarts," Melinda said. "Tell me again what happened when you got there? What did she say? What she do, your ex?"

John told her what had happened again. She could tell he was skipping some of it and slowed him down.

"I'm in a bind here," he said. "I don't know what to do next. I had any brains, I'd hop a train somewhere."

"Let's just figure this out," she said. "Step by step, what happened? Go slow."

He huffed a few times in frustration. Melinda coached him along. "She waved you inside, brought you to the back of a tent, then out to a parking lot and grabbed your arm?"

"I was furious when she told me it was a bet," John said. "I told her she was crazy, then tried to head back to the car. She grabbed my arm and apologized."

"What do you mean? Why?"

"I don't know. She was trying to explain herself. She told me about Nathan and the bet she made with him."

"Did you talk to him, to Nathan?"

"No, why would I? It's not his fault she's crazy. He's a decent guy."

"And then you went back out and the car was gone."

"Yeah," John said. "Why? I don't get it."

Melinda sighed.

"What?" John repeated.

"Think about it," she said.

"I have. I did. What?"

"Unless I'm completely off, John, it sounds like your son being abducted was one big diversion. And your ex-wife getting you inside the tent and then out to the parking lot was the biggest part of it."

John stared blankly.

Melinda huffed. "Think about it," she said.

Chapter 40

The note Kathleen had left him was a confirmation of Billy's worst fears. No matter if the police suspected him, his wife always would. Her fear of being linked to his guilt was apparent. As much as he loved her, Billy couldn't permit another betrayal.

The first thing he did after reading the note was search the yellow pages for a dog-eared page or pen or pencil mark Kathleen might've made. He found several at the top of a page with advertisements for hotels and motels. Kathleen was beautiful but not very clever. He closed his eyes and imagined her searching the book he held open on his lap. She'd held a pen. Either she'd memorized the number or written it down. Billy stood up to look around the kitchen. He spotted the newspaper on one of the kitchen chairs and set it on the table. A piece had been torn off one corner of the cover page. He leaned over and could see the outline of the number on page three. He used a pencil and lightly brushed the tip over the number until he could read it. He checked the number against those in the telephone book and found a match.

"Bingo," he said.

The motel was in Sheepshead Bay, less than a ten-minute drive from the house. He could call and ask for her name or make a quick pass with the car, but he preferred to give Kathleen one last chance. If she came home or called and agreed to meet him, they might be able to salvage their life together.

First, though, he needed to kill John Albano. For the sake of speed and efficiency, Billy had already equipped his .308 Savage 99 with a 2X-7X variable power scope. He would be able to make a kill shot from 100 yards.

When the phone rang, he was hopeful Kathleen was ready to come home, but their conversation became a cat-and-mouse game that could've been taped. The tone of her voice suggested she was convinced he had killed Victor Vasquez. The fear in her voice suggested she would give him up as the murderer or at least point the police in his direction.

Billy ended their conversation abruptly. He went down to the basement and added a few more weapons to his portable arsenal. Fifteen minutes after he finished packing, Billy made a pass through the Sheepshead Bay motel parking lot. He saw Kathleen's car parked between a Dodge pickup truck and a recently washed Oldsomobile Toronado.

■ ■ ■

Nick found the bar was unusually crowded for a Sunday night. The atmosphere seemed tense. He recognized a lot of muscle from other crews in the neighborhood and wondered what it was about. Then he was told to see Eddie in his office right away.

He used the kitchen stairway down to the basement and saw the office door was slightly open. He knocked on it anyway.

"Eddie?" he said.

"Come in," Vento said.

Nick sat in one of the two folding chairs across from the desk. "What's up?" he asked.

"You tell me," said Vento, staring hard into Nick's eyes.

"I had a thing with the family, my sister-in-law," Nick lied.

"Yeah, and?"

"It took a little longer than I expected."

"Where's John Albano?"

"What?"

"Albano. Johnny Porno. Isn't that what you call him? Where is he?"

Nick shrugged. "No idea."

"Yeah, well, he's MIA right now. So's my money."

"You're kidding?"

"I look like I'm telling jokes?"

Nick nearly choked trying to swallow. "What happened? He didn't call?"

"No, he didn't. Neither did you until half an hour ago."

Nick understood. He held both his hands up. "Wait a minute. You don't think I had something to do with him? I hate that fucking guy."

Vento continued staring.

"I'll be the first one to whack him, you want," Nick added.

"So it wasn't staged, that little beef you two had?"

"What? No fucking way. He japped me, just like I said."

"Except everybody saw it said it wasn't a jap shot. They said you asked for it and he gave it to you. You better live with that story because right now it's the only reason I haven't put your fucking legs through a meat grinder."

Nick stuttered.

"Shut up," Vento said. "There's close to fourteen grand out there somewhere."

"You really think he robbed us?"

"Me, cocksucker. If he robbed anybody it was me."

"Sorry."

"His wife called here with some cock-and-bull story about his kid being abducted or some shit. Then Gene upstairs passed the message to Albano and he called back later asking for you. Why'd he do that? He's not here,

you're not here. All the bullshit between you two makes me wonder."
Nick's hands were up again. "Hold on," he said. "I had to borrow Mike's
car because my wife had ours today. I wasn't anywhere near Albano."
Vento went silent.

Nick was too afraid to admit what he'd done to Albano's windshield earlier, but it might help get him out of this mess now. He was about to tell
Vento, but couldn't. He took a moment to gather his composure, then said,
"Look, I have problems with the guy, I'll admit it, but I'm no friend of his.
I had this thing, my sister-in-law, her husband roughed her up a little and
my wife got all crazy. I went for the sake of keeping peace at home. As far
as Albano goes, like I said, you're ready to take him out, I beg you to put
me on it."

"Regular tough guy, you are."

Nick knew to keep his mouth shut.

Vento pointed a threatening finger. "I find out you had anything to do
with this you won't go easy, jerkoff. I'll feed you to the sharks over the
aquarium myself. A quarter fuckin' inch at a time."

"On my kids," said Nick, making the sign of the cross. "I got nothing to
do with Albano."

"Get upstairs and don't go nowheres until I say," Vento said.

"Right," Nick said. He got up out of the chair. "You want the door
closed?"

"What?"

"The door?"

"What about it?"

"Open or closed?"

"Leave it."

"Right," Nick said. He stepped around the door on his way out. He was
halfway up the stairs when he thought he heard Vento call him an asshole.

"I must be," Nick whispered, "working for you."

■ ■ ■

They had gone to Melinda's place after John called the bar back and
finally spoke to Eddie Vento. The mobster had been too cordial. John suspected he was in trouble. He'd called Nancy's house a few times since
without reaching her. He tried again now but there was still no answer.

In an attempt to ease some of the stress, Melinda joked about different
ways he might escape the mob.

"I could drive you up to the mountains, to one of the Catskill resorts,"
she said. "I read somewhere it's what they used to do, hide in the mountains."

John was preoccupied wondering if his ex-wife had really set him up.

"If you can do a Yiddish accent, I have a yarmulke my ex had to wear at Jewish funerals," Melinda added. "I'll put a kerchief over my head and we go up there as a couple."

"Huh?"

"Or I could drop you off at JFK. You can head for Mexico."

"I'm afraid of flying," he said. "Going back to when we were kids."

"We?" Melinda said.

"Me and my brother," John said. He realized she didn't know about Paul and explained, "He was killed in Vietnam."

"Jesus, I'm sorry."

"I've got to find Louis," John said.

"What?"

"Nancy's ex. If she did this, she did it with him."

"Do you know where to find him?"

"I doubt she does. The guy's a snake."

"Would she tell you?"

"She won't volunteer it. Maybe once she understands how serious it is. Maybe."

"I like her less and less."

"I have to assume they're already wondering about me and the money," John said. "It won't be long before they look into Nancy. Then my son won't be safe."

"Bring him here. You'll both be safe here."

"For tonight, then tomorrow you'll be in the shit, too. There's no running away from this. And if Nancy really did have something to do with it, her dopey first husband's behind it, he's got the cash and is probably long gone. The only justice in it for her is she'll never see two cents if she helped him."

"You can't still think she's innocent in this?"

"I don't know. I don't. The real problem will be convincing Nancy she's the one needs to hide. She's clueless, though. She'll tell me I'm paranoid."

"Convince her? You don't give her enough credit. If she's still in town, she's probably scared shitless right now."

"Maybe."

"Maybe nothing. And if—what's his name, the ex?"

"Louis."

"If Louis has the money and takes off, she'll know she's been had and she'll count on what she told you, your mother bailing you out or whatever, but she'll be a train wreck while she's waiting for that to happen. She's not that stupid. By now, if Louis is gone, she knows she screwed up. It's you I'm worried about, the fact you're still not sold she had something to do with this. Speaking of which, it's time to give her another call."

He tried Nancy's phone again but there was still no answer. He thought about what Eddie Vento had said over the telephone earlier and repeated it. "'Hey, buddy, where you been?'"

"You said he sounded friendly."

"Why I knew I was in the shit," John said. "Sounded like my best friend."

"Shit, John. Where might your ex be?"

"I don't know. Nathan's maybe, but I don't know where he's staying now he's left. I don't know he's got family or what."

"What about her? Any family?"

John shook his head. "Mother lives in Florida, but they're not close."

Melinda could tell he was still struggling with the idea of his ex-wife setting him up. "What?" she said.

"Santorra," John said. "I can't get past him."

"Except why would he draw all that extra attention breaking the windshield?" Melinda said.

"I don't know. None of it makes any fucking sense."

"You're a terrible sleuth, John."

"Not to mention a dope."

"You've got a good heart. Too good. You wanna believe in people, even Nancy. It's what she counted on to distract you."

"On the street they call that a sucker."

"We're not on the street now."

She leaned over and kissed him. It was a long kiss, but when he went to hold her, Melinda held up the telephone.

"Business first," she said.

John started dialing.

CHAPTER 41

After his impromptu meeting with Special Agent Stebenow first and Kaprowski immediately after, Levin had spent the rest of the night reviewing surveillance audio tapes. He was close to falling asleep when the doorbell rang. He yawned in Brice's face when he answered the ring and had to squint to make out the fifty-dollar bill the junior detective was holding against his chest with both hands.

"He left it in my car," Brice said.

"Kelly?"

"Can I come in?"

"Sure, I already slept it must've been two, three minutes."

Levin stepped back to let Brice inside.

"You want coffee, make it yourself," he said. "I'm going straight to bed after you leave."

Brice went to the kitchen, opened the refrigerator and took a beer. He brought it to the living room and sat on the sofa.

"He wanted me to go out for drinks with him," Brice said. "After sitting in the car with him all day, he wanted to 'spend some time,' the way he put it."

Levin sat in the armchair facing the couch. "You should've offered him a few bucks to go home."

"Clever," said Brice before taking a sip of the beer.

"Any callers?"

"What?"

"At Berg's place. Anybody come back today?"

"Zilch."

Levin yawned again, this time long and loud. "Why he probably left the fifty," he said. "Keep your interest."

"Keep it or feel for it?"

"Both."

"You know he's dirty, right?"

Levin rubbed his face to avoid answering the question.

Brice said, "You know because you're investigating him."

"Excuse me?"

"You heard me."

The detectives stared at one another until Levin lit a cigarette. He took a long drag, exhaled the smoke, and said, "Would it really make a difference?"

"The fuck is that supposed to mean?"

"I'm only asking so you think it through, whatever's on your mind. The man's dirty, what's an investigation got to do with anything?"

"If you're part of it? Plenty, it seems to me. Where do I come in? How'm I being used in this? Are you selling me down the river, too?"

"You give yourself too much credit, kid."

"And you're a lying sack-of-shit rat bastard."

"Hey," Levin said, "that's how you feel, there's the door."

Brice took a long drink from the bottle this time but didn't move.

"Kelly say anything?" Levin asked.

"You want to get a tape or you have one running now?"

Levin didn't respond.

Brice said, "Outside of his normal rants against the Italians, the Jews, queers and the black man? No, not really. Was his usual charming self. I offered to drop him off his car we were done. He mentioned going out for drinks."

"And left a fifty when he got out?"

"It wasn't my fifty."

"It is now."

"What?"

"You can mention it to him, you found the fifty in your car, but I doubt he's gonna say it was his."

"And then I'm guilty of taking a payoff, great."

"You could wait and see if he mentions it first. Maybe he lost it. It fell out his pocket or something."

"Yeah, right."

Both men stared at each other.

"And if I don't mention it, or if I do and he says it wasn't his, and then I keep the money, I'm on the take," Brice said. "It's a lose-lose from where I sit."

"Technically, but who's gonna charge you?"

"What, you won't? You're my friend? I can trust you?"

Brice finished the beer. He set the empty bottle on a coaster on the coffee table. "I don't want Kelly thinking I'm okay with it. I don't want him assuming that shit."

"Why it was a clever move, dropping that fifty," Levin said. "You turn it in, the money, he knows he can't trust you. You keep it, it's an implicit acceptance."

"I don't want the money," Brice said. "And I won't rat."

"Nobody will need your testimony, kid, so you can get off your high horse. A guy like Kelly, when the time comes, will give himself up and cut a deal before the cuffs are on."

"That's true. Or maybe he'll kill himself and really make your day."

"I'd rather see that than he cuts a deal. You feel sorry for him, I won't."

"Yeah, and what happens to me?"

"Why should anything happen to you?"

"It comes out you're the guy behind busting Kelly, no matter he makes a deal or not, I was there and nothing happens to me, my rep is trashed anyway and you know it. Either I'm part of the bust or I'm a rat. Thanks a lot."

"Nobody is gonna be sympathetic to Sean Kelly, I can tell you that much."

"Or to me," Brice said. "Why would they?"

"We'll do what we can to help you out of it," Levin said. "But I have to tell you this much, you can't go anywhere with this or you will have trouble."

"You prick."

"I'm not a prick. I'm doing what I can for you. It isn't much, but I don't have to do anything."

"Okay, so, what? I resign today or wait the week out?"

"I can't tell you what to do."

Brice set the empty bottle on the coffee table. He looked at Levin a moment, then started for the door.

"You can ride with me tomorrow," Levin said. "I'll note it officially I was forced to inform you of the investigation. I advised you stay with me. It's the best I can do."

"You busting him tomorrow?"

"That I won't say."

Brice turned toward the door.

"I'll let you know," Levin said.

"When?"

"When I know."

■ ■ ■

Even though he'd promised to put the money in the safe-deposit box the next day, Nancy knew that Louis would keep his distance until she could assure him it was safe to return.

In the meantime, she was supposed to learn how John was going to deal with the situation. She would arrange for John's mother to watch Little Jack, and when she was sure it was safe, she would let Louis know. The problem was how to go about it, letting Louis know. Nancy had no clue where he was and was totally dependent on him calling her.

It was eleven o'clock when she finally made it home. She had eaten a slice of pizza after dropping her son at John's mother's house, where Nancy had hoped to hear something, but apparently John hadn't called the old bag yet.

Nancy went upstairs to begin packing a bag just in case Louis called sooner rather than later. She was hoping it was Louis when she heard the phone ringing. She picked it up before putting down her purse.

"It's me," John said.

"Oh," Nancy said. "How'd you make out?"

"Why don't you tell me how you made out?"

"Excuse me?"

"Louis have the money?"

Nancy paused a moment. "Wha-what money? What are you talking about?"

"Jesus Christ, Nancy, how the hell could you do this?"

"Do what? What are you talking about?"

"I'm not the only one they'll come after, you dumb shit. Remember you called the bar? They passed the message along to me. They'll just assume you were part of it."

Nancy felt the blood drain from her face. She braced herself against the kitchen table and lowered herself into a chair. "Part of what?" she said.

"Where's my son?"

Nancy took a moment to compose herself.

"With your mother," she said

"Good. Leave him there."

"Why? What's going on? What are you talking about?"

"I'm not going to argue," John said. "I'm telling you to get in touch with Louis and tell him not to bet the money you two stole today because you didn't steal it from me. That was mob money. They break legs for a fifty, never mind what that asshole is driving around with right now."

Nancy couldn't speak.

"Nancy?" John said.

"What?" she managed.

"Call him."

She was about to say she couldn't, that she didn't have his number, when John hung up. The reality of her situation was jarring. She tried calling Louis's apartment and counted ten rings before she gave up.

Nancy couldn't move. How had John known she was involved? How had he known it was Louis?

The doorbell rang. She looked at the clock and saw it was ten-twenty. She went to the living room to look out the window. Two husky men were at the door. Cops, she thought; detectives probably.

She knew she was mistaken as soon as she saw their faces. Neither of the men presented identification. The shorter of the two did the talking.

"Mrs. Albano?"

"Actually, it's, uh, Ackerman."

"You know a John Albano?"

"He's my ex."

"Oh, okay. We're friends of your ex. You know where he is?"

Nancy shook her head for effect. "No. Is something wrong?"

"How's your kid?" the taller one asked. "You get him back?"

Nancy stuttered. "Ah, yes, wa-we did. Tha-thank you."

"Can we come in?" the short one asked.

"Uh, I was about ta-ta-ta to go to to-to, uh, to bed."

"You could let us in or we'll break the fucking door down," the tall one said.

Then he pushed her hard and she fell back on her ass. When she looked up, they were already inside.

■   ■   ■

After John called his mother to check on his son and to warn her to stay put, he felt conflicted about scaring his ex-wife. Melinda wasn't hearing it, saying Nancy deserved feeling scared and should develop ulcers for what she had done and that John was still being too god damn nice about it all.

"She's the kid's mother," he told her. "Anything happens to her, it's my son who suffers. She's still his mother."

Melinda bit her upper lip.

"I'm not saying she's a model mother," he said. "But she is his mother."

"Then she's the one should return the money she stole."

"How's she gonna do that?"

"Jesus Christ, John," Melinda said. "She's not half as stupid as you think. I'm sure she's got quite the little stash someplace."

"She won't give up Louis. Those two have a history. A sick one, but it's there all the same."

"Is there even time to do any of that? These people will want their money right away, won't they?"

"If they can squeeze more money out of it, they'll take it like an annuity. They'll probably charge interest on what was stolen and turn thirteen grand into twenty. It comes to money they'll make whatever deal nets them the most."

"Would they still hurt somebody?"

"You bet your ass they will," John said. "I already owe them for nailing one of their own, the punk who broke my windshield. This, now they think I'm involved, they'll come after me with baseball bats."

"Jesus Christ. What about the police?"

"No thanks."

"Why not?"

"They can't do anything that can help. And if Eddie Vento thinks I went to the police, they'll put a contract out on me."

"Contract?"

"I'm not going to the police, Melinda, so let's drop it."

She covered her head with both hands.

"You okay?" he said.

"No, I'm not."

"You got aspirins?"

"Aspirins, Jesus Christ. Look, stop worrying about other people for a minute. Worry about yourself."

"I'm gonna have to give myself up," John said. "Or they'll go after Nancy and maybe my kid. I can't risk that."

"That's crazy. I have a few dollars. I can help."

"No way, Melinda, forget it. I still feel like a deadbeat for when you paid for my coffee."

"If you tell them you have money and they see it comes from me or somebody else, you make them go with you to the bank, they'll have to believe you were robbed. You can pay me back later. I don't need the money. It's just sitting there anyway. It's not going to make me rich."

"And how do I pay you back?" John said.

"Whenever, I don't care."

"No."

"John, damn it."

"No."

"Forget your pride for two minutes," Melinda said. "This is your life we're talking about."

John glanced up at the clock. "Can I borrow your car?"

"What? Why? Where are you going?"

"To see Nancy."

"What for?"

"Convince her to leave my son at my mother's, for one thing. Maybe she knows where her ex is and I can get the money back before he blows it."

"You going to protect her now?"

"Jesus Christ, Melinda."

Melinda was clenching her teeth. "Go," she said.

"The keys?"

She got them from her purse. He leaned in to kiss her on the mouth. She turned her head and he kissed her cheek instead.

"Thanks," he said.

"Be careful," she said.

He started for the door, stopped to look back at her, then nodded and was gone.

CHAPTER 42

"I used to come here when I was a kid," Eddie Vento said. "My grandfather used to take me on the boat rides they had. Was a nickel or something."

"My old man said it was a swamp, Canarsie," Kelly said.

They had met at the pier a few minutes earlier. Vento led the detective around it starting from the east end, where he pointed toward the sanitation fills off the Pennsylvania Avenue exit on the Belt Parkway.

"Still stinks when it's humid," he said. "The shit the city dumps there. I used to gag sometimes."

"You sure it's the garbage?" Kelly said.

Vento didn't understand until he saw Kelly was pointing at a group of Hispanics sitting around a late-night barbecue. He ignored the remark and said, "I got a guy missing in action. He's missing and so are copies of the film and a lot of money."

"How much money?"

"Enough I'm looking for help."

"He's one of yours?"

"I just said."

"Any ideas?"

"Not really. Only something ain't right. I just give him a bunch of new stops, he doubled up what he had and then this. There's some other shit going on between him and another guy don't make sense either. Run his plates. I already sent people where he lives. I need you to track his plates."

"I can't put an APB on a guy robbed the mob, Eddie. I'd need more of a reason. Legally, I mean. Wouldn't look good."

"Now you're being a jerkoff."

Kelly stopped walking. They were at the north end of the pier. Kelly pointed out across Jamaica Bay.

"I once took a broad there, the island out there," he said. "Jewish broad worked for my brother wound up ruining his life."

Vento waited for more.

Kelly said, "He was a happily married man, my brother. Very religious. Sanctimoniously so, until the Jewess with the big tits had him eating out of her hand."

"He was getting some on the side. So?"

"Point is, except for under her bra, he never bothered looking into the twat he was banging. She stung him for close to twenty grand."

"You couldn't help him?"

"We weren't talking. When I say he was religious, I mean it. My brother should've been a priest instead of a lawyer. He didn't approve of my lifestyle."

"He knew you were dirty?"

Kelly flashed a sarcastic smile. "No, he didn't," he said. "But he knew I screwed around on my wife and that I drank. Until his girlfriend, those weren't venal sins. Screwing around he thought of as mortal sin. Seriously so."

"Okay, I bite. What happened?"

"She went and dropped some pictures in the mail. This after he'd remortgaged his house and handed over twenty grand. My sister-in-law saw them and ran to the pastor of their parish, nitwit that she was, and when my brother found that out, his priest knew, he went down his basement and blew his brains out."

"Jesus Christ, over a broad?"

"Over his sins. I'm convinced it had to do with her going to the priest, his wife. Which was one reason she never saw the cash he'd stashed in a safe-deposit box, which is another reason I don't use one. I like my cash close at hand. A good old American safe with a loaded thirty-eight inside the event it's some dumb bastard comes to rob me, has me open the thing for him. Anyway, I found one of the safe deposit keys on Michael's St. Christopher metal. God only knows who had the other one. I know it wasn't the broad he was screwing because there was still money inside when I opened it."

"Tell me you went after her."

"I did the due diligence he should've, albeit too late."

"And?"

Kelly pointed to the island. "Like I said, he was a sanctimonious asshole, Michael was, but he was still my brother."

"And I needed to hear this why again?"

"Your girlfriend," Kelly said. "Something tells me she's not as intimidated of you as you think."

"Explain," Vento said.

Kelly had to be careful. He couldn't let Vento know he'd tried to have her killed and had failed. He said, "You know about her other boyfriend, right, the one died in the joint?"

"The jerk she was all goo-goo over, yeah."

"She was busted with him. You know that?"

"I'm the one told you. Yeah, she got caught transporting or some shit. Big deal."

"So, when he died, they had to know she was working for you and they never followed up on her. You know if she gave the boyfriend up?"

"Do you?"

"When she start with you?"

Vento shrugged. "The guy was already inna' joint I put her to work."

"When'd you start fucking her?"

"Week or so after he was locked up. So?"

"It's worth looking into is all."

"You know this cunt is talking to the law or not?"

"I don't, not officially. I'm just saying is all, you'd be smart to perform some due diligence of your own."

"The fuck does that mean?"

"Maybe you should take a look-see around that apartment of yours and make sure there aren't any electronic devices you didn't put there yourself."

Vento took a moment. "Okay," he said. "I will."

"As for the other thing," Kelly said, "maybe your MIA saw an opportunity and took it. He was carrying a lot of cash, it had to be tempting. He have any roots?"

"A wife and kid. Ex-wife."

"Then the kid is the one we should work through."

"We don't fuck with kids."

"You can always farm it out. I don't mind mercenary work."

"No," Vento said.

"You want the money back?"

Vento glared at Kelly.

"I'm just saying," the detective said. "There's a reward for this money, I'm not shy about getting things done. The guy gives a fuck about his kid, I'll get to him."

Vento remained silent.

Kelly said, "I'll take that as a yes."

■   ■   ■

Louis took the Garden State Parkway to exit 40, then the White Horse Pike East. He told Holly they would spend the night at one of the motels outside Atlantic City and go to the Boardwalk the next day for some saltwater taffy, maybe go on the rides on the Steel Pier.

He pulled into a motel parking lot with a view of the water three miles from the famous Boardwalk. The Wind Bay Inn featured a sad-looking swimming pool out front, color television and electric-fingers beds. He paid cash for the room and asked for three dollars in change for phone calls he might or might not make, depending on his mood after getting a few hours sleep.

Holly was still excited about their adventure. She pulled off her bell-bottoms and paraded around the room in her white panties and halter. Louis used the bathroom first, taking a shower after he was finished with the toilet. He wrapped a towel around his waist when he came out. It fell off when he went to lift the gym bag.

"You shaved yourself?" Holly asked.

Louis followed where she was looking and realized he'd exposed himself.

"Had to," he said. "Jock rash."

Holly pointed. "What's that white stuff?"

"Cream for the rash."

Holly wasn't convinced. "They made you shave for that?"

"It's not VD," Louis said, "if that's what you think."

"Okay, rash from what then? From where?"

Here we go, he thought.

"I don't know what," he said. "Running probably. I went for a jog last week and felt a cut there, a burn, and I didn't take care of it."

"You're sure it's not crabs?"

Louis set the gym bag on the bed. "Where would I get crabs?"

"From another woman."

"I didn't sleep with another woman."

"Your ex-wife."

He unzipped the bag. "Let's not ruin this, okay?"

Holly put a hand across the gym bag.

"The rash is why we didn't have sex this morning, isn't it?"

"Partly. Move your hand."

"No, tell me. Is it really a rash or something else?"

Louis pulled the bag away. "It's a rash, Holly. That's what it is, a rash. Men get those sometimes. It isn't the end of the world. I went to the doctor and he gave me the cream, told me to shave myself and apply it."

"Okay, if that's the case, then we can fuck."

"Don't take it the wrong way, but right now I'd rather count this money."

Holly reached behind her and undid the halter. It dropped from around her neck to her lap, exposing her breasts.

"And now?" she said.

Louis looked from her breasts to the bag and said, "Just a rough count first, but let me chain that door lock first."

■ ■ ■

Nancy hadn't been slapped that hard since the fifth grade when Sister Mary Michael caught her and two of her friends smoking in the lavatory at Holy Family during homeroom. She remembered she couldn't even cry it had hurt so much.

It's what she was thinking about after swallowing two Bayer aspirin at the kitchen sink. The tall one had pushed his way inside the house and then helped her up with one hand before slapping her across the face with the other. She remembered gasping from the slap and then there were bright lights she saw in her head just before she hit the floor.

She'd heard footsteps on the stairs behind her when she sat up, but the tall one was still standing there right in front of her, daring her to get up. She hadn't moved.

When the short one had finished looking through the house, he stood over her, too, then pointed a threatening finger at her and said, "This shit you and your ex pulled today isn't going away until the money turns up."

She had been too scared to reply. She was thinking she had nodded and might've said, "Okay."

Then the short one had kneeled down alongside her and reached a hand up her skirt and grabbed her there hard and she gasped again.

"I'll pull them out one a time, your cunt hairs, I have to come back," he had said.

After they left, Nancy had managed to crawl to the kitchen and use a chair to stand up again. She glanced at her reflection in the small mirror alongside the wall phone and could see the right side of her face was puffy.

Then she was sick and had to use the toilet. She was still dry-heaving when she heard the phone ring. Her ribs hurt too much to move. She ignored the call.

A few minutes later the phone rang again. Nancy had managed to make it back to the kitchen. She answered the phone in a weak, cracked voice.

"Hello?"

"Nan?"

She couldn't speak.

"It's John."

"Oh, God!" she cried. "What have I done?"

■ ■ ■

John's emotions ran the gamut from guilt to rage after Nancy told him what had happened. As much as she deserved the trouble she had brought on herself, he couldn't deal with a woman being slapped around. He did his best to calm her down and walk her through what she had to do, but it wasn't easy. Now that she was finally remorseful, it was getting in the way.

He told her to go upstairs and turn on the lights in her bathroom and bedroom and to try and peek out a window to see if the two goons that had been inside the house were gone. He was guessing they weren't, and when she returned to the phone downstairs a few minutes later crying hysterically again, she confirmed his suspicion.

The next part was tougher. He had her go down to the basement and then out through the cellar stairs to the backyard. Then she was to climb the fence to their neighbor's yard and walk out the driveway on the next street where he would pick her up. If she met anybody along the way, if one of the neighbors saw her or walked into her or whatever, she was to keep going until he picked her up.

He'd made the call from a telephone booth on Cross Bay Boulevard, close enough to be there in a few minutes, but also exposed enough to be seen from a passing car. "Don't say anything to anybody," he'd told her. "Just get out of that driveway and head up toward the far end of the block. We don't want anyone spotting the car or they'll give a description."

"I won't," Nancy told him.

Five minutes later he positioned himself low behind the steering wheel of Melinda's Valiant. He had parked half a block from the house directly around the block from Nancy's. Six minutes later he spotted her in the middle of the street, not where he had told her to go. If one of Vento's men were circling the block, they would spot her.

So would anybody looking out their windows.

He pulled away from the curb and raced up the block. He was waving at her to get in when she screamed about as loud as a woman could.

"Jesus Christ," he said once she was inside the car.

He could see the windows of the nearby houses light up as he pulled away.

"I'm sorry, John," Nancy said. "I'm scared. I'm so scared."

"Okay, calm down," he told her as he sped through the neighborhood toward the highway.

"You get their names, the guys hit you?" he asked.

"No, but it was just one guy hit me," Nancy said. "And he grabbed me, too. Down there."

John felt his teeth clenching.

"Where can I take you is safe?" he said.

"I don't know. Nathan's, I guess. His sister."

"Did you call him?"

"No."

"Why not?"

"He left me, John. I told you."

"He's still your husband."

"What could he do?"

He knew she was right. It wasn't Nathan's problem to start with and shouldn't become his now.

"What about your boyfriend? You call him yet?"

She was sniffling again. "I don't have his number."

"What do you mean, you don't have it?"

"He's not home. I don't know where he is."

"It was him, though, right? Louis took the money."

She began to cry again.

"Son of a bitch," John said.

"I'm sorry," she sobbed. "I really am."

As soon as John had figured out she was still screwing her first husband, he'd started divorce proceedings and moved out. The marriage had been a mistake, but they'd had a child together. He could live with his bruised ego, but there was no way he'd walk away from his son.

He had never confronted her about Louis when he found out because it didn't matter. He and Nancy weren't happy together and it wasn't Louis's fault. John had done what he had to do instead of making a bigger drama than was necessary. He'd moved out and filed divorce papers and seen his kid whenever he wanted until she'd started dating Nathan Ackerman and instituted new visitation rules.

Then when he'd lost his union job, John was too busy hustling odd jobs for an income to support his son and himself. The biggest mistake had turned out to be taking the weekend job Eddie Vento had offered him at the bar in Williamsburg. The way John saw it, even though Nancy had set him up so Louis could rob him, at least some of the responsibility was his own for getting involved with people he knew he shouldn't have.

Those people.

It was the only reason he didn't throw her out of Melinda's car right then instead of pulling into a hotel parking lot on Conduit Boulevard near JFK and helping her hide from the people who were really after him. He escorted her up to a room on the third floor overlooking the Belt Parkway and sat her down on the bed while he dialed Nathan's sister's house. The phone rang three times before a woman picked up.

"I'm very sorry to trouble you at this time, but is Nathan there?"

"He's sleeping. Who is this?"

"My name is John Albano. I'm Nathan's wife's ex-husband, one of them."

"What's this about?"

"It's an emergency. Can you please put Nathan on?"

There was a pause on the line John assumed was the woman waiting for more of an explanation. Then she said, "Hold."

John tried to hand the phone off to Nancy, but she waved him away.

"He won't talk to me," she said. "Please, John."

"Hello?"

It was Nathan.

"It's John, Nathan. I'm very sorry to bother you."

"What's wrong?"

John gave him an abbreviated version of the story, then asked if he would help Nancy.

"Is your son okay?" Nathan asked first.

"Jack's fine, Nathan. He's with my mother."

"Thank God for that."

"Can you help Nancy in the meantime?"

"I was supposed to travel to Boston in the morning, but I already canceled. I told them it was a family emergency. It is, I suppose. I was planning on getting my things from the house. Where is she?"

"Right here at the hotel. She just checked in. I have to get going soon, though. I can't stay."

"Her first husband used her to rob her second husband and now her third husband is going to hide her from the mob," Nathan said. "Is that about it?"

John couldn't help chuckling. "It's almost funny, you put it that way," he said.

"You're a better man than me, John."

"Not in a million years, but I'll understand if you don't want to get involved."

"Give me the address," Nathan said. "I'll come by but not tonight. I'll pass by in the morning. I can't make any promises after that."

"Understood," John said. He gave Nathan the hotel address and said goodnight.

"Good night," Nathan said.

John hung up and turned to Nancy.

"Is he coming?" she asked.

"You don't deserve his help, but he's coming tomorrow. Try not to blow it when he gets here."

"He wants me back?"

"Jesus, Nan, no. I doubt it. Just try not chasing him away before this is over."

Nancy started to cry again, then noticed the bruise on his forehead for the first time and pointed at it. "What happened?"

"What's it look like?"

"Oh, my God. Now you, too."

"Save it," John said. "There'll be plenty more to be sorry about if we don't get that money."

"They said they'd come back."

"And they will. You can bet your ass on that."

"Can't you stay?"

"No."

She covered her face with both hands.

"You should've thought about this before you helped that asshole rob me," John said. "He's probably in Vegas gambling it away while you were getting slapped around, your hero."

"I hate him!" Nancy yelled.

"Yeah, for now," John said. He got up and headed for the door.

"John!"

"What?"

"I'm sorry."

"Sure," he said. "I almost feel sorry for you."

"Please," Nancy said.

John left.

CHAPTER 43

"The man tells me I have to stay, I have to stay," Nick told his wife over the phone. "I can't come home yet."

"Are you in trouble?" she asked.

"No, but I would be if I left, so I'm staying."

He saw Eddie Vento leave earlier and although it didn't look like he was coming back, Nick wasn't sure he could take the chance and leave. That had been a few hours ago. Now it was after one in the morning and none of Vento's crew was there.

To top it off, word was they were out searching for John Albano.

"It's not fair you have to stay," Angela said. "Nick, I mean it. You're always the one getting stuck. I wish he'd find himself another driver."

"Okay, that's enough," he said. "I can't leave yet and you're starting to talk stupid. I'll be home soon as I can, but don't forget I don't have the car. I'll have to take a cab."

She was saying something else when he hung up.

Nick wound up staying until closing. At three o'clock he called a local car service. He waited outside where he lit a cigarette at the curb. He was alone on the street and anxious to get home. He leaned against a car and took a nervous drag on his cigarette. Headlights turned onto the street at the corner and got his attention.

He assumed it was his cab and tossed the cigarette as the car pulled into a space alongside the fire hydrant about five yards from where he was standing.

Nick put his arms out. "What the fuck?" he said.

The car's brights flashed, blinding Nick. He shielded his eyes and didn't see it was John Albano until it was too late.

He took the first punch to his gut and doubled over. He was gasping for air when a knee smashed his face. Nick dropped to his knees first, then the rest of the way face-first against the pavement.

He lay there unconscious a good fifteen minutes before the local car service driver woke him.

■ ■ ■

John had called his mother again from the lobby of the hotel when he left Nancy. Marie Albano had been asleep but still managed to answer on the second ring. She said she'd gotten a phone call from his ex-wife earlier, something about the mob wanting their money back. It took John ten minutes to calm his mother. When she was listening again, he told her to take his son someplace safe the next day and not to tell Nancy or anybody else where they were.

It took him another few minutes to reassure his mother that Nancy had been lying. When Marie Albano finally let her son hang up, John rushed to get to the bar in Williamsburg. He hoped for an opportunity to talk with Eddie Vento alone.

He drove to the bar using the Belt Parkway and BQE, speeding the entire way. He parked off the corner of South Second and Hooper Streets, less than a block from the bar. John figured it was the last place Eddie's crew would look for him.

He waited until the place emptied out, but still there was no sign of Eddie Vento.

He waited another half hour and was about to leave when he spotted Nick Santorra. The punk had stepped into the street with a cigarette and seemed to be waiting for somebody. All the bullshit Santorra had pulled over the last week ran through John's head; the verbal abuse, the fifty bucks it had cost him for knocking the punk out, the flat tires and the windshield. It was like that last poke in the chest the first time John had hit him.

He drove and parked alongside a fire hydrant. Santorra approached the car with his hands out wide and was shooting his mouth off about something when John turned on the brights. Then he got out and did a quick number on the punk. A few minutes later he saw he had blood on his pants. He stopped for a red light about three blocks from where he'd left Santorra in the street. He found a packet of tissues in Melinda's glove compartment and wiped his pants as best he could.

On his way back to her place he took a slight detour to see if the Buick had been found yet. He saw a police car double-parked alongside it and kept driving. He figured Eddie Vento already had somebody in the police department looking for him or why else would they stop to search a car with a broken windshield in the middle of the night?

When he got to her place, Melinda was waiting up for him. She looked exhausted and angry when she answered the door, but then she kissed him long and hard on the mouth.

"I was so worried," she said when their mouths separated. "I want you to leave phone numbers where I can reach you. I can't stand waiting around like this. I didn't know where you were or what was happening."

"It's okay," he told her. "Everything is okay."

"I mean it, damn it. I want phone numbers there on the fridge so I can call someone. This was horrible waiting here like this."

John kissed her. She kissed him back, this time getting more involved. He used his foot to shut the door behind him as she squeezed him tight against her. They were still kissing when Melinda locked the door.

■ ■ ■

It was a simple note, but telltale nonetheless.

I'll call you.

—K

It had not been easy for him to kill his wife. He had loved Kathleen and had hoped they would last, but the brief note she had left on their refrigerator door back at the house and how she'd seemed to try and trap him over the phone afterward told him it was over.

He had used a credit card to break into her hotel room and was waiting for her outside the bathroom while she showered. She had just stepped out of the bathroom and was turning toward the bed when he shot her in the stomach. The force of the bullet knocked her to the floor flat on her back.

The shock registered in her eyes. She was gasping for air as Billy took one of her hands.

"It's okay," he'd told her. "Lay quiet."

Her arms had started to twitch when she tried to sit up. Blood spurted from her mouth. Billy felt a tear run down one side of his face when she began to choke.

He squeezed her hand tight as she tried to speak. She could only manage to say part of his name.

"Illy... Illy."

After she'd passed, Billy dragged her body inside the bathroom. He left the Do Not Disturb sign on the motel room doorknob. It would probably be maid service that discovered Kathleen when they went to clean the room later in the morning. Then Billy took his wife's Karmann Ghia from the motel parking lot just to delay the inevitability of the police looking for and finding it. He had figured he would use Kathleen's car rather than his own and then dump it when he was finished with John Albano. He could always steal something off the street to escape with afterward.

Now that he could focus on Albano alone, he headed east on the Belt Parkway toward Canarsie. Unless he had spent the night with his girlfriend at her place in Queens, Albano would have to return home for work Monday morning.

He'd made it to Canarsie within fifteen minutes of leaving the motel. He was careful with the lights on Rockaway Parkway, making sure to stop well in advance of them rather than take the chance on running one and being stopped. He drove past the firehouse and then the building where Albano lived and saw the old man was sitting on the stoop again.

He parked the Karmann Ghia on the next block and took his time walking back. He hoped the old man would go inside so he wouldn't have to pass him, but the guy was still sitting there when Billy crossed the street.

"Who you are?" the geezer asked.

"I'm looking for a friend," Billy said.

"Who?"

"John Albano."

"He's not home."

"You sure?"

"I doesn't see him."

"I'll try his door. Excuse me."

The old man wouldn't move. Billy stepped around him.

■   ■   ■

Nearly fifteen minutes had passed and the guy that had gone upstairs to look for John wasn't back yet. Alexis Elias hadn't seen where the man had parked, but he'd recognized the sports car when it passed in front of the building earlier. It looked like the one that had nearly hit John Albano a week ago.

Unless he'd gone out through the back, the man was still upstairs. Elias decided to go see. He climbed the two flights of stairs, then stopped to remove his shoes when he reached the third-floor landing. John's apartment was off to the right. Elias shuffled to the door and listened. He heard a chair being dragged along the floor and quickly knocked on the door.

There was no answer. Elias knocked again, then put his ear to the door, but the movement inside the apartment had stopped.

"Hey," he yelled. "What you're doing in there?"

He knocked one more time.

"I call police," he said.

The footsteps inside the apartment moved quickly. Elias was still leaning close to the door when it opened. Then, before he could react, a hand reached out and grabbed him by the front of his T-shirt and pulled him inside the apartment. He was half dragged, half shoved into an armchair in the living room. Then the man stepped back and Elias saw he had a gun.

"Mobster," Elias said.

"Not exactly," the man said. "But who are you?"

"What you are doing here?"

"You first."

Elias sat back in the chair.

"Okay," the man said. "Have it your way."

He raised the gun. Elias didn't flinch.

"Tough old bastard," the man said. Then he lowered the gun a few inches and whipped it up fast and hard under Elias's chin. The old man's eyes fluttered a few times before they closed.

CHAPTER 44

"You look terrible," Nathan said.

"I haven't slept a wink," Nancy said.

He had come as promised, but earlier than she had thought. She had been asleep when the phone rang. The front desk said a Nathan Ackerman was in the lobby. She told them to send him up and wondered why he hadn't said he was her husband.

She answered his knock wearing her panties and bra and was surprised when he didn't kiss her hello.

Now he was keeping his distance, sitting in one of the chairs at the tiny table across the room while she sat on the edge of the bed.

"I appreciate your canceling Boston for me," Nancy said. "I hope it isn't a problem."

"It's not a problem and I canceled for myself to get my things from the house."

"Do you hate me?"

"I guess I feel sorry for you," Nathan said, "but you don't make it easy."

"I'm sorry I hurt you."

"No, you're not. You're sorry this turned to shit, whatever crazy thing you did."

"I did love you, Nathan. Really. I'm sure I still do."

"Baloney, Nancy, let's not kid each other. I feel foolish enough. I've felt foolish enough. Being here now isn't easy."

She apologized again, then said, "I need to contact Louis. For John. He says I should try."

Nathan ignored her.

"I don't know where he is or where he's gone," she continued. "He can only reach me at my, our home number. We need to go back to the house. I was afraid to stay last night."

"You have a bruise and your face is swollen," he said. "Did they do that?"

Her eyes welled with tears. "They hit me so hard."

Nathan shook his head. "How can a man do that?"

"John had me sneak out the back," Nancy said. "They might still be there."

"We'll call the police first to make sure they aren't."

"I'm not sure we should involve the police."

"I won't go there without calling them."

"What can I tell them?"

"You don't have to mention whatever you did, but there's nothing wrong with saying what happened last night. Show them your face, tell the truth about that."

"They'll want to know why?"

"Lie."

"What?"

"It's what you do best. Make up a story. At least that way the police will stay there. Tell them you were robbed."

"You think that'll work?"

"Come on, Nancy, get dressed. I want to get this over with. I don't want to waste more time than I have to."

She got off the bed and went to him. "I want to thank you," she said. She put a hand on his shoulder. He removed it.

"I'm doing this for your son," Nathan said. "And John. No other reasons."

"You won't even look at me."

"Get dressed, Nancy. Then you can call the police."

Forty-five minutes later Nathan pulled up in front of their house, where a police cruiser was waiting. He invited the policemen inside. They took Nancy's abbreviated report: Two black men pushed the door in when she answered their knock. One of them slapped her and stood watch while the other went through the house. Some jewelry was missing and they took all her cash, about two hundred dollars, she'd told them.

The policemen told her detectives would probably pass by later in the morning. Once they left, Nathan told her she shouldn't have said they were black men or lied about the cash.

"You're the one told me to lie," Nancy said.

Nathan stared at her a moment. "You're right," he said. "I should've known better. I'm going to make coffee."

Nancy rolled her eyes when he turned his back to her. She went upstairs to shower. When she came back down the phone was ringing.

"Why didn't you answer?" she asked before picking up the receiver. "Hello?"

"It's me," Louis said.

"God damn you," Nancy said.

The connection was broken. Nancy screamed Louis's name when she realized he had hung up. Then she kicked at one of the kitchen chairs and hurt her foot.

"He'll call back," Nathan said.

"What?"

"He'll call back. Next time don't curse him."

"Don't curse him? What are you taking his side too now?"

Nathan sipped his coffee, set the cup down and headed for the front door.

"Where are you going?" said Nancy, limping behind him.

Nathan didn't answer. He opened the door and walked out. She stood in the doorway yelling his name until it was clear he was leaving. Then she started cursing and kept it up until she heard the phone ring again. She limped back to the kitchen and answered.

"Louis?"

"Who's Louis?" a strange voice asked.

"Who's this?"

"The guy grabbed your snatch last night."

Nancy couldn't speak.

"You tell the cops about the money you robbed?"

"Na-no," she managed to say.

"Good. Now, who's Louis?"

"A friend."

"He the one has the money?"

"No. He's a friend from the school."

"A boyfriend?"

"No, just a guy. Our kids go to school together."

"Where's your kid?"

Nancy didn't answer.

"We'll talk again," the caller said.

She was trembling when he hung up.

■ ■ ■

Stebenow had tried and failed to convince the special agent in charge of the Eddie Vento investigation that their key informant's life was in danger. Clive Flynn, a fifteen-year veteran of the bureau, the last two as a special agent in charge, had recently been admitted to the bar and was hoping to become a federal prosecutor. Taking down Eddie Vento would go a long way toward advancing his political future.

When Stebenow told Flynn about Bridget Malone's bruised face, the SAC said, "She's been sucking Vento's dick the last six months. You really think she can't handle a few slaps?"

The comment had infuriated Stebenow. "I think the cop on his payroll is investigating her," he'd said. "I think he's already figured her out."

"Was that why you had our people hold some Westie inna safe house? They aren't for your personal hunches, safe houses. There's something going on I should know, you best tell me now."

"That was a guy attacked me is all."

"Except you were guarding the Princess Malone at the time. Or watching her anyway, I'll bet, and without keeping us informed. Then you order the punk held like you're J. Edgar himself. The fuck you think we're slow?"

"Alright," Stebenow said. "It looked like he was going for her. Yeah, I was there."

"And you think the guy with Vento sent him."

"I know Kelly sent him."

"You can prove it?"

"No."

"Because the Westie isn't saying fuck all. Quinn his name is, right?"

Stebenow hadn't answered.

"It's fine by me," Flynn had said. "Kelly is NYPD's problem. At least until we take Vento down."

"That cop can give us Vento just as easy."

"Except that would make us look like we've been wasting our time with Malone, wouldn't it?"

"Us or you?"

It was the wrong thing to say and Stebenow knew it.

Flynn had smirked. "I'll make believe I didn't hear that," he said. "You concentrate on keeping our girl active. The sooner she brings us something we can convict Vento with, the sooner she's living under a new identity. We bring him in because he slapped her we'll all look stupid and the only thing she'll get is an order of protection."

That had been late last night. This morning, after another sleepless night, Stebenow had called his wife and was surprised when a man answered her phone. Their separation was less than six weeks old. Although they had stopped seeing each other more than three weeks ago, Stebenow had been caught off guard by the new man in his wife's life.

Rather than asking to speak to her, he'd hung up.

As much as it hurt, Stebenow felt a strange sense of relief knowing his wife had moved on. His efforts to save the marriage had been half-assed. If it wasn't his job that had come between them, it was his discontent with what his job entailed. Either way, Stebenow knew both his marriage and his work had become dead issues. It was time to leave both behind.

He thought about calling Flynn and quitting the Bureau, but that would require turning his back on a witness and Stebenow knew he couldn't do that. Not anymore.

He left the house with his weapon of choice, a Sig-Sauer.

CHAPTER 45

The phone call from her former daughter-in-law and her son had kept Marie Albano up most of the night. First Nancy had said John owed the mob money, but later John had said his ex-wife was lying. Marie couldn't trust her ex-daughter-in-law, but the fact her son wanted her to take Little Jack someplace safe was cause for concern.

This morning she was thinking she might take her grandson to the theme park in Hershey, Pennsylvania. Marie was thinking she'd book a room in a motel nearby the amusement park. Little Jack was eating cereal in the living room while watching television. She didn't mention anything to her grandson while she looked over her road atlas.

She took notes of the roads and highways she would have to take and had just written the directions through Pennsylvania using Interstates 78 and 81 when the doorbell rang. Marie glanced out the kitchen window and saw a tall man with red hair standing at the front door.

"Grandma!" Little Jack called to her.

"I got it," Marie said. She looked through the peephole and asked who it was.

"Police, ma'am."

She was about to ask him to show his identification when a badge appeared. Marie opened the door enough to show her face.

"Morning, ma'am," the detective said.

"What is it?" Marie asked.

"I'm looking for your son."

"My son? What for?"

"It has to do with money he owes, ma'am. I'm not here officially this morning. More as a favor. Your grandson here?"

"My grandson? Why?"

"I was asked to ask, ma'am."

"Why? Who asked you to ask?"

"A friend. If you could pass along a message to your son, that he needs to speak to the man in Brooklyn today, it'd be much appreciated."

"What man? What is this about?"

"Money, ma'am."

"What money? I don't know what you're talking about."

"Your son does."

"And you're police?"

"A detective, ma'am."

"Says you," Marie said.

The detective smiled, then turned and walked away.

■ ■ ■

Detective Levin was sitting up high in the passenger bucket seat of the surveillance van. Brice had joined him a few minutes ago with two fresh coffees and a couple of packs of Yankee Doodles. Levin had been sitting surveillance on Detective Sean Kelly since just after midnight. He yawned before taking a sip of his coffee.

"Last night he meets Eddie Vento on the Canarsie Pier and this morning he's doing house-to-houses," Levin said.

They had just watched Kelly approach the front door of Marie Albano's home about half a block away.

"I guess you didn't get any sleep," Brice said.

"I almost missed him," Levin said. "Somebody stopped over last night and put a bug up my ass."

"Think about the bug up my ass," Brice said. He was watching Kelly. A stocky woman with gray hair opened the door the detective had just knocked on.

"Who's that?" he asked.

"Albano's mother's the woman lives there, owns the house."

"The guy, Johnny Porno, his mother?"

"The same."

"And Kelly's visiting her why?"

"Something to do with missing money from the porn flick."

Brice adjusted the van's rearview mirror so he could see through both rear windows.

"So, Kelly is working for Eddie Vento," he said.

"Oh, yeah."

The two detectives sat silent the next few minutes while Kelly and the gray-haired woman continued their conversation.

"I'm sure it has something to do with last night," Levin said. "This Albano, Johnny Porno, he's supposed to be missing with cash and some bootlegged copies of the movie they're peddling. That's off an OC bug in Vento's bar."

"You have somebody with OC?"

Levin ignored the question. "Whatever's going on, it looks like Kelly's helping to find him."

He wrote the time down in a notebook and started the van's engine. He waited until Kelly's car was a full block ahead of them before pulling out.

"Where's he going?" Brice said.

"Pay phone," Levin said.

"You're sure of yourself."

They followed Kelly through the streets before he turned onto a busy commercial street. Four lights later, Kelly pulled into a gas station and used a pay phone there.

"What's going on?" Brice said.

"I was a betting man?" Levin said. "Kelly's checking in."

■ ■ ■

Louis returned to the pay phone at the motel office and dialed Nancy's home number again. This time she was a lot more pleasant when she answered.

"You calm?" he asked.

"Yes."

"Can we talk?"

"What do you mean? Of course."

"Is it safe?"

"It is now. I'm alone."

"What happened? Why were you so crazy before?"

"Because men came here looking for John last night and one of them hit me," Nancy said. "They went through the house and then they grabbed me down there and said they'd be back."

Louis had to be careful with her. Nancy was loyal but not crazy. If mobsters had come and smacked her around, there was a chance she was setting him up now.

"What else did they say?" he asked.

"Nothing."

"Nothing?"

"They'd be back. They said they'd be back."

"And John?"

There was a pause that unnerved Louis.

"And John?" he repeated.

"He thinks it's some guy he had a fight with at the bar," Nancy said. "Somebody broke his windshield on the Buick. He thinks it's the same guy."

Louis remembered the broken windshield. "Great," he said. "That's great he thinks it's somebody else."

"Where are you?" Nancy asked.

"I'll be back tonight."

"What time?"

"I can't come there, Nan, to your place. Not yet."

"You going to the apartment?"

He didn't like the question. "Maybe, I don't know yet."

"Louis, where? I can meet you."

He could see Holly crossing the parking lot.

"Look, I'll call you tonight or tomorrow morning."

"What time? Nathan left me and I'm all alone now."

"Just hang on and I'll call you."

Holly was waving at him.

"Okay?" he said into the phone.

"I miss you," Nancy said. "And I'm afraid."

"It'll be okay," he said.

Then Holly yelled his name and he tried to hang up but missed the cradle and had to try again. He missed a second time, while Holly yelled she was hungry, and then he finally hung up.

"Shit," he said under his breath.

"I'm starved," Holly said. "Let's get breakfast."

"Sure," Louis said. "And maybe a stiff drink."

CHAPTER 46

This morning Louis told her they were heading back to New York so he could broker a car deal for some big shot with deep pockets. He said it had something to do with a car that had been used in the porno film, *Deep Throat*; a Cadillac some rich guy supposedly wanted to buy as an investment.

Holly had already lost her appetite from the way Louis had been acting since they stole all that money. She dropped the piece of rye toast she'd been holding.

"Come on," Louis said. "This is exciting stuff we're doing. Don't get down on it now, Nan."

Holly's eyes opened wide. "Excuse me?"

"Fuck," Louis said.

"You just called me Nan."

"I did?"

"Yes."

"Sorry. Probably 'cause you're looking so down. A woman gets bitchy, it reminds me of Nancy."

"Really? And who'd you call from the parking lot?"

"I already told you. The guy with the car."

"I don't believe you."

"I can't help that."

She watched him scarf down two pancakes. He sensed her stare and set his fork down.

"What?"

"It was Nancy you called," Holly said. "Admit it."

Louis tried to return her stare, but blinked first. "Fine," he said. "It was Nancy. Happy?"

"Why?"

"To make sure she didn't give me up."

"How would she do that? What's she got to do with it?"

He avoided her eyes while he reached for his coffee.

"Louis?"

"She helped me set the guy up," he said.

"She what?"

"It was her ex-husband's car we took."

"Are you kidding me? Is this some kind of joke now?"

"I didn't tell you before because you'd think the wrong thing, but he's the one peddling the movie."

"He's a mobster?"

"Not a mobster, no. He works for them."

Holly's eyes narrowed. "Isn't that the same thing?"

"It's not what you think."

"Of course not. Nothing is what I think, but then it turns out exactly what I thought. What's going on, Louis?"

"What I told you. We took money from bad guys. Nancy's ex, he's a bad guy works for other bad guys."

"And Nancy did this why, out of the kindness of her heart or because you're still screwing her?"

"I'm not screwing her. Would you get over that already? Look at you and look at her. No comparison, okay."

What Holly noticed was he still couldn't look her in the eyes. It was the same when she had asked him about his rash and mentioned it looked like what they did for people who had crabs. He couldn't look her in the eyes then either.

"I've known people who had crabs before," she said.

"What?" he said. "We're back to that again?"

She waited for eye contact, but there wasn't any.

"Never play poker, Louis," she told him.

"What's poker got to do with anything?"

"I want to go back to the dorm."

"What?"

"I want to go home."

"Fine, I'll drop you off. You can give the professor a call. See his dick is still hard."

"You're disgusting."

"If you say so."

Holly slid out of the booth. "Let's go," she said.

"In a minute," Louis said.

She stood over him. "Now," she said.

"You mind I pay the check, maybe take a piss?"

"I'll wait in the car," she said.

She was on her way out when she spotted him giving her the finger in the mirrored wall's reflection. She stopped and turned around.

"Fuck you, too," she yelled loud enough for the entire diner to hear.

Then she left.

■ ■ ■

John's mother told Nancy that a cop had come to the door asking about John and money he owed and then asked about Little Jack, if he was there

in the house with her, but she didn't believe he was a cop, even though he
had a badge.

Now she was in a hurry on her way out and didn't have time to talk.
Nancy asked her to hold on a minute. She told Marie to put her son on the
phone, but the old bag said they were in a hurry and promised to call back
when John told her it was okay.

"You know how much he owes?" Nancy asked.

"What? He didn't say he owes anything."

"It's a lot."

"How do you know?"

Nancy rolled her eyes. "Because he told me."

"Why would he tell you?"

"Fifteen thousand," Nancy said. She figured why not make it more than
it was. The old lady probably had that and more.

"How much?" Marie Albano asked.

"You heard me."

"I don't believe it. I don't believe you."

"Then ask your son."

"I will."

"Good."

Marie hung up.

"Bitch," Nancy said.

If there was a way out of this mess without someone getting hurt, Nancy
assumed it was John's mother. There was no way the old bag wouldn't bail
her son out. The problem would be John and whether or not he'd allow
his mother to help. Probably not, Nancy was thinking, which was why she
might have to negotiate the situation herself.

It wouldn't be easy.

She was still pissed off at hearing Louis's blonde bimbo's voice in the
background of their telephone conversation earlier. Wherever he was with
their money, the blonde was right there with him. Nancy wondered if
there wasn't some way to implicate little Miss Oklahoma in the robbery.
Chances are she had been there for that too and was guilty anyway.

Nancy had made Louis promise he was finished with that one and had
believed him until she heard the blonde calling his name through the
phone. The man couldn't be trusted.

She had even started to get beyond the smacks she took the night before,
figuring they had been a small price to pay for the money Louis had net-
ted; money that would get them started together somewhere else until her
half of the house from her divorce would provide a small windfall. She
would go back to work and Louis would find something new and then
maybe they could go back to being married again.

She had heard of couples that had done that, break up one year, have other relationships that didn't work out and then start over again. It wasn't a complete pipe dream.

She looked at the time and realized John would be calling soon wanting to know if she knew where Louis was or if he'd called her. It had been a mistake admitting Louis was involved, but now that she'd done it, she'd have to string John along.

There was still a lot to do, Nancy was thinking, when the telephone rang at ten-fifteen.

"Hello?" she answered.

"It's me," Nathan said.

"Oh, okay. What do you want?"

"When will you be out of the house?"

"Excuse me?"

"I need to get a few things."

"And why can't I be here?"

"You can. I'd rather you weren't."

"Don't you think you're being silly?"

"I can't make you leave, Nancy, but I'd rather do this without you."

"Nonsense. You can come whenever you're ready. I won't get in your way."

"Fine. My sister will be coming with me."

"What for?"

"We'll try for noon."

"What? Wait a minute."

Nathan had already hung up.

"Bastard," Nancy said. "How dare he hang up on me."

She started to call him back, stopped herself, then dialed again anyway.

"Hello?" Nathan answered.

Nancy hung up.

"There," she said. "How do you like it?"

CHAPTER 47

Melinda was awake when Jill called to complain about a fight she'd had with the guy she'd just dumped. It would've been a long conversation, except Melinda said she couldn't tie up the phone and that Jill should come over instead. Jill said she'd be over later in the morning. Melinda said she'd leave a key under the doormat if she wasn't home.

She watched John sleeping afterward, his face toward her, his abdomen and chest rising and descending ever so slightly. She had to stop herself from reaching out to touch him.

At nine-fifteen she slipped out of bed to make the coffee. She scrambled some eggs, put up the bacon and prepared four slices of toast while listening to the news on her kitchen radio. The weather report... sports... the time.

She woke him at nine-thirty.

"What time is it?" he asked.

"Nine thirty-five."

"Shit."

"What?"

"I have to call the bar."

"Why?"

"I have to talk to Vento."

"Who's he?"

"Eddie Vento."

She remembered the gangster. "Why?"

"And Nancy," John said. "I should probably call her first, see if she spoke to Louis yet."

"Louis is probably in Las Vegas."

"Probably, but I need to know. And my mother. I have to call her and see what's going on there. I told her to go someplace safe."

"Jesus," Melinda said. "You made all these plans... when exactly?"

She was feeling left out and it scared her. She called to him as he made his way to the bathroom.

"John?"

"I'll be right out," he said.

She saw the bathroom door close.

"You're shutting me out," she said.

"What?"

She stood there staring at the bathroom door. She heard the toilet flush, then the sink running.

"John?"

He opened the door and kissed her on the cheek as he tried to brush passed her.

"John!"

He slipped through her hold and headed for the kitchen. Melinda followed him.

"You're ignoring me," she said, then waited for him to turn and face her again. "You made all these decisions and none of them include me."

"I don't want you involved, Melinda."

"I am involved, damn it."

He hugged her.

"I'm afraid for you, in case you haven't noticed."

"I notice you made breakfast."

She slapped his arm a bit harder than she intended.

"Ouch."

"Pay attention to me," she said. "I'm trying to help."

"I'm sorry."

Melinda could feel herself turning red with frustration. "Eat something," she said. She motioned at him to sit, then poured the coffee while he started on the eggs.

"Aren't you hungry?" he asked between bites.

"I was. I'm not now."

"You should eat."

She grabbed a piece of toast.

"Jill is coming over."

"Your waitress friend?"

"She had a fight with some guy she was dating and he won't stop calling her house."

"Why doesn't she leave the phone off the hook."

"Because then he rings her doorbell."

"Cops?"

"John, I don't know, but she's coming over and I don't want to talk with anybody right now. I mean it."

"Okay," John said.

"Except you."

"I'm right here."

"Can I ask you something?"

"Sure."

"Why are you calling Nancy?"

"To see if Louis called."

"And if he did?"

"Maybe she knows where he is."

"You think she'll tell you? She loves him. She isn't going to give him up."

"She's scared enough she will. She was terrified last night."

"I'm not so sure."

"I saw her. She was scared."

He was doing it again, defending the woman who had tried to set him up to take a fall with the mob.

"And why call that other guy from the bar?" she asked.

"Because he's the one who counts," John said. "It's Eddie Vento's money. I need him to know I didn't rob him. He already knows about me and Santorra." He grabbed a strip of bacon. "Not what I did last night, but that I popped him at the bar last week. Vento should know what Santorra did to my car."

"Why would the mob guy care about what Santorra did to your car or that you beat him up?"

"Because Eddie Vento knows Santorra is a fuckup. He told me so himself."

Melinda was confused. "I don't see how that helps."

"Let him suspect Santorra or that he had something to do with it. The punk deserves it."

"But you won't give up Nancy, right?"

"I won't. It was Louis did this. I know she helped, but he's the one with the money. She's my son's mother. I may not be able to find Louis on my own, but they sure can."

"And how does that help you? If Louis spent it, I mean. You said the mob won't care anyway, they'll still look for you."

"Eddie will, probably, but maybe he won't kill me."

It was too much to contemplate. She suggested the obvious. "What about the police?"

"Only if I want to kill myself," he said. "There's no turning to the law on this, Melinda. I'm not going that route, looking over my shoulder the rest of my life. No thanks. It was my choice to take that work. It's my headache."

There was no talking to the man, she thought. He was stubborn to the point of suicidal.

"I was thinking I'd follow Nancy," he said. "I'll have to be careful because Vento's guys are probably doing the same. I doubt Louis goes to meet her. She'd have to go to him."

"And he'll spot you if you're there and then he'd disappear for sure, right?"

"It gets tricky."

"If it's all about the money, I think you should consider my offer again. You could go find Louis after you're safe."

He ignored her comment and reached for a piece of toast.

"John?"

"Can I use your car again?"

"Can I come along?"

He sipped his coffee.

"I might be able to help," she said. "They don't know me."

"I don't want you involved."

"I know that. And I won't be, but you might need me."

"What about work?"

"I already called in."

"So you made some plans too?"

"Don't fight me on this."

He rubbed his temples.

"John?"

"Alright," he said. "But we do it my way. No arguing."

She didn't like giving in, even temporarily, but it was better than watching him leave and then having to spend the day waiting again.

"Okay," she said. "Deal."

■ ■ ■

Billy wasn't sure if the old man had survived being hit so hard with the handgun, but he'd tied and gagged him anyway. If the geezer wound up suffocating from the gag or choking on his own blood, it'd be his own fault for being nosey.

That had been hours ago. Still impressed by the old man's nerve, Billy hoped he'd been found.

After leaving Albano's apartment, he'd driven to the girlfriend's house. He'd made a few passes around the block, but didn't see the Buick or the Valiant. It was possible they had gone out to breakfast. It was also possible Albano had started back to Brooklyn and the girlfriend had gone to work, but then Billy spotted movement through the living room window and pulled to the curb two houses from the corner.

The street was quiet except for a few kids he could see in his rearview mirror playing stickball at the far end of the block. Billy put the Walther in a small gym bag alongside his AGA Campolin stiletto before getting out of the car and heading back toward the girlfriend's place.

He had brought the knife along with the rifle and the Walther because he didn't have a sound suppressor. Billy figured it was best to stab whoever answered the door.

He was hoping to use the Walther on Albano but was prepared to take him out from a distance with the hunting rifle.

Now he held the knife inside the bag as he pressed the doorbell with his free hand. He released the blade when he heard footsteps behind the door. He held the screen door handle with his free hand and pulled on it as the front door opened.

"Yes?" the woman said a split second before Billy plunged the knife into her stomach.

Her eyes opened wide as she fell back against the pantry wall. Billy stepped inside and closed the front door behind him. The woman was spitting blood. Billy looked into the kitchen but didn't see anyone. The woman grabbed at his leg.

"Sorry, hon," he said before squatting down to cover her nose and mouth. Her body jerked, but Billy's eyes remained glued to the open area in the kitchen. A full minute passed before she stopped moving. Billy continued to cut off her air another thirty seconds, then pulled the Walther from the gym bag and made his way through the house.

He found the note on the kitchen table on his way back to the front door.

Jill,

Sorry, I had to leave. Make yourself at home. There's leftover Chinese in the fridge. Talk to you later.

Mel

"Who's Mel?" Billy said. "What's your name, hon, and where the hell'd you go?"

Then he saw the other piece of paper taped to the refrigerator. A list of names and phone numbers in different handwriting:

John: 241-6331

John's Ex: 696-2001

John's Mom: 696-4891

Billy reached for the phone hanging on the wall. "Let's not call and ruin the surprise," he said, lowering his arm. "But let's do go visit Mom."

■　■　■

"No, you won't pay them," John told his mother over the phone. "I won't let you."

"You can't stop me," Marie Albano said. "I'm not going to let anything happen to you or my grandson. These people are animals and I don't know why you bothered with them in the first place, you could've come to me if you needed money, but now that they're coming to my door, I'm going to pay them and that's it."

"What do you mean they came to your door?"

"This morning, a little while ago, a tall guy with red hair. He had a badge, but I don't think he was a cop."

"What did he want? What did he say?"

"He wanted to know where you were and when I told him I didn't know he said to give you a message to go see the guy from Brooklyn. Then he asked if Little Jack was home."

"He knew Jack's name?"

"No, he said grandson. He asked if my grandson was home with me."

"Jesus Christ."

"Exactly, and that's why I'm paying them whatever you owe."

"I don't owe them a thing, Ma. I was robbed yesterday. The guy who stole the money owes it."

"Well, then they'll get their money because I'm not taking any chances with loved ones. Good-bye."

"Ma!"

It was too late, his mother had hung up.

"God damn it!" John yelled.

Melinda had been listening alongside him at the pay phone. "They went to your mother?"

"They sent somebody to scare her and it worked."

"You can't blame her for being scared."

"I know that. Obviously they do, too."

"This is getting out of control."

John motioned toward the car. "Let's go," he said.

"Where?"

"My mother's."

"What if they're watching?"

"Then they'll see me."

She stopped before getting in. John slid behind the steering wheel. He put the key in the ignition and started the engine, then turned to Melinda as she got in.

"It'll be okay," he said.

■ ■ ■

Bridget Malone was extra nervous today. Two nights ago she'd nearly been killed by somebody Special Agent Stebenow insisted had been hired by the red-haired cop on Eddie Vento's payroll. She had assumed the government would bring her in off the streets, but they hadn't. Stebenow said her life was still in danger and that she should stay with him, but Bridget knew her only real freedom would come when she gave them something to convict Eddie Vento with. After spending the night wondering what to do, she decided to give it one last try.

She'd returned to the bar the following day and was lucky to learn Eddie had spent the night with his wife. Then when he turned up early this morning, she was in the shower when he yelled at her to hurry because he wanted to get laid.

Concerned he might want to fuck as soon as he saw her, she was forced to remove the recording device she had taped to her right thigh. She wrapped it with a pair of black panties and stuffed them in the hamper.

Vento said he needed to use the bathroom when she came out. Bridget used the opportunity to move the backup recorder from the bottom drawer of a night table in her bedroom to under the couch in her living room. Then she removed her clothes to expedite their sex and Vento made her put on high heels when he was ready. He made it rough, bending her over the arm of the couch and not bothering to use a lubricant. He insisted she remain naked but continue wearing the heels afterward.

She used the bathroom again, making sure to flush while she checked the hamper to make sure he hadn't discovered the tape. Then she plugged herself with a tuft of tissue and returned to the living room. Vento was on the couch. He had lit a cigar and had his feet up on the coffee table. He made her stand in front of him while he peppered her with questions about where she had been the night before.

"Out," she said. "Why?"

"Because I called and you didn't answer," he said.

"So? Where were you? With wifey?"

"That's my fuckin' business where I was."

Bridget set her hands on her hips. "So?" she said.

"You fucking somebody?"

"Besides you, no."

"You sure?"

"Are you serious?"

"Extremely."

"That's ridiculous."

"Unless you are and I don't know about it."

"I'm not fucking anybody, Eddie. Jesus."

Vento stared at her until she was nervous enough to smile. "What?" she said.

He didn't answer. He got up off the couch to use the bathroom again.

Bridget noticed a wire under the couch skirt and quickly dropped to the floor to hide it. She heard the toilet flush and stood up. The tissue plug she'd used dropped to the floor without her noticing. She quickly moved to the windows and adjusted the air-conditioning from high to medium as the bathroom door opened.

"You got any coffee?" Vento said.

"I can make some."

"Make it then. I need to stay awake."

"Sleepy, baby?"

"Fuck tired's more like it. The hell is that?"

Bridget stopped midway to the kitchen and turned around. Vento was pointing to the tissue plug on the floor.

"Oh," she said. "That's me."

"You?"

Bridget went to the tissue and picked it up. "Actually it's you," she said. "It must've fell out."

Vento still didn't get it. Then he looked to where she was pointing and saw his milky liquid had run partway down the inside of her right thigh.

"Jesus Christ," he said. "Take a shower."

Bridget wiped her leg and proceeded to the kitchen. "After I make the coffee," she said. "Takes two minutes."

"Shower first, for Christ's sake," Vento said.

The telephone rang. Bridget picked up in the kitchen.

"It's me," someone said.

Bridget remained silent.

"Eddie?"

Bridget recognized the voice. It was Mister Horse. "It's for you," she told Vento.

He shooed her out of the kitchen.

"Yeah, it's me," she heard him say.

Bridget removed her heels and hustled into the bedroom where she could listen in on the other phone. She slowly, carefully released the receiver and put it to her right ear.

"Where?" Eddie said.

"The mother's house in Queens."

"You're sure?"

"Positive. Kid's there, too."

"Albano?"

"Not that I could tell. I don't think so, but he'll probably be there soon enough now I scared her."

"What's the address? Hold a second, let me get something to write on."

"I'll hold," the cop said.

"Fuckin' cunt doesn't own a note pad. I gotta use a pizza box out the garbage. Go ahead."

Bridget heard the cop rattle off an address, then Eddie said, "Anything else?"

"You could take a look-see while you're there, the apartment."

"Those things you mentioned?"

"Due diligence. Something's there it won't be hard to spot."

"Okay, I'll see you in a little while."

"Don't take your time, I'm not comfortable being around here after my initial appearance."

Vento hung up.

Bridget hung up behind him, then went to the door and quietly stepped out into the hall. She went up as far as the kitchen wall and peeked around the corner. She saw Vento was on his hands and knees looking for something under the chair. Then he seemed to see something under the couch and Bridget headed back to the bedroom. She locked the door behind her, slipped on a pair of low-heeled flats and opened the window leading to the fire escape. Then the bedroom door was kicked open.

CHAPTER 48

Angela Santorra bypassed the crowd because her husband had been brought in by ambulance. She waited for him in the partitioned area he'd been assigned a few hours earlier.

She didn't hear the curtain open when Nick was back from having his broken nose set.

"Air a kids?" he grunted more than said.

Angela could see his upper lip was very swollen along with his cheeks around the bandage.

"At Mom's," she said.

"Ors or ine?"

"Mine. You okay?"

"I ook it?"

She saw there was black and blue around the edges of the bandage near his eyes. His lip was gross. She wondered if he had lost any teeth.

"What happened?" she asked.

"I ot umped. Ee eyes."

"What?"

He held up three fingers. "Eee," he said.

"Does it hurt?"

"Ony en I eeth."

"What?"

"Es, it urs."

She tried not to talk to him during the drive home. He had that look that scared her, the way he sometimes got when he'd made a big bet and lost. Like a few months ago when Secretariat won the Belmont Stakes and Nick kicked the television screen in because he had wheeled all the other horses on top of Secretariat, four fifty-dollar exactas he had sworn would make them rich. His eyes had that same look then they did now.

Angela didn't know what had happened the night before. She assumed it had to do with what had happened last week when he came home with that knot on his forehead and said some guy had given him a cheap-shot. Maybe it was the same guy again. She wasn't sure she believed it was three guys.

She managed to keep him calm until he told her to turn left rather than right on Cross Bay Boulevard near their home.

He grumbled when she asked why.

She didn't understand what he'd said and asked again.

"A un," he repeated.

"I'm sorry, Nick, I can't understand. What?"

"A un. A un."

She saw he had those eyes again. "I can't make out what you're saying."
He pumped his right hand a few times until she realized he had made a
gun out of it. "A un," he said. Then he pointed left for her to turn that way.
Angela didn't bother asking anything else.

■ ■ ■

Holly hadn't said a word the entire trip. Louis stopped at a service area
along the Garden State Parkway to call about the Cadillac Eldorado.
Sharon Dowell yawned into the phone when she answered after six rings.

"Hey, doll," Louis said.

"Huh?" Sharon said.

"It's me, Louis."

"Oh, you woke me," she said with no emotion.

"Sorry."

"Can you call back? It's not even noon yet."

"Late sleeper, huh?"

"What do you want, Louis?"

"You're the one told me to call."

"To call, not to wake me."

"Sorry."

"It's here."

"What?"

"Your car."

"It is?" Louis felt a tingle of excitement.

"In the driveway," she said.

"You serious?"

"Louis, it's too early in the morning for me to joke. You can come see it
this afternoon, but not before three o'clock."

"This is great. How's it look?"

"Like a car. A big one."

"Great. And you have the paperwork?"

"Yes. He already signed it over to me."

"To you?"

"Don't worry, I don't want it. You buy it from me and I'll sign it over to
you."

"Wait a minute. You bought it? For how much?"

"I bought it as a technicality. He's waiting on the money."

"How much?"

"Original sticker price."

"What was that?"

"Seventy-five hundred."

"Seventy-five? I thought it was closer to six."

"Look, hon, we can argue about it when I'm awake."

Louis huffed. "Alright, but the car looks good?"

"It's beautiful, yeah."

"Okay, I guess."

"You guess?"

"Okay. It's okay."

"Good. I'm going back to sleep now. We'll talk again later."

"Alright."

He didn't like the twist to the car deal, but Louis was still excited when he hung up. He glanced at his watch and saw he could make it back to New York by mid-afternoon. When he returned to the car Holly was gone.

"Now what?" he said.

He decided he'd give her two minutes.

■ ■ ■

"Put me through to Eddie," John told Eugene.

He had stopped on his way to his mother's and made the call from a pay phone on Metropolitan Avenue.

"This John?" Eugene said.

"Yeah, Eugene. He in?"

There was a pause before Eddie Vento said, "It's me."

"I didn't steal that money," John said.

"I'd like to believe that, but you don't make it easy."

"I'm telling you I didn't steal it. I figured you'd think it was me is why I didn't call or come back to the bar."

"And I'm telling you I can't just take your word."

"Why not ask the little prick busted my windshield when I was in Northport," John said. "Last night I busted his nose."

"Excuse me?"

"Santorra, Eddie. The prick gave me flats during the week, then busted my windshield the same day I was robbed."

"You fuckin' kidding me?"

"I broke his nose and I'm not about to apologize for it."

"After I told you hands off? You're talking an awful lot of shit for a guy in your position."

"I'm no tough guy, but I'm not gonna let some punk like Santorra take potshots at my car and then maybe set me up for the crime of the century."

"The way you two talk about each other makes me suspicious of both of yous."

"You're joking, right?"

"Remember who you're talking to, jerkoff."

John could see Melinda watching him from the car.

"You there?" Vento said.

"I'm here," John said.

"The point is I need to see your face up close where I can read your eyes better than through a phone."

"I'm sorry, Eddie, but I can't do that yet. I need to clear myself of this bullshit and getting my legs broken won't make it any easier."

"Who said anything about breaking legs?"

"I'm not coming in yet."

"You'll do what I tell you to do, my friend."

"Don't take this the wrong way," said John before he hung up.

"How'd that go?" Melinda asked when he was back in the car.

"It didn't."

"Where to now?"

"My mother's place."

"You sure?"

"I need to make sure she's out of there. I don't trust these pricks. They get to her, she'll sign her house over."

"It might buy you time if they think they're getting paid. Why you should tell them you have it. I have it."

"I'm not letting you or my mother get robbed."

"Maybe we don't see it that way, saving your life."

John was preoccupied wondering why Nancy had gone along with such a crazy scheme. Melinda turned east onto the Brooklyn-Queens Expressway when he finally realized why.

"That bitch!"

"What?" Melinda said.

"Nancy."

"Excuse me, but about fucking time."

"She told my mother about the money," John said.

"She was probably counting on telling her."

"It's how she justified this from the start."

"They steal from you and your mother pays it off so nobody gets hurt."

"Only Nancy'd be stupid enough to think nobody'd get hurt."

"She knew exactly what she was doing," Melinda said. "Stop telling me how stupid she is. Right now you're the stupid one in all this. You're the one protecting everybody else."

John saw a sign for an exit and pointed to it. "Take McGuinness Boulevard."

Melinda checked her rearview mirror and switched from the middle to right lane.

John leaned across the console. "I appreciate your concern," he said. "I do."

"It's about time."

"Now how 'bout a kiss?"

"How 'bout I break your face?"

"Never mind," John said.

She was glaring at him again. He winked.

"I'll kick your ass," she said. "I swear it."

■ ■ ■

Brice was growing anxious waiting for Kelly outside the Sutphin Boulevard subway stop. He knew Levin was watching from the van parked half a block behind the Mustang and was nervous Kelly might spot the surveillance. The two had trailed Kelly to a Queens precinct less than an hour ago. When Brice called the precinct, Kelly had left a message for him to meet outside the subway stop. That was ten minutes ago.

Brice finished the last of a Yoo-Hoo drink and stuffed a napkin inside the mouth of the bottle before setting it down on the floor beneath the passenger seat. As he straightened up, he glanced at the *Daily News* and saw the headline: Agnew's Lawyers Start Own Probe.

"Everybody's dirty," he said.

A moment later he yawned into a fist. A loud knock on the passenger window made him jump.

"Jesus Christ!" he said.

Kelly removed the *Daily News* from the passenger seat as he got in the car. "Morning, boyo."

"More like afternoon," Brice said.

"I got a lift," Kelly said.

Brice pulled the fifty-dollar bill from his pants pocket and held it up. "I think you dropped this in my car."

Kelly waved it off. "Careful, boyo, we're in the jungle here. They'd cut your nuts off for a pound, never mind something that big."

Brice went to hand him the bill.

Kelly waved it off again. "Isn't mine," he said. "I haven't seen one of those since I was married."

"It was on your seat after you got out," Brice said. "I didn't put it there."

"You ask Levin? He sat up front the day before, right?"

"Only till you came, but there was too much traffic back and forth between you two for it not to've been noticed. I know it isn't mine."

"Looks like it is now."

Brice was still holding the bill. "You gonna take it?"

"It's not mine. Keep it, boyo. Get yourself laid tonight. At least put it away before you get us both killed."

"Shit," Brice said, stashing the bill in his pants pocket.

"You talk to Levin?" Kelly asked.

"Nope."

"Give him another few minutes. At least it's not a sauna again today. Rain last night must've helped. Maybe it'll keep the apes in this jungle in their trees. I'm on the train here once a few years ago, this part a the Congo, there was a guy must've shit his pants six years ago the stench was so foul. Which is one reason I don't like Jamaica. A guy has to piss, his tires could disappear. But don't talk like that in front of Levin. Guy's a bleeding heart faggot it comes to the darkies."

"There's a rash of stolen cars over in Canarsie," Brice said. "Worse than anywhere according to a friend a mine in the precinct there, the Sixty-ninth. That's a white neighborhood."

Kelly didn't get it. "Yids and dagos," he said. "Going back to forever, they had that turf, Canarsie."

Brice checked his rearview mirror and saw the van was still there. The few minutes they were supposed to wait for Levin turned to twenty while Kelly read the newspaper. Brice finally mentioned the time and Kelly got out of the car to use the pay phone. It was noon already.

A few minutes later Kelly returned to the car thumbing toward the street.

"What is it?" Brice said.

"He's out sick again, the lazy fuck. But I need you to drop me off some-wheres."

"Where?"

Kelly got in the car. "Queens," he said.

"What's there?"

"Me, when you get me there. You're going to Levin's place to see if he's really out sick or just jerking my chain. I had it with that guy."

"What? I'm not spying."

Kelly motioned toward the street for Brice to start driving. "It's an order," he said. "Now, let's go."

■ ■ ■

The pain in his nose had shifted to his mouth and then his teeth. Then it turned into a headache and he couldn't blink it hurt so much. Nick was on Quaaludes and codeine and had taken half a dozen aspirin as soon as he got home, but now that he was awake again, his head felt as if it would explode. He took a bunch of his wife's diet pills to help him shake the grogginess.

He had made Angela take him to a guy he knew sold guns. It was right after they left the hospital when he was still numb enough not to feel the pain. The guy had showed him three pieces, all used, which meant they had all been stolen, found or pawned, not the best weapons in the world to use because of their prior history, but Nick was obsessed with getting John Albano and didn't care. He paid seventy-five dollars for a semiautomatic handgun that looked and even felt a little shaky when he pulled the trigger on an empty clip.

"Is ing onna all a-art en ah oo it?" he'd asked the seller.

"What?" the seller said.

Angela helped translate. "The way it looks, he said," she said after Nick mumbled something unintelligible. "He thinks if he shoots you from across the room it'll fall apart in his hands."

"I'll tell you what," the seller had said to Nick. "Go stand over there and I'll shoot you with it. It falls apart, I'll give you your money back."

Now that he couldn't sleep anymore he was anxious to shower and get a start on searching for John Albano. All he could think about was the beating he'd taken outside the bar and how he'd have to face everybody a second time, except this time it was even worse, his nose had been broken, the discoloration would be with him for weeks, not to mention his nose would be crooked.

And then there was Eddie Vento. How was he supposed to deal with that cranky fuck after this?

Nick was half out of the bed and about to give up and go back to sleep when the phone rang. He couldn't move fast enough. His wife said hello into the receiver and told the caller to hold on before passing it to Nick.

"Aloe?" he said.

"It's me," Eddie Vento said.

"Air," Nick said.

"What?"

"Air."

"The fuck you saying?"

"I ant alk," Nick said.

"You can't talk?"

"O."

"Okay, then listen," Vento said. "I got a call before from a mutual friend said he kicked your ass again, broke your nose or some shit. Maybe that's why you sound like a retard. All I know is I want some answers about what the fuck he told me, some of which I already confirmed, which you didn't tell me the other day when I asked you."

"Ott?"

"Never mind what," Vento said. "Just get your busted ass down the bar and wait for me there so's I can see for myself the number this guy did on you again."

"E umped me."

"Yeah, right."

"E id."

"Yeah? Okay, uck ooo."

Nick tried to clench his teeth in anger. Biting down sent a jolt of pain up through his jaw to his head.

"Uck ee!" he said, then it hurt all over again.

■ ■ ■

Stebenow had called the old lady Bridget Malone looked after in the building where she lived with Eddie Vento. He left a message for Bridget to call her uncle at his office. The number Stebenow gave was a pay phone at a diner around the corner from Fast Eddie's where he was having breakfast. He ate a western omelet, toast, a corn muffin and drank five cups of coffee before he gave up waiting and went to the apartment.

He used the pay phone to leave Detective Levin an emergency message. Then Stebenow called Bridget's home phone number. Nobody answered.

The bar had already been open for business a few hours when Stebenow parked off the near corner. He walked past the front window without looking inside. He walked a dozen or so yards past the bar, then turned and approached the front door alongside the bar entrance.

There were two floors above the bar, each with two apartments; one at each end of the hallways. Stebenow stood close to the front door while he picked the lock. He walked up the first flight of stairs to the landing and listened before going further. Vento's apartment faced the street. The door was at the far end of the narrow hallway. Stebenow had no idea whether the wiseguy had spent the night there or not. He removed the Sig-Sauer as he made his way to the apartment Bridget shared with Eddie Vento.

He knocked on the door and listened for a response.

Nothing.

He knocked again, this time a little louder. He waited, heard nothing again, then glanced down the hallway as he slid the handgun into the waist of his pants. He picked the lock, then carefully opened the door. Using the door as a shield, he looked down the apartment hallway. The bathroom door was open at the far end of the hall, but the light was off. He quietly closed the apartment door, took another glance around the apartment from where he stood, but noticed nothing out of order. He raised the gun and stepped into the living room. He scanned the room from one end to the other. Again, nothing seemed out of place.

Stebenow took careful steps toward the back of the apartment. Halfway between the kitchen and bathroom was a door he assumed led to the bedroom. He looked down and noticed scuff marks on the floor. He raised the Sig-Sauer to chest level with his right hand as he opened the door with his left. The door stopped after no more than a foot. Stebenow called Bridget's name, but there was no answer.

He pushed on the door with both hands until it opened enough so he could pass through. He stepped into the bedroom with the gun leveled out ahead as he scanned the room. One of two windows leading to the fire escape was open. Stebenow looked down and saw the tip of a pair of shoes sticking out one end of a rolled-up rug, what had been blocking the door.

"Oh, Jesus," he said. "Oh, fuck."

CHAPTER 49

Holly had returned a few seconds before Louis pulled away.

"The hell'd you go?" he'd asked her.

"The bathroom. To check myself. That a problem, Louis?"

"Get in."

He had tried to explain himself, but Holly wouldn't hear it. She claimed her brother had once had crabs and that he too had had to shave his testicles and that she recognized the cream as well because it looked exactly like the one her brother had used. She hated him, she told him later, for letting her go to bed with him, and when he asked her why the hell had she insisted they do it, especially if she was so damn sure he had crabs and not just some rash, Holly had said because she was leaving it up to him to be honorable and not lie to her again.

Louis had told her she was certifiable.

"And what're you?" she'd said.

"I'm just a guy trying to make a living," he'd told her.

"You're a thief is what you are," she'd said.

They were close to the city when she decided she wanted to chat or break his balls, he still wasn't sure which. She had turned on the seat so her back was flush against the door. He imagined the door opening and her falling out.

"So, you were fucking Nancy and me at the same time, but neither of us have crabs so who'd you get them from?" she asked.

"Neither of you," Louis said.

"Obviously. So, who?"

"What's the difference?"

"I'd like to know."

"Some broad in the park."

"What park?"

"Washington Square."

Holly's face turned red. "Near the dorm?"

"Yeah, the night you dumped me for Professor pervert."

"You're kidding?"

"Get over yourself, honey."

"I can't believe it. You fucked some slut at the park and got crabs and then gave them to me?"

"From the park, not at the park. And you're the one insisted we fuck. I tried not to. You get crabs, although I doubt you will, they're probably all dead already, but if you do, it's your own fault."

"I can't believe you, Louis. You're insane."

"For taking you along, yeah, I must be."

"I guess the money isn't going to a woman's organization."

"Not unless you have a gun."

"You are a thief. You really are."

"Oh, stop it. You enjoyed what we did. You said so yourself."

"Because I thought it was for a cause."

"And now that you know it wasn't, that makes it less exciting? I believe that's the word you used."

"It's wrong. Stealing is wrong."

"Even though we're driving around with thirteen different copies of *Deep Throat*? Thirteen copies that'll never be played again, I might add. What about that?"

"You're full of it, Louis. You'll probably sell those to somebody else. You're a thief and that's what thieves do with stolen property, they sell it."

"You can still help me with the car," he said. "I'll pay you for that. Up front if you want."

"No thanks."

"I said up front. Two hundred."

"You have close to fourteen thousand dollars in that bag and you want to pay me two hundred? How much will you make off the car, another ten thousand?"

"I wish."

"I hope you get robbed for a change."

"Is that nice?"

"I can't believe I fell for your bullshit."

Louis sighed.

"So, what happens now?" she asked. "You have to get back to Nancy and make sure she doesn't tell on you, right?"

"Don't strain yourself, kiddo."

"I better not have crabs, Louis."

This time he laughed.

"I mean it," Holly said.

"I'm sure you do," Louis said.

■ ■ ■

Eddie Vento had been rushed after the call from Eugene this morning. After learning Kelly had found where John Albano's mother lived and that Albano's kid was with her, Vento discovered a tape recorder under the couch and had to deal with that. He'd called Tommy Burns to see if the kid was available to dispose of the body, but the young Irishman hadn't answered. Vento was forced to delegate the removal of Bridget's body to his own people later in the day. He spent the rest of the morning preparing it.

It was early afternoon when Vento drove himself to the address Kelly had provided. To avoid being spotted, he left his Cadillac parked in front of the bar and used his wife's Buick Riviera. Instead of his usual neat attire, Vento wore cutoff shorts, a black T-shirt, and a navy blue Yankees baseball cap.

The address was in the middle of the block. Vento drove two blocks past it before making a U-turn, then drove back toward the house, turned right at the near adjacent corner and parked. He turned his sun visor down and took note of the cars already on the street. Vento paid particular attention to a UPS van parked at the curb on the next block.

He smoked some of his cigar and was about to relight it when the UPS van pulled away. Vento checked the time. He was expecting Kelly within the hour. If Albano didn't show shortly thereafter, he would send a few of his men to watch the house. Once Albano's mother saw what was going on, chances were she'd offer to pay the money her son was responsible for losing, whether he was guilty of stealing it or not.

Vento was still wondering about Albano and whether or not he was stupid enough to rob mob money when a white car passed the Riviera and pulled into a driveway about mid-block. A few seconds later John Albano got out of the car along with a blonde. Vento sat up straight.

■ ■ ■

"He thinks I'm following you," said Brice when he got inside the van. "He wants to make sure you're really sick this time."

Levin had stopped to pick up Brice alongside a fire hydrant on McGinnis Boulevard after Brice had dropped Kelly off at a gas station three lights further up the street. Brice had circled the block to park the Mustang where Levin could spot it.

"How'd he act?" Levin asked.

"Like his usual charming self. What's going on?"

Levin pointed up ahead where Kelly was pulling out of the gas station in a brown Chevrolet Impala. He kept a safe distance behind Kelly, then moved up when the Impala turned off the exit for the Long Island Expressway.

"He heading back?" Brice asked.

"Definitely," Levin said.

It was all that was said for the next twenty minutes while they followed the Impala onto Woodhaven Boulevard heading south. Confident he knew where Kelly was heading, Levin let the Impala gain some distance.

"Something's going down, right?" Brice said. "You could at least give me the option I want to be here or not."

"What time is it?" Levin said.

"Two-ten," Brice said.

"Shit. I need to make a call."

The Impala turned right onto North Conduit Boulevard. Levin fed the engine gas to catch up.

"Now what?" Brice said.

"This is about Albano."

"Johnny Porno? What about him?"

Levin followed the Impala a few blocks before it turned right at 84th Street. Kelly parked in the first open space.

"I have to make that call," Levin said. "I passed a phone booth about a block back the other way."

Kelly was out of the Impala and walking. Levin drove passed 84th Street and turned.

"I'm gonna pull over," he said. "You wait here."

■   ■   ■

Melinda poured the coffee at Marie Albano's kitchen table while mother and son continued to argue about the money John insisted he wouldn't let his mother pay.

"I didn't steal it, I'm not paying it," he told his mother. "Neither are you. Or her."

Marie Albano looked up at Melinda.

"She offered, too," John said, "and I told her the same thing. I know the guy stole it. He can pay it. I'm not letting either one of you get robbed because of him."

Melinda had finished pouring the coffee. She sat across from John. His mother was at one end of the table. Little Jack was in her room watching television.

"I appreciate what you offered to do for him," Marie told Melinda. "But this is a family matter. I'll pay."

"What am I, a mirage?" John said.

"No, but you're thick," Marie said. She looked at Melinda then motioned at John with a hand. "Stubborn like his father."

"I'm getting the stubborn part," Melinda said.

John ran his right hand through his hair. "Look, neither of you understand how these guys operate," he said. "They sense weakness and they go for the jugular. Pay them once and they'll come back for more. They know they have a soft touch, they won't forget it. And, if we pay them, the guy robbed it gets away with it, which is not gonna happen."

"And what else are we supposed to do, wait for you to get jumped again?" Marie said. "What, you didn't think I noticed that on your head? I won't bother asking how it happened."

"Weren't you supposed to take off with Jack?" John said.

"Yes, and we were until all this happened. I was going to Pennsylvania. Then there were the calls and that cop showed up and now I'd just rather pay them and get it over with."

John looked to Melinda.

"You can't even go home," Marie said, then turned on her chair when the doorbell rang.

"I'll get it," John said.

"Who is it?" his mother yelled.

John was already up from the table to answer it.

■ ■ ■

Billy spotted the white Valiant parked in the driveway and pulled to the curb. He checked his rearview and side mirrors and saw there was a van parked off the far corner with two men sitting up front. He wondered if they were surveillance.

He could wait for Albano to come back out or go and knock on the door. Billy wouldn't kill Albano's mother or his son, but the girlfriend was another story; somebody had to make up for Kathleen.

He was about to get out of the car when he saw two men approach Albano's mother's front door. Billy slid the Walther out from under the front seat and set it on the passenger seat. He covered it with a two-day-old *Daily News*.

■ ■ ■

"Yeah?" said John to the two men standing on the stoop outside his mother's front door.

"You John?" the taller of the two asked.

"Who're you?" John said. He was guessing Eddie Vento had sent them and didn't see the point in being polite.

"Eddie sent us," the shorter man said.

"Come out and talk a minute?" the tall one said.

"No," John said.

"You want us to take you out?"

"Won't look good in front of whoever else's in there," the short one said.

"Why don't you come out, take a walk with us."

"Who is it?" Marie Albano asked. "I'll call the cops."

"Tell her not to do that," the tall one said.

"No need," John said over his shoulder. "I'll only be a couple minutes."

"Smart man," the tall one said.

"John!" Melinda yelled. She had opened the front door.

"I'm right back," he said.

He stepped out on the stoop. Both men chose a side and grabbed John by an elbow. His mother yelled from a living room window as Melinda stepped out on the stoop.

"We're just gonna talk," the tall one yelled. "Tell the old bag to keep the cops out of it."

John hadn't liked being grabbed. He took extra exception at his mother being called an old bag and slammed an elbow into the tall man's stomach. His right hand free, he shifted his weight onto his right leg and came up with a half uppercut, half hook, but the punch barely glanced the short man's forehead.

John tried to recover his balance when the short man threw an uppercut of his own, a perfect shot to the crotch. John gasped a moment before he doubled over and then dropped to his knees. Then he was being dragged and he could hear Melinda and his mother screaming from the stoop.

CHAPTER 50

Billy stepped out of his wife's car with the two-day-old newspaper folded around the Walther. He crossed the street and was heading for the car
John Albano had been forced into when it suddenly jerked away from the
curb. He watched as it made a quick U-turn across the lawn alongside
Albano's mother's house. He heard tires screech and had to hustle back
onto the sidewalk as the Marquis bounced off the curb and sped away.

Billy turned toward the car thinking he might be able to shoot the tires
out, but yelling from the Albano house distracted him. He could see an
older woman on the stoop. He flashed his phony badge with his free hand
and told her he was police. Then he saw the girlfriend heading for the
Valiant and Billy rushed up the driveway, opened the driver's side door
and showed her the Walther. He told her to move over.

He saw the key was in the ignition and started the car. He shifted into
reverse and quickly backed out of the driveway. As he straightened out the
car in the street, Billy saw someone holding up a hand in his rearview mirror. On his right the old woman had started down the stoop and was
yelling something when Billy turned to Albano's girlfriend.

"Don't get nervous," he told her.

He leaned to his right and extended his right arm out across her chest.
He leveled the Walther at the house and fired one shot at the stoop behind
the old lady. Then he shot at one of the tires of a parked car at the curb. As
he drove away, Billy turned to his left and swore he saw Sean Kelly lying
on the street in front of somebody holding a gun.

■ ■ ■

Brice had been watching Kelly sitting in his car more than twenty minutes before the lieutenant detective finally got out of his car. Kelly walked
to the far corner, turned as if he'd forgotten something, then turned again
and continued walking until he was standing alongside the passenger side
of the Riviera parked off the corner. Kelly spent the next five minutes in a
crouch talking to the driver through the Riviera's passenger window.
When a dark sedan pulled up at the curb directly across the street from
the Albano house, Kelly stood up and headed back toward his car.

Brice could see Levin approaching the van in the right side view mirror.
He leaned out and motioned toward the street. "Kelly," he said. "He's coming this way."

"Cuffs," Levin said.

"You're busting him?"

"Right now."

Brice handed Levin his handcuffs, then saw the scuffle going on in front of the Albano home. John Albano was being half led, half dragged across the street by two goons.

"What's this about?" he said.

Levin had pulled his service revolver from his ankle holster. "Two-to-one they're Vento's goons," he said.

Brice watched Albano being shoved into the back of a navy blue Mercury Marquis. One of the two goons sat in back with him; the other sat up front.

"We gonna sit here and watch?" Brice said.

"That's OC, kid. I'm not. Now excuse me a minute."

Levin stepped out in front of the van to block Kelly.

"And I'm not you," Brice said.

He removed his weapon from its ankle holster, got out of the van and crossed the street in a low crouch. The Marquis had already pulled away. Brice was about to fire a warning shot when he saw a white compact car backing out of the Albano driveway. He put up a hand for it to stop when a shot was fired from inside the car.

Brice dropped to the ground. A second shot had him roll toward a parked car for cover. When he looked up again, he saw the white car was headed in the same direction as the Marquis. Then he saw the old woman clutching her chest at the curb and ran to give assistance.

■ ■ ■

Kelly had already stopped in his tracks when he saw Levin holding the department issued .38 in one hand and handcuffs in the other.

"The fuck is this?" he said.

"Your buddy killed the girl, but you're mentioned on a tape," Levin said.

"Excuse me?"

Levin was about to explain when the first shot rang out from somewhere across the street. He crouched at the knees, but continued to hold his weapon on Kelly. A second shot sounded a moment before a white car raced passed them. Both men hit the pavement.

Kelly, on his stomach now, glanced to his right.

Levin said, "I'll shoot as soon as cuff you."

Kelly motioned toward Brice as the junior detective was getting inside a car parked at the curb.

"He a rat, too?"

Levin heard the engine start and then tires screech when Brice pulled away.

"He had nothing to do with this," Levin said. "You wanna blame somebody, look to your ex-sister-in-law. She's the one tipped off IA about you a long time ago. Something to do with a safe-deposit box?"

Kelly's eyes narrowed. "You two're gonna have a great future with the department after this, Jew-boy."

"I'm fine with what I'm about," Levin said. "And Brice'll always have you he ever needs an excuse to join IA."

"You think so, huh?" Kelly said.

"Sure," Levin said. "A piece of shit like you? No problem. Now, extend your hands before I break them."

■ ■ ■

Nancy knew little Miss Oklahoma lived at one of the NYU dorms on Bleecker Street from following Louis there one night last month. She had parked off the corner of Bleecker and LaGuardia Place more than an hour ago and was feeling antsy when she spotted Louis's car in her rearview mirror. It had just turned onto Bleecker Street. Nancy ducked behind her steering wheel as Louis pulled up to the curb across the street from the dorm.

Her teeth clenched when she saw the blonde getting out of the Cutlass holding a beach bag. The blonde took a step away from the car, then turned back to say something to Louis. Nancy's eyes opened wide when he flipped the blonde the bird.

Nancy heard the blonde yell, "Fuck you, too!" before she slammed the car door shut.

Louis was still holding his middle finger up. Another few seconds passed before he brought his hand down and pulled away from the curb.

Nancy was smiling. The lovebirds had obviously had a fight. She wondered if Louis had shorted the bimbo on her end of the robbery or if he had outright cheated her.

Or maybe it was something else.

Nancy wasn't taking any chances. She pulled out of her spot and followed Louis.

■ ■ ■

He'd already reconfirmed the car would be there when they stopped for gas. Sharon Dowell had said it was parked in her driveway. Louis still wasn't sure what the car looked like, he hadn't actually watched the movie yet, but Jimmy had a sucker willing to buy it for five thousand dollars above the original sticker price. Louis needed to find out what the original sticker price was before he agreed to buy the car from Sharon.

The night he'd gone down on her, Louis had asked why the director of the porn movie was being so generous.

"Two things," Sharon Dowell had said. "One, I gave him something he never had before or pro'bly since. And two, he needs to get rid of everything has anything to do with that movie. Government wants his ass now. Lawyers probably want him to get rid of any connections he has to *Deep Throat*, the car included."

"Too bad for him," Louis said. "But good for us."

"I guess so," Sharon had said. "Or just luck. Right place at the right time."

Louis had liked the idea of it having been luck, then remembered she had said something else he wasn't clear on. "What was one again?" he'd asked. "What you say?"

"Gave him a back-to-backer," Sharon had said.

"One after another?"

"Without coming up for air. You didn't have crabs, I might've treated you."

"Wow," Louis had said, genuinely impressed at the time.

Now he was thinking about Florida again. He remembered when the Jackie Gleason show had first moved to Miami in 1964 and he was introduced to one of the original June Taylor dancers, a long-legged bisexual woman with a live-in bisexual girlfriend. After a night of smoking dope and drinking, they had formed a threesome that lasted through a long weekend and might've gone on longer except for a huge professional football player with the newly formed Miami Dolphins—the dancer's girlfriend's boyfriend. Louis had been intimidated by the burly competition and had opted out of the relationships.

Aside from the retirement community it had become since the sixties, Louis still had fond memories of the female talent available on Miami beach and throughout the sunshine state. Young women in bikinis were what he was thinking about as he drove across the Williamsburg Bridge. A Manhattan bound train on the same bridge brought him back. He glanced to his left and realized how close he was to Fast Eddie's bar, the joint run by the same mob guy John Albano had been working for. He wondered what was going on with Albano and whether or not Nancy had fallen apart and confessed yet. He hoped not, but it would be her own problem if she did. Until Louis was positive he was safe, he wasn't going anywhere near his ex-wife.

He glanced at his watch and saw it was close to three o'clock. If things went right, he could be on the road heading south within a day or two.

Louis turned on the radio hoping to hear a few baseball scores, but the rock-and-roll station Holly had switched to was promoting an upcoming concert by the Allman Brothers and playing their music. Louis sang along with "Ramblin' Man," making up the words when he didn't know them.

■ ■ ■

Kelly had been giving him shit about having to meet him so close to the address he'd provided over the phone because, he'd said, "How the hell would it look for me if some Organized Crime unit is there to bust you?"

Eddie Vento had to reassure the dirty cop he'd fatten his monthly envelope. Then the cops showed up alright, except it appeared they were there to get Kelly.

It's what Vento feared dealing with the dirty cop, that he'd get cocky and sloppy and it would come back to haunt everybody else, which was why he'd made a follow-up call to the Irish kid, Tommy Burns, when he stopped for gas.

He didn't see where the gunfire had come from, but when he pulled away from the curb, he saw Kelly was on the ground and he wondered if the cop had been shot. He didn't stick around to find out. He took off instead and managed to get away because the police hadn't bothered to seal off potential escape routes.

Still, he couldn't be sure the men he sent to grab Albano hadn't been caught. Their original plan was to meet at a car wash on Rockaway Boulevard after the Marquis took a detoured route to make sure it wasn't being followed. There would be a few extra men and a third car waiting for them.

After speeding away from the scene outside John Albano's mother's home, Vento pulled up at the curb a block from the car wash and waited for the Marquis. Two minutes passed before he saw it approaching from 101st Avenue. A few minutes later he saw Albano being moved from the Marquis to an Oldsmobile Delta 88. When he saw one of his men drive the Marquis into the car wash, Vento made his way to the Oldsmobile. He quickly scanned the street for police pursuit, saw none and sat up front in the Delta 88. The two men who had abducted Albano sat in the back. Both men put on baseball caps.

"Nice of you to join us," said Vento over his left shoulder. "And don't think I forgot how you hung up on me." He tapped the driver on the leg and said, "Let's go."

"This is bullshit," Albano said once the car was moving.

"You know anything about the cop they just pinched outside your mother's place?" Vento asked.

"No."

"You sure?"

"I don't know anything about any cops."

"Because he's probably throwing up his guts right now," Vento said. "Which means they're gonna come knocking on my door before the end of the day and I don't need the extra exposure."

"Which is probably why you shouldn't kill me," Albano said. One of the two men in the back kicked him. Albano grunted.

"Easy, fellas," Vento said. "He's right about not killing him. At least not until I know what the hell all the cops were doing at his mother's place. You wouldn't have gone running to your mother, John, would you?"

Albano grunted again. "I get a shot at you later, I'll break that foot," he said to the guy kicking him.

A loud thump followed. This time Albano remained quiet.

"Warehouse, Eddie?" the driver asked.

"The bar," Vento said. "Use Third Street. We'll go in the back so's I never left. They're gonna come for me sooner or later. This way it don't look like I had something to hide."

"And this piece of shit?" the driver asked.

"He don't talk to me at the bar," Vento said, "yous can take him the warehouse after you remove that other package from upstairs in the apartment."

■ ■ ■

Angela had dropped him off at the bar half an hour ago. In the time since John Albano had attacked him, the bruises on Nick's face had turned a nasty shade of purple. It still hurt him to do more than sit still, which is what he was trying to do outside Eddie's office.

The bar noise had hurt his headache too much to stay upstairs. Between the stares from some of the crew and customers, Nick figured he was better off waiting for Vento alone. He had brought the gun just in case the wiseguy went crazy. It was wrapped in a towel inside the small gym bag he had brought with him. Nick believed in loyalty up to a point. He wasn't about to take any more abuse than he'd already taken at the hands of John Albano.

It was close to three o'clock when Nick heard the back basement door open. Eddie led the way, followed by John Albano and two husky guys he knew were with another Brooklyn crew.

"I forgot about you," Vento told Nick. "Wait there."

Albano was shoved inside Eddie's office, Nick noticed his hands had been tied behind his back. The husky guys went inside the office and the door closed a second later.

There was some laughing before the door opened and the two husky guys stepped outside. One of them was holding a fresh fifty-dollar bill. The other looked at Nick and said, "Gotta learn to duck, buddy."

Nick was too embarrassed to reply.

"Get in here," Vento yelled.

Nick nearly stumbled getting up from the folding chair. He squinted from the overhead light inside the office.

"Si'down," Vento said.

Nick sat in the chair alongside the one Albano was sitting in. He saw Vento was holding a handgun. Nick dropped his right hand to the gym bag.

"What'd you bring your lunch?" Vento said.

Nick started pulling the zipper.

Vento tossed him a pocketknife. "Untie his hands."

Nick dropped the pocketknife, but used the opportunity to finish opening the bag. Albano leaned forward to give him easy access to his bound wrists. Nick made sure to nick Albano's back after cutting through what looked like shoelaces.

"Fuck," Albano said.

Nick slashed sideways to get him again. He drew blood the second time, but then Albano snapped his head back and Nick thought he heard a gunshot before everything went dark.

CHAPTER 51

Brice had made sure the old lady wasn't hit before escorting her to the curb behind the Dodge. She had been frightened more than anything and insisted he take her car. Brice took her keys and used the six-year-old Rambler to pursue the men who had taken her son. He drove less than a few feet when he realized the front left tire was flat. He fed the engine gas anyway. If not for the white car, he might've missed seeing John Albano being hustled from one car to another. Brice pulled into an open spot on the street about ten cars behind the Valiant. He could see two people inside the car, the driver and a woman.

He removed his service revolver, set it on the passenger seat and waited.

■ ■ ■

The Mercury Marquis had gone around the Cemetery before it turned left on Pitkin Avenue, then right on 80th Street, then right again on Liberty Avenue. It turned left on 84th Street and then right onto 101st Avenue.

Billy had followed the Marquis onto Rockaway Boulevard but pulled up at the curb when he recognized the Buick Riviera parked about six cars ahead on his right.

"Five'll get you ten your boyfriend'll be getting out of the Marquis into another car any minute now," he told the girlfriend.

Then he could feel her cold stare.

"I hope you're not thinking about jumping out," said Billy, turning to her. He showed her the Walther again. "You'll be dead before your feet touch the ground."

"What do you want?" she said.

"Your boyfriend."

"Why?"

The Marquis had pulled alongside the line at the car wash up ahead. Billy saw Albano being hustled out of one car into another, an Oldsmobile it looked like. A few seconds later Eddie Vento was out of the Riviera.

"Why?" the girlfriend asked again.

Billy turned to her. "Shush," he said.

Eddie Vento was getting in on the front passenger side of the Oldsmobile. The Marquis cut in ahead of the car wash line and was next to go under the spray. The Oldsmobile took off. Billy put the Valiant back into gear and followed.

That had been little more than half an hour ago. Now Billy was walking the woman through Fast Eddie's bar using her like a shield. He pointed the barrel of the Walther at her head as he told the old man behind the bar it was best to close the place down for an hour or so. When the old man didn't move fast enough, Billy shot him in the chest.

He fired another shot into the ceiling and the place emptied.

The woman collapsed back into his arms and he had to carry her down the stairs.

■　■　■

The blue 1970 Cadillac Fleetwood Eldorado was parked in Sharon Dowell's driveway. It had been freshly washed and waxed and was gleaming in the afternoon sunshine.

Louis was all smiles as he pulled into the driveway and parked directly behind the luxury coupe. Even if he paid seventy-five hundred for the car, Jimmy's contact had agreed to pay at least five thousand above the sticker price for the same car. Assuming he threw Jimmy a five-hundred-dollar finder's fee and maybe handed off something smaller to Sharon, Louis stood to make an extra four grand. Considering what he was driving around with and the way things had gone so far, Louis felt the worm had finally turned; Lady Luck had finally smiled his way.

Twenty minutes ago Jimmy had said the buyer was excited about the car before he reminded Louis about a kickback.

"I hope you intend to do the right thing," the loan shark had said. "There's a dozen other guys I could feed this thing didn't make me wait for my money every week."

It was the first time Louis wondered why the big man had let him in on the sale in the first place.

He asked why and Jimmy had said, "Because with you I get a finder's fee."

"Right," Louis had said. "What was I thinking?"

Now he peered into the passenger window of the Cadillac and admired the white leather upholstery. He saw the huge dashboard and said, "It's a beautiful thing."

"It sure as shit is," he heard someone say.

Louis turned and saw it was Jimmy. The big man was standing at the gate entrance to the backyard. Louis was surprised.

"Here," Jimmy said. He held out an open can of beer.

Louis was speechless. He grabbed the can and drank deep. He finished half the can before he stopped to belch.

"Excuse," he said, then finished the beer.

"Gimme," Jimmy said. He took the empty can from Louis, crushed it between his meaty hands, then tossed it toward a garbage pail, missing it by at least four feet.

Louis was led up a short flight of wooden stairs to a deck connected to Sharon's living room. He stepped inside and nearly gasped when he saw a couple of guys he knew were muscle for the two bookmakers he owed money. He thought about running when Jimmy's huge shadow blocked the sliding glass doors.

■ ■ ■

John's head was sore from the head butt he gave Santorra, but then he heard the gunshot and dove to the floor in front of the desk. He heard Vento scramble behind the desk and then there were two more shots before a grunt and a loud thud.

John looked up from behind one of the folding chairs and saw Melinda dangling from a choke hold. He stood up without thinking. He didn't recognize the man behind her until it was too late. The gunshot knocked him back over the top of the desk. His head struck Vento's chair before he landed on the wiseguy's body.

It had happened so fast he didn't feel the piercing burn just below his right shoulder until he tried to stand again. He stumbled on one of Vento's arms and had to use the desk to support himself. Melinda was being held from behind in the office doorway. John saw it was the cop he'd knocked out a few months ago and he had a gun pointed at Melinda's head.

"Don't," John told him. "It's me you want."

Billy Hastings had his weapon pointed at Melinda's head. He looked at John and said, "I watched mine die, now you watch yours."

Then there was another gunshot. Then another two as John scrambled across the desk.

■ ■ ■

The blood running into his mouth caused him to choke and regain consciousness. Then there was a gunshot that made him flinch. By the time Nick could focus again, John Albano was rolling across the top of Eddie Vento's desk.

Nick was on the floor, where he must've dropped to when Albano headbutted him, but now his hand was inside the bag and he could feel the grip of the handgun. He pulled it out slowly when he heard movement behind him in the office doorway.

He saw it was the undercover cop they'd had trouble with in the past. Billy Hastings had been the guy Vento always joked about and the one

John Albano had knocked out. The dirty cop had an arm wrapped around some woman's neck and was holding a gun to her head.

Nick realized it was Hastings that had shot Albano. He looked across the floor and saw Eddie Vento lying on his back with thin rivers of blood flowing from one side of his mouth.

Albano said something and then Hastings said something and Nick shot the cop at least three times before the sound was too much and he fumbled the gun. Albano tumbled from the desk to the floor and pulled the woman to him as Nick reached for the gun he'd just dropped.

■   ■   ■

She had tried to make herself deadweight after the bartender was shot, but then her abductor carried her down the stairs anyway. When they were in the basement he pulled her hair and she'd yelped.

"I thought you were faking it," he'd said.

He draped an arm around her neck and shoved her inside the small office. Melinda had closed her eyes when she heard the gunshots. When she opened her eyes again she saw John a moment before she heard another gunshot. Then she saw he was hit and Melinda struggled to try and free herself until the pressure on her windpipe tightened and she couldn't move.

She heard John say something and then there were more gunshots as she fell back in the doorway. Her ears were ringing when she sat up and saw John reaching for her. She glanced to her right and saw a man with a bandage on his face. Blood was pouring from his nose. He had a gun in his hand and was pointing it at John.

Melinda cocked back her right leg and then kicked up at the gun but missed and caught him under the chin. His eyes rolled a moment before he collapsed against the back of a folding chair. The chair slowly slid from his weight until it was against the far wall and the man was lying on his back. Then John was holding her against him and she squeezed him back as hard as she could.

There were footsteps on the basement stairs and someone shouted "Police, freeze!" but Melinda didn't let go of John.

CHAPTER 52

Nancy had followed her ex-husband to Woodhaven in Queens. She watched from half a block away as he parked at the curb in front of a blue colonial house with a Cadillac parked in the driveway. Louis got out of his car and looked the Cadillac over, leaning on the passenger door to look inside before walking down the driveway and disappearing from her view. She drove to the far corner and parked in front of a small discount store. It was a one way street and Louis would have to pass her when he left.

She decided to make a few calls from a pay phone while she waited. She started with Marie Albano to see what was going on there but the old bag hung up on her three times in a row before Nancy gave up. She had two dimes left when she called Nathan at his sister's house.

"It's me," she said as soon as he picked up. "Please don't hang up."

"What is it now?" Nathan said.

"I'm sorry, Nathan. I really am."

"What do you want, Nan?"

"I need your help."

"You can't have it."

"It's for John. For my son."

"I wish I could believe you, but I don't."

"Please, Nathan. I mean it."

"What happened?"

"Meet me someplace."

"No. Tell me what happened or I'm hanging up."

She sniffled into the phone.

"I'll count to three," Nathan said.

"I need money," Nancy told him.

Nathan hung up.

She returned to her car and waited for Louis.

■　■　■

"You two live together?" Louis asked Sharon and Jimmy.

"He wishes," Sharon said.

"I'm serious," Louis said. "Are you two an item I don't know about?"

"You count an occasional blow job," Jimmy said, "call it whatever you want. Why? What's the difference?"

"Bricklayers should have to work as hard," Sharon said.

The three of them were alone in the house after the others had left with the money Louis had to pay them because they knew he had it to buy the car. He had to use more of the money he'd taken from John Albano and the mob. Louis picked up on something between the big man and Sharon, something that wasn't right. He'd asked if they lived together and could feel his color drain when he learned they were friends.

It was then Louis knew he'd been scammed. The paperwork for the car was on the coffee table where he'd dropped it once he saw the book value was a lot less than Sharon had said.

First off, he had no idea the car was three years old. The blue book on it was almost two thousand less than what he had agreed to pay. Even if the guy Jimmy claimed to have waiting to buy it paid five above book, Louis would still be coming out with a lot less than what he had when he walked in the place.

Then there were the dents he found on the driver's side door, the side he hadn't bothered to look at because he'd just assumed the car was in mint condition. At the least it needed bodywork. God knew what the engine sounded like.

"I'm feeling kind of fucked here," he said. "I mean those guys being here and all. I feel like you set me up."

"Those were friends of mine," the big man said. "Just like you're a friend of mine. I did them a favor and I'm doing you one. You think about it, I did you one letting you pay them before they did a number on you."

"And how much they gonna kickback to you for getting me to walk in here all flush?"

"If you're talking about their appreciation, I may well see a small gratuity, but what's that got to do with you and this car you don't seem so anxious to buy anymore?"

"That car is a piece of shit," Louis said.

"Except you got a guy on the hook wants to buy it."

"What he wants is the car in the movie," Louis said. "Something tells me that one didn't have the dents this one has."

"Now you're accusing me of hustling you? That supposed to be gratitude?"

Louis looked to Sharon. "Thanks," he told her.

"Hey," she said. "I did what you asked me to do."

"Look, kid, you want the thing or not?" Jimmy said. "I got someplace I gotta be soon and you're looking like you might be on the toilet all night. I could've asked you where the fuck you got that money you're lugging around in that bag of yours, you're so flush all of a sudden, but I didn't. It's not my business. You're a bright kid and a hustler, I figure you had a score selling that shit the kids smoke or maybe you actually won a few bucks somewhere. Whatever the fuck, I don't really care. I got other business besides yours. What's it gonna be?"

Louis took a deep breath and said, "This guy gonna show up with the money and buy the thing?"

"What he told me, yeah."

"He gets here and he still wants the car at a price I won't lose on it, I'll buy it."

"He gets here, he still wants the car you didn't buy yet, I'll sell it," Sharon said. "Whatta ya take me for, a moron?"

Louis looked from the paperwork on the table to Jimmy to Sharon and then back to the paperwork. His knees nearly buckled when he stooped to open the bag.

■ ■ ■

Detective Levin restrained Detective Brice from a fistfight with a federal agent outside the Brooklyn House of Detention. Brice and the fed had gotten into it over a temporary court order charging Detective Sean Kelly with police corruption rather than granting federal jurisdiction. After an exchange of several sets of insults, Brice had suggested the fed remove his sunglasses since it was about to rain. When a group of NYPD officers laughed at the comment, the fed took the first swing. Brice swung back and a short melee ensued.

Levin walked an out-of-breath Brice toward the curb. "You're taking things pretty personal for a guy wants nothing to do with IA," Levin said.

"It's got nothing to do with IA," Brice said. "That brownnosing punk. The hell does he care about jurisdiction?"

"You're probably right about him being a brownnoser, but you need to get over it before we go back inside. You really commandeer a car or just robbed one?"

Brice wasn't smiling.

"Look, you should get six commendations for following Albano," Levin said. "That turned out to be smart."

"And you should get fired," Brice said.

"Let's not get into that now. I still may get fired."

Levin took Brice's left arm and tried to guide him toward the building. Brice jerked his arm away.

"Why go back there?" he said. "I thought it's settled."

"It'll piss Kelly off."

"What will?"

"My being there."

"You want to go back inside just to piss off Kelly?"

"Yes."

Brice spotted a hot dog vendor across the street. "I need a soda first," he said.

They had crossed the street and were drinking Yoo-Hoo chocolate drinks when a special agent in charge identified himself. "Flynn," he said. "I'm the SAC on a federal investigation involving Eddie Vento."

"Congratulations," Levin said.

"You're his friend," Flynn said. "He here now or what?"

"I'm whose friend?" Levin said.

"Don't fuck with me, Detective. I'm not in the mood."

Levin turned to Brice. "You know what he's talking about?"

"Not a clue," Brice said.

Flynn handed Levin the badge. "Special Agent Stebenow," he said. "He left this for me. He left it here. Where is he?"

"Hey, I barely know the guy," Levin said. "He left a message for me to contact you. I did that. I don't know anything else." He handed the badge back to Flynn.

"He left a message means he knows you. How would he know you?"

Levin gave it a moment.

"Detective?" Flynn said.

"I contacted him," Levin said.

"You contacted him?"

"Yeah, about a tape I listened to from Organized Crime. A woman was mentioned on it I thought was in danger."

Flynn offered a sarcastic grin. "You wanna float that shit to a federal prosecutor, it's your funeral," he said.

"Hey, what can I say? Your boy wasn't very discreet. I spotted him during surveillance. Then I approached him."

"You expect anyone to believe that?"

"Personally, I don't give a rat's ass what you believe."

"You do realize we'll have Kelly under our jurisdiction in a day, two at the most."

"Then you're on a roll. Congratulations again."

"You're a smart bastard, aren't you?"

"I have my moments."

"He here or not?"

"I don't know."

"Or you won't tell me."

"That, too."

Flynn pocketed the badge. "Well, if you see him, your new friend, tell him he's in the middle of a shit storm. And if or when I find out how much you're involved, so will you be."

Levin turned to Brice. "I guess you're off the hook."

"Hey, you know what?" Brice said. "Fuck the both of you."

Flynn mumbled something under his breath before walking away. Levin pulled a dollar bill from his pants pocket and motioned at the frankfurter vendor. "Two more," he said.

■ ■ ■

A member of the Army's Green Beret, Darrel Stebenow was part of a search-and-destroy mission outside the village of Dak To in early November 1967. The North Vietnamese had begun a border battle strategy attacking from villages along western Kontum Province. Hill 1338 was the dominant hill mass south of Dak To and where several bodies of a South Vietnam Civilian Irregular Defense Group unit were discovered during a reconnaissance patrol. Shortly after securing themselves in a position at the base of the hill, Stebenow's unit came under heavy fire. The unit was immediately pinned down and within hours they were overrun. Stebenow was forced to cover himself with the bodies of colleagues to survive and spent the next several hours nearly motionless waiting for a chance to escape. Fighting went on throughout the night, but when two NVA troops began scavenging the bodies Stebenow was shielding himself with, he quickly and stealthily broke their necks and found his way off Hill 1338.

He'd snapped both men's necks in such a way as to sever the spinal nerve pathways above the heart and lungs, insuring death. Stebenow had killed other enemy combatants during the war, but never with his hands. As it turned out, the two he killed with his hands were the last. Three months after his escape from Hill 1338, Stebenow's tour of duty was over and he returned to the States.

Now he observed Detective Sean Kelly looking cocky sitting across from his expensive attorney inside the small conference room in a subbasement of the Brooklyn House of Detention. Stebenow had expected United States marshals to guard Kelly, but there weren't any. Unless they hadn't arrived yet and were on their way, Kelly's only protection right then was a single Department of Corrections officer.

Stebenow had managed to avoid Detective Levin and Special Agent in Charge Flynn as they argued in the lobby by conversing with a defense attorney on his way to visit a client. After flashing his credentials to access the subbasement, Stebenow went to a tiny kitchen area where he poured himself a cup of coffee. He stirred in some sugar while he observed Kelly and his attorney.

The attorney stepped out of the small room to use the bathroom around the hallway corner. Stebenow waited a few seconds, then crossed the short hallway and approached the corrections officer.

"Some guy just went down in the men's room," he said.

"Excuse me?" the corrections officer said.

"Some guy in a suit. Might be a heart attack."

The officer took a quick look into the conference room and saw Kelly had put his legs up on the corner of the table.

Stebenow flashed phony identification. "I got this," he said. "Go 'head."

The corrections officer nodded before heading for the bathroom. Stebenow counted three full beats before he stepped inside the conference room.

Epilogue

"I think I miss your ponytail," Nancy said. "I'm not used to your hair short like this."

Louis was watching the engine temperature gauge to the left of the odometer on the dashboard and getting nervous about the needle edging back toward hot. The Cadillac had already overheated once since they'd left New York.

"Then again, now it'll match your balls," Nancy said. "And I do like that look."

They were heading south on the New Jersey turnpike and were less than thirty miles from Delaware. Half an hour after Jimmy's *Deep Throat* enthusiast had turned down buying the Fleetwood Eldorado, Louis had stopped for a crew cut at a barbershop on Queens Boulevard and in walked Nancy. She'd followed him, she told him, from when he dropped off little Miss Ohio.

"Oklahoma," Louis had told her. "And she was a runner up."

Nancy didn't have much money with her, but Louis knew she had some stashed in a bank she could get to in the morning. The problem was he couldn't wait overnight, not with Jimmy and two bookies knowing he was flush with newfound money. Sooner or later word would get back to Eddie Vento's crew.

Nancy said she could always sneak back to New York and withdraw the money another time, maybe when she visited her son. Louis wasn't about to argue with her. All he wanted now was to get far enough away from New York so he could sell the bootlegged films he still had.

It was after one in the morning and they had been on the road since after sunset, stopping three times in total; once for dinner, once to fill the Cadillac's huge gas tank and once to let the radiator cool down after it overheated outside Trenton.

"I'm excited about this," Nancy said. "A new start and all. It'll be good for us."

Louis turned the radio on to drown out her overenthusiastic conversation. He wasn't about to tell her about the money they didn't have.

"*And here's a song that debuted back in June of this year,*" the announcer said. "'Manu Dibango, Soul Makossa'."

"What the hell is that?" Nancy asked.

Louis listened to the repetitive lyrics and felt himself starting to relax.

"Mama what?" Nancy said. "What's he saying?"

"I don't know, but I like it," Louis said.

"Sounds like jungle music."

"It is. Guy's from Africa somewhere."

"You know this song?"

"I've heard it before. I like it."

"Sounds like nonsense to me. I don't get it."

"I can't hear it, you keep yapping."

"Excuse me."

She hadn't shut up since they left the gas station in Brooklyn. Louis had just over a few grand in cash, what was left after he'd been scammed into paying off his gambling debts and buying a car he didn't need. Nancy was potentially worth a lot more, but he wasn't sure he could put up with her perky spirit another thousand miles, what was left before they reached Florida.

"I'll bet this song is big in Bed-Stuy," Nancy said.

Louis tried to ignore her commentary. He was thinking about the films he could sell once he was comfortable with the distance they'd traveled from New York. That would take at least another few hundred miles, but would mean some extra cash.

"Can I at least change stations when this shit is over?" Nancy said.

"Yeah, fine," Louis said.

"Honestly, I don't know how you stand it."

"I can't hear it."

"What's to hear. Mumbo jumbo. Mama bama Aunt Jemima."

"Jesus Christ."

"Jungle music is all it is. What, are you into black now?"

"Go 'head, change it, you want."

He had to keep her happy or she'd make it impossible for him to finish the trip with her. He'd already thought about leaving her when they made the last stop. He would've if he still had half the money he'd had before he tried to buy and sell the car. He didn't, though. Not anymore.

Louis hadn't doubted she'd leave the kid behind and was surprised about the note she'd left John.

"I wrote I'd come up to see Little Jack at least once a year and that he could always come and stay with us for the summer once school was out," Nancy had said.

"The summer, huh?" Louis said.

"He is my son."

She hadn't even mentioned the note until they were through the Holland tunnel. He wondered if she'd even felt guilty about the kid.

Now she changed stations while he thought about it again, leaving her someplace.

"Yeah!" Nancy said when she found a song she liked.

She sang along to Three Dog Night's "Shambala."

Louis said, "You wanna explain the difference between this shit and what I was listening to?"

"I like this," she said. "What's wrong with it?"

"The fuck does it mean?"

"I don't know. Shine the light, I think."

"Shine the light, what?"

"I don't know, Louis. What's the difference, I like it."

Louis rubbed his face with his free hand.

"At least it's white music," Nancy said. Then she was dancing in her seat, waving her arms, snapping her fingers and singing the next verse.

Louis saw the temperature gauge had touched the red spot. Then there was steam coming from under the long hood. He let off the gas pedal and coasted the Cadillac off the road.

"What's the matter?" Nancy asked.

Louis pointed to the steam.

"Oh," she said. "That again. Where'd you get this piece of shit anyway?"

Louis turned the engine off and rubbed his face again, this time using both hands.

"Whadda we do?" Nancy said.

"Wait."

"For what?"

"Until it cools again, same as we did last time."

"Then what? Won't it heat up again?"

Louis felt his teeth clench.

Nancy said, "Now what are you mad for?"

"Nothing," Louis said. "Just leave it alone."

"I'm sorry, baby," Nancy said. She rubbed his right leg with her left hand. "Want a blow job until the engine cools?"

"Jesus Christ."

"What? You don't want a blow job?"

"That mouth," Louis said. "No."

"Why not?"

"I'm not in the mood."

"Since when?"

Louis glared at his ex-wife.

Nancy drew her hand back. "Excuse me," she said. "Let's just sit here and do nothing. That'll be fun."

■   ■   ■

Eddie Vento was buried at the Greenwood Cemetery in Brooklyn on Friday, August 31. Angela had gone to the two-day wake but had skipped the burial. Nick had used the opportunity to skip both the wake and the funeral as a sign he was retired from the life.

The afternoon of the burial the Santorras took a ten-thousand-dollar home equity loan. One thousand would cover the legal fees for an illegal gun possession charge, but leaving the life would also mean losing his no-show union truck driving job.

For the first time in five years Nick was forced to consider his employment options. Walking home from the bank, his heavily bandaged face a road map of bruises, Nick argued against working for his brother-in-law in the used car business.

"The fuck do I know about cars?" he said. "I can drive one, that's it."

"Neither did Larry know anything," Angela said. "He was a shoe salesman, for God's sake. He learned on the job. That's what you'd do."

"I'm not standing around a used car lot like some jerkoff needs to sell somebody a lemon, okay? Forgetaboutit."

Angela knew better than to get into it with him now. It was his pride getting in the way. It had been hard for him to accept losing his dream of being a gangster, but after Eddie Vento was killed, Nick had said his chances had been flushed down the toilet along with all the other bullshit he'd been taking the last few years, that it was a blessing in disguise. Angela agreed.

She was grateful he was finished with that life and anxious for him to find work doing something more normal. She had never really bought into it anyway, the Mafia. All those wiseguys and goodfellas or whatever it was they called themselves. All she knew was her husband had been abused and for not much more money than he might make selling used cars and probably with a lot less aggravation, not to mention the risk.

"There's plenty things I can do besides that," Nick said after a while.

"Such as?"

"Business. I can go into my own, for one thing. Not work for somebody like some schmuck."

"What kind of business?"

"I don't know... something. Maybe we'll open a store or something. A bagel joint or a pizza parlor. Something the kids can get into, they can help out they get older. We can leave them a store they can leave to their kids."

Angela knew Nick was trying to be optimistic. It was one of the good things about him and she loved him for it now more than ever.

■ ■ ■

Melinda had learned about her best friend's murder at the hospital where John had been taken after the shootout in Eddie Vento's bar. Grief-stricken and overwhelmed with guilt, she spent the night at the local police precinct, where she stayed until Jill's body was removed. The next day Melinda listed her house for sale with a local realtor.

John had tried to contact her after he was released from the hospital, but the police relayed her message that she needed time. When he finally tracked her down at a motel five days later, he was told she had just checked out and hadn't left a forwarding phone number.

It was the Labor Day weekend and John's mother had planned a Saturday barbecue. Last night he had taken his son to the Yankees game against the Orioles. Although the boy was still questioning where his mother had gone, he'd enjoyed himself at the game, especially after securing a few autographs on a baseball one of the players had tossed into the stands. The fact the Yankees had won was an added bonus. Today Little Jack was still excited as he played running bases in the driveway with a couple of other boys that lived on the same block as his grandmother.

Old man Elias, Nathan, John and his mother sat on beach chairs spread around Marie Albano's yard. A cooler half filled with beer and soda was set against the house in the shade. A large serving tray with sandwiches, potato salad and coleslaw was centered on a portable folding table. Plastic Tupperware bowls filled with potato chips, pretzels and popcorn were spread across a small wooden picnic table.

The grown-ups could hear the boys laughing in the driveway. It was close to game time for the Yankees, but Little Jack was having too much fun to remind him.

"I never seen him so happy," Marie said. "He's got Jim Palmer and Brooks Robinson's autographs, whoever they are. He must've told me two dozen times."

"Who they are?" Elias asked. His mouth was still sore from the stitches along his gums and a slight fracture of the jawbone. Although he could speak, it was painful to do so.

"Orioles," John said.

"It's baseball, Mr. Elias," Nathan Ackerman said. "They're baseball players."

He had returned to orchestral practice with the Philharmonic upon their return from Boston. He had come to visit Little Jack, but was waiting for a private moment to speak with John.

"He mention Boog Powell?" John asked his mother.

"Probably. Who's he?"

"First base," Nathan said.

"He got three hits but the Yankees still won," John said. "Robinson didn't play. I don't know why."

"He was so happy," Marie said. "Thank God they won."

"You hear anything from Nancy?" John asked Nathan.

"Me? Not a word."

"Unbelievable, that woman," Marie said. "Good riddance."

Elias stood up, took Marie's right hand and helped her up. "Come," he said. "We prepare coffee I brought. I show you." He stopped and turned to Nathan. "Greek coffee. The best."

"I know it's very strong," Nathan said.

"Puts hairs on your chest."

"Just what I need," Marie said.

"On you they look beautiful, I'm sure."

"Hey, hey, hey," John said. "Watch yourself, old man."

Elias waved him off as he followed Marie up the back steps to the kitchen.

Nathan used the opportunity to talk privately with John.

"How's the shoulder?" he asked.

"Not too bad," John said. "I'm almost used to the sling. Should be fine in a few weeks."

"Good, because I have a job offer."

John's eyebrows furrowed. "Not cleaning your yard, I hope. I'm already driving for a car service here in Queens. I have to take the sling off, but at least it's something. You're a great guy, Nathan, but I'm not looking for charity."

"No, it's nothing like that," Nathan said. "This is real. The Metropolitan Opera has a carpentry staff. Men who build the sets they use for the operas."

"Really?"

"A dear friend from the old days has some clout there. He can put you on."

"Seriously?"

"Yes. The pay is union scale, whatever that is."

"I don't have a union card anymore, Nathan. I lost it."

"He'll get it back."

"How?"

"These are very influential people, John. They do whatever they want, trust me."

"I'm talking about a delegate got me tossed," John said. "I had a fight with his brother was a foreman on the job I was working and they had me out like that." He snapped his fingers for effect. "The guy killed a stray dog for the fun of it and I hit him."

"My God, that's terrible," Nathan said. "Good for you, you hit him."

"Except it cost me my union card."

"The people behind the Met are old money. They have lots of clout."

"That'd be great. Is it steady?"

"You'd be on staff. Unless the Metropolitan Opera goes out of business, you'll have a job."

"Won't they want me to apprentice or something? I'd be coming in cold."

"You were a union carpenter how many years?"

"Ten."

"I told them eight, what Nancy told me once. You'll be fine."

"Jesus, Nathan, I don't know what to say."

"Say you'll take it?"

"Of course I'll take it. I don't know how to thank you."

"You just did."

John grabbed Nathan's right hand and shook it. "Nancy really blew it with you," he said.

"And you," Nathan said.

One of the boys in the driveway yelled out the Yankee game was starting. Little Jack ran into the yard to ask his father if they could watch it inside in the living room.

"Ask Grandma," John told him.

The boy ran up the back stairs and inside the house. He was back a few seconds later calling to his friends. Two boys entered the yard, said hello to John and Nathan and headed up the stairs and followed Jack inside.

"He look happy or what?" John said. "Which reminds me. Thanks for those tickets."

"No problem," Nathan said. "Now can I ask you a favor?"

"Anything," John said.

"Can I teach him to play an instrument?"

"Seriously?"

"Yes, seriously."

"Sure, why not. Is he interested? He never mentioned anything to me."

"Honestly, I don't know. I thought I'd give it a try."

"This about visiting him? Because you can always do that, Nathan. Forever as far as I'm concerned."

"Thank you, John. I appreciate that. May I teach him?"

"Only if I can pay."

"If you insist."

"Can I afford it?"

"We'll work something out."

John took Nathan's hand, shook it again, then leaned over and half-hugged the musician. "Thank you," he said, "for everything."

■ ■ ■

Detective Sean Kelly woke from the sting of cold water against his face. He coughed a few times before sitting up and acknowledging the short wiry man with cold blue eyes standing at the foot of his bed, a Colt Python .357 Magnum in his right hand. Kelly immediately recognized the gun. It was his.

"Name's Tommy," the man said. "Tommy Burns."

"Am I supposed to know you?" Kelly said.

"I highly doubt it," Burns said.

It was early in the morning. Kelly had been alone in the house since his wife and three daughters left to visit family on Long Island the day before. He tried bluffing the short man with a warning about waking his daughters.

"Not home," Burns said. "Labor Day weekend and all."

"You're sure of that, are you?" Kelly said.

Burns flung the basin he'd used for the water against an armoire to the left of the bed. Kelly jumped from the crash.

"Nervous?" Burns said.

"The fuck you want?" Kelly said.

"It's not what I want. I don't know you from Adam."

"Who sent you? Can't be Vento, he's dead."

"You're warm."

"Who?"

"What's the difference?"

"You're gonna shoot a cop in his bed in his house? A detective with rank?"

"A disgraced detective."

"Except I'm not dealing with the feds yet, am I? Or what am I doing in my bed? I'd be guarded at some military fort the middle of the fuckin' country I cut a deal. Whoever sent you take the time to think about that?"

Burns was smiling.

"Fuck you and your mother," Kelly said.

"You ever see *Kiss of Death*?" Burns said. "Guy's my fucking hero, Tommy Udo."

"You wanna tie me up first, put me in a wheelchair?"

Burns smiled again.

"You're a sick one alright, but you're no guinea," Kelly said. "You're a mick same as me. How's that make you feel?"

Burns stopped to light a Camel filterless cigarette. "My old man said I had two choices this life. Work the docks, be another donkey, or I could be a cop. I chose the streets. You're working a hook the docks, there's too many people you gotta answer to. Way too many of 'em Italian."

"Except you're working for one now, right? Unless you're with those crazy bastards on the West Side."

"I'm no Westie, pal."

"Then who? You're here to whack me, at least gimme that."

Burns grabbed the single chair in the room from in front of the secretary. He moved it to the side of the bed and sat.

"Make yourself comfortable," Kelly said.

Burns said, "Except for the uniform and chain of command, fuckers like you are just as dirty as me. Dirty as a nigger's outhouse, my old man used to say about cops on the take."

"He was a philosopher was he, your old man?"

"Was a drunken longshoreman with a spiteful mean streak used to beat my mother the same night he'd fuck her sister lived with us. That's what he was, my old man."

"Your hero, no doubt."

"You're looking to push my buttons, but it won't work. I'll kill you when I'm ready."

Kelly tried to swallow, but couldn't.

"Not being a dago myself," Burns continued, "one of their rank and file, I don't have a chain of command. There's people I answer to, yeah, but only after I'm retained, money up front. I work for the dagos this way, Eddie Vento included when he was still around, but it's for proper wages. Those I set up front."

"And that makes you proud, killing your own kind for greaseballs like Vento?"

"That's funny comin' from a piece of shit like yourself. How long you on his payroll was it? Five years? Ten? The problem with guys like you, thieves in uniform, you get soft playing make-believe. Can't handle the pressure when it comes."

"Says you," Kelly said.

"Or what the fuck am I doing here?"

Kelly exchanged a long hard stare with Burns. He said, "You're gonna kill me, get it over with. I don't enjoy conversing with bog Irish."

"First things first," Burns said. "The safe combination."

"Fuck you."

"Yeah, I know, except I'm getting inside it with or without your help. Without, I might have to bend your wife over a table first, give her a little Roto-Rooter through the back door. Supposed to work wonders for the incontinent."

"She don't know the combination. What do you take me for?"

"Then she'd be getting all that action for nothing."

"Those the terms you set up front, you fuckin' genius? You kill me but then you gotta rob my house? There's nothing in the house, you moron. I keep mine in the bank."

"I've already been down the basement. There's a safe and you're going to give me the combination."

"I'm gonna do that, I might as well open it."

"And reach for the piece inside? I don't think so."

"Then I guess you're fucked once you shoot me," he said. "That's too bad."

"Let me ask you this then," Burns said. "You have three daughters, correct?"

■ ■ ■

"Stebenow's lucky you went back inside," Captain Edward Kaprowski said, "now Kelly's dead anyway."

"I almost didn't," Lieutenant Detective Neil Levin said. "We had that beef with Stebenow's SAC outside and then Brice wanted a soda. I wound up having another one after the first. We just made it back down the sub-basement in time."

They had been eating Nathan's hot dogs in Kaprowski's Catalina parked near the ramp leading to the Coney Island boardwalk on Stillwell Avenue. Levin licked a dangling onion from his frankfurter bun, then bit off the end of the hot dog.

"You think he would've done it?" Kaprowski asked. "Killed him, I mean."

Levin nodded as he finished chewing. He swallowed, wiped his mouth with a napkin and nodded again. "The look in his eyes? Oh, yeah."

"You think it was him farmed it out?" Kaprowski said.

"Could've been with copies of the same tapes he gave us."

"Lord forgive me, there is one, I like to think it was the mob cleaning up their own mess," said Kaprowski before taking a bite from his frankfurter. He wiped his mouth with a napkin, then took a sip of Coke through a straw. He set the soda on the console and forced a belch. He excused himself and wiped his mouth again, this time with the back of his right hand.

Kaprowski had come to inform Levin of his promotion and the fact that Detective Steven Brice's sexuality had been exposed in a separate Internal Affairs investigation.

"Conducted at the behest of Lieutenant Detective Sean Kelly," he explained, "back when Brice was first assigned to him. Claimed he wanted his new guys vetted."

"I'm glad he's dead," Levin said.

"Kelly had an issue with Brice's car. Thought he shoulda been using it to chase tail."

"Mach One."

"What?"

"Nothing. What do they have?"

"Your guess is as good as mine, but it's an easy bet there are pictures involved. Nothing naked, unless they're doin' it in some park someplace, but they probably have whatever was public between them. The boyfriends'n advertising. Apparently they weren't as careful up in Connecticut, where the guy lives, they were down here."

Kaprowski started on his fries. He stopped after a few. Levin took a long drink of Rheingold beer from a can.

"There anything we can do for him?" he asked.

"Bring him over to us," Kaprowski said. "I can expedite that, but it's only a matter of time before some asshole lets it out, whatever they have. Kid's in for hell when that happens."

Levin set his fries on the console. "What if I team up with him?"

"He's still the one's gonna have to deal with this, my friend. It isn't going away."

"Kid has balls," Levin said. "How he went after Hastings. Could've walked into the middle of that shootout. Shots fired and he went down those stairs anyway. Didn't wait for backup or anything else."

"Nobody'll doubt his courage, but speaking of that bar, guess who took it over, Fast Eddie's?"

Levin shrugged.

"Jimmy Wigs."

"Valentine?"

"The same," Kaprowski said. "Him and Vento were friends going back to forever. Probably robbed hubcaps together, the other kids were in kindergarten. Either the bosses figure Valentine is going places or Jimmy was already in on what Vento was doing, figured he'd grab it before somebody else did. Word is he's being upped, but there's no confirmation of yet."

"Which is another possible explanation for Kelly," Levin said. "Valentine cutting all loose ends."

Kaprowski nodded. "I like it better that way than it was Stebenow."

"Me, too. And if Valentine gets his stripe, he'll be branching out and fast. He's got a good sized crew in Canarsie. He gets a piece of Williamsburg, he'll be in position for one of the top spots down the road."

"Then we'll set our sights on him."

"Think he'll spend time in Williamsburg?"

"Pro'bly, yeah, at first. That bartender Hastings shot survived, he used to run the place for Vento. Very low-key, he is. Not saying a word about what happened, except some cop used to shake him down shot him in the chest. Great publicity for NYPD, Hastings was."

Kaprowski had dropped a string of sauerkraut on his lap. He picked it up with two fingers, held it up to his mouth and dropped it on his tongue.

"What's next for me?" Levin asked.

"Canarsie, I'm thinking."

"The stolen cars?"

"We got a name now. Confirmed. Roy DeMeo."

"Feds on it?"

"I don't know, nor do I care. You'll be straight surveillance to start, until you're familiar with the players. Supposedly DeMeo's got a crew of kids working for him. Canarsie locals, but there's a bar they work from over to Flatlands, the Gemini, I want to keep an eye on it."

"Sounds exciting, watching a bar. I hope it's not from some roof."

"We can get an apartment we will, but you'll start on a roof so get yourself a parka for when it rains."

Levin tossed the rest of his fries out the window. A flock of sea-gulls descended on them. A few seconds later, the fries were gone.

"I guess I owe Brice," Levin said.

"Yeah, you probably do," Kaprowski said.

Levin took one of Kaprowski's fries and tossed it to the pigeons. "Sometimes I hate this job," he said.

Kaprowski offered him the rest of his fries. "Yeah," he said. "Sometimes I do, too."

THE END

Stark Houлe Preлл

REPRINTS OF CLASSIC MYSTERY AND NOIR FICTION

1-933586-01-X **Benjamin Appel** Brain Guy / Plunder $19.95

1-933586-26-5 **Benjamin Appel** Sweet Money Girl /
Life and Death of a Tough Guy $19.95

0-9749438-7-8 **Algernon Blackwood** Julian LeVallon /
The Bright Messenger $21.95

1-933586-03-6 **Malcolm Braly** Shake Him Till He Rattles /
It's Cold Out There $19.95

1-933586-10-9 **Gil Brewer** Wild to Possess / A Taste for Sin $19.95

1-933586-20-6 **Gil Brewer** A Devil for O'Shaugnessy /
The Three-Way Split $14.95

1-933586-24-9 **W. R. Burnett** It's Always Four O'Clock / Iron Man $19.95

1-933586-12-5 **A. S. Fleiлchman** Look Behind You Lady /
The Venetian Blonde $19.95

1-933568-28-1 **A. S. Fleiлchman** Danger in Paradise /
Malay Woman $19.95

0-9667848-7-1 **Eliлabeth Sanxay Holding** Lady Killer / Miasma $19.95

0-9667848-9-8 **Eliлabeth Sanxay Holding** The Death Wish /
Net of Cobwebs $19.95

0-9749438-5-1 **Eliлabeth Sanxay Holding** Strange Crime in Bermuda /
Too Many Bottles $19.95

1-933586-16-8 **Eliлabeth Sanxay Holding** The Old Battle Ax /
Dark Power $19.95

1-933586-17-6 **Ruллell Jameл** Underground / Collected Stories $14.95

0-9749438-8-6 **Day Keene** Framed in Guilt / My Flesh is Sweet $19.95

1-933586-21-4 **Mercedeл Lambert** Dogtown / Soultown $14.95

1-933586-14-1 **Dan Marlowe/Fletcher Flora/Charleл Runyon**
Trio of Gold Medals $15.95

1-933586-02-8 **Stephen Marlowe** Violence is My Business /
Turn Left for Murder $19.95

1-933586-07-9 **Ed by McCarthy & Gorman** Invasion of the
Body Snatchers: A Tribute $17.95

1-933586-09-5 **Margaret Millar** An Air That Kills /
Do Evil in Return $19.95

1-933586-23-0 **Wade Miller** The Killer / Devil on Two Sticks $17.95

0-9749438-0-0 **E. Phillips Oppenheim** Secrets & Sovereigns:
Uncollected Stories $19.95

1-933586-27-3 **E. Phillips Oppenheim** The Amazing Judgment /
Mr. Laxworthy's Adventures $19.95

0-9749438-3-5 **Vin Packer** Something in the Shadows /
Intimate Victims $19.95

0-9749438-6-x **Vin Packer** Damnation of Adam Blessing /
Alone at Night $19.95

1-933586-05-2 **Vin Packer** Whisper His Sin / The Evil Friendship $19.95

1-933586-18-4 **Richard Powell** A Shot in the Dark / Shell Game $14.95

1-933586-19-2 **Bill Pronzini** Snowbound / Games $14.95

0-9667848-8-x **Peter Rabe** The Box / Journey Into Terror $19.95

0-9749438-4-3 **Peter Rabe** Murder Me for Nickels /
Benny Muscles In $19.95

1-933586-00-1 **Peter Rabe** Blood on the Desert /
A House in Naples $19.95

1-933586-11-7 **Peter Rabe** My Lovely Executioner /
Agreement to Kill $19.95

1-933586-22-2 **Peter Rabe** Anatomy of a Killer /
A Shroud for Jesso $14.95

0-9749438-9-4 **Robert J. Randisi** The Ham Reporter /
Disappearance of Penny $19.95

0-9749438-2-7 **Douglas Sanderson** Pure Sweet Hell /
Catch a Fallen Starlet $19.95

1-933586-06-0 **Douglas Sanderson** The Deadly Dames /
A Dum-Dum for the President $19.95

1-933586-08-7 **Harry Whittington** A Night for Screaming /
Any Woman He Wanted $19.95

1-933586-25-7 **Harry Whittington** To Find Cora /
Like Mink Like Murder / Body and Passion $19.95

If you are interested in purchasing any of the above books, please send the cover
price plus $3.00 U.S. for the 1st book and $1.00 U.S. for each additional book to:

STARK HOUSE PRESS
2200 O Street, Eureka, CA 95501
707-444-8768
www.starkhousepress.com

Order 3 or more books and take a 10% discount. We accept PayPal payments.
Wholesale discounts available upon request. Contact griffinskye3@sbcglobal.net

Danger in Paradise / Malay Woman

A. S. Fleischman

1-933586-28-1 **$19.95**

Two south sea, cinematic adventure thrillers, with a new introduction by the author.

"Filled with a colorful cast of characters and wonderful noir dialog." MICHAEL CART, *Booklist*

SUMMER 2010

Thief of Midnight

Catherine Butzen

1-933586-31-1 **$15.95**

A startling original dark fantasy from a new author on the horror scene.

"The Thief of Midnight is a book to be appreciated and savored for its moody prose... and to be read with the doors locked by those who still believe in the bogeyman." JEAN RABE, *USA Today* BESTSELLING AUTHOR

SUMMER 2010

One for Hell

Jada M. Davis

1-933586-30-3 **$19.95**

The quintessential bad cop novel from 1952.

"A boxcar bum named Willa Ree enters a small town with the intention of picking it clean, and in the process all kinds of secrets and corruption come to light. It's a fine noir story with a powerful ending that Jim Thompson would have been proud to have written." BILL CRIDER'S *Pop Culture Magazine*

FALL 2010

The Silet Wall / The Return of Marvin Palaver

Peter Rabe

1-933586-32-x **$19.95**

Two previously unpublished novels by one of the top noir authors of the 50's and 60's—a serious study of Mafia revenge, and a crazy con from beyond the grave.

"With Rabe, you never know how the plot is going to unfold." MICHAEL SCOTT CAIN, *Rambles*

WINTER 2010

EVERYBODY'S OUT TO GET JOHNNY PORNO!

It's the summer of 1973 in New York City and John Albano is just trying to make ends meet. They've taken his union card and work is hard to come by. Weekends he picks up the cash from illegal showings of the recently banned porno flick, *Deep Throat*, for local wiseguy Eddie Vento. Vento has a nephew, a penny ante mobster who can't stop riding Albano. When he pushes one too many of Albano's buttons, the nephew winds up with a knot on his forehead and an even bigger grudge to nurse.

Then there's Albano's ex-wife, now re-married for a third time but still hung up on her first husband, Louis, a wannabe hustler with a gambling problem.
She'll do anything to get Louis back, no matter what it means to Albano. Or to his new employers.

Albano has another problem he's unaware of, a dangerous, drugged out ex-cop named Billy Hastings. Convinced Albano once tried to put the make on his wife at a mobbed up bar, Hastings took a swing and missed, but Albano didn't miss when he swung back—and knocked the cop out. Hastings was caught on tape starting the fight and was forced to retire. So here's another guy with a grudge, only this one's a psycho.

Over on the other side of the legal fence are detectives Neil Levin and Steven Brice, who may or may not be on the same side, and Lt. Det. Sean Kelly, a cop who looks out for himself above all else. The NYPD has been given a new priority—rid the streets of porn, especially *Deep Throat*. At the center of it all is Johnny Porno—god, how Albano hates that name! He's just a guy trying to earn a few extra coins to pay his way; just a guy trying to stay alive.

CHARLIE STELLA BIBLIOGRAPHY

Eddie's World (December, 2001, Carroll & Graf)

Jimmy Bench-Press (December, 2002, Carroll & Graf)

Charlie Opera (December, 2003, Carroll & Graf)

Cheapskates (March, 2005, Carroll & Graf)

Shakedown (June, 2006, Pegasus)

Mafiya (January, 2008, Pegasus)